Praise For Abigail Rose-Marie

"When the young Michigan artist Antigone Costello receives an invitation to small-town Kentucky to paint a portrait celebrating her grandfather, she finds a region haunted by the past. Tales of murder, betrayal, and escape emerge, along with the hidden history of heroic women and the secrets of her own family. Read *The Moonflowers*—a novel as dark and moody as the deep woods where it's set, yet ultimately inspiring."

—Lawrence Coates, author of *Camp Olvido*

THE
MOONFLOWERS

THE MOONFLOWERS

a novel

ABIGAIL ROSE-MARIE

LAKE UNION
PUBLISHING

Published by Lake Union Publishing, Seattle

www.apub.com

Amazon, the Amazon logo, and Lake Union Publishing are trademarks of Amazon.com, Inc., or its affiliates.

ISBN-13: 9781662522970 (paperback)
ISBN-13: 9781662522987 (digital)

Cover design by Caroline Teagle Johnson
Cover image: © Nuntiya / Shutterstock; © DEEPOL / Plainpicture; © Brezina / Getty

Printed in the United States of America

*for my mother and grandmother,
and for all the strong and courageous women
who live in the hills*

Prologue

Up from the barren, parched earth, a statue grows. A man, for a woman is too malleable to be immortalized in stone. His rigid body, standing on a two-foot pedestal, rises ten feet into the air. He wears a military officer's uniform: a thick overcoat with gilt dress buttons and two collar discs pressed on either side of his neck. On his head is a dress cap with a medallion placed in the center, directly above the lip. He stands with one leg slightly bent at the knee and carries a musket. Its thin, tubular mouth points upward, eager to spit a bullet from pursed bronze lips.

The man's eyes are large, and his cheekbones are much too long and sharp. Benjamin Costello was never an angular man. He was slight and refined. Feminine in features and mannerisms. I see him now as if he is sitting before me, one leg crossed casually over the other with long fingers folded together on the knee. His head bends slightly to the right, and his round cheeks flush from the glass of red wine he sips before setting it back on the table between each taste. He taps his fingers lightly on his knee, and a slow smile creeps across his face as the tip of his tongue teases the curve of his upper lip.

This is how Benjamin Costello looked the night of March 27, 1948. The night he sat at the dining room table inside Whitmore Halls and ate lemon meringue pie before drinking the hot mug of tea steeped with poisonous leaves that stopped his heart and curdled his organs so fast that he was dead on the floor before I had time to clear the table.

It is now 1997, and I have been imprisoned for nearly fifty years for the murder of the man they are commemorating with a large statue erected in the center of the square in Darren, a town that's not much more than a stray pebble kicked from the hollers of the Appalachians, home to the state asylum where they placed me and the other eighteen geriatric inmates after the women's penitentiary became overcrowded. It's also the hometown of the late Benjamin Costello, former mayor of Darren and heir to Costello Railways, a line of rails that brought hope and prosperity to the people in rural Appalachia.

At least, that's what the travel brochure says.

From the window of my room, I watched it all. The crane was only a gnat in my vision, but I saw the scene before me as if I were standing at the base of the statue myself. It took three days to erect. The cement was poured first. Then on the second day, a pedestal was placed in the center of the square. And on the third morning, before the sun was fully awake and her early-morning glare was still hazy with fatigue, the crane rolled in, Benjamin's bronze body clenched in its mighty jaws. A crowd had gathered. They applauded as the figure landed heavily on the cement podium and the crane removed its teeth from around his neck.

At night, I close my eyes, and the moon shines down on the memorial. The light makes the monument glow like freshly baked skin after a morning spent in the sun, creating a fine layer of sweat on Benjamin's upturned face. The room is quiet, and I am alone. Fluorescent lights flicker out in the hall, and the water-stained walls lean closer as I hum a song Benjamin once sang to me while picking crab apples in the woods.

Here we go round the mulberry bush, the mulberry bush, the mulberry bush. Here we go round the mulberry bush, on a cold and frosty morning.

I think of the first time I saw Benjamin. He was just a boy then, stumbling out from the trees with an apple in either hand. *Sweet Galas,* he told me. The ones that grow on the low branches of the fruit trees. Benjamin always did have an affinity for sugar. He juggled the apples in his hands before catching the last in his mouth to make me laugh.

When I did, he took a large bite and grinned, a thin line of sweet juice trickling through the gap in his teeth and down his chin.

When the moon is at her highest peak, the ghosts come. They crawl up Benjamin's hands and feet, wrap their arms around his broad shoulders and thick neck. They claw and pull at the bronze overcoat, the polished boots, the erect musket, and I wonder if they have enough strength to push the statue over, to make it crumble at their feet. All the while, Benjamin stares straight ahead, never looking down at those who writhe beneath him.

One

I leave for Darren by train. It's a long nine hours from the Amtrak hub in Ann Arbor to the station in Morehead, Kentucky, and my body lurches and sways with the rails. As the train departs, I pick at my nails and watch the brick university towers that mark the urban college town shrink. They never looked small to me before. Even when I left for graduate school at the School of the Art Institute of Chicago, my car weighed down with paints and blank canvases, the university still loomed large in the rearview mirror.

I am somewhere in the southern corner of Ohio when the land begins to fold into rolling hills pigmented with green trees. If I were to paint them, I would use acrylics, not oils. Their dark-olive complexion is too rich for the denser paints; they would smear. It's the mountains that need the oils. Their shadowy ridges and hazy peaks. Acrylics could never adequately capture the uneven textures and smoky light.

The train is hot and full of people. The leather seats are covered in deep scars that scratch against my legs. The material pulls at my skin when I cross one knee over the other.

A woman sits next to me. She is slight and petite and holds a small boy, who draws shapes on the window with his wet fingertip. The woman reminds me of Anh Nguyen, the owner of the Vietnamese market in Chicago. I used to stop there almost every day for a cup of pho or ramen. Anh would always send me home with a large bowl, even when I paid for a small.

This is the first time I've been on a train since leaving Chicago, but, looking at the woman sitting next to me, the scent of pho tangled in her hair, I feel calmer than I thought I would. My fingertips tap against my thigh, but the rhythm is steady, controlled.

I pull out the letter from the mayor of Darren. It's addressed to my father, a professor of Medieval Art History at the University of Michigan.

"Darren County," Dad said when he first handed me the letter a month ago. "It was where my father lived."

I looked up in surprise. Dad rarely mentioned his father. My grandmother, Valerie Costello, had never liked to talk about him. All Dad knew was that his father had grown up in the Kentucky hills, had fought in the Second World War, and had become the town's mayor. He was the son of a man who had founded a railway company, and when Benjamin had taken over the business, he'd built a line that had added Darren to the midwestern trade routes. Dad hadn't even known Benjamin had been murdered until I'd read about it in an old newspaper clipping I'd found while researching my family's history for a sixth-grade genealogy assignment.

"How odd," Dad said when I showed him the article. The fragile clipping looked small in his hand, and I realized how easy it would be for him to simply wad it up inside his fist and throw it into the wastepaper basket.

Benjamin had been twenty-eight when he was killed, the article read. He had been murdered by a woman named Eloise Price, who was still imprisoned at the women's penitentiary in Morehead, Kentucky.

When I'd asked Dad why he wasn't more upset, he'd just shrugged and said, "I never met the man. How can I mourn his absence?"

It was true that Dad had never known Benjamin. My grandmother had been pregnant when she'd left Darren after Benjamin's death, taking a train north to Chicago, where she'd gotten a job serving eggs and hotcakes at a corner diner on the south side of the city. When I'd first moved to Chicago, I looked for the diner, but it had burned down over twenty years before and a laundromat had been built over its remains.

After Dad left for college, his mother had lived in a small cottage just off the coast of the Atlantic. It had a red roof and a pink door that cried like a hungry kitten when you pried it open. She'd lived there for twenty-six years until she came down with a bad case of double pneumonia six months ago that sent her to the hospital. She'd died three days later. I'd driven with Dad to Maine for the funeral, and on the way home, he'd handed me the box of Valerie's ashes. All I could think about was how it was so much lighter than my mother's porcelain urn.

The train jerks, and I smooth the letter over my kneecap and reread the now-familiar words written in bold, sharp ink:

28 August 1997

Dear Dr. David Costello,

I write to you as mayor of Darren Township. I'm sure it's not lost on you that this March will be the fiftieth anniversary of the death of your father, Corporal Benjamin Costello. Corporal Costello is held in the highest esteem here in Darren for his acts of bravery and selflessness during the Second World War and after. We consider ourselves much indebted to your family.

On the anniversary of the corporal's death, we would like to commemorate his achievements, courage, and contributions by erecting a statue in his honor in the town square. We also plan to create an exhibit in memoriam for Corporal Costello in the Darren County Historical Museum. We have numerous items of memorabilia that will be displayed, along with photographs, testimonies, and personal letters, graciously contributed by several townsfolk. If there are any of your father's personal items that you would be willing to donate, we would be most grateful. However, that is not the reason for my writing.

The Darren County Literary Society wants to commission a member to paint a portrait that will be hung in the museum. However, as the society is quite small, frankly, no one feels up to the task. I've learned you are an artist and art historian in Ann Arbor and, since he is your father, I write to ask of your interest in taking on this project. We can offer 500 dollars as compensation, a single room for lodging, and a small stipend during your time here in Darren. If this is suitable to your needs, we do ask that the project be completed by the end of January, as we hope to have the full exhibit open to the public with the coming of the new year.

On a more personal note, I had the pleasure of meeting your father once as a small boy. I was riding my bicycle down the street when a large stick got stuck in the rear cog. The wheel creaked and jammed, nearly sending my body flying onto the road. Corporal Costello came by as I was bloodying my fingers trying to remove the spur. He knelt and worked the stick out himself, with fingers like a wood peddler and the patience of a fisherman. He patted me on the shoulder and sent me on my way with a military salute. I am pleased to report that many others had similar encounters with the corporal, for he was as competent and willing as he was amiable.

We do very much hope that you will consider our offer. It would be an honor to have the offspring of Corporal Costello in Darren Township once again.

Yours,

Mayor Anthony Grant

"A memorial?" I was sitting with Dad at the dining table when he first showed me the letter. "I didn't realize Benjamin was that big of a celebrity."

Dad shrugged and leaned against the high-back chair that was a gift from the University of Michigan's Medieval Department to celebrate his tenure. Dad loved anything old and ornate. Anything that had a history. When the Medieval Department presented him with the cherrywood chairs covered in carvings that bled down the chairbacks and arms, he spent the better half of the following week researching their origin. He was always more interested in an object's history than a person's. It was safer, I liked to think. Not so messy.

"Are you going?" I asked.

He reached into his shirt pocket and pulled out a pack of cigarettes, tapping the head of one on the inside of his wrist before placing it between his lips and lighting a match. Dad never used a lighter. He said they dampened the experience for him.

He slid the pack across the table toward me as I pulled a lighter from the pocket of my jeans.

"So?" I gestured to the letter.

He took off his glasses. Dad never rushed. He ran a hand over his thinning gray hair and looked past me, toward the reproduction of Boltraffio's *The Adolescent Saviour* that hung on the wall above the buffet. It was a portrait of the Virgin Mary that was harrowing and ghostly in appearance. "I was thinking you might want to," he said.

"Want to what?"

He nodded toward the letter, which had become like a golem sitting between us. "To go to Darren."

"To go to Darren," I repeated.

"Yes."

"But the letter is to you." I was baffled. I couldn't go to Darren. I could paint a portrait, sure, but Dad had always been the better artist. Though he studied art more than he practiced, our house was still adorned in his work. I was only a mediocre art student who had dropped out of the program after being awarded the School of the Art Institute of Chicago Fellowship for the following year, an offer I'd declined when I'd decided to move back home to Ann Arbor and never think about the city again.

"Antigone, don't get ash on the table."

I looked at my hand. A small pile of ash had fallen from the tip of the cigarette and onto the wooden tabletop. I wiped it to the floor.

Hey diddle, diddle, the cat and the fiddle, the cow jumped over the moon.

The old nursery rhyme scratched against the inside of my ear, and I cringed. It was the same aggravating tune that had plagued me ever since I left Chicago.

"I can't go to Darren," I confirmed. "You should go. You're on sabbatical soon." My palm itched, and I scratched the soft skin just above the flower I'd had inked on the inside of my wrist: Monet's water lily. I had two tattooed, one on each arm.

Dad frowned and leaned forward to rest both his arms on the tabletop, flicking ash into the dish at his side in a single fluid motion. Even his filth was orderly. "I'm working on a grant. It is out of the question."

"I'm barely an artist," I protested. It wasn't entirely a lie. It had been months since I'd picked up a paintbrush.

"Bullshit," he countered.

"They asked for you."

"I think they will settle for any Costello descendant."

Dad looked at me, and for the first time since I had come home from Chicago, I felt like he was really seeing me, his dark eyes searching my face.

I thought of my sixth-grade genealogy project. It had been somewhat of a joke. Dad had no siblings, and his tree branches were as bare as the dogwoods in the middle of a Michigan winter. My mother's family was small, names etched onto twigs that would snap when the winter snow became too heavy. Mom had never known her father. She and Dad had that in common when they'd met.

"Aren't you curious?" My voice softened. "He was your father. Don't you want to see where he lived? Where he died?"

Dad looked pensive for a moment, as if he wanted to say something but the words were too far apart to form. He put out his cigarette, a quick push down into the ashtray, before turning toward the window. The light shining on his skin made him look twenty-five years younger, and I saw my father as the man he'd been before I was born, the man he'd been when he'd met a young woman and asked her to be his wife: young, proud, and fearless.

"I think it might be good for you to get away for a while," he said. The words held me in place. "You've been home for over a month now, and after Chicago"—his voice caught on the name of the city, like it was a bad taste in the back of his mouth—"it might be good to be somewhere new. A fresh start for a couple months. Get your mind off things."

I nearly laughed. *Get my mind off things.* Forget what happened. Forget the way the alley had felt underneath my skin, the way the gravel and cement shards had stayed lodged in the divots underneath my knees, against my shins, wedged in the bloody scratches that had bruised and scarred. I had picked them out for days.

I pushed back from the table. The chair legs screeched against the floor, and the wood trembled. "It would be easier for you if I did, wouldn't it?" I said, standing. I was angry now. Angry that Dad didn't care more about his family than his work, angry that he'd suggested I do what was asked of him, angry that he'd brought up Chicago.

"You should go. He was your father. He is your history." I turned to leave.

"Antigone." Dad called my name as I was leaving the room.

I paused.

"There are some parts of a man's history that he cannot learn for himself. They have to be told to him through a funnel. That way, if it all becomes too much, he can put out his hand and simply stop the flow."

✦

In Morehead, a man is waiting outside the station. I see him even before I disembark. He stands to the side of the small brick building and looks miserably hot. He has a mop of thick, unruly hair that is pressed down with a backward baseball cap and wears dirty jeans and a flannel shirt that covers wide shoulders. He can't be more than thirty years old. Dad told me that someone would be waiting for me at the station.

The man looks past me, watching the other passengers. I can tell from the way he rocks back and forth on the heels of his feet that he is waiting for someone he has never met. I know that someone is me.

I roll my heavy suitcase behind me and walk over to him. My pulse beats in my eardrums. He is tall but not tall enough that I couldn't reach his eyes if he grabbed the inside of my wrist. His legs are shorter than his torso, and I'm certain I could outrun him if I had to. I glance down at my black-soled loafers. I should have worn sneakers.

I grip the handle of my suitcase a little tighter. "Are you waiting for someone?"

The man turns. In the light, he looks older, his skin weathered from too much time in the sun.

"I'm supposed to be meeting someone here," I tell him.

"Sorry," he says. "I'm waiting on a man from up north." His voice is low, a deep burgundy, much lower than my father's.

"You're looking for David Costello?" I know I'm right when a confused expression crosses the man's face. "I'm his daughter, Tig," I explain. "My father sent me on his behalf. I'm here for Benjamin's memorial."

The man startles but recovers well.

"I'm an artist," I tell him, as if this makes me less of an impostor. "Dad thought I might be able to hold the paintbrush better than he can."

The joke falls at the man's feet.

He takes off his hat, and his hair looks like a wet head of lettuce. The flattened curls and cowlicks are thick with sweat. He wipes a hand over the dark mess before setting the cap right back where it was. "We weren't expecting a lady," he says. At least he's honest. "Mae will be pleased. She wasn't too keen on having a man living up above her."

He holds out his hand and introduces himself as Jason, personal assistant to Mayor Grant.

"We don't have many visitors passing through." Jason bows his head to the gravel walkway, and a shy smile traces his lips. "And not many come this way carrying a suitcase on wheels."

I look down at the hard plastic shell, cringing when I notice the dirt roads and cracked asphalt. "Leave it to plastic to give me away then," I joke awkwardly. My hand loosens around the handle.

Jason laughs graciously before offering to carry the case.

"I got it," I insist when he reaches for the handle the second time. My voice has a bite to it that still tastes unfamiliar.

Jason takes a step back, wiping the sweat from his upper lip. He brushes a hand on the front of his jeans and looks up. "It's been hotter than normal this fall."

I rearrange the suitcase in my hand and lift it off the ground, determined to carry it the rest of the way. Jason is right: it is hot here. I am used to midwestern summers, the streets heavy with sweaty bodies and recycled air, but the humidity in Darren is as thick as the smoke I pull into my lungs every time I draw from a cigarette.

The station sits at the bottom of a foothill and is surrounded by trees. In the distance, the mountains roll their shoulders at the birds that fly overhead. In Chicago, and in Ann Arbor, there were pockets of color. The vibrant bouquets and flower arrangements from Patty's Petal Shop. The heavy dark blue of the Chicago River after it rained. The stream of yellow taxis strung like Christmas lights flickering across the streets. But nothing like here. Here the trees are on fire, the red and orange and yellow leaves stained with colors so rich that the paint couldn't be diluted.

"The hills look like they're burning," I murmur.

Jason squints. "Yep, I suppose they do." When I look back at him, I catch him eyeing me warily.

"Something wrong?" I am instantly uncomfortable.

He blushes. "No, ma'am."

I am suddenly very aware of myself. Not only of the suitcase I am holding but of my hemmed pants, fitted top, long dark hair pulled back in a plastic clip that digs into my scalp. I press my hand against the side of my pants, searching for a pocket, for something to hold on to.

Jason leads me to a green pickup truck. It is freckled with rust and has a large dent on the right front side as if it has recently encountered a metal pole. As he lifts my luggage over the tailgate, I see a wooden structure in the truck bed. It looks like a cedar box missing a wall. Placed inside is a black bucket full of wood shavings. Two paint cans are pushed against the back, and a red toolbox holds them in place. The plastic bed liner is a wig of dirt and pine needles. When I slide onto the front seat, I'm careful not to sit on the large coffee stain that blossoms on the edge of the fabric.

I roll down the side window. "You mind?"

The train ride has made my stomach churn, and the air here feels light. It draws the city noise and smog from my body.

Jason pulls the shifter into gear. "I think you'll like it up here just fine," he says as I stretch my arm out the open window to grasp a fistful of air. "Once you get those wheels off that damn suitcase."

I bite the side of my cheek to hide my chuckle. Damn suitcase, indeed.

Two

On the night Dad asked me to go to Darren, I sat in my bedroom and pulled out *The Woman in the Woods*, the last painting I'd ever made in Chicago. It was settled in a crate of work I had sent to Ann Arbor when I left the city. It was a large canvas, and I had secured it in many layers of Bubble Wrap that I unwound slowly before leaning the painting upright against the far wall.

It took a meticulous gaze to notice the woman. At first, all you saw were the tall trees illuminated by the dark-purple sky and the moon-light. Oaks, not pines. This had been important to me at the time. The woman in the painting stood below the tallest tree on the canvas. A silhouette with a pool of light spilled around her feet.

"The light source is brilliant," I had been told by my professor. His voice was bloated with New York. "What inspired this?"

"I don't know," I'd replied truthfully.

Later, I pulled out an old shoebox full of photographs that I had collected over the years. Most were of me when I was young: soft and fawn-eyed. Toward the bottom of the box, hidden beneath a handful of ticket stubs, was a picture of my grandmother. She was standing up to her knees in a river, wearing a paisley-print dress that she had bunched up in her hands to keep from the water. Her body bent forward as she laughed at someone standing on the other side of the lens. Her hair was dark and wild and familiar. Behind her, growing along the river's edge, were hundreds of trees. On the back of the photograph, written in fine penmanship, were the words "Darren, KY, 1935."

As I knelt in front of *The Woman in the Woods*, my father still sitting at the dining table studying the words of a letter sent from a place he had never been, I thought again of the photograph. Valerie would have been only a teenager then. Before she was married, before the war, before she was pregnant and her husband was murdered. Why did she leave Darren? I wondered. She must have had relatives there, family.

I reached forward and traced the outline of the woman standing among the trees. There was a quiet pulsing inside me. *I could go to Darren,* I thought. *Find this river my grandmother stood in and walk through the trees that I painted on a piece of canvas.* I closed my eyes, and the sharp sting of tears settled near the bridge of my nose.

My hands were shaking when I reached up and took a set of keys off the desk, the cool metal licking my palm. I took the corner of the key and rubbed its sharp teeth over the woman's legs. Four inches of canvas sheared like the skin on my knees when the man from the bar had pressed me against the dumpster as he unbuckled his pants. Did I want this? He hadn't given me a chance to answer. I dragged the key across the woman's stomach, her shoulders, her face. And finally her hands.

A woman erased.

I placed the painting in the dark corner of my closet and stood. When I looked down, my hands no longer shook.

✿

Darren is a thirty-minute drive from Morehead and a steady incline up into the hills. From the station, Jason takes the old truck down a paved road that winds and curls between two red-rock cliffs. The road is smooth, but I am dizzy from watching the hills pass so closely. Ahead, the Appalachians loom, raising their sugary peaks into the dazed sky.

"There's a reason they call them the Smokies." Jason nods toward the voluptuous skyline. "You see that blue mist over there?" He points to the fine peaks of the rocks. "It never goes away. Just settles there. Even the hot sun can't shine it away when it gets going."

He leans close to the wheel and peers up through the fogged windshield. "Natives used to call it Shaconage—Place of Blue Smoke. Used to think them hills had a bit of magic deep in them. Easy to get lost up in those parts."

When I was young, Dad took me to Arizona to see the Grand Canyon. We stood on the edge of the cliff, and Dad put me on his shoulders. I thought no one had ever seen so much of the world at one time. We took a boat tour on the river, and Dad pointed out the small hollows high up on the canyon walls. They were like foxes' eyes glowing in the middle of midnight woods. He was quick to tell me that the caves had once belonged to the Navajo, who had settled there far earlier than the Europeans had. They're empty now, but legend holds that all the hollows were connected in a labyrinth of elaborate tunnels that twisted and turned like intestines inside the body of the canyon.

Many men have gone into one hollow never to come out again, Dad said. *They tried to retrace their paths, but once inside, the caves and tunnels were like trees in a forest: too thick and dense to know north from south. Easy to hide there. Easier still to get lost.*

"And there is Whitmore Halls. In all her awful glory." Jason points to a large estate halfway up the hills, an ominous presence shadowing Darren. It is made of stone, with long pillars holding a large veranda up above the front entrance. The right of the house has a three-story tower that leaves the home strangely lopsided, as if she were stuck with a permanent frown. The mansion is freckled with windows, most boarded up, though some, near the top, are just black holes left open. A sheet of ivy grows up the side of the home and curls into the exposed windows. The forest is thick around the property, and I'm not sure I would have been able to find the estate had Jason not pointed it out to me. This is the former home of Eloise Price. This is where my grandfather was murdered.

"Was quite beautiful once, I'm told." Jason taps the wheel with the palm of his hand. "But a place can only contain evil for so long before it gets to spilling out. That's what my pap always used to say."

I stare out at the estate until it is swallowed by the trees, and Jason turns the truck into town. There is a river running alongside us. It flows from the hills down through the left ventricle of eastern Kentucky. Jason tells me it's called Mud River, and that it floods almost a dozen times a year, leaving the county covered in muck and trash. It's been dry this season, and the water is low, moving sluggishly three feet down from the outer banks as it follows us into town.

We turn onto the main street, and I see that it is lined with flags. They stand along both sides of the asphalt, hung from a series of electrical poles, and each one is coupled with a poster of a war veteran.

"Our boys of war," Jason says when he notices me eyeing the black-and-white photographs. Most can't be more than seventeen years old. "Seventy-eight of them. Many served in the Second World War, but there is a good handful of World War I vets up there."

"How long have they been up?" I note the worn colors and frayed edges.

"Long time," Jason says reverently. "A long time."

He slows the truck to a stop in front of a small store. The name on the sign was once painted in thick black letters, but now most of the color is chipped and peeling. There is a smaller sign hanging from the front screen door that says GENERAL STORE. The building looks as if it could sigh and collapse.

"Got to make a quick pit stop." Jason gets out of the truck and strolls up the stairs. He pulls on his loose jeans as if he has recently lost a bit of weight and is still getting used to his new physique.

Two men sit on the front porch of the store. Both wear dirty jeans and loose shirts with cutout sleeves. One, a lanky man with dark hair that looks a week past a good washing, stands and leans against the front of the building. He lights a cigarette and presses the sole of his right shoe against the back wall. He glances at the truck and grins.

My eyes dart toward the screen door. A car pulls up in front of the store, but the slouching man's gaze holds firm on the truck's windshield. He lifts the cigarette to his mouth, and gray smoke rushes from his nostrils. A crow lands on the telephone wire and calls out in distress for his mate.

The screen door shrieks, and Jason appears. The man on the porch turns at the sound. I take a deep breath and look down at my feet. My right knee is bouncing up and down, and my fingers are curled inside my palm. When I release them, four perfect crescent-shaped moons are left on my skin.

Jason climbs back into the truck. "Sorry about that," he says. "Just had to get a couple of things for the wife. Not good to be on her nasty side." He waves a brown sack in his hand.

I give Jason a tired smile and reach in my pocket for a cigarette, cursing when I remember they are in the suitcase that is sliding back and forth across the floor of the truck bed. I tell myself that this is the perfect opportunity to quit the habit but, God, does it do wonders for anxiety. A small spider lands on the dashboard, and I jump. It's black and the size of a nickel, sunning its bulbous body twelve inches from my face. I recoil.

"Just a little one." Jason reaches over and crushes the spider with his bare hand. He wipes his palm on the front of his shirt. "All right, now," he says, shifting the truck into first. "Let's get you home."

✿

Mae's Soap and Spool Shop sits between a tanning salon with bikini tops hanging in the windows and a pawn shop that advertises WE BUY GOLD AND GUNS. SOLD CHEAP! The building is made of brick, much of it crumbling, and there is a freshly painted sign hanging from a shepherd's hook on the right side of the door. The front window is wiped clean and has a large display of roses in one corner. Inside, in the display window, two baskets sit on an iron bench. One is filled with bright-colored yarn, the other with handmade soap. On the floor, next to the bench, a large orange tabby cat is lying in the sun.

"That's Cougar. Don't like cats much, but that one's all right." Jason pulls my bag from the back of the truck and leads me up the front steps.

Inside, the shop smells like lavender and vanilla and honey. The space is small, not much larger than the apartment I rented on Dahlia Street in Chicago. The walls are a series of shelves that run from floor to ceiling and are covered with baskets full of yarn, all organized by color. Together, they look like the wildflowers that grow in the arboretum back home. Along the back wall sits a counter with a cash register next to a glass jar full of mints. Three tables are placed in a sort of triangle throughout the space, each one covered with rows of soap.

Cougar saunters over to greet us, pressing his well-fed body against the side of my leg. I jump at the sudden pressure and then kneel to stroke the cat between his ears. His fur is soft, and running my fingers through the long strands is as pleasurable as opening a fresh tube of paint.

A woman sits on a rocking chair in the far corner of the shop. Her shoulders are so straight against the chairback that I wonder if she is leaning against the wood at all. She is hand sewing the bottom cuff of a pair of pants and doesn't look up when we come inside. "You're late," she says without taking her eyes off the needle. Her voice has a hardness to it, a grit, as if it has deepened over years of hardship. It is the voice of someone who has lost.

"I told you sometime this afternoon, Mae." Jason pops a mint in his mouth. "Besides, I had to stop at the General to get a few things. The clock's been killing me."

Mae glances up at us for the first time since we came into the shop. "Thought they were sending a man." She looks me up and down slowly. Cougar purrs at my feet.

"This is Tig Costello," Jason introduces me. "Benjamin's grand-daughter. Her father couldn't make the trip."

"The mayor know that?" Mae stands and folds the pair of pants she is hemming in two squares, taking time to make sure each crease is flat and pressed.

I shift my weight from my left foot to the right and back again, feeling less sure of myself than when I got off the train.

A fan churns in the corner of the shop. Its steel blades cackle. "You'll be staying here with Mae," Jason tells me. "She has a place she rents out upstairs." He gestures to a staircase I hadn't noticed before.

I nod. Mae still hasn't said one word to me, but her eyes follow my slight shifts before settling on the suitcase at my feet. Cougar is busy rubbing his head against the hard plastic.

"I used to live above an antique shop," I tell her. This is a lie. When I first moved to Chicago, I began my apartment search as if I were a forty-year-old professional with disposable income. I looked at places with two bedrooms, central air, an electric stove. One apartment was above a small boutique that sold clothes and jewelry secondhand. The woman who owned it didn't want to rent to a nineteen-year-old student because, she said, college students were messy and poor. She was right.

"Mae's owned this shop for thirty years now. About right, Mae?" Jason says. "And her family before that."

Mae has a round, wide face with a voluptuous nose standing between brown eyes that darken when she hums in agreement. "We've been around a long time in these hills." Mae's eyes trail unapologetically over my freckled neck, thin wrists, the undercurve of my knee peeking out from a rip in the denim. I have the sudden urge to pull the wings of my jacket tighter, to conceal the parts of me that feel like they are no longer my own.

When Jason says he has to get back to the office, Mae looks relieved. He bends down to give Cougar one last pet on the head and then reaches up to adjust his baseball cap. "I'm sure I'll be seeing you, Tig," he says to me. "Be good to Miss Mae. She's the heart of this town."

I expect the corners of Mae's mouth to turn upward at the endearment, but they stay in a firm line above her chin. When he leaves, she sighs, and her shoulders drop an inch.

"He seems nice." I immediately blush at my banal comment. It tastes like Dad's watered-down lemonade.

If Mae notices my awkwardness, she says nothing until Jason starts the truck and pulls away from the shop. "Folks always seem nice till they're not. He works for the mayor. It's best if you remember that."

I'm about to ask more about the mayor when she looks at me fully, her eyes like two eclipsed suns.

"And he's married," she says. "Best if you remember that too."

I nearly laugh at the unexpected insinuation. Part of me wants to ask what it is about me that screams "sex-crazed home-wrecker," but I lost what little nerve I had after Chicago. I give her my most reassuring smile and tell her she has nothing to worry about. "I have no interest in men," I say. "Only in my work."

She folds her arms over her chest. "Women can cause trouble. And I stay away from trouble." I'm surprised when she reaches over and places her hand under my chin. She tilts my head upward. "You have a pretty face," she says. "Soft skin. Lonely eyes."

I haven't let many people touch me since the night in the alley, and I still. Tremors tickle the bottoms of my feet.

"When the mayor told me Benjamin's son was coming to stay for a few months to help with the memorial, and that he was to stay here above my shop, I was downright angry. Can't say no to the mayor." Mae shakes her head. "Doesn't matter if I lose the extra income from renting the space."

Mae pulls her hand from my face. "So I tell him all right. As if he were asking. Now, here you stand, a young woman from the city, and I'll tell you again that I don't want any trouble. I don't make trouble, and I don't go asking for trouble." Mae pauses as Cougar rubs against her legs. "Now, that's not to say that trouble hasn't gone and found me from time to time. But I have a nice life here, and I don't intend to let trouble take that from me anytime soon."

I feel a softness toward Mae. "I understand," I tell her. "Trouble's found me too."

The corners of Mae's mouth pull up. "Honey," she says, "your trouble don't look nothing like my trouble."

Mae turns and waves her hand for me to follow her up the set of narrow stairs. It is humid, and the heat makes the scent of old cat urine steam from the warped wood. Mae opens the door at the top of the steps and leads me into a small apartment. The kitchen is to the right, hardly big enough for the card table placed in the corner. There is a stove and a refrigerator that is the color of mustard with a long silver handle that looks like a butter knife dipped into margarine. The walls of the sitting room are covered in peeling forest-green wallpaper with a rose trim border settling under the top of the baseboards. Even inside, I can't escape the forests.

The bedroom to the left is only large enough for a twin-size bed and a four-drawer chest. "And the bathroom is right through there." Mae points to it. The room is dark, but I can still see the flowered wallpaper and furry pink toilet seat cover. I think of Dad's horrified expression if he'd been standing here now, and I hide my smile.

"It's great," I tell Mae truthfully. "I'm used to tight spaces. The apartments in Chicago are notorious for being small and dirty." I instantly cringe at the blunder. "Nothing like this," I recover. "This place would be picked up in an instant."

Mae's mouth sharpens into a straight line. "Well, a little dirt never hurt anything." Her head tilts to the right, and her eyes drift over my thin frame.

I tuck my hair behind my ear and look around the room nervously.

"I'm a simple woman, Ms. Costello . . . ," Mae says.

"Tig."

Her mouth tightens at my interruption. "Pardon?"

"I go by Tig."

"All right then. Tig." My name sounds like a curse word. "Now, like I was saying, I'm a simple woman. I have a couple rules that I follow, and as long as you'll be staying here with me, I expect you to do the same."

I dig my hands in my pockets. I'm not used to rules. Dad never had any. I never needed them.

"I don't want you coming in all hours of the night," Mae says. "I sleep in that room downstairs, in the back part of the shop, and I'm a light sleeper. I spend my days making soap and sewing hems for pretty ladies, and when I go to sleep at night, I want to sleep." She reaches over to turn the rim of a glass vase sitting on the bureau. It is filled with wildflowers. "Second rule. When the shop's closed, it's closed. When I'm gone, no one comes in this shop. No exceptions. And last"—she pops off the wilted head of a pink flower with the quick press of a finger against thumb—"there is going to be a lot of attention on you. Everyone is excited about the memorial, and people will be curious about what you've got to say. I don't want to hear of you attracting any more attention than necessary. A woman attracting attention is trouble, and I already told you that I don't want trouble. Do you understand?"

A squall of unease stirs around my feet. I am beginning to realize that my time in Darren may not be as peaceful as Dad assured. I knot my hands together and wonder if Mae can see the tension.

"I understand," I confirm.

"Good, then I'll let you get settled."

Mae turns toward the staircase. She has a light walk for a woman of her size, and the pads of her bare feet touch the floorboards in the soft, worn places where the wood is pliable and absorbent. The floor is darker there, sanded down by skin and oil. Somewhere, from down in the shop, a grandfather clock chimes. For the first time since I arrived in Darren, something turns loose inside me: a rusted bolt cracks, and the pipes shudder.

"Mae?" I call before she leaves the room. "Where is the statue?"

Her eyes close for a moment and lips purse as if she's swallowed a sour pucker. "Down the main street about three blocks. You can't miss it." She points out the window. "Blocks out all the sunlight on West State Avenue."

I turn and look out the glass as if the statue will suddenly appear on the other side of the frame. "I think I may take a walk to see it."

"Not a bad place to start," Mae replies. I feel like she already knows I'm at a loss as she shakes her head once and walks down the stairs.

I kick off my shoes and take a moment to digest my new surroundings. The counters are scrubbed clean, and the stove is spotless around the paint chips and rusted burners. It looks twice as old as me, but I'm fairly certain that there aren't mice living underneath. On the card table is a vase full of flowers. They are green and yellow and red and purple and made of plastic. I open the refrigerator and see the bulb has burned out, but the shelves are wiped, and there is a loaf of bread and a stick of butter sitting above the crisper. In the side door, there is a half-empty jar of milk. I decide to wait to smell it.

The light in the living room is perfect for sketching. A pink-and-green-striped sofa is pushed against the far wall. It will have to move, I decide, just a little to the right. Enough to set the easel to the left of the window where the sunlight will strike the canvas midafternoon. *Just like a cat stretching out on a windowsill,* Dad used to say to me, *you always paint in the sun.*

I unpack quickly. I don't like to waste time, and I want to see the statue before it gets dark. In the bathroom, I slip a worn T-shirt over my head, tucking the hem into the waistband of a pair of newly cut-off shorts. The faces of the *Beverly Hills 90210* cast are plastered across my chest, and I wonder if the Walsh twins felt as displaced in Beverly Hills as I do now in Darren County.

The air in the apartment is stale, and I use the bottom side of my palm to push up on the window, breaking it free from the sill and closing my eyes when a warm rush of fresh air filters in. I kneel on the floor and lean my upper body against the screen as I light a cigarette. Through the mesh, Darren is made of a thousand tiny squares: the red tin roofs that shimmer in the sun; the blinking streetlight; the old, rusted pickup truck that sits across the road; the brick peak of the county courthouse looming behind the trailer park; the red-white-and-blue flags that have waved tirelessly for the last fifty-five years.

Cubism is a distortion of reality. I learned this in a second-year art seminar focusing on the avant-garde movement in the early twentieth century. You can never be certain about what you see. There is always something more happening underneath, in the soil just beneath the surface.

I lean forward, the tip of my nose pressing against the rough screen, and see Darren come undone into a thousand pieces under my gaze. Up in the hills, like the silhouette of a bird in flight, a building appears. It is no larger than my pinkie nail, bitten to the quick. *It must be miles away,* I think. There is a silent stirring in my stomach, much different from the rough teeth of hunger. This is a dull pulse, something dark and bitter that leaves me unsettled, and even though the humidity coaxes sweat from my skin, not even autumn's tired sun can stop me from shivering.

Three

Darren County is sinking. As I stroll toward the town park where the statue stands, I follow a sidewalk in desperate need of repair. The soil under the concrete has uprooted many of the cement slabs and left them cracked and slanted, creating a mountainous terrain that threatens to trip me with every step. The eyes of the boys of war look down at me, hiding smirks and snickers. Across the street, a woman waters a jungle of potted plants that decorate the rail of the cement patio attached to her trailer.

The park is on the east side of Darren, two blocks from the main drag of shops and convenience stores. It's bordered by a residential street to the right and Mud River on the left. I hear the water but can't see it through the tall trees and high bank.

When I reach the statue, I am disappointed to see that my grand-father's bronze body and rigid stance is much too imposing. The monument looks out of place in a town like Darren, where the buildings are made of wooden planks and tin roofs, and the homes, built nearly a century ago, are tired and beaten and placed haphazardly between double-wides that have sunk into the soil. The statue is more like a ghoul, a gargoyle fallen from a cathedral perch.

The words COURAGE, BRAVERY, HONOR are carved in the stone pedestal my grandfather stands on, his name and dates of life printed beneath. Benjamin himself is carved from bronze, and I stare at the square jaw and dark shadow beneath his chin, searching for some piece of him that is familiar. With the sun pouring over the park, his skin is radiant. On the center of his chest, in the hollow directly above his heart, a ring of sunlight strikes so violently that I'm forced to shield my eyes.

Bronze is an expansive metal, I remind myself. It breathes. Before it sets, it grows and expands. This is what allows the artist to create and refine the details.

"Impressive, isn't it?"

A man comes up beside me. He is short and has a thin, pointed nose that is red at the tip. His hair is trimmed close to the scalp, and his ears are like perfectly cut orange slices.

I take a step back, instinctively, and look to my right. A woman is carrying a child on her hip as she walks down the street. Her long hair is pulled back in a tight ponytail, and the ends whip against the side of her wide waist. Her shoes clap loudly on the cement.

"Mayor Anthony Grant." The man holds out his hand, and I notice an old shoebox tucked under his arm. He wears a dark suit coat, fraying at the hem but clean and pressed, over a white collared shirt. "Mae said you would be here."

The mayor. I lick my upper lip and shake his hand. The sunlight tickles the tops of his black leather shoes, and I spot a circle of dried mud on his heel. Somewhere to my left, the river rushes.

"You've come to see the statue." The mayor looks up at the monument with pride. "A beauty, isn't it?"

"It does make a statement," I say. I think of the first piece I ever created in Chicago, a sixty-two-pound papier-mâché uterus. I pieced it together on the floor of my dorm room after spending months collecting and scouring old newspapers. I would use only articles about women, I had decided. I wanted to fill the uterus with everything a woman is: books and pictures and tools and spices. I wanted to show the world that women are more than just baby ovens. It would be a statement piece. Every day I went to school smelling like wet dog.

"Pride of Darren." The mayor's eyes soften as if he were looking at a grandchild. "Was a good man."

His pointed pupils follow the lines of my body like a mortician assessing a cadaver. "It sure is a pleasure to have you here, Ms. Costello." He tugs on the corner of his jacket. "I assume you are comfortable with Mae?"

I tell him I am, and he nods. "She's been around these parts longer than I have. Salt of the earth." The mayor leans back on his heels, and the box under his arm shifts. I think of the way Jason and Mae wondered how he would react to my presence.

"I look forward to getting to know this place better." I am anxious for him to leave. "The flags are a nice touch." I gesture toward the nearest pole. The face of a boy of war stares back at me.

"Many good men have served from around here, sweetheart," he says. "Those men you see, up on those flags, are the same men who lived here fifty years ago, seventy years ago, some of them." He squints against the sun.

Mayor Grant looks back at me, then at the statue. I wonder which one of us appears more real. "So, you paint?"

I'm not sure if it's a statement or question, so I simply nod.

"Yes," I say when he remains silent. "I'm a graduate student at the School of the Art Institute of Chicago." Or was, six weeks ago. Before I walked to the enrollment center and told them to take my name off the list. *No, I don't need financial assistance. I'm not coming back.*

A car honks and tires screech. A man pushes his head through the window and yells. The flag on the street corner flaps.

"The thing is . . ." The mayor clenches his jaw as if he's ready to spit on the ground but thinks better of it. "I want to make sure this is done right. This memorial means a lot to us here in Darren. It represents who we are. People got the wrong idea about us. Truth is, we're hard workers and good people. And Benjamin is all of us now."

I think of my sixth-grade genealogy tree. Benjamin's name was so close to mine. Me and my father and his father and his father and his father. Branches of people I wouldn't recognize even if they were made of bronze. I look at the mayor and think of the story he wrote in his letter. Of how Benjamin fixed his bike when he was a child. I realize then that maybe Benjamin does belong to Darren, maybe more than he belongs to me. Maybe even more than he belongs to Dad.

I find myself suddenly wanting to comfort Mayor Grant. "I never met him," I say, looking up at my grandfather's stoic face. "But I think he would be really touched."

The mayor nods, only once. "Have you seen the museum yet?"

I shake my head, and he points across the square, down the long paved road that Jason and I drove in on. A large plantation-style house sits at the end. It is adorned with six tall pillars that support the upper half and a dozen more running parallel down either side of the home. An American flag dangles over the door.

"The Costello House," Mayor Grant says. "Marked a historical site about three years back. Was bought by Benjamin's father. One of the oldest places still in this town. A lot of history here." The mayor looks at me with interest, and I look away, feeling exposed. His tongue wets the corner of his mouth. "It's important to know your roots."

"That's why I'm here," I admit.

Mayor Grant chuckles, put at ease. "You should go there sometime. To the house, I mean. Talk to Anna. She knew Benjamin back in the day." A group of gnats fly around the mayor's neck, and he pulls at the collar of his shirt impatiently. A train whistle sounds, off in the distance, on the other side of the river.

"The river." I motion toward the sound of rushing water. "How far does it run?"

Mayor Grant turns and looks out at the tree line. The branches are colored in red and yellow and orange as the leaves purr in their autumnal prime. "About a hundred and fifty miles, give or take. Most people think she's part of the Cumberland, but she's got a mind of her own. Mud River. Makes a big mess during the rainy season. Meets up with the Mississippi at some point. Near the border."

I think of the photograph of Valerie, the water rippling around her knees. "Is there another around here?"

"River?" He shrugs. "Quite a few streams and eddies, but this is the only one that really amounts to much. The railways were built alongside it back when your grandfather was running things." The train blows its low whistle again, and the mayor chuckles as if he has just told a joke. "See what I mean? Used to be part of the canal system back in the 1800s until the railways came and replaced the steamboats. Your grandfather built the rails when he first became mayor back in '46. Was going to make this town a fortune. But then the rains came. Wasn't until after his death that the rails got to working right. It was such a shame that he never got to see his success."

The ground rumbles as the train wheels churn past. From here, I can't see the engine through the trees, but my body radiates with its hum.

I can't imagine Darren ever blooming with wealth. I'm about to ask the mayor more when he tells me he has to get back to the office. Linda doesn't like it when he's away for too long.

"I have something for you." The mayor hands me the shoebox. "This is what we have of Benjamin's."

I run my finger over the lip of the box, not sure if I should open the lid. It feels both weightless and ruinous, like I am holding something that should have been thrown out long ago.

"It's not much," the mayor concludes. "Just some old articles from the *Darren Daily*—that's the paper around here—and some things of Benjamin's that folks found and donated."

I thank him and place the box in my bag. Something shifts inside, and a warm weight presses against my rib cage.

"The thing is . . . ," the mayor begins.

I pause.

"All we really know about Benjamin was passed on to us, like everything in Darren." He looks up at the statue. "We got it secondhand."

The sunlight reflects off Benjamin's bronze shoe and onto the mayor's round cheeks. "He was such a private man," he muses.

"Sounds like my dad."

The mayor looks at me, his face painted with pity, and I suddenly worry that he is about to tell me something terrible. Dad called and he is sick. Dad left the coffeepot on, and an electrical fire burned down the house. All my artwork is gone. *The Woman in the Woods* is now a pile of ash.

"Such a tragedy. His death," the mayor says.

My mind scrambles. I look at the statue of Benjamin, and he is my touchstone.

"Don't you worry now, sweetheart." Mayor Grant stomps the heel of his left foot hard against the ground in indignation. "We keep our eyes on her."

I cock my head, perplexed. "I don't understand."

"Eloise Price." He spits her name into the air as if it were the shell of a sunflower seed. "That damned woman straight from hell. She used to be in the penitentiary two towns over, but last fall she was moved to the asylum. It's right up that hill over there." He points to a sterile-looking square building about five miles from where we stand. I lift a hand to my forehead to shield my eyes. The building looks familiar, and it takes me a minute before I realize this is the same structure I saw from my bedroom window. The dark silhouette is so similar to that of a bird in flight.

"A place for the elderly and criminally insane." The mayor grimaces.

I squint, and my gaze roams over the tall brick walls and circular peaks that rise from the four corners of the facility. Most of the property is hidden among the trees, but I can just make out the tall fence posts that circle the area. *Not much different from a prison,* I think. Are there iron bars in front of the windows? The wind picks up, and the trees fluff their feathery leaves. The river churns.

"Don't you worry, Ms. Costello," Mayor Grant repeats. "She's locked up real good."

✿

At the shop, Mae is sitting at one of the tables toward the back of the room. She is bent over a pot resting on a single electric burner plugged into the wall and placed atop the table. With one hand, she stirs the spoon, and with the other, she weighs cups of water on a small scale. The room smells like lavender and lemon.

"You see the statue?" She doesn't look up.

I nod. "Yes."

On the table, to Mae's right, are four wooden molds. Each is the size of a loaf pan and lined with parchment paper. Mae is making soap.

"Hand me that lye on the floor," she commands. "Be careful, it's nasty when it spills."

I reach down and lift the heavy bottle.

"I met the mayor." I grunt as I set the lye between us. "He gave me a box of Benjamin's things." I pull out the chair across from Mae and sit down, half expecting her to tell me to leave. She lifts her eyes, brows raised, but says nothing.

Mae turns the heat down on the burner and pours a cup of lye into a bowl full of water. "You ever make soap before?"

I shake my head.

"Here." She hands me the wooden spoon sitting inside the pot. "Stir. Slowly."

I lean forward and mix the watery substance. It's dark purple, and I think of the grape Jell-O I used to make in Chicago. "It smells heavenly," I tell Mae before coughing at the fumes.

"Don't breathe it in," she directs. "It's nasty in the lungs."

She pours lye into the glass cup and sets it on the scale. "The most important part of making soap is the measuring," she says. "It's not like cooking. There is no guessing. Everything must be precise."

"Sounds daunting," I admit, leaning back. "Where did you learn?"

Mae places a thermometer in the pot and frowns when the temperature rises. She turns down the heat and tells me to stir slower. I have to give the oils time to settle.

"From my momma, I suppose," she says, answering my question. "But I don't remember learning. Making soap is kind of like stories in that way. Gets passed down from one person to another along the way."

"You've lived in Darren all your life?"

"You're still going too fast."

I slow the course of the spoon once again.

"All my life," she says. "I've never even been in another state. Imagine." She leans back in her chair and looks around the shop. "These walls are the only ones I've known, and they've been plenty. My father worked in the coal mines until the accident. Those mines take more than they give to the people in the hills, but that's just the way of things. Better than the tobacco fields, if you ask me."

I ask Mae if she still has family in the area.

"Oh yes. My momma had eight children, and then her heart gave out. I was mostly grown by then. My sister Rosie and me took care of the house and made sure all those children were fed and right in the head."

It feels nice talking with Mae. When I moved back to Ann Arbor, I didn't reconnect with any of my hometown friends. Most had gone off to different states and schools, and I avoided the ones who remained. They were pieces of a life I had outgrown.

I hadn't expected to make friends with anyone in Darren. I wasn't expecting to ever come back after I finished my grandfather's portrait, but sitting at the table making soap with Mae, I feel a piece of me taking root, like some part of Darren will be coming home with me, even if it is just the recipe for making a bar of lavender-scented soap.

I clear my throat. "You're not married?" I assume.

Mae's eyes narrow. "You're a nosy one, aren't you?"

"I didn't mean . . ." My cheeks flush.

She waves a hand in front of her face. "Nobody ever means . . ." She sighs and turns the burner off. "Married for about ten years back in the fifties. Then he took up with the bottle, and it about killed him. Always sneaking off and hiding. Finally, one day he takes off for a night or two and never comes back." Mae smacks her lips. "Can't say I was too surprised."

She takes the spoon from my hand. "The funny thing is, I don't think I ever really loved him. I married him, sure. Thought I loved him. But when he skipped off, it was like a deer taking off for the woods after stopping in your yard for a salt lick. Nice to watch for a while but was always going to leave after a bit. And when he did, I just got on with life such as it was before. Maybe a little flutter in my heart, but then things got back to normal."

I stay quiet.

Mae shakes her head. "Glad we had no kids, though. Would have hurt them pretty bad."

I think of all the ways children are hurt by their parents, most of the hurt passed on from generation to generation, like stories and soap.

"So what did he give you?" Mae asks.

"Pardon?"

"The mayor." She glances toward my bag where the shoebox is settled.

I reach behind me and extract it from the fabric, setting it on the table beside the burner. The heat snaps at the back of my hand, and I slide the worn cardboard closer to my belly.

The box is filled with a handful of newspaper clippings, a handkerchief, a pipe, and a book of stamps.

"Not much." I frown. Benjamin's statue, three blocks down from the shop, stands tall and proud, but the rest of his legacy doesn't even fill a dusty shoebox.

I skim over an article about my grandfather's contributions to Darren and an announcement printed when he became mayor. Both features in the *Darren Daily*. I set them aside.

"All the girls were in love with him." Mae's eyes drift over the articles.

"You knew him."

Mae curls her fingers into her palms and rests the knuckles on the table's lip. "I was young. Just a child. But everyone knew him. He was the mayor. And a war hero. One of the ones who made it back."

"It's hard to imagine Benjamin," I confess. "I would love to know what he was like."

"Wouldn't we all." Mae grunts. "Benjamin wasn't the type of person who was easy to get to know, if you know what I mean."

I don't know what she means at all.

I pick up the handkerchief and trace over Benjamin's initials that are sewn into the top right-hand corner. A gift from his mother? The fabric is rough and yellow with age. I try to imagine Benjamin strolling down the street with the handsewn handkerchief in his pocket, but all I see is Gregory Peck walking along with a briefcase.

Underneath the cloth, there are more newspaper articles. A marriage announcement and an obituary. Both are short and formal, but below the marriage announcement there is a photograph of Benjamin and his bride, Valerie Dunn.

"It's my grandmother," I say quietly, holding the photograph gingerly between my fingertips.

"I was only a girl when he married Valerie," Mae says, "but that wedding. Lord, it was something." She shakes her head, and the yellow sweater she has tied around her shoulders falls to the side. "Valerie was only about nineteen."

I think of her. She was so small for a grandmother, so fragile. Every morning, she walked the shoreline before sunrise with a cup of bitter coffee, collecting sea glass. Greens and blues and a handful of yellows that she kept in wine bottles on the windowsill.

"He married her right when he came home from the war, and boy, did that get people talking." Mae pours another cup of lye into the pot.

I tell Mae that I don't understand.

"Only one reason why a wedding would be set up so fast like that." Mae hands me the spoon and nods for me to stir. "She was in a delicate condition."

"She was pregnant?" That can't be right. Dad was born three years later in the months after Valerie moved to Chicago.

Mae nods in confirmation. "Benjamin became mayor, the baby was born, and then the awful incident at Whitmore Halls." She shakes her head.

I look down at the photograph of my grandparents. This is the first picture I have seen of my grandmother with Benjamin, and I hold the newspaper clipping close to my face. She is younger than me, and her hair is dark and curled close to her shoulders. She wears a white dress that covers nearly all her skin. The train spreads out around the young couple's feet. They stand by a flower garden with white blossoms peeking out from behind their heads. Benjamin is to Valerie's right. He wears a black suit coat that looks a size too tight around his waist, and his left hand holds hers. They look happy, I think, standing in the garden in Darren.

Valerie was pregnant? It couldn't be true. Surely, Dad would've known if there had been another child. Unless Valerie lost the baby? I lean in to the aged picture. My eyes unapologetically scrutinize my grandmother's body, searching for a tight seam, a swollen curve, but the photograph gives nothing away. She was nineteen years old, newly married, possibly carrying a child. What was she feeling then, I wonder, on her wedding day?

Benjamin's obituary is underneath the marriage announcement. It is short and has thick creases down the middle as if it has been folded many times. I smooth the lines and read through the death announcement quickly. Obituaries always make my stomach clench.

There are several articles about Benjamin's passing: the suspected murder, the sentencing, and the verdict. Looking at all three together, I see a sketch of what happened on the night of Benjamin's death.

Eloise Price lived in Whitmore Halls with her aunt, Ulma. Both had been present the night of Benjamin's murder. The police found the body in the woods near the back of the home. He had been poisoned. Six days later, Eloise confessed to the murder.

From the article, I read that Eloise killed Benjamin because she was jealous of his marriage to Valerie Dunn. A crime of passion? It sounds like something out of the eye-rolling murder mysteries Dad always reads.

I clear my throat. "He was killed up at Whitmore Halls."

I say this as if Mae doesn't already know. The pads of her fingers twitch against the tabletop.

"Whitmore Halls," she repeats. "People thought that place was full of evil." Her voice is quieter now, but there is an edge to her words that gives me pause.

"Eloise and her aunt lived up there," I say, skimming the articles. "Did Benjamin know Eloise well?"

Mae coughs, a sharp spring of sound that makes my head snap upward. "Quite well. Those two were nearly inseparable as children. Created a lot of trouble. Darren was full of tragedy back then. The war. All that death. And then Marjorie Thomas went missing. People swore Eloise was up to no good in that house."

"Missing?" This is the first time I have heard about this. "Where did she go?"

The air shifts in the room, and suddenly I feel like I'm stepping closer and closer to the edge of the Chicago River. One wrong move and the current will pull me away. Mae's lips purse, her shoulders tighten, and for a second, I think I see fear flash across her features.

"Doesn't matter." Mae shakes her head brusquely. "I shouldn't have said anything about it. It was a long time ago, and what's done is done."

I nearly rear back from the accusatory look in Mae's gaze. Her eyes have darkened, and she pushes away from the table so violently that hot liquid slips over the lip of the pan. She grabs the handle. "There is work to be done," she snaps. She gathers up the molds and pulls the plug on the electric stove.

"I'm sorry." I stand. "I didn't mean to upset you."

"Oh, you didn't upset me." She turns and takes two large steps over to me. This is the closest we have been, and I feel the heat from her body.

"Listen, Tig." My name sounds like a curse word. "You can start with these scraps of paper and newspaper articles and whatever else the mayor gave you, but the truth is, the people around here know that great big statue much better than they knew Benjamin Costello." She takes a breath as if she is trying to calm herself.

"The funny thing is," she barks, "the person who probably knew your grandfather best is the woman who killed him."

She turns and walks to the back of the room. The closet door opens, and I hear boxes and cartons being shoved around on the shelves. I look out the front window of the shop. It's dark, and there are no streetlights here. I fight to see past my own reflection.

I think of the sanatorium sitting on the hilltop overlooking the town. *She's locked up real good,* the mayor said. I think of the large building, more like a prison than an asylum. I think of Eloise Price sitting inside her room and looking out the glass panes. Could she see the statue being erected? What does she know of Benjamin? What stories could she tell?

Cougar pads over and presses his warm body against my legs. I kneel down and pet his soft fur, my fingers following the line of his spine as I realize what I will do. I will go talk to the woman who killed my grandfather. I will go talk to Eloise Price.

Four

I meet Eloise Price the following Thursday. She is slender and diminutive yet sits at an old white desk with a rigidness that lengthens her spine and broadens her shoulders. There is a music box winding on the corner of the tabletop, and its tinny sound burrows into the folds of the room. I study Eloise, poised and severe, and even before she turns her head, I feel the walls of the room bend in toward her. When I look down, my hands are shaking.

I left Mae's Soap and Spool Shop with a bag full of pens, a sketchbook tucked between the blank pages of a lined notepad, a handful of charcoal, the 1960 edition of *To Kill a Mockingbird*, a pack of cigarettes, and a haphazardly made peanut butter and jelly sandwich.

Once I had decided to speak with Eloise Price, I realized that I faced a problem. There was no public transportation in Darren, and the sanatorium was nearly five miles away, most of those winding up a mountain. When I asked Mae if I could borrow her car, she laughed.

"I don't own any car," she said. "It's been a good decade since I've been behind a wheel. No need around here."

I soon learned that owning a car wasn't something most people did in Darren. The town was so small, most didn't need one, especially not a single woman like Mae, whose whole life had been lived within a two-mile radius. While taking my walk to the statue, I had puzzled over the lack of traffic. Now I understood why.

I decided to ask the mayor if he had a vehicle that he could loan me during my stay. "I need it for research," I told him. I stood in the middle of a wood-paneled office in the back of the courthouse.

The mayor sat behind a large desk that was covered in papers and file folders, one with a coffee ring stained on the front. The room was cold, as if all the air-conditioning in Darren County had been used to fill this single square space. There was a shelf behind the desk, and on it were two bowling trophies and a baseball in a glass case. A fake tree was pushed into one corner, and on the wall hung a photograph of a woman and two small boys. The frame was bent to the side, making the trio lean precariously to the right.

The mayor scratched his head. "What kind of research would you be needing a car for?"

I didn't tell the mayor about my plans to visit Eloise. I was certain he wouldn't be happy to hear that I wanted to talk to the woman who'd murdered Benjamin Costello. "I want to drive around a bit," I said. "Get a feel for where Benjamin grew up. Maybe see his house, maybe even see Whitmore Halls." My voice was casual, loose.

The mayor massaged his chin. "Can't get up there," he said. "Road's closed off."

He leaned back in his chair. "When are you wanting to do all this . . . *exploring*?" He folded his hands behind his head, and his stomach ballooned forward.

I had read in an old brochure that Dusty Hills' visiting hours were Tuesday and Thursday from one to four. I told the mayor I needed transportation then.

His arm caught the corner of an open folder on the desk, and the papers fell to the floor. The mayor swore but made no motion to pick them up. "You come back here on Thursday." He looked down at the mess. "I'll have a way for you to get around by then."

I thanked him, and on Thursday afternoon I walked back to the courthouse, eager to see what kind of car the mayor had given me. I turned the corner and saw Jason standing outside the office, his back leaning against his old pickup truck.

"You get yourself into trouble?" I greeted him.

He smiled and shook his head. "Not today," he said. "I heard you're needing a ride?"

Jesus Christ. Of course, the mayor never planned to give me my own car to drive around. How different this small town was from the city. I nearly groaned. I crossed my arms in front of my chest. "Well," I said. "It's awfully nice of you to loan me your truck for the day." I held out my hand for the keys.

He laughed. "Never gonna happen, Tig. I have strict orders. I'm to take you wherever you want to go." He held his arms out to his sides. "Think of me as your personal chauffeur."

"I don't need a chauffeur," I countered. "I need a car."

Jason reached into his front pocket and pulled out a candy bar. He peeled open the top corner and took a large bite. "Well, then, just think of me as a happy addition." He grinned through a mouthful of caramel.

I shrugged my bag higher on my shoulder and walked to the passenger side. In the bed of the truck there was a large wooden frame separated by planks. It looked like the shell of a child's playhouse. "Are you building something?" I asked.

"Dollhouse. Just a hobby of mine." He got into the cab.

My brows rose. The woodworking was clean and refined. When I reached out to touch the frame, the surface was smooth, as if it had recently been sanded.

"Do you build them often?" I climbed into the cab.

He shrugged and turned on the ignition. The truck rumbled beneath us. "I've built a few." Before I could ask more, he interrupted me. "We're going to Costello House then?"

"No," I replied as he shifted the truck into first and we pulled away from the courthouse. "We're going to the sanatorium."

Jason's head swiveled, and he stared at me. "Dusty Hills?"

"That's right."

"I don't know, Tig." His voice was heavy with trepidation. "Most people don't go up that way unless they're itching to see someone important to them. And the others, well, they usually don't leave again."

Dusty Hills Sanatorium was a self-contained facility that housed patients and staff. Before I'd left Ann Arbor, I went to the university library and found out all I could about Darren. There wasn't much except for an old article about the facility printed in a *New York Times* exposé on the history and rehabilitation of state sanatoriums. The building was erected in 1842 and used to home tuberculosis patients when they needed to be isolated from the public. Originally, it was able to accommodate forty patients, but after the epidemic spread, the building needed to expand to a capacity of over two hundred.

Since the patients could not live among the general population, the building had to be self-contained. It had its own water treatment plant, post office, vegetable garden, and lake. At one time, it even had its own farm and slaughterhouse. By 1965, tuberculosis had been cured in Darren County, and the facility became a resting place for the geriatric. Only recently had Dusty Hills begun taking in elderly inmates from the women's penitentiary when area prisons became overpopulated.

"I want to go," I insisted.

Jason pressed on the gas. "I'm figuring you want to meet Eloise Price."

"Pretty clever, Sherlock," I teased.

Jason nodded, and the corners of his lip turned up. If I didn't know any better, I would say it was in admiration. "Well, all right then," he said.

"Well, all right then," I repeated.

The truck lurched and sputtered over the broken asphalt that folded into a gravel two track as it neared the entrance of Dusty Hills. My eyes skirted across the windshield, and I leaned forward, desperate to see the compound in one frame. It was useless. The building stretched on to my left and to my right, much farther than I could see. It was made of brick and cement, and the entrance, guarded by a pair of gargoyles perched on twin pillars, rose far above the building's five-storied walls.

A nurse stood near the entrance, arms crossed, a cigarette dangling between two fingers. She watched the truck as she brought the burning paper and tobacco to her mouth and inhaled.

"You sure you don't want me to go up with you?" Jason asked as I gathered my bag and moved to open the door.

"I'll be fine," I assured him.

I shut the door and turned. The building loomed before me, as imposing as Benjamin's statue in the middle of the town square. I gripped my bag a little tighter and walked toward the entrance. As I approached, the nurse quickly snuffed out her cigarette and hurried into the building. So much for southern hospitality.

The wooden front door looked ancient, and above it, carved into the frame, was a small angel peering down at everyone who entered the building. Dad would love this.

I opened the door and took a step up. Inside, the building was a maze of long yellowed halls and faded-blue-speckled linoleum covered in black scuff marks. There was a reception desk to my right, and to my left hung a sign stating EAST WING in hospital red. I glanced down the hall when a flickering light caught the corner of my peripheral vision.

"You looking for someone?"

A woman in maroon-colored scrubs stuck her head out of a sliding glass window at the reception desk. She was holding a phone to her ear and had thick black hair. Her lips were a bright slash of crimson lipstick.

I hurried to the desk.

"Yes," I said. "I'm here to see Eloise Price."

❋

I step into room 402 and clear my throat. "Ms. Price?"

Eloise's head tilts slightly to the right. It is the only indication that she has heard me. I clear my throat, and the floorboards beneath my flats grumble.

"Beethoven's Fifth Symphony," I say when she doesn't turn, referring to the song the music box was playing moments before. "It's one of my dad's favorites."

Eloise is still. I continue, convinced my voice will beg her attention. "I never had much interest in the piano myself," I say. "I wasn't musically inclined."

An understatement if there ever was one. In fourth grade we were required to try an instrument. I chose the clarinet, and for five tired months, Dad sent me outside to practice. It never did any good. On the night of the grade school recital, my music teacher put his hand on my shoulder and told me to put my mouth on the clarinet but refrain from blowing. I played the whole concert in silence.

Eloise tenses. "They didn't tell me I would be having a visitor." Her voice is lower than I expected, made of an old tree's rich tenor. "I assume you are from the state?"

"No, I'm not."

"You're too young to be a doctor." She places her hands on her knees and turns slowly. In profile, she looks younger than I imagined, less severe.

I slowly approach. "I'm not a doctor," I say. "My name is Tig Costello, and I'm an artist."

"Costello," she repeats softly. Her eyes rise to meet mine, and I startle at their rich color, blue as the darkening sky painted on the ceiling of Graffiti Alley in Chicago.

"I was asked to paint a portrait of Benjamin Costello." I watch her eyes for the slightest change in demeanor. Her face stays set. "Darren County is creating a memorial. Collecting a few items for a museum. They erected a statue." I glance toward the window.

Eloise scoffs. Her lips part briefly before locking together. She places a hand on the large yellow dictionary sitting on the desk beside her. Its thin pages are pregnant with pressed flowers.

"I'm sure you've heard about it," I prompt. "Can you see the statue from your window?"

"A waste," she mumbles. Her hands slide over one another, the tip of her middle finger running over the curve of the neighboring thumbnail.

"The people in Darren seem to think Benjamin was a fine mayor." I am fishing for a reaction.

"He was a fool." Eloise chuckles.

"He was an honored war hero."

"He was a coward."

"He was my grandfather." I'm surprised when I admit this so readily.

The right corner of Eloise's mouth pulls up, and she lifts her chin to look at me, meeting my gaze for the first time. "Why are you here, Ms. Costello?"

The use of my last name leaves me flustered.

"I want to know more about Benjamin." I wipe my nose with the outside curve of my palm. It is a childhood habit that follows me when I'm nervous. "I came to Darren to learn more about him, but the people around here don't seem to know very much. They say he was a private man."

I step closer, trying to exude more confidence than I have. "I've heard that you knew Benjamin better than most." I expect her to correct me, but she remains quiet.

My eyes flit around the sparsely furnished room. White walls. A rickety bed shoved into the corner, covered with a thin blanket the color of burned toast. A wooden chair pushed against the closet door. A blue-and-white-striped rug. There is a yellow stain near the middle, the size of my palm.

"So that's why I'm here. I want you to tell me about Benjamin."

When Eloise looks back at me, her thin face is like stone. Her bottom lip presses against her front teeth, forcing her chin forward, and in the subtle movement, I see the profile of a much younger Eloise Price, still striking but rinsed with a softness that smells like Miss Mae's soap.

"Do you like flowers?" she asks.

I glance over her shoulder at the dictionary. "I do," I say.

"And which is your favorite?"

I think about this for a moment. In Chicago, there was a garden near my apartment on Dahlia Street. It was small and grew behind the building, mostly a plot of soil and weeds. But along the back fence line, sunflowers often sprouted in the summer heat. In the afternoons, I would look out the living room window and see them, their bright yellow heads glowing like twenty-five July-bred suns.

"Sunflowers," I tell Eloise. "Sunflowers are my favorite."

She cocks her head, studying me. "Are you sure about that, Ms. Costello?"

Her gaze unnerves me, and I scratch my forearm absentmindedly. "I'm sure," I confirm.

Eloise traces the cover of the book, the pad of her thumb rubbing over the worn spine. "Moonflowers were always my favorite," she says. "Most think they grow best in pots and gardens, but they love the Appalachians. They grow wild out there, though they're hard to find. They only bloom at night, after all. You have to look deep in the pines to find them, and too few are willing. So many people fear the forest."

Eloise opens the cover of the dictionary, and a white flower falls into her lap. I recognize it instantly.

"Lily of the valley," I say.

"You know flowers better than you think."

"I've always loved lilies."

"Yes, I suppose you would."

My brow furrows at the assumption, but I let it slide as she continues.

"The lily of the valley is one of the oldest flowers in the Appalachian Mountains," she explains. "They grow in patches. More widespread than the moonflowers. You'll see them when you're walking through the foothills. They're the most beautiful. The most enchanting."

She looks at me fully. "And the most deadly."

I breathe in sharply.

"Kills more people in the mountains than the bears and wolves." Eloise chuckles at my wide-eyed stare.

Now that she's talking, I'm determined to extract her story. I reach for the chair pressed up against the closet door and bring it closer to the desk. I pull down the hem of my skirt and sit on the wooden frame. The palm of my hand catches on a splinter, and I jump, folding my fingers around my throbbing skin.

"Have you been hurt, Ms. Costello?" Eloise asks. Her voice is coated with sobriety, and I pause, wondering if she is talking about my hand at all. I look down at the red scratch and shake the pain from my skin.

"I'm fine," I tell her.

I set my bag on the floor beside me. "How are you liking it here? At Dusty Hills? I heard you were moved six months ago. I assume the change is nice."

She sucks on her bottom lip and fans the pages of the book. I glimpse reels of red and yellow and orange and realize they aren't flowers at all. Eloise is pressing leaves.

"I'm sure there must be more freedom here," I continue.

"Freedom." Eloise snorts.

She flips a hand through the air. It is the first relaxed gesture I have seen from her. "This place is a sinking ship. A roof for the dying. Gray walls, stained floors, food that tastes worse than what they serve in the prison. When you are old," she says, "the world becomes somewhat dull."

Pity stirs in my stomach. She killed a man, I remind myself. She killed my grandfather. "I want to ask you about Benjamin." My voice is firm.

"You want to know why I killed him?" Eloise inquires matter-of-factly.

"I want to know more about who he was."

"Who he was . . ." Eloise looks at the ceiling and then back to her hands. "Well, he was charming." She snickers. It is a sound of disgust. "He was a Costello, after all."

She shoots me a sidelong glance, and I think that maybe the rumors were true. Maybe Eloise was jealous of Valerie.

"What else can you tell me about him?" I am ready to pull out a piece of paper.

A teasing smile toys at the corners of her lips. "You think I can tell you about Benjamin in one afternoon? A few highlights, perhaps, so you can paint your picture. Tell you about the *honorable* man who is erected in the square?"

I rest the still-closed notebook on my lap. "I've heard that you and Benjamin were once quite close."

Eloise twitches as if she has eaten something that soured her taste buds.

"That the two of you used to be inseparable." I watch her body tense. "Until he married Valerie. . ."

"Valerie." Something in Eloise's demeanor shifts. She sits up a little straighter, her shoulders broaden, and her ankles cross in front of her. "You want to know more about Whitmore Halls," Eloise says.

I'm not sure if it is a question or a statement. My instinct tells me it is the latter.

"I want to know about Benjamin," I reiterate.

"Are you sure about that?"

When I don't answer, Eloise regards me intently. "Are you a reader?" she asks.

I think of the copy of *To Kill a Mockingbird* in my bag and nod.

"Then you must know there are many tales, Ms. Costello," she says. "Perhaps the one you're chasing is in a different book than the one you've been given."

"Okay then." I sigh, reaching down into my bag to pull out a sharpened pencil. "Tell me a story," I say. "All I ask is that it be true."

Eloise glances out the window and then down at the dictionary full of dried leaves. The daylight shifts, and the colder side of autumn lifts her head. "All right," she agrees. "I'll tell you about Benjamin Costello and Whitmore Halls. But then you must do something for me."

She splits the dictionary open at the seam and peels a crisp red leaf from the page, holding the thin stem between her fingers. "I would like you to bring me leaves," she declares. "From the red oak trees. They're changing colors about now."

She looks around the room as if seeing it for the first time. The plastic clock on the wall. The white popcorn ceiling. The crack in the floorboards just in front of the doorway. The harsh fluorescent lighting.

My lips part in confusion. She wants me to bring her dead leaves?

Eloise holds up her hand. "You'll come here twice a week and bring me the red oak leaves. Not maple. Not beech. Red oak. That is the price. No more, no less." Her voice is unwavering. "And in turn, I will tell you the story you need to hear."

An unusual request, certainly, but Eloise Price has been locked up for fifty years now. Surely, she is entitled to some odd demands. I run a hand through my hair, already knowing my decision. Perhaps I knew it from the moment I walked into room 402. Perhaps from the moment Dad received the letter and I set foot in Darren County, or from the moment I first stood up from the ground and let go of the dumpster in that Chicago alley. Perhaps, from somewhere just outside myself, I always knew I would come to this place, deep in the caverns of Appalachia, and meet a woman who would tell me the story that my father could not.

"All right, Ms. Price," I agree. "But we begin today." I keep my own voice steady.

"Very well, Ms. Costello." She sets the leaf back in the book and turns to face me fully. "I will tell you a story. And this one, like many before it, begins with a house."

Five

Richard Price bought Whitmore Halls with the $300 in his pocket and the gold watch on his wrist. He had found the home by chance. A broken-down train kept him in Morehead, Kentucky, for an overnight on his way westward to meet a young girl at an orphanage. While at a local pub, he met a man who was selling the house. "It's quiet, secluded. No one will bother you," the man said. Richard agreed to see the home, and when he stood outside Whitmore Halls, the manor like an ominous gargoyle perched on the mountainside overlooking the city, he lit his last cigar and knew that this was where he would continue his research.

Richard was a neuropsychologist who studied those whom the state had deemed insane. He had lived all over the country. He spent his early years in the Iowa plains and Nevada deserts before moving his practice to the East Coast, where he worked and studied cases from Maryland to the northern border of Florida. He was well traveled. His work took him from city to city, with scandal nipping at his heels. Richard Price was an intelligent and well-educated man, but his affinity for studies that involved young girls left him with an unsavory reputation.

There had been a nasty case where a young patient of his was found in a garden shed, barely alive and bleeding both vaginally and from the abdomen. Her hand was wrapped around a garden hoe that was covered in blood. The woman survived, barely, and was sent to an asylum upstate. She was pregnant. There wasn't much doubt about what had happened.

When Richard came to stay in Darren, he brought with him a young girl named Joan Abrecht. Joan was an orphan, diagnosed as insane because she had never uttered a word. No one could agree on the age Joan was when she was brought to the Halls, but everyone was certain that the young girl had arrived dressed only in white.

When Joan first saw Whitmore Halls, her face was blank, clear as the pale moon, as she stood holding only a large book of pressed flowers. What could she have been thinking, this child meant to live in the hills? Perhaps she'd been afraid, terrified of the broken window-panes and rusty hinges. Or perhaps she'd been hopeful, sure that her life was to be better now that she was away from the orphanage's dark, cold walls. With Joan, one could never be sure. Whatever the case, she walked up the front stairs, through the great oak door, and into the first room she found on the second floor. She closed the door, and everything in the house was still.

Richard spent the next four weeks readying the home. He painted the walls in shades of cool blue and warm beige, sanded the old oak railing of the staircase, and nailed down the broken floorboards that blemished the steps. He hung doors on the kitchen cabinets and filled them with glass dishes and copper cups. He patched the holes in the roof, repaired the broken windows, and hung large photographs of flowers and wildlife on the walls, wanting Joan to feel safe and calm while living in the hills.

Joan loved the garden most of all. It wasn't a surprise, Richard always said. He tilled the large plot of land to the west of the house in the afternoons when Joan was most tired and liked to sit in her bedroom and look through her book of pressed petals. The soil was rich, and it was easy to churn the moist black dirt. Richard didn't want to plant any seeds in it before he showed the space to Joan. He wanted it to feel like her own. He would buy her whatever she wished to plant.

Richard brought Joan to the barren plot of dirt early one morning. "For your flowers," he said.

She stood there for a moment, her gray eyes searching the land, and then she carefully took off her shoes and socks and walked out into the soil.

"You'll get filthy," Richard called, but the girl was already sitting in the dirt, her dress stained and crushed. Joan thrust her hands into the ground as if she were trying to unearth something deeply buried. She held fistfuls of dirt in her palms and sifted it through her fingers like sand. She looked up at the gray sky, freckled by the dark silhouettes of a flock of geese, and marveled at the great expanse of it above her. She looked down at her hands, her skin covered in a muddy film, and brought her fingers to her mouth, sucking the dark marrow like a newborn baby at its mother's breast.

What a strange girl, Richard must have thought. *What a strange and marvelous girl.*

✿

Whitmore Halls flourished. Over the next year, the house was molded and shaped into a fine residence. A barn was built in the back field, behind Joan's garden and to the right of a large pond filled with lily pads and bright-colored koi. Books lined shelves, photos hung on walls, and the house on the hillside purred in the morning sunlight.

Richard hired two housekeepers, a cook, three caretakers for the animals and property, and four nursing assistants to help with the patients who came to stay at the Halls. And they did come, some for longer than others. After that first winter, when a brutal wall of midwestern snow came down without warning, killing a half dozen livestock and all of Joan's flowers with one icy gasp, word got around that a new doctor was living up on the hillside. He worked with the loonies. Fixed things in the brain.

The patients stayed in the West Wing of the house, on the second floor, in locked rooms where they were only taken out when accompanied by a member of staff or by Richard himself. This isn't to say that the patients were neglected, for Richard Price was an involved and meticulous physician. He never allowed more than six patients to stay at Whitmore Halls at one time, and never for longer than a year. He slept two patients to a room and monitored their actions and interactions obsessively.

In the mornings, Richard met with each of his studies individually. He brought them into his office, a large room with little light and high ceilings, where he let them explore a wide variety of trinkets he kept on the shelves. He noted how they handled the objects, their nonverbal gestures, and the words they used.

During the afternoons, Richard brought them to the library, let them stroll around the grounds, and taught them how to tend to the animals in the barn. All this he charted in a set of thin, leather-bound journals. And by the end of the day, Richard Price could name every meal and bowel movement a patient had taken, as well as which activities each of them had engaged in.

The patients were happy at Whitmore Halls. Richard, with his business thriving and his good name restored, was boisterous and attentive to the needs of those around him. He was inventive in his practices and used a variety of medical techniques. Music therapy, animal therapy, taking his patients on long outdoor walks around the pond and into the woods. Yes, Richard Price would have made a fine doctor, if he didn't have such an affinity for his female patients, of course. For in those early days, Whitmore Halls was marvelous.

But then again, not all was well inside the home. Over the months, after the first hard frost, Joan became gaunt and withdrawn. Her pale skin was nearly gray, and her thin wrists were so frail that Richard could wrap his fingers around them and nearly touch his second knuckle. Richard took Joan's declining state to be the result of the colder weather. Her flower garden was dead, and Joan was brushing against the hard ribs of grief.

"They'll come back," he promised her as they stood by the window overlooking the garden. "They're only gone for a short time, my love. When the rains come, everything will grow more beautifully than before."

Joan was silent.

✿

No one was surprised when Joan became pregnant. There were rumors in the house. Richard spent too much time in her room. He took Joan to the pond and into the forest for hours on end. Richard bought her gold jewelry and clothes made of silk. His eyes followed her. His hand often reached up to cup the back of her neck as they walked.

The baby was born in Whitmore Halls. The midwife was called when Joan went into labor, and the birth lasted over eighteen hours before the baby slid from her mother's womb and cried. Richard adored the child. He held her in his arms, her round face and cherry-drop nose so similar to his own. And her eyes, so startled and suspicious, before they fluttered closed. Richard brought the infant to his nose and inhaled.

He named her Eloise.

As Eloise grew, Joan shrank. She hated being a mother. She refused to feed the girl, clutching the collar of her dress between her fists when Cook begged her to breastfeed. She wouldn't hold the baby when she cried and only shrugged when Cook announced that Eloise had taken her first steps across the kitchen tile. Most days, Joan was hard to locate. She roamed through the halls like a ghost, never still long enough to be found.

Richard wasn't concerned. He was certain that once the baby blues passed, Joan would show progress. He made it his mission to dote on her. He came back from town with bouquets of red roses and boxes of Swiss chocolates wrapped in purple ribbons. He bought bottles of red wine and laughed when Joan sipped the alcohol and her nose twitched. He placed a piano in the front room and hired a man to come in once a week and teach Joan how to play. He gave her paint sets and easels, handwoven blankets, and books full of watercolors printed across a two-page spread. He rinsed her hair in coconut oil and her skin in honeysuckle, feeling radiant when Joan's eyes softened and closed. He did all these things, never noticing the small, golden-haired child watching from behind the door.

Eloise grew within the confines of Whitmore Halls. She spent her mornings following Cook around the house and her afternoons running between the legs of the grazing horses beside the barn. She was an imaginative child, and she created games for herself while in the house, scurrying from room to room as if crossing state lines. One room for the plains in Nebraska, another for the mountains in the west. The library became the shoreline of the Pacific and, two rooms away, was New York, the Statue of Liberty only as tall as the flowering bird-of-paradise growing in the corner of the room. It was in this way that Eloise traveled the country, talking with the locals as if she were a tourist only passing through.

There was only one place in Whitmore Halls that Eloise wasn't allowed to explore. The West Wing. Eloise knew about the patients. She often saw them wandering the grounds with a nurse or caretaker, but Richard made certain that she had no contact with them.

"They are sick," he told her. "You must stay away. You don't want to get hurt."

But Eloise was a curious yet lonely child, and she liked to play with marbles in the upstairs halls after her daily tutoring lessons. One day, when she was six years old, a marble rolled from the East Wing to the West, and Eloise watched as the blue-and-white ball stopped directly in front of a patient's bedroom door. She looked to her left and to her right, and when she saw that she was alone, she walked slowly, cautiously, into the barren hallway as if she were creeping into forbidden land.

When she reached the marble, she knelt on her hands and knees and peered underneath the door. She heard footsteps on the other side and the soft murmur of voices, but the words were unintelligible. Eloise thought of her father. It was midmorning, and he would be busy in the study. She was alone. No one was coming.

Eloise placed the tip of her finger underneath her thumb and released it against the side of the hard glass ball. It rolled across the hallway and underneath the door. She waited. And then the ball came back, slipping under the thick wood and stopping at her feet as if she were pulling the smooth globe back to her with an invisible string tied around her middle finger.

Eloise ran.

The next day, Eloise returned. She sat in front of the door and rolled the marble under the wood, her face brightening when it came racing back. She rolled it again. This continued for weeks. Sometimes Eloise would bring multiple balls, rolling one, and then after counting to ten, rolling another. They always came back to her in the same order they were sent.

One day, Eloise was just about to shoot a large green marble under the door when she turned and saw Richard Price standing at the end of the hall. From the ground, he looked taller than he was, and his hands were rolled into fists that looked like two turtle shells sitting in the sunlight beside the pond.

"I told you to never come here." Richard took long strides down the hall, grabbed his daughter by the shoulders, and dragged her back to the East Wing. Eloise's sharp nails scratched his arms, and twin lines cut across his skin. When he pushed the girl into her room, his face was red and hot, and a sick smile bloomed on his face when she stumbled onto the floor.

"If I ever catch you up there again . . ." His threat fell flat when he saw Eloise stand. Her eyes were as wild as the coyotes that roamed the estate after nightfall.

"You keep them locked in there like animals," she accused. Her voice was so thick with contempt that Richard startled.

"You dare speak that way to me?" He broadened his shoulders.

Eloise took a step toward him. "This place is no better than a prison," she spat. "We're all like caged animals in here."

Richard slapped his daughter across the face. She winced but did not cry. Her bedroom door slammed, and Eloise pressed her palm against her cheek. Her skin was as hot as the anger that coiled within her.

❋

Eloise had only one clear memory of her mother. It was on the night that she died. Eloise was sitting in her bedroom, watching the moon rise over the pond from her upstairs window, when she saw a figure gliding across the grass. It was Joan. She wore a long white nightgown, and her hair, normally secured at the base of her neck, floated behind her like a veil. Her feet were bare, and yet, when she walked across the sharp branches and hard stones surrounding the bank of the pond, it was like she was hovering above the earth.

When Joan reached the water, she stilled. Eloise watched her standing in the moonlight, and a familiar ache settled against the inside of her chest. Eloise hated her mother. She hated how Joan walked past her without a glance, how she spent all day in her garden, pressing dead flowers into books. If Cook asked Eloise where her mother was, she would simply shrug.

Eloise watched Joan pick up the rocks. Her motions were slow, and she held each stone to her breast before placing them in her pockets. When she ventured into the water, she held her arms out to her sides as if she were walking on a tightrope, steadying herself with the added weight.

Eloise thought about running to the pond. She could stop her. She could wake her father. They could get there in time. But she looked at her mother, so beautiful in the moon's wide-eyed light, her lithe body sinking lower and lower, and she thought of the patients locked in the West Wing. She thought of her mother sitting in the garden, her face gaunt and expressionless, trapped in the cage of foliage that Richard Price had locked her in. Under the water, Joan would be free of this place, Eloise thought.

When Joan sank, her body slipping away as slow and lazy as a sunset, Eloise saw the moonflowers. They were tangled around the fence posts that traced around the back half of the pond. In the morning, Eloise would pick all the white blossoms from the stems and take them back to her mother's library. There, she would pull a heavy book from the shelf and press the petals between the pages of a novel she would never read but always remember as the book that held the flowers that bloomed on the night her mother died.

Richard was the one who found Joan. He was strolling the grounds the next morning when he saw her body, half-submerged and stuck in the weeds. Cook said his cries were as sad as those of the nightingales. Eloise sat on the floor of the West Wing and slid a marble under the door. She was disappointed when only the sound of low moans came rolling back.

Eloise didn't go to her mother's funeral. Instead, she went through the things that were left behind in a cedarwood chest at the end of her mother's bed. She found dozens of books that Joan had never read. They were all filled with hundreds of dried flower petals. She found a pale linen handkerchief, a frayed bookmark, a bottle of half-empty perfume, and, folded in a bottom corner, a small, dirt-stained white dress. It would fit a child, Eloise thought.

After Joan's death, Richard no longer cared about his meticulous routine, and instead, spent his days wandering the woods outside the manor. He dismissed ten members of the staff and kept only Cook to prepare the meals. When the money began to thin, the animals in the barn were sold at auction and the two caretakers let go. And then only the patients remained.

Richard built a bonfire. The flames burned like a giant's torch, reaching nearly as tall as the second-story windows where Eloise stood, looking down. Her father was next to a wheelbarrow full of loose papers and lined notebooks. Eloise recognized the brown leather of his journals. Over twenty years of medical notes and observations huddled in the wheelbarrow's dirty bowl. Richard threw them into the fire. The air smelled of smoke and rot and decay.

The next morning, Richard Price was gone. No one would ever be able to say exactly where he went. Some thought he stepped into the fire himself, his body becoming one with the ashes of the hypotheses and conclusions he'd spent his whole life compiling. Others thought he left town, crossed state lines, and went west toward the mountains.

Things moved quickly then. The patients inside Whitmore Halls were led out in handcuffs by men wearing uniforms and placed in black cars. What remained of the livestock was sold, and a slew of phone calls were made behind closed doors. Cook was the last of the staff members inside the house, and why she remained as long as she did, Eloise didn't know.

On the day the patients were taken from Whitmore Halls, Eloise put on her mother's old dress and sat on the front stairs of the house, where she watched the row of long, sleek black cars crawl down the hill. Eloise heard Cook behind her, standing in the doorway, but she did not turn. *What to do with this child sitting on the front stairs,* Cook must have thought. *What to do with this small, strange girl dressed only in white.*

Six

"So. What's she like?"

Jason and I sit side by side at the far end of the bar inside Mitt's. It's late afternoon, and the tavern is quiet and dim. A couple sits at a table toward the back, directly beneath the dartboard. The woman casually glances up at the three arrows stuck in the red heart above her. A reedy older man is at the other end of the bar, his hand wrapped around a beer, and his eyes stare vacantly up at the television. A sports game is on. Muted. Behind the counter, Mitt washes cups and wipes down bottles.

I take a bite of the sandwich I'm holding.

"Best Reubens in town," Jason told me as we drove away from Dusty Hills. "It's hot and I'm hungry."

I wrinkled my nose and told him I had no interest in going to a bar.

"Nothing beats the sandwiches at Mitt's." He opened his mouth wide, stretching his jaw. "You'll never have a better Reuben."

Jason looks younger now, inside the bar, with slanted, sun-shy eyes and a bud of mustard on the corner of his mouth. He holds the sandwich in both hands, elbows on the counter, body hunched over and leaning toward the bread like a book lover leans into an open page. I know almost nothing about Jason, but I am comfortable sitting beside him.

Mitt's is a place that would never make it in the city. The walls are brick and painted with figures that are both repulsive and strangely endearing. A crocodile dressed in a Hooters shirt laughing at an Elvis impersonator drinking a pint of beer. An ostrich peering down the chest of a blonde woman drinking a martini. Her large, barely concealed breasts rest on top of a painted bar. A man wearing overalls with no shirt underneath, revealing a handful of curly black chest hair that peers over the top hem of the denim. I am oddly drawn to this detail, this ball of wiry twine. My eyes keep coming back to it, again and again.

The figures remind me of those spray-painted on the cement walls of Graffiti Alley, a tunnel adjacent to the Chicago "El," thirty steps down from the street. It runs about fifty feet in length before taking a sharp turn to the right and trailing on a bit more until it hits a dead end. It is dirty and wet and foul and the perfect place for Chicago artists. I went there nearly every afternoon after my introductory print class. It was there I found the elephant, painted bright purple with a spray of flowers bursting from its trunk. It was exuberant and gaudy and ridiculous, and I loved it fiercely.

Jason wipes the corner of his mouth with the back of his hand and looks at me expectantly. He is waiting to hear about Eloise.

Eloise.

Something pulls tight inside me, and for an instant I feel like I'm going to be sick. My muscles clench, and I release a breath of steam that burns my esophagus and fills my mouth with stale saliva. It feels no different from the nausea that plagued me in the city. The hard pit of sickness that settled in my stomach every time I ate a burrito from Taco Tim's or sat in front of a blank exam. It was the same nausea that coursed through my body, seedy and salty, when I tossed back a shot of tequila before asking for another and another, all the little glasses lined up in front of me like bottles at the carnival. Pick the right one and win a prize. A dollar more for another chance.

"She's different," I tell Jason and pause. How can I accurately describe Eloise Price? There is something strange about her, calculated, yet oddly appealing. I think of how abruptly she ended her story this afternoon. Joan was dead, Richard was gone, and the child was sitting alone on the front steps of Whitmore Halls. What happened next? What happened to the young girl wearing white?

Eloise dismissed my questions. "Another day," she said. "That is all for now. I am tired."

It wasn't until I left room 402 and was back in Jason's truck that I realized I had spoken of the child Eloise as if she were someone different from the old woman sitting before me. As if she were someone other than the woman locked in an insane asylum for murdering a man fifty years ago.

Was it her unusual upbringing that made her kill Benjamin Costello all those years ago? Was there something about Eloise, something dark and dangerous and budding, that was planted inside her? Perhaps Richard could see it. Perhaps that was why he struck the child that day when she stood up from the ground and looked at him through dark and troubled eyes.

Jason takes another bite of his sandwich and looks at me, waiting.

I haven't been back to a bar since the night in the alley, and the rows of glass bottles look dusty and sad. I used to love looking at all the alcohol, lined up like the Ziegfeld Follies onstage, lights shining on their sticky labels. *Give me a shot of your best tequila. Top shelf,* he said. I was so impressed. Top shelf. Bottom shelf. The clear alcohol poured like hot water from a kettle. It burned when it went down. My throat was boiling.

I reach for my soda and take a small sip. "She's going to talk to me about Benjamin."

The man sitting on the opposite end of the bar glances toward me. Everything about him is too large. He has a face that is gaunt and sullen yet populated with bulky features: a wide nose and round grasshopper eyes that sit high in their sockets, giving him a slightly bewildered look. He wears a brown corduroy coat that makes him look heavier than he is and a black flat cap with a red rim that hangs low over his forehead. Tufts of gray hair stick out in odd places: behind the ear, on the corner of his neck, over his right eye.

"That's good, right?" Jason cuffs his shirtsleeves at the elbow.

"She has a lot to say." I shift so I no longer see the old man's hard glare. There's something unnerving about him, and I am keenly aware that he is watching me.

I saw you staring from across the room, I said that night in the city. The bar was full of people and lights and music and alcohol. The bottom of my shoe was sticky. I stuck to the floor when he walked over.

How could I not? he said. *You are intoxicating.* He had such lovely teeth, straight and wide and square. There was no space between any of them. It was bold of him to have teeth like that. Teeth with no gaps.

"You need to see her again then?" Jason bunches the sandwich wrapper in his hands and aims for the trash five feet to our left. It lands in the can soundlessly. He flexes his fingers.

"Twice a week," I say. "During visiting hours. She wants me to bring her leaves."

The man at the other end of the bar clears his throat and looks back at the television. It is a dirty sound, hoarse and ripe with phlegm.

Jason rolls his shoulders and stretches his neck. "Looks like I know what I'll be doing Tuesday afternoon then."

I scoff. The mayor will never let me drive around Darren alone. He will never let me off his leash. "The mayor keeps you pretty busy then?"

Jason shakes his head. "Mayor's a side gig," he says. "I have my own business. Landscaping, mainly. In the winter, snowplowing." I picture Jason's truck with a plow head attached to the front of it. I ask if they get a lot of snow.

He shrugs. "Enough for a plow every couple days."

"You'd make a fortune in Ann Arbor," I tell him. "The snow comes in piles up there. Even more in Chicago."

Jason laughs. "No reason to move anywhere else."

I think of what it would be like to grow up here, what life Dad would have had if Valerie Costello had decided to stay. He would have lived in Darren, the only child of his mother, Valerie Dunn. He wouldn't remember his father; Benjamin had died before Dad was born.

His world would have been small and simple, living in the hills, and a part of him would always wonder if there was more, if he should leave this town and travel north to the city.

People would have watched him because he was the son of Benjamin Costello, and they would have wondered if one day he, too, would become town mayor. He would have married, probably a girl from his high school, a girl he had grown up with who lived the next street over. He would have had a child, maybe two, and he would hang reprints of famous paintings throughout the small house he owned with his wife because they both liked to look at beautiful things. And when he was fifty years old, he would decide to build a statue in memory of his father, a man who brought the railway to Darren County and who died in the hills.

"Hunting season's about to start up," Jason says suddenly.

I blink and he grins. "People talk about hunting in the same way they talk about the weather around here. I took my daughter once. Scared the shit out of me. Having her out there and hearing all those gunshots."

I am surprised to learn that Jason has a daughter. "You have kids?"

"Well, now, don't act so shocked, Tig," Jason teases.

I blush. "I'm sorry. I just haven't heard you mention them."

"Yep," he says. "Two of them. Nine and seven, now. Way too good for me."

Jason looks at the watch on his wrist, and I know he's getting ready to leave. I think of the evening before me, alone in the apartment above the Soap and Spool Shop. I think of the empty refrigerator, of the loaf of stale bread on the counter, and of Dad's voice roaming from room to room. A fresh pull of nausea threatens to crest within me.

"Jason," I say before he stands. "What do you know about Whitmore Halls? About what went on there fifty years ago?" I am being selfish. Jason doesn't have time to sit with me inside a bar, discussing the mystery of my grandfather's death.

"I was wondering when you were going to ask me." A lopsided grin floats over his features as he settles back in his seat and relaxes.

"Mae mentioned something about a missing woman? That Eloise Price was involved somehow?" I am fishing for answers, already knowing that the pond is empty. Jason is too young. Everything he knows is now rumor.

"Missing woman? There wasn't just one that disappeared."

I sit back in surprise.

Jason reaches for a cold fry left on the corner of my plate. "People liked to tell all kinds of stories about Whitmore Halls. Benjamin wasn't the first person that Eloise killed. Eloise wasn't right in the head. She placed curses on the town. Those kinds of things. All lies. People love a good story more than anything else."

"What do you think happened to the women?"

"Personally, I think they drowned or just took off. Most of the men from around here had been gone to war. They came back not quite the same as when they had left. The women may have been bored, met someone else, and left. My wife thinks Eloise poisoned them or something. But I hate when she talks like that in front of the girls."

"Those are old stories you're telling." The man from across the bar gets up and walks toward us, sliding onto the empty stool beside Jason. He smells like cigarette smoke and cheap beer. It is the scent of Chicago on a Friday night.

"Get me another, will ya, Mitt." He holds his empty glass up in the air, and I see the edge of an eagle's wing peek out from under the cuff of his jacket.

Mitt tilts the rim of a pint-size mug under the Bud Light spigot. The amber beer spills into the cup, and white foam slides down the sides of the clean glass. Somewhere, behind the closed kitchen doors, someone drops a pan and curses. The couple at the table behind us stands to leave. The door chimes, and we are alone in the bar.

"Last one for today." Mitt places the mug in front of the old man, who scowls and waves him away.

"How're you doing, Stan?" Jason holds out his hand in greeting. "I thought that was you down there."

Jason's posture changes when Stan sits beside him. He shifts slightly back, toward me, just an inch or two, and sits up straighter, more alert. He folds the rim of his baseball cap with the cup of his hand before leaning on the bar top. I'm surprised when Jason tells Mitt to pour him one too. He looks at me. "You want one?"

I shake my head.

"How've you been feeling, Stan?" Jason asks. Then, before Stan can respond, Jason adds, "This is Tig Costello." He places a hand on my shoulder. The weight of his palm is both friendly and uncomfortable at the same time. "She's here for the memorial. Mayor brought her in to paint a portrait. She's an artist from Chicago." Jason's face fills with pride, and I suddenly feel like his daughter, standing next to her father for an introduction to an old friend.

Stan takes a long drink of beer. His fingers are like twigs, all knuckles and veins. "How is your pop doing these days?" he asks as if we were talking about Jason's father the whole time. I wonder how much alcohol he's already consumed this afternoon. He comes here every day, I figure. Sits at the same stool at the end of the bar and drinks the same beer while staring vacantly at the same muted television set. Only the games change. Football. Soccer. Boxing. Hockey.

"Oh, keeping busy." Jason thanks Mitt as a large glass of ale slides toward him.

Jason rests his forearms on the bar and ducks his head down, inadvertently cutting me off from conversation. Stan's voice is weathered, deeper than Jason's but soft, the words slow to matriculate from his lips. I have trouble hearing what the two are talking about. No matter, I think, sucking on the end of a straw. I've never been good at small talk.

On the back wall, hanging in the space above the liquor bottles, are twelve framed photographs of soldiers. They all look the same with their tailored uniforms, set jaws, and young, bold, expectant eyes. They must have been told to look emotionless. *Look straight ahead at the camera. Don't blink.*

A slow sickening feeling tickles my nerve endings and lifts the hair on the back of my neck and forearms. This is much different from the waves of nausea I've become so familiar with. This is more primal. It's the feeling that something is about to change course. The feeling that something is about to shift.

"I knew Benjamin," Stan says, forcing me out of my thoughts and into the conversation.

Jason leans back on the stool.

"We were in the army together. Stationed not far from combat. He was a fine corporal, even if he only got the job because of his pop." Stan talks to his glass, looking into the liquid as if it could reveal something about life, something that is unknown and pure.

Jason points to one of the photographs hanging on the wall. It is of a young man, a boy, really, wearing a garrison cap and looking out at the bar. "That's you, right, Stan?"

I see it now. The same long, narrow chin and round, wide-open eyes. The photo is in black and white, but there is a flush to the boy's cheeks, a shadow on the smooth, hairless skin. His eyes are dark, much darker than they are now, over fifty-five years later, where they look almost amber, the same color as the beer in the half-full mug.

Stan barely glances at the photograph. "Some version of me, I suppose." He grunts and picks up his drink.

"Everyone 'round here has a war story," he says. The fingers on his left hand tap his knee rhythmically. An old tic, I think. One that the young boy in the photograph must have picked up when he went overseas. "But them women over there in that house. They were up to no good, I'll tell you that. A lot of bad doings going on up in those woods."

It takes me a minute to realize that he is talking about Eloise. I work to relax my jaw and keep my face a perfectly clean palette of beige. "Eloise Price," I say, more in confirmation than question.

"Humph." Stan shrugs off her name like a pesky fly that has landed on his shoulder. "She's a dirty woman. Always has been. She and her aunt. A bad lot. Even Ruth. Though she was never much of a problem."

"Come on now, Stan." Jason lifts his beer to his mouth.

"What do you know about it?" There is an edge to Stan's voice, a gravity to his words as if they were gaining weight inside his mouth, making them sharp and bulky. "You weren't even born yet, boy."

My head feels heavy, and I'm struggling to keep pace. I lean forward on the counter so I'm able to see Stan completely. "What do you think happened up there?" I ask. "Up at Whitmore Halls, I mean."

Stan shakes his head, and suddenly, he looks overcome with sadness, like a small child releasing the hook from a fish's mouth only to put it back in the water and watch its wet, slippery body float lifeless and open-eyed atop the waves. "I was a young boy when Ulma Price came into town," he says.

"Eloise's aunt," Stan clarifies when I frown. "She was some kind of witch doctor. Worked with plants." He looks up at the photographs on the wall, and it's as though he's speaking to the boy he once was, telling him a bedtime story. It must be startling, I think, to see your younger self gazing at you from the other side of the bar, watching you drink pint after pint and still ask for another.

"What did people think they were doing up at Whitmore Halls?" I ask again.

"Brewing potions, of course!" Jason winks, reminding me that he thinks Stan's story is only myth.

Stan ignores Jason's mockery and leans toward me for the first time as if he's about to tell me a secret he's been holding in since he was a young boy. His eyes are larger now and clear. Their color is striking, a deep ochre, and for an instant, I wonder if alcohol does that to a person. Makes one's eyes burn gold.

"They were killing babies," Stan growls. The air in the room changes. Mitt sets down a mug, and the sound of the glass hitting the countertop is everywhere.

I don't have time to react before Stan continues. The story falls from his lips in that easy, slippery way that stories do around picnic tables and bar tops.

"Women started going up those hills around the time the war started," Stan says. "A bit before. Most of the men down here wouldn't let their wives go. Didn't want anything to do with those women and their medicines. We had perfectly good doctors down here." Stan swallows the last of his beer and looks to Mitt. Mitt shakes his head from the other side of the bar, and Stan grumbles.

"Those women, Ulma and Eloise, they did things that would kill the babies." Stan wipes his nose. "Took them out of the mamas and buried them up in the hills. Whole cemetery of them up there."

"Jesus Christ," Jason swears. "Stan, these are old wives' tales you're telling. Those women didn't bury dead babies all over the woods."

"You don't think I'm telling the truth?" Stan bristles. "Just ask your daddy. He'll set you straight, boy."

I expect Jason to laugh, to tell Stan to quit spreading lies, but something in Stan's tone makes him settle.

"Abortion," I say aloud, realizing the rumor.

Jason recoils from the word like a horse jumping from a snake underfoot. I shoot him a disapproving glare, and he opens his hands toward me in surrender. The gesture is so familiar that I long for Ann Arbor.

"That's right." Stan twirls his empty glass from left to right on the bar top. "Them women were murderers long before Benjamin Costello was killed in that house."

I look back at the portrait of Stan as a boy and imagine the day the photograph was taken. It would have been the morning he left for war. The morning he boarded a train that took him to an army camp, where he trained for the next several months. He would be given a rucksack full of cooking equipment, a sleeping bag, food rations, extra socks, and a wool hat his mother had made for him before the war. He would be handed a gun and a spare box of ammunition. *Don't be afraid to use it,* he would be told. *Don't be afraid.*

An eerie calm settles me. "What do you think happened to the women who went missing?"

Stan is more subdued now, as if the story has run its course. "I think those women found themselves in a bad way and went up to Whitmore Halls to have it taken care of."

He thinks they were pregnant, I realize.

"There's a reason why that kind of stuff shouldn't be done." Stan turns on his stool, and his feet rest on the metal bar circling the chair legs, knees bent and spread outward.

"It's damn complicated. You play God and get yourself in trouble." He fumbles with a chain around his neck, pulling a silver cross out from underneath his shirt. "Something went wrong up there in that house. The women bled too much. Eloise and Ulma couldn't stop it. So they died. The women and the babies." He rubs his fingers over the silver medallion. The metal's worn down around the middle, in the center crux where it's been rubbed dry for many years.

I look over at Jason. He hasn't spoken in several minutes, and the air around him feels thick and sticky. It's the kind of air that follows children around when they come in from an afternoon outdoors.

"Well." I set down my chewed straw and fold the napkin in my lap. "That's quite a story."

An alarm sounds on Jason's watch. He looks down, flustered, as if he can't figure out how to turn it off. He fumbles with the side buttons until it quiets.

He stands. "I better be going," he says. "I have to be at the Kelley house by five o'clock, and you know how Lorrie gets when I'm late." Jason looks at me when he says this as if, during my three-day stay in Darren, I couldn't possibly *not* know who Lorrie is and how she gets.

Stan mumbles something I can't hear, and suddenly I'm afraid to be alone, not because of what waits for me in the Soap and Spool Shop but because of what is already here, in Mitt's Bar. I am afraid to be left alone with the stale smell of smoke and cheap beer, the laughing crocodile and bold, misogynistic ostrich, and Stan's stories about Eloise and Ulma and all the women who went up the hill.

"Give me a ride?" I ask Jason as I slide off the stool.

He nods and pats Stan on the shoulder. I follow Jason to the door, glancing back only once to see Stan sitting at the bar, empty glass in hand, staring at the eyes of a boy who once looked so much like himself.

MISSING

MRS. MARJORIE THOMAS. MISSING SINCE DECEMBER 20, 1945. WIFE OF CHRISTOPHER THOMAS. Last seen at her residence in Darren County, Kentucky.

OFFICER THOMAS IS OFFERING A $100 REWARD FOR ANY PERTINENT INFORMATION ON THE WHEREABOUTS OF HIS WIFE.

DESCRIPTION OF MARJORIE THOMAS FOLLOWS:

Age: 42 (forty-two) years. Blue eyes. Brown hair. Wearing long blue dress, brown coat, black shoes.

Seven

It was raining when Ulma Price came to Whitmore Halls. She expected as much. The clouds had been low and heavy for miles as the train neared Darren. Ulma came to the hills with two suitcases, three crates full of jars and dried herbs, and a seven-year-old boy carrying a rocking horse made of soap. He had a slight limp in his left leg and, for much of his life, he always leaned a bit to the left.

Ulma stood on the front walkway and looked up at Whitmore Halls, much like Richard Price had done years before. She frowned. *There is darkness here*, she thought, *but also something else, something softer, more malleable.*

Ulma was a strong woman who was made of thick limbs and a round middle that made people think she was heavier than she was. Her husband had died four years back and left her with a small boy named Charles. She did well for herself, making a business of selling dried herbs and spices at the local market. She hadn't spoken to her brother-in-law in years and hadn't known he had a child until she received news of his death. His young daughter would be placed in her care or put in an orphanage.

Since the passing of her husband, Ulma had been feeling unsettled in her home in the upper half of Minnesota, so she'd decided to pack up everything she deemed necessary and travel with Charles the few hundred miles to Darren, Kentucky, where they would start again.

Charles was such a quiet boy; surely it would be good for him to have his cousin to play with.

I will be of use here, Ulma thought as she took the young boy's hand and led him up the front steps. Whitmore Halls leaned toward them as they walked through the great oak doors.

Inside, the house was dark and quiet. Thick curtains were pulled shut, and there was a thin layer of dust coating the wooden banister that led upstairs. The foyer was nearly empty of furnishings, and the chandelier hanging above swung lightly from left to right, the bulbs pulsing with dull light. Ulma stood for a moment, closing her eyes and breathing in the home's stale air. The backs of her knees tingled. She had been right about this place. She was needed here.

Somewhere inside this house is a child, Ulma thought. *A girl, barely older than Charles.* The cook had stayed with her until the morning of Ulma's arrival. It was out of kindness, not obligation, the letter had said. Eloise was a strange child, it was true, but she was such a fiery little thing. She had gone through so much.

Ulma had set the letter down and lit a cigarette. She hadn't been surprised by Richard's disappearance. He was always such an erratic man, obsessive really, with his curious fascinations and questionable ethics. Ulma had no doubt about what had happened to this girl's mother. Ulma would come and care for the girl, but she wouldn't seek her out in this house. No, she would wait. She would wait for Eloise to come to her.

Ulma went ahead and made herself at home. She placed her bags in the room upstairs, the one that looked the most well kept, supposing it once belonged to her brother-in-law, though she couldn't be sure. When she pulled the thick, bulky burgundy-colored curtains away from the large window that faced the back pond, a pale ray of dirty sunlight shone through the fogged glass. A startled mouse ran to the shadows, and Ulma frowned.

She turned and saw Charles standing in the doorway. His thin legs were trembling. Charles was a kind boy, sweet and tender and terribly afraid. Ulma told him to put his things in the room closest to hers.

❋

For three days, there was no sign of Eloise. Yet during that time, she watched. From the dark corners of the house, Eloise stalked about, lurking in the shadows as she observed the new residents of Whitmore Halls. Ulma, a woman so different from fragile Joan, spent the early afternoons and evenings covered in dust. Eloise was startled when her aunt first emerged from the bedroom wearing a pair of Richard's old slacks, for Eloise had never seen a woman wearing pants before. Her aunt's hair was held back with a folded-over bandanna, and she wore a dark shirt with rolled-up sleeves as she got down on her hands and knees and began to wash the floors. How peculiar, Eloise thought, seeing a woman dressed as a man, scrubbing the floors.

"There's no need to keep things so closed up," Ulma said as she opened the doors and windows. Wild gusts of autumn air swept golden leaves across the halls. Eloise drank in the clean, milky forest air while lying on her stomach beneath the bed.

"Go find a bucket," Ulma told the boy on the second day. "Fill it with water. Go on, now." Her voice was stern but calm. It was the voice of a mother, a voice so unfamiliar to Eloise that her dry fingers tapped together when she heard it.

Ulma pulled the sheets from the beds, dusted the cabinets and dressers, polished the fine wood with a spray that made the rooms smell like freshly squeezed lemons. She scrubbed the windows, standing on a stepladder and stretching her arm high above her head to reach the top of the glass, and placed candlesticks on the dining room table. When she finished, Whitmore Halls was warm and ripe with summer.

Ulma and Charles ate in the dining room at a grand table that Eloise couldn't remember owning. There was fine china placed on the polished oak each night, plates and bowls and pitchers of ice water sitting between two white candles that always stayed lit. Ulma placed three table settings, and when the boy asked why, she simply poured the glasses full of water and said, "One is for your cousin, if she cares to join us."

It wasn't long before Ulma moved on to the gardens. Like Joan, Ulma held an affinity for soil. But, unlike Joan, Ulma saw the plots of overgrown weeds and tangled brambles and sighed. There was just so much work to be done. For three sweat-filled afternoons, Ulma tugged and toiled with the overgrown shrubs, filling wheelbarrows with piles of dead foliage that she dumped into the woods. The planting would have to wait until spring, but she could already see the rows of tomatoes and vegetables that would sprout in the tilled square of land.

Eloise watched this all from behind the stone wall that ran along the property. She was curious about this woman and her son. She wanted to hate them, but she wondered about Ulma and the ways that she had already changed Whitmore Halls. When Eloise snuck into the bathroom, in the hours when Ulma and Charles were outdoors, there were clean towels that felt soft under her hands, and in the kitchen, something was baking in the oven. Something sweet and buttery that made her mouth water. At night, when the house had always been at its quietest, Eloise listened to Ulma's low voice as she read to the small boy inside the library. There was a burning fire, warm and bright in the fireplace, and Eloise found herself sitting on the other side of the wall, her small palms pressed flat against the floor.

Ulma knew Eloise was in the house. She also knew the girl did not want to be seen. Ulma didn't mind. The child would come out when she was ready.

Still, Ulma cared for her young niece. It was the bedroom at the end of the hall, the one with pencils and books and dead flower petals thrown across the floor, that Ulma cleaned first. She chuckled to herself when she pulled back the curtains and caught the quick shadow of a small hand slip under the bed. She smiled again when she was tidying the study and saw the black tip of a shoe stuck out from behind a bookcase.

While Ulma worked in the gardens, she talked aloud. "We will have juicy ripe tomatoes in the summer, and in the spring, we will have beans and cabbage and carrots. They will make a delicious stew." Ulma hated talking. She was a quiet woman and found chitchat frustrating and unnecessary. Yet she pressed on, narrating her day as she walked from room to room inside the house, talking to the girl as if she were a baby growing inside her womb.

Every third morning, Ulma went to town. It was a long trek down the hill, and after, she was covered with sweat. Those first weeks, Ulma and Charles came back with bags full of canned beans, fresh mushrooms, pounds of sugar and flour, and a fair amount of butter and cream. Later, after the days had cooled and the house was no longer saturated with darkness, Ulma came back from town with different items, glass jars and vials that she brought down into the cellar and placed on shelves too high up for children's curious hands to reach. Or so she thought.

Ulma had a system. She organized her dried herbs and oils alphabetically with the labels facing forward and running from *Aloe barbadensis* to Yohimbe, a rare bark found in Africa that was used as both an aphrodisiac and a cure for high blood pressure. She was meticulous with her labeling, a skill she learned in Minnesota when she served as a midwife in a small town too far away from the main hospital.

One morning, when Ulma went down to the cellar to collect vegetables for dinner, she saw that many of her jars had been rearranged. The *Lavandula angustifolia* was no longer beside the *Lawsonia inermis* and the *Papaver somniferum* was placed next to the *Sambucus nigra*. She frowned and set to the task of reordering them correctly.

The next day, Ulma went to the cellar and found the same thing. The glass bottles and plant-filled jars were all wrong.

"Strange," she said aloud, looking around the cellar as one does when searching for mice. "This will not do." Ulma set the jars right once again. But this time she left a note.

These are important jars to be left alone. Please do not disturb.

When Ulma stood in front of the shelves the following morning, she found another note. This one was written by a child, the words made with large loops and sharp angles.

These are important jars to be left alone. Please do not disturb.

Ulma studied the jars on the shelves. This time, nothing had been moved out of place. Ulma reached up and righted a bottle of lemon balm, turning the label toward the front as she bit the inside of her cheek where the flesh was warm and moist.

Ulma flipped the paper over and, in her own tight, refined cursive, wrote:

I can teach you.

That night, Ulma and Charles sat at the dining table, eating steaming bowls of vegetable stew. Charles sat across from his mother, a ring of wooden horses circling his dinner plate. It was a stampede, he told Ulma. Charles would spend the better part of his life devoted to the care of horses.

When the floorboards in the hall creaked, Charles jumped, his brilliant blue eyes stretched with fear. He always had such beautiful eyes, the kind you see on children before life dilutes them. Charles somehow kept that vitality. Life was never quite able to make his eyes dull.

"It's just the wind," Ulma reassured him. She placed her hand on his forearm and glanced quickly at the door. It had been nearly three weeks since Ulma and Charles had settled in at Whitmore Halls, and

Ulma knew the girl's willpower was waning. She was more careless now in her hiding. Even Charles had begun to spot her. Still, Ulma was steadfast. The girl would have to come to her.

Charles galloped a wooden horse across the tabletop, knocking down a pair of sheep. He laughed. Ulma dipped her spoon into the bowl of soup.

The last rays of autumn light slipped behind the barn, cloaking the dining room in a peculiar haze. The breeze seeped through the open glass, and Ulma shivered. The days were shortening. Ulma rose to shut the window, and there, standing in the doorway, was the girl.

"Hello, Eloise," Ulma said simply. "Come and have some supper."

Eloise followed Ulma. Gone were the days of waking when the sky was at its darkest, the long afternoon naps, and the luxury of eating whenever she pleased. Now, with the arrival of Ulma and Charles, Eloise was put on a schedule. She rose each morning and followed Ulma outside to feed the chickens large handfuls of cornmeal. She learned to cook, though she was dreadful in the kitchen and much better outdoors taking care of the poultry and horses that were brought in the following spring. There were goats too—a pair of them. Troublesome and conniving. Eloise took to them instantly.

Under Ulma's care, Eloise grew, her childish limbs spreading long and lean like those of a colt weaned from its mother. And she learned. Eloise was an excellent study. She was a quick child and had a sharp memory that was rich soil for knowledge.

Ulma took Eloise to the apothecary shop in town. It was a delightfully small store on the edge of Darren, pressed into the county by cornfields to the left and back of the building. It had a chimney, unusual for a shop even in the thirties, and the exterior walls were nearly black with soot. Inside were rows and rows of shelves lined with bottles and vials labeled with words Eloise couldn't pronounce. There was a certain smell there, odd but familiar, like dead flowers left on the windowsill for too many days. It was earthy and organic. It was the smell of Joan's fingers after she licked off the soil during her first days at Whitmore Halls. Eloise could stay there for hours.

Immersed in the shop's foreign perfume, Eloise ran her fingers over the jars slowly as she read the labels aloud, wanting to taste how the words felt on her tongue. *Sambucus nigra. Foeniculum vulgare. Nerium oleander.*

"For insomnia." Ulma handed her a bottle full of green leaves and dried purple flowers. "Also used to help the respiratory system and relieve menstrual cramps."

Skullcap. It was heavy in Eloise's hand, and she yearned to open the lid. Were the leaves soft, or would they crumble at her touch? Would they taste bitter when mixed into tea, or would the lavender-colored petals make them sweet?

"You must recognize it," Ulma said. "It grows in thick patches in the forest behind the barn."

The woods behind Whitmore Halls were rich with herbs. Each morning, after the animals were fed and breakfast was made, Eloise followed Ulma into the trees, where they gathered bundles of witch hazel and black haw that were hung to dry on clotheslines strung across the kitchen ceiling.

"Find three more herbs that have similar properties," Ulma instructed.

This became a game the two of them played when they went into town. Inside the apothecary, Ulma would hand the girl a jar. Sometimes the contents were familiar and sometimes not. She would explain the plant's uses and ask Eloise to find others like it. It was a quick game, one Eloise took very seriously as she studied the glass bottle in her hands, noting the size and shape of the leaf, the color, the texture, the smell.

There was a stepladder in the shop, and Eloise would scale the wooden planks and stare at the rows of jars before her, tapping the very tip of her nose as she studied the labels.

While Eloise searched for similar herbs, Ulma spoke with the shop-keeper, Erika, a brittle woman with leathery, bruised-looking skin and large, clumsy fingers. Eloise was never sure how the woman handled such fine and delicate materials. She was the last descendant of a family line that stretched across continents, and she spoke with a thick Russian accent that made her sound more abrasive than she was. Erika had a tender heart. She took to Ulma, impressed by her knowledge of herbal medicines, but she was wary of the girl with deliberately piercing eyes and carelessly eager fingers. *Too young to be in a shop like this,* Erika must have thought.

"There are items that I need," Ulma said to Erika as she slid a folded piece of paper across the counter.

Eloise, standing on the stepladder, holding a vial of safflower oil in her palm, turned. She had never seen Ulma ask the woman for specific items, nor had she ever submitted a request written on a piece of paper. What items could Ulma possibly be searching for that she couldn't ask Eloise to find?

Erika held the paper close to her face and squinted. "Pennyroyal. Colocynth," the old woman muttered, her eyes narrowing. "What you want with these kinds of plants?"

The air in the old shop turned stale, and Eloise stilled. Pennyroyal. Colocynth. The plants were unfamiliar. She itched for their Latin names, for the roots of the words that she could separate and dissect. English ruined such things.

"You won't find any of these things here." The woman slid the note back toward Ulma with a short, deliberate shove.

"I figured as much," Ulma said, though she seemed unfazed by the old woman's denial. "Though I wondered if you might have some in the back, perhaps? I'm willing to pay more than fair price."

Ulma opened her pocketbook, and Eloise saw the sheets of crisp dollar bills fan outward.

Erika peered over the countertop, then glanced behind her as if someone were standing on the other side of the room. Eloise chilled when the old woman met her gaze. Erika looked at the girl the way that her father had after her mother's death, his eyes dilated with utter contempt.

Erika grumbled, and her old lungs rattled in her chest. "And how often would you be needing these?"

Ulma's face turned upward. "Often," she said. "As much as you can spare. I know they aren't easy to obtain."

Erika clutched the counter. Her thick, bony knuckles turned white. They looked like bulbs, Eloise thought, like Erika was grown from the same soil that rooted the hills.

"I understand you know what they're used for?" the old woman asked.

Ulma's hand tightened around her clutch, and the silver buckle snapped shut. A cloud buried the sun, and a long shadow crept across the shop floor. "Of course," Ulma said. Her face slipped into darkness.

The two women studied each other until Erika's shoulders sagged. "Very well then," she said, and Ulma smiled.

When they arrived back at Whitmore Halls that first morning, and for many after, Eloise collapsed on the stiff high-back chair sitting in the foyer. Her small fingers were wrapped around a jar full of dried lavender leaves, and the unfamiliar scent of Darren soaked through her clothes. She closed her eyes and saw the streets with their metal grates and cracked veins, smelled the thick smoke billowing from the apothecary shop's chimney, heard the sharp cries of the children racing across the park, and trembled. She was exhausted by the enormity of it, by the immensity of being alive.

❁

"I had never thought much about the world that existed outside Whitmore Halls until Ulma arrived," Eloise says. "And then everything began to change."

Eloise is more relaxed today. She sits at the same wooden desk with her back turned away from the sun, but she looks softer, painted in pastel. The sky was a smoky gray when Jason dropped me off at the front door of Dusty Hills, but now the clouds are beginning to thin, giving the sky a rather bruised look, and the murky swamp-water light filters into the room in patches.

A nest of red oak leaves is scattered across the desktop. I brought them to Eloise in a plastic bag I found in Mae's shop. Mae had scowled but hadn't asked what I was up to. Ever since I asked about the missing women during our talk while making soap, she's seemed wary of me. I hadn't mentioned that I was seeing Eloise, but something told me she already knew.

Most of the leaves were found on the sidewalks. Red and orange swatches of color that I stooped to pick up on my walks around town. I found them in gutters, behind trash cans, under bushes that grew wild near the river. I found them along the street in front of Dan's Deli and beside the drive-through that was lit up with a series of neon lights advertising liquor, beer, cigarettes, and suds.

I was proud of my finds, some of the leaves larger than two of my hands put together, and at night, I spread them out on the floor of Mae's upstairs apartment and wondered about what Eloise had planned. They were beautiful, the perfect autumnal palette of paint, bright and bold and brilliant, until I watched them sink right into the wastebasket in room 402.

"No good." Eloise tossed one after another into the plastic bin by her feet. Too brown. Too dull. Too fragile. Too wet. By the time she had finished sifting through the bag, only a dozen leaves were stacked beside the dictionary, and I felt smaller than I had before, as if the lines of my charcoal-drawn body had been smeared by the back of a hand.

I sit beside Eloise in the same wooden chair I occupied during our last visit, pen and paper in hand. I feel heavy with questions, weighted by Stan's words that still ring in my ears days later. *The women in the hills were murderers: They killed babies. Practiced bad medicine.*

After my lunch in Mitt's Bar, I felt repulsed whenever I thought of Stan, but then I remembered the way he looked as I left the bar, lonely and hollow, gazing at the eyes of a young boy he used to know.

"As much as I was fascinated with Ulma herself," Eloise continues, "I was also fascinated with Charles, for I had never been around another child, and this boy was so, well . . ." Eloise laughs, and the sound is harsh and sterile as it slaps against the white walls. "Peculiar," she finishes. "So timid."

She looks at me for a moment, her eyes holding me captive until I glance away. I feel nervous around Eloise, vulnerable.

"My life has been full of peculiar people." She reaches for the white mug on her desk. Tea, I decide. Eloise would be drinking tea.

"I was awfully cruel to him." She shakes her head as if she is baffled by herself. "Charles. He was just so *good*. He never did anything wrong. Never yelled, never ran, never cursed. He was always just there. Always following me around, following Ulma."

Eloise is quiet for a moment. It would be easy to draw her here, sitting at this desk, in this light. It would have to be done in pencil. It didn't seem right to put her in color.

"I was terribly lonely before they arrived." She continues her story, and I right the pen against the page. "Painfully lonely. Though I wouldn't have been able to say why. I hated my own mother with her dark silence and blatant indifference toward me. She was so weak. I wasn't wrecked when she died. I don't think I ever thought about it again."

Eloise is testing me, gauging my reaction.

I think about when my own mother died. How she was there and then she wasn't. How I was three years old and searching for something that had been lost. I looked under the beds, inside the closets, behind the bushes in the backyard. I opened cedar chests and boxes and hanging coat bags, which made everything around me smell aged. I peered around curtains, behind books tilted to the side, and between the slats of the wooden floor. I searched until I was tired and hungry and empty, and then I sat in the laundry room, my body red and shaking, because what was lost was not inside the washing machine, and I had found a pile of my father's clothes in the hamper, and it still wasn't enough.

"I lost my mother too," I disclose. "She got sick when I was very young. I don't remember much about her at all."

Eloise hums, and I have the inexplicable feeling that I'm telling her something she already knows, but she lets it go. "Ulma was so different from Joan," she begins again. "She was so steady, so solid. Not merely in appearance, though she was a rather large woman, big bones and strong muscles, but she was just so . . ." Eloise closes her eyes for a moment. "Real. And I wanted to learn everything from her."

"Do you remember the first time you met Benjamin?"

Eloise looks surprised. It's as if she has forgotten that I came to her asking about Benjamin. "Do I remember?" she repeats. "Of course I do."

She shifts back into her chair like a cat kneading a warm blanket before settling. "It was one of those glorious summer days," she says, "and I tried to kill him."

Eight

As much as Eloise loved Ulma, she detested Charles. Never having lived with another child, the boy was endlessly fascinated by Eloise and followed at her heels like a stray pup. It didn't matter that Eloise wanted nothing to do with him. He was relentless in his pursuit. Wherever she went, Charles was never far behind.

He was a loud child with heavy feet and always dragging along some wooden horse tied to a rope behind him. He was dirty, snot running from his nose, dried bits of food crusted on the corners of his mouth, knees scabbed over from stumbling on the stones around the pond. Still, much to Eloise's bafflement, Ulma doted on the boy, scooping him into her arms when he cried and kissing the top of his blond head. Eloise couldn't understand how this grimy child could so thoroughly possess Ulma's love.

Eloise played countless tricks on Charles.

"We'll play hide-and-seek," she'd tell him. His round brown eyes were as wide as two perfect chestnuts hanging from a tree. "Go on and hide while I count."

So starved was the boy for another child's affection that he ran quickly through the halls of the house, where he would hide inside cupboards, under stairs, or wedged between the wall and the bookcase, waiting to hear the faint sound of his cousin's footsteps coming near.

They never did, of course. Eloise waited until she was sure Charles was hidden, and then she promptly went outdoors to join Ulma in the gardens.

"Charles is inside playing with his animals," Eloise would tell her as she pressed her small body tightly against her aunt's while their cold hands dug deeply into the soil. "He doesn't want to be bothered."

Once, while Charles was napping in the nursery, Eloise collected all the wooden animals that Charles so deeply loved and hid them in the closet. There were so many of them. Horses, gorillas, zebras, giraffes, elephants, rhinos, even a wooden kangaroo that was missing a left foot. *What a ridiculous collection,* Eloise thought. She was certain that she would never have toyed with such things at Charles's age.

Charles was frantic when he awoke. The boy had never been without his toys, and he coursed around the room with a certain fury that Eloise almost found admirable. She watched soundlessly as he ripped the sheets from the bed, tore the books from the bookshelf and threw them into a heap on the floor, pushed open the heavy lid of the wooden chest and sifted through the stuffed bears and the wooden blocks and the metal train set that had never been placed on a track.

When he finally noticed Eloise leaning against the doorframe with her arms crossed over her chest, he stared at her, his eyes wet. They looked like glass, Eloise thought, like the eyes of the porcelain dolls that sat in the china cabinet her father bought for Joan fifteen years ago.

"It will be a game," she said, righting herself. "You search the house, and I'll tell you if you're getting hotter or colder."

Charles blinked at her. His small fingers trembled at his sides.

Eloise rolled her eyes. Such a dim-witted boy. "If you're getting warmer, then you're closer to those stupid animals," she explained. "Try not to be so dull."

So poor Charles searched the house with Eloise strolling behind him, growing more and more bored with every wrong turn and misguided direction.

"Wrong," Eloise hissed when Charles looked underneath the cushions of Ulma's reading chair only to find a ball of lint and a stray penny. "Cold. So cold your teeth should be chattering. You'll probably freeze up and turn blue in the hands and feet. Won't even be able to play with those animals when your fingers fall off."

Charles fell to the floor, his small body nearly convulsing as his limbs seized and a belt of sound poured from his open lips. His skin was red hot, and streaks of tears ran down his flushed cheeks. The corners of Eloise's mouth turned down in disgust.

The boy was still sobbing when Eloise came back into the room with the basket of wooden animals. She dumped the heavy figures on his chest. "No one is going to want to play with you if you carry on like that," she spat.

Still, no matter what games and tricks she played on the boy, Charles loved Eloise. A terrible fault in his character, she thought, for no human being should show such devotion to someone who treated them so poorly.

Not long after Eloise's eleventh birthday, a great change was taking place in Darren. A new family had moved into the area and was buying up much of the land surrounding the small town, taking with it the ownership of several local businesses. The family's name was Costello, and they were from Texas with ties to rail companies in the southern states.

Ulma, being a quiet woman without interest in local gossip, didn't pay much attention to what was happening away from Whitmore Halls. She had heard of the Costellos, but she had lived in small towns before and knew this was nothing new. Families with big money were always coming into small counties to settle and monopolize. Most made their fortune and then moved on to another small town to capitalize there. Money travels, after all. It rarely stayed in one place for long.

It was one of those heavy summer days, the kind when the air outside feels bitter and damp, when Eloise realized she was irrefutably bored. She felt she could learn no more from the books and lessons that Ulma gave her, and even the games inside the apothecary shop had begun to dull.

She was tired of walking around Whitmore Halls, of feeding the chickens and collecting bunches of witch hazel out in the woods. Even torturing poor Charles had lost its appeal, for the boy no longer followed Eloise around like a duckling but was content to sit on the back porch of the house and whittle away at a piece of old driftwood, carving out his own wooden horse for a collection that now lined the shelves of his room.

"Let's go to the pond," Eloise said to him that morning. Maybe she could dare him to walk into the murky water in his undergarments, then take his clothes and hide them in the trees. He wouldn't go in there without a fight. He didn't love the forest like she did.

"Not today," Charles replied, using the side of a razor to smooth the curve of a wooden horse's back.

Eloise kicked the side of his shoe, and the knife sliced into the wood.

"Cut it out!" yelled Charles.

She was pleased when she saw that the horse was ruined. Charles shook his head and got up to leave. Eloise sighed. Even Charles couldn't be bothered by her boredom.

She went to the gardens and sat on the stone wall that separated the house from the woods, tossing handfuls of nuts into the air before catching them in her mouth. How bland life seemed, living in the hills and licking salt from her fingers.

An unfamiliar shadow moved inside the woods. Too large to be a rabbit or raccoon, too noisy to be a fox or deer. Eloise frowned.

A tall, gangly-looking boy stumbled out from behind the trees. He was carrying two ripe apples in his hands.

Eloise stood on the stone wall and crossed her arms. "You're on private property," she called out, feeling large and grand atop the stones.

The boy shrugged. "My father owns most of this town," he said. "One day, I'll own it too."

Eloise scowled at the smug look on his face. The boy was lanky, with dishwater-colored hair that hung too low in front of his eyes. He was clumsy, like Charles, yet tried to cover it up by moving too fast, his feet breaking twigs and stepping on anthills as he walked.

"Well, he doesn't own this place," she shot back.

The boy glanced about as though he were seeing Whitmore Halls for the first time, as though he hadn't been sneaking around the forest peering out from behind trunks and branches.

What was he thinking? Eloise wondered. She knew that people in Darren hated her and her aunt. The men especially. They watched Ulma visit the apothecary shop and warned their wives to stay away from the woman in the hills. After all, Whitmore Halls had always been a shadow over the town, a place reeking of dark history and mutilated scandal. It didn't take long for the whispers to start up again.

A sly sort of smile crossed over the boy's face. "You want to see a magic trick?" he asked.

Eloise's nose twitched. She was suspicious of this boy who wandered out of the woods, her woods. Yet Eloise couldn't deny she was curious. And at the very least, he might alleviate the cloud of boredom that surrounded her.

The boy didn't wait for her answer. He simply took three steps closer to the stone wall and threw the pair of apples into the air, turning them in circles as he caught them in opposite hands.

"Big deal," she scoffed, though her arms fell to her sides and her shoulders relaxed. "So you can juggle two apples. Let's see you do four."

A messy grin knocked his features off balance as he caught an apple in one hand while tossing the other much higher in the air. The ripe fruit spun as the boy tilted his head back and caught the apple in his open mouth. When he reached up to grab the fruit, his teeth crunched down on the crisp flesh, and a dribble of juice trickled down his chin and onto his shirt. "Pretty good, huh?" he said, waggling his eyebrows.

Eloise rolled her eyes to mask any signs of awe. She sat back down on the edge of the wall. Her legs were covered in mosquito bites, and a red rash of bumps snaked up the side of her knee. Poison ivy? The woods were full of it. She would rub baking soda and vinegar on it later.

"I'm Benjamin." The boy took another large bite of the apple. "Benjamin Costello. My father is Ralph Costello." He gave Eloise a hard, knowing look.

She shrugged. She didn't know who Ralph Costello was, and she didn't care.

"You know . . . ," Benjamin said, gesturing grandly. "The man who just bought out the railroad company." He said it like she should know this, like it was a fact she should have learned in a history book.

"Never heard of him."

Benjamin's eyes darkened. Then he stared hard at Eloise, a sickly smile sliding across his face. "Hey," he said. "Is it true that your father murdered your mother?"

Eloise had heard the rumors about her family. How could she not? She heard the cold gossip before it ever left the hills. The hushed murmurs traded between the staff inside Whitmore Halls, secrets passed through open windows and quiet hallways. People were never quite as alone as they seemed.

"I didn't mean anything by it," Benjamin added hastily, noting her reaction. "I just heard things, that's all. I don't believe it or anything."

Who was this rich and entitled boy who came onto her property, tossing apples into the air and talking about her parents? He shouldn't even be here, Eloise thought, up in the hills away from town. And what did he know about Richard Price? Eloise hadn't thought much of her father since Ulma arrived, and his memory left a bitter taste in the back of her mouth. She thought for a moment, looking past the boy and out into the trees that grew for miles along the hills.

Eloise tilted her head to the side, and she, too, smiled.

"You think those apples taste good?" She scampered down from the wall and walked toward the woods. "Wait until you see what I found the other day."

Eloise waltzed straight into the forest without looking back. She knew a boy like Benjamin Costello would follow. She led him through the trees, jumping over broken branches and weaving around the small creek that ran into the heart of the forest. It was the same creek that fed into the pond that killed her mother.

"Where are we going?" Benjamin panted as he struggled to keep up, his soft skin not used to the scrapes and scabs that the overgrown pricker bushes liked to leave on bare calves and ankles. He stumbled and cursed.

Eloise stopped abruptly before a thick cluster of green bushes with long spiky needles, much like the pine trees hovering to the right. These were a lighter green, almost glowing in their enticement, and covered in bright red berries.

"Yewberries," Eloise announced, plucking two ripe fruits. "They taste like raspberries, but much sweeter." She rolled the smooth fruit against her skin, staining the pads of her fingers crimson. "My aunt makes the most wonderful yewberry pies."

She held her hand out to Benjamin. "Want to try?"

Benjamin took a step closer and grabbed a set of berries from the nearest branch. He brought them to his nose and took a long sniff.

"Nettie makes the best pies," he insisted. There was no room for debate in his voice.

Eloise tossed the berry into the air and caught it back in her palm. "That your mom?" she asked.

"Of course not," Benjamin said. He threw the fruit into his mouth.

Eloise smiled.

"She's one of our cooks." Benjamin chewed loudly. "Hey," he said, "these aren't half-bad." He took another pair of berries and devoured them.

Eloise dropped the two she'd been holding, smacking her hands together like she was dusting flour from her skin.

Never trust a plant you don't know. Ulma had told this to Eloise more than once. Plants must protect themselves. Learn to adapt. Just as a porcupine spreads its sharp quills when it senses danger, plants, too, must learn to look soft. But never be fooled. Only a fool eats from the plant he doesn't recognize.

"Maybe I'll tell Nettie to come on up here and get some of these." Benjamin's voice was loud in the forest. And then, quite suddenly, he went still. The trees pulled in the last tremors of sound, and the boy grew pale, his hand moving to his stomach.

"Say," he mumbled, "I don't feel so good."

Eloise took a step back. A cool calm ran through her as she let out a satisfied whistle. "That'll teach you not to talk about my father again."

A look of horror crept across Benjamin's face. "What did you do?"

"These are yewberries," Eloise explained in a voice that sounded much older than her age. She was surprised, at first, by the sound of it, and she looked over her shoulder. "They're poisonous to humans."

Benjamin's eyes widened, and he leaned forward as a cramp pierced his abdomen.

"You didn't eat enough to kill you, if that's what you want to know."

Eloise bent down to pick some wildflowers. The black-eyed Susans were beautiful this season, and she knew Ulma would love to have a fresh bouquet on the kitchen table. They would sit nicely beside the candlesticks. Eloise could already taste the braised ham Ulma was making for supper.

"You should apologize to Nettie when you get back," she said. "She'll have a lot of laundry to do."

Eloise took one last look at Benjamin Costello, all sweaty and pale and bloated, before turning back toward Whitmore Halls, calling out as she ran, "You'll be shitting for days!"

Nine

"You poisoned him." I bite back a smile. It's easy to fall into Eloise's story, to imagine myself sitting on the other end of the stone wall watching Benjamin toss a red apple into the air. I should be appalled. I should be disgusted by Eloise and the calm, playful way she talks about her first meeting with him. I still can't reconcile the fact that the young boy in the story will one day grow into my grandfather.

"He was such a smug child." Eloise rests her elbow on the back of the chair. "I figured I had had my fun that afternoon. Taught some mindless boy a good lesson and gave the town another sticky piece of gossip about the strange girl who lived up in the hills. However . . ." She pauses and her eyes lose focus. "Benjamin surprised me. Three days later he came back. I walked out of the house that morning and there he was, sitting on the stone wall, tossing apples into the air."

He came back.

"Was he angry?" I ask, incredulous.

"Not in the least," she replies. "He simply looked at me with that sly smile and said, 'I won't be falling for that one again.'"

Eloise stares off at the far corner of the room, puzzling through a memory. Her body is present, fingers rubbing at the underside of her chin, but her mind is elsewhere. I search her face, following the thin lines that web across her skin. She has a scar on her left temple. It's an old one, hardened like wax.

Why did she do it? I ask myself for the hundredth time. Why did she kill Benjamin Costello?

"From then on, things changed," Eloise continues, returning to room 402. "Benjamin and I roamed Whitmore Halls together. The forest was a land to be conquered, and the hills were ours to own." She looks at me through the same eyes she had that day when she stood on a stone wall, watching a boy catch apples in his mouth, audacious and wild and eleven years old. "How much larger the world suddenly becomes," she says, "when another child enters it."

"What about Charles?" I think about the young boy sitting on the porch of Whitmore Halls, carving horses out of old pieces of wood.

"Oh, he often tagged along." Eloise picks at a hangnail with the edge of her thumb, brushing her cousin's presence off as if he were here in the room. "He loved Benjamin. Took to him instantly. A boy coming into his life to teach him how to be a man."

Her mouth narrows into a line and then relaxes. "Charles was useful, though," she says. "Later in life."

Eloise is contemplative, her gaze locked on the window where the naked limbs move synchronously in the hills, the tops of the pines swaying back and forth. From here, they look like water, like looking down at Lake Michigan from the upper end of the pier.

"Benjamin saved me once," she says, suddenly.

I am instantly alert.

"We were in the river. Swinging into the water from an old rope Benjamin tossed over some tree branch, hoping it would hold. The river was slow moving that fall, and I was standing in the water when a cottonmouth bit me right in the calf. I didn't even see it until Benjamin grabbed that snake out of the water and threw it onto the riverbank. Have you ever been bit by a cottonmouth, Ms. Costello?"

I shake my head.

"How can I describe the pain?" Eloise taps a finger pad against her lip. "I suppose it feels something like dipping your skin into a vat of hot wax. The pain is instant. Consuming. And by the time Benjamin had dragged me out of the river, my calf was a horrible mix of purple and blue veins and had swollen to twice its size."

"What did you do?"

"I was just about ready to lie down under that willow tree and let the coons find me, but Benjamin had other plans. He grabbed his pocketknife. It was a useless thing that could barely cut a twig in half, and he dug the blade right into the bite."

My stomach clenches.

"When the cut was deep enough, he bent down and put his mouth right over the wound, sucking a mix of blood and venom right out of my leg." I am surprised when Eloise chuckles.

"I can still see it," she says. "The determination on his face as he spat my blood on the ground before leaning down and sucking out more. Five times he did it until finally he leaned back on his knees, wiped his bloody mouth with the palm of his hand, and said, 'That ought to do it.'"

I am working to see what Eloise saw. A young girl lying on the bank of the river with a boy kneeling over her, his mouth latched on to her leg like a leech, leaning back to spit blood onto the grass. "What happened next?"

Eloise puffs out her cheeks. "He helped me up, wrapped an arm around my waist, and brought me up the hill to Ulma. We must have been a sight walking up to that house. My leg a sad mess of ravished skin and Benjamin stained with my blood. Ulma didn't even blink an eye. She knew Benjamin's methods didn't do any good."

"I can't imagine." I close my notebook. This is a story I won't need to write down to remember.

"We were back in the woods in a week's time, playing around in the Oak Rocket."

"The Oak Rocket?" I haven't heard Eloise mention it before.

She takes a long sip of her tea, and I wonder what these memories cost her, what price she pays for recalling the long days filled with the laughter of a boy who would grow into the man she would kill one spring evening when something had changed.

"It was a hollowed-out log that had fallen down in the woods," Eloise describes. "Sitting inside it felt like being in the cockpit of a large rocket ship. Benjamin loved it there. Inside that tree." She lets the memory drop and places an orange-red oak leaf between the pages of the dictionary.

Something about the red and yellow and orange leaves reminds me of Chicago, and I think of the night I was awarded the School of the Art Institute of Chicago's fellowship for my painting *The Woman in the Woods*. The art show was at the college, and the downstairs gallery was saturated with student work. *The Woman in the Woods* was toward the back of the building, and a collage of bodies surrounded the gold plaque with my name carved into the metal. Students and professors came by to congratulate me, shaking my hand and offering to buy me drinks after the show. I was flushed with pride and excitement. It didn't matter that the show was in a basement student gallery, because I was a starving artist in Chicago and the dirty bulbs swinging from the concrete ceiling used the same electricity that powered the lights shining down on Georgia O'Keeffe's *Sky Above Clouds*.

"Are you the artist?"

A woman wearing a bright-yellow coat shuffled up to me. It was raining that night, a fine spring mist that felt too kind and tender for the city. It dampened the woman's graying hair and highlighted the freckles on her cheeks. I looked past her to the doorway. Professor Newman caught my eye and raised his cup of water. I forced my mouth into a tight smile.

"I know these trees." The woman's voice pulled me back. She gazed at the painting, and her hand reached up as if to trace the lines of the thick trunks. I almost warned her not to touch, but something in her stance told me she already knew. *She's an artist*, I thought.

I told the woman I created the piece in a single sitting. The trees seemingly appeared on the canvas faster than I could paint them. There was something familiar about her, but I couldn't place it. *She must have one of those faces,* I figured.

"Red oak trees." She turned toward me, her face bright as if she had just solved a curious riddle. "I use them in my work." The woman told me she was in Chicago to see a show. She'd seen the art exhibit flyer on the front door of the institute and thought she would stop by.

"I'm glad I got to meet you, Tig." My name stumbled from her mouth a beat too late. Much later, after the drinks and the purple elephant and the cow that jumped over the moon, I thought of the woman in the yellow coat and of the way she said my name, the way it sounded stilted, like an afterthought, and I realized I had never asked for hers.

❀

"Season's turning," Eloise says, and I am back in Darren, Kentucky. "Soon it will be too dangerous to go up into the hills."

"I hear winters are pretty brutal." I think of Jason plowing the streets in town, wearing a stocking cap, and drinking hot coffee from a thermos. "What did Ulma do in the winter?" I ask. She must not have been able to get to town so easily. "Where did she get her herbs?"

"Not everything dies in the winter, Ms. Costello." Eloise watches the tree branches shudder outside. "Erika sold the apothecary shop a few years after Ulma arrived. Too much fear and suspicion and not enough profit."

Eloise dunks a homemade tea bag in and out of her coffee mug. She never drinks the tea the facility provides. She always makes her own with leaves and flowers collected around the facility. "It was no matter," she says. "By then, Ulma had enough for her practice."

"Her practice?"

"She was a midwife, Ms. Costello." Eloise slides her finger across her upper lip before sucking on the tip. "Rural medicine is always lacking. Even now, sixty years later, it's hard for people to get the treatment they need. Women especially. The nearest hospital is in Morehead, and even then, people are often airlifted to Lexington. The drive to Morehead is more than thirty miles, and the roads are never clear, even without the snow. It's a terrible drive. Imagine being in labor. The woman's life would be in danger, and the infant's."

There is a mechanical sound in the hall, the loud whine of a drill. A woman yells, something loud and abrasive, but the words are buried beneath the noise.

Eloise cocks her head. "There were always women coming up to Whitmore Halls. Most came in secret, wearing shawls over their heads, speaking in whispers as if they had been followed. They came for all sorts of things those early years. Ointments for blisters, lathers for rashes and bumps, teas for headaches, and oils for lubrication. Contraceptives.

"They were all so afraid," Eloise says. "Afraid of their husbands, afraid of scandal. There is such shame surrounding women's medicine, and by then the rumors were rampant. But they still came. Mainly in the night. Their husbands could never find out, you see."

They were killing babies up in those hills.

I reach up and scratch the long edge of my earlobe. "Eloise," I say. My voice sounds strangled, and I cough quickly into my hand. "What happened to the women who went missing in the '40s?"

I had been searching for a way into the topic for days now, the question pressing against the roof of my mouth. "Were they killed?" The words sound harsh, and I flush.

"Is that what they say?" Eloise looks pleased.

"A man in Mitt's was talking about it the other day. Your name came up." I press my hands together, crossing my ankles and tucking them far under the chair. A sharp screech of metal echoes in the hall. It sounds far away, as if the work were being done three houses down.

"Bad vents." Eloise peers over my shoulder toward the door. "No airflow. It barely gets above fifty degrees in here at night."

I frown.

"Better than the prison, I suppose," she continues. "Used to get hives from the cold. Would wake up shivering and bleeding from scratching at the sores."

It's hard to imagine Eloise in a cell, sleeping in a room with cement walls and mice scurrying across the floor. Used to find droppings in her pillowcase, she told me.

It's different for her here, I tell myself. The lights overhead buzz.

"Eloise," I venture, "you must know that people suspect you were involved. With the missing women, I mean."

She looks at me, and there is something in her gaze that is so strikingly familiar that I sit straighter, wanting to put more distance between us. My skin feels hot, and I'm worried that when I stand, a damp circle will have spread across the back of my skirt.

"Ms. Costello." Eloise speaks to me as if I were a schoolgirl brought to the front of the class to write sentences on the board. "No women are murdered in this story."

"So you *do* know what happened to them." I'm careful to make this a statement, not a question. With Eloise, there is no room for ambiguity.

A door slams down the hall, and the walls rattle.

"Patience is a virtue." Eloise lays a worn hand on top of the closed dictionary, flattening the red and orange and yellow foliage.

"But . . ." My mouth opens in protest.

Eloise raises a hand to stop me. "I have one more story for you today," she says. "And listen carefully. Here is where things begin to change."

Ten

Eloise and Benjamin were in the woods stalking squirrels when they found the woman.

"Just you wait, Eloise Price. I'm telling you that the rails could be run from north to south with Darren right there in the middle. I've been thinking more about it, and that canal goes all the way from Mississippi on up to the Dakotas. What's stopping the rails from doing the same thing?" Benjamin was spitting out words and ideas that Eloise wouldn't pay two cents to hear on a damp, no-good-for-trapping day. Nothing like today when the woods were quiet and the sun was just beginning to rise over the hills.

"Would you shut your mouth already," she snapped. "You're scaring away anything worth catching with your loud yakking and horse-clomping feet. What are you doing, wearing those city slickers in the woods, anyways?" Eloise had howled with laughter when she met Benjamin earlier and he'd stood under the chorus of red oaks in his leather loafers with a tie wrapped around his neck. It was Sunday, and church started within the hour.

"Get down." Eloise grabbed the end of Benjamin's silk tie and yanked hard.

Benjamin fell to his knees on the hard dirt beside her. "Jesus!"

A squirrel sat to the left of the brush only a rock's throw away. It was gnawing on the head of an acorn, its black, beady eye skirting from left to right. Eloise rose on her knees behind a log and lifted the slingshot out of her pocket, pulling the thick bands back to the corner of her mouth as she squinted. Benjamin was restless beside her, tugging at the knot of his tie and breathing much too hard for hunting.

Eloise released the rock, and it bit to the left. The squirrel scurried up the tree and out of sight. "Damn," she swore.

"Guess you're not such a good shot, after all." Benjamin shrugged, a smug smile pulling up the left side of his mouth. It had been two years since Eloise had first met Benjamin, and she still hated that smile. "Must need more practice."

"Must need to leave you at home." Eloise stood and wiped the sweat from her palm. It was a crisp December morning, and the woods dripped with winter. The branches of the oaks were bare, and the ground was soddened with dead leaves and hard patches of ice. Only the pines held their color, the green needles shouldering clean rags of snow.

Benjamin looked through the trees and toward the path leading back to town. "Let's get out of here, anyways. It's too cold to be hunting."

Eloise was about to tell Benjamin to go on home then—she wasn't leaving this forest until she had a pelt of squirrels, fat and ready for Ulma to cook up for dinner—when she heard a loud cry pierce through the trees.

Eloise stilled. "You hear that?"

Benjamin tugged on the knot around his throat. "I don't hear—"

Another cry. Sharp and raw and unmistakably human.

"This way." Benjamin turned and fled through the woods, Eloise tight on his heels. It was strange for Eloise to be the one who followed, yet as clumsy as Benjamin's steps were only minutes before, he was now as sure-footed as a three-point buck moving soundlessly over the hills.

They found the woman collapsed on the ground. Her body had folded in on itself as she rocked back and forth, clutching her swollen abdomen. She was young, not more than twenty years old, and undeniably pregnant. Her long brown hair was matted with twigs and leaves as if she had run wildly through the woods, and she wore a housedress that left her exposed skin nearly blue with cold. Whatever this woman had been doing, she hadn't intended to do it running through the forest.

The woman moaned, and Eloise knelt and brushed the hair away from the woman's face. "It's okay," she said softly. "I'm going to help you."

The woman's knees pulled upward, and she pressed her face into the hardened dirt. When her arms shifted, Eloise saw that there was blood on her dress, a large dark stain blooming on the cotton tucked between the woman's thighs.

"She needs Ulma," Eloise announced. She was sure the woman was in labor, that the child was coiling inside, writhing and angry. Eloise was also sure that the woman could not walk and that the trail back to Whitmore Halls was not close enough. She would have to get Ulma herself, bring her aunt down into the woods to place her hands on this woman's body.

Eloise was just about to turn and run when Benjamin hooked an arm under the woman's knees and the other around her thin shoulders as he lifted her up from the ground. Eloise faltered, startled by the realization that Benjamin was a boy who could lift a grown woman into his arms and carry her up the hill. Eloise suddenly felt small and helpless, and she tucked the image of Benjamin Costello holding the limp woman in his arms in the back of her mind. She would think of it later, close her eyes and imagine him standing there underneath the trees, and know that it was then, in the middle of the forest, that Benjamin first began to shed the fragile silk of boyhood.

"Get moving, Ellie," Benjamin commanded. "Now!"

The woman was quiet, and as Eloise ran ahead through the forest, she felt unmoored. Not only by Benjamin's strength but also by the haunting realization that the woman's silence was so much louder than her cries.

Ulma told Benjamin to set the woman in the back bedroom. This was where Ulma always brought those who were in labor. It was the room where the medicinal herbs were kept in cabinets and on shelves that were once used to hold the books Richard Price bought for Joan.

"It's Margaret Owens," Ulma gasped when she saw the woman.

Margaret Owens. Eloise hardly recognized her.

Margaret lived down by the river in a double-wide, fifty feet from the one she'd grown up in with her mother and seven sisters. She was married to Cliff Owens, a hardened man with a shaved head and eyes that never fully opened. He had worked in the tobacco fields for fifteen years before he lost his arm on a blunt splitter. Eloise saw him sometimes, sitting out by the river, just staring at the water with those eyes that never grew wide. Benjamin said that Margaret only married him for the compensation check that came every month and Cliff's weak promise that he would help take care of the girls. The money never did any good. Margaret worked at Hot Cakes most mornings, serving up plates of eggs and sausage and lukewarm coffee.

Eloise brought a pot of hot water into the room, and Benjamin laid Margaret on the bed. His arms shook as Eloise handed him a clean towel to wipe off the blood. She didn't want to think about the story he would have to tell his father when he got home.

Margaret was awake now, her head rolling to the right and then back again, her frozen fingers curling and uncurling in their search. Eloise wanted to reach out, to take the woman's hand in her own palm, but she was afraid. It had been six years since Ulma had first come to Whitmore Halls, and in that time, Eloise had become used to the frequent visitors. They came in the night asking for herbal teas to ease headaches and stimulate arousal, for pills to help with cramping, for creams to be rid of the nasty fungal warts and blisters on their hands and feet and between their legs.

During this time, Eloise had also borne witness to the dark underbelly of labor. She had heard the low and guttural moans of women giving birth and seen the way the contractions wrapped around a body like a riptide, twisting and pulling. She had pressed down on a woman's abdomen when a baby was breech and watched as Ulma reached up inside to unhook a lodged shoulder. But now, standing beside Margaret Owens, Eloise felt unprepared for the raw pain on this woman's face, and she had the unsettling realization that something was terribly wrong.

"What do we do?" Benjamin asked repeatedly. His voice was shaking, and he looked like a young boy again, standing there in the middle of the room. His face was as pale as Margaret's. "What do we do?"

Ulma worked quickly. She cut Margaret's bloodstained dress right down the middle and exposed the white globe of her stomach. It seemed larger now than it had in the woods, and Eloise wondered again at Benjamin's ability to carry this woman and her unborn child up the hill.

"She's lost too much blood," Ulma muttered to herself. "And it's dark. Too dark. Hard abdomen. Swollen labia." Ulma registered symptoms as if she were reciting a grocery list.

Margaret moaned, and her eyes shot open wide as a contraction gripped her body.

"The placenta's abrupted," Ulma said. "We need to get the baby out."

"No." Margaret shuddered, and something hot and wet spat from her mouth. "It's too early. I'm only twenty weeks."

Eloise stilled. Twenty weeks. The baby wouldn't survive outside the womb.

"If we don't induce labor, neither you nor the baby will make it through the night." Ulma's voice was sharp and clinical. It was the kind of voice that had been mechanized through years of working with women in pain.

Margaret gripped the white bulb of her stomach. Eloise looked across the room at Benjamin, who stood rooted to the floor in leather loafers that were covered in dark swatches of blood. His whole body trembled, and Eloise was reminded that he was too soft for this. He wasn't used to seeing so much suffering. Eloise was just about to tell him to leave, to go on and get to church, but Ulma needed him.

"Benjamin, get on the bed behind Margaret. Hold her up," Ulma demanded.

Benjamin paled.

"I'll do it," Eloise interjected. She couldn't stand to look at the fear that ghosted across Benjamin's eyes.

"No." Ulma's voice was sharp. "I need you over here. The baby will come fast, and so will the blood." Eloise held her breath as Ulma explained that the placenta had detached from the uterine wall. The gauze would have to be dipped in witch hazel to stop the bleeding. Blue cohosh and primrose oil would induce the labor.

"We'll use the moonflower seeds for the sedative," Ulma decided. "They are dry and crushed in the cellar. Mix a pinch with a cup of water. Now, Eloise. Go."

Things moved quickly after that. Eloise soaked a strip of cloth in the sedative and placed it between Margaret's teeth. Benjamin climbed up on the bed. His thin boyish limbs folded around Margaret as he held her upward and Ulma opened the woman's legs. A gush of something hot and black darkened the sheets and Ulma's hands as she smoothed a thick lather of cohosh and chamomile over the woman's abdomen and vagina.

The fetus was delivered in a rush of water and blood and embryonic fluid. Its skin was a ruined blue and purple, and Eloise knew that it was already gone. Margaret had gone slack in Benjamin's arms, her skin coated in sweat and blood, and the room smelled of the woods in the hours after something had laid down and died.

Ulma would keep Margaret overnight, sew up what she could, rub the thick lather of cream over the woman's body every two hours. The moonflower oil would keep her asleep, and tomorrow, when she woke, Ulma would take her back to the double-wide on the side of the river. The next morning Margaret would be back at Hot Cakes, serving up a plate of bacon and waffles with an ache inside her stomach that would never quite heal.

Ulma wrapped the infant in a blanket. She would wait until Margaret was awake before doing anything else.

"You can get up now," Eloise told Benjamin. Her voice was thin and strained. She hated the sound. "It's over."

Benjamin looked horribly wounded, and Eloise thought of the fawn she once saw in the woods after Benjamin brought the doe to her knees with a bullet. Benjamin wanted to let the fawn go, but Eloise told him it would be cruel to send it off into the woods without its mother, that it wouldn't survive the night. *It will die a terrible death, Benjamin,* she'd said.

The air inside Whitmore Halls was stagnant and filled with something that felt sinister and cold. Eloise hadn't felt this presence since she was a small girl and Richard Price walked up and down the halls. "Dad," she almost called out. And then Benjamin shifted from the bed, and he was the same thirteen-year-old boy he had been before. Eloise watched as he stumbled across the room before he vomited, and the sick smell of bile was everywhere. Eloise reached for a fresh towel, but by the time she turned, Benjamin was already gone.

❀

Eloise found Benjamin sitting inside the Oak Rocket.

"It's not always like that," she said quietly as she climbed onto the log and slipped into the tree's hollow, folding her knees to her chest. They were too old to be sitting like this now, and her shoulder pressed against his. "We were lucky to save the mother."

Benjamin was silent, and Eloise smelled the metallic scent of wet blood still on his clothes. She ran her hand over the oak's withered bark and thought of all the times they had played in this log, all the times they had run through the woods, screaming and yelling because they were uninhibited and fearless and eleven years old. Eloise felt now

113

that something was changing between them, that something had been unearthed. She felt almost certain that this would be the last time they would sit like this, side by side inside the oak tree that had grown in the woods for over two hundred years.

"That was the first time, you know," Benjamin said suddenly.

"What are you talking about?"

His head hung forward as he picked at the dried blood on his fingernails. "The first time I'd ever been in that house."

Eloise thought for a moment, thought of all the times they had caught frogs in the pond where her mother died and had climbed into the hayloft and hidden behind the great wooden beams, snickering when Charles came into the barn calling out their names. She thought of how they had covered the expanse of the woods and had jumped into the river in the dead of winter, just to prove they could. She thought of all these things and of how she had never once considered bringing him into Whitmore Halls. There were reasons. Ulma made it very clear that what went on in the home was to be protected, and that meant that no one was allowed inside without her approval. But Eloise suddenly found it strange that Benjamin had never looked up at the home's great peaks and suggested they go inside. Now she wondered why.

Eloise hoped Benjamin couldn't feel the way her pulse had sped up. "You never asked," she said.

Benjamin looked out into the woods. "I never believed what people said about you. About what you and Ulma do up in that house."

Eloise felt her chest tighten. She and Benjamin never talked about the women who knocked on the door of Whitmore Halls. Eloise wasn't even sure he knew about all the ways they came. One night, Eloise might be kneeling beside Ulma, coating a woman's swollen vagina with eucalyptus to calm an angry red rash, and the next morning she would be back by the river, hooking worms with Benjamin. It seemed to Eloise, in these moments, that she lived in two very different spheres. That there was some version of herself growing and learning inside the walls of Whitmore Halls, while another version of herself sat inside the hollowed-out center of a dead red oak tree with Benjamin, imagining the old trunk could take them someplace outside the hills.

"But now I've seen it, Eloise." Benjamin looked at her fully, and Eloise thought of all the ways she and Benjamin were not the same. "I've seen all the things you keep in that back room. All those bottles filled with God knows what and that rag you put in Margaret's mouth. The smell. It was like she couldn't breathe."

Eloise felt something between her and Benjamin rot.

"We shouldn't have brought her there." Benjamin flinched. "We should have taken her to Dr. Reed. She needed a professional. Maybe then the baby would have survived."

"You think that old bat could have saved her?" Eloise seethed. "She would have been dead on the table before we even got there."

"At least the baby would have had a chance!" Benjamin grabbed Eloise's wrist and tightened his fingers, bruising her skin. Eloise winced.

Benjamin's eyes widened and he looked bewildered, dropping her wrist before rubbing the heels of his palms into his eyes. His shoulders shook. Eloise was certain he was crying, but when he looked up, his face was dry and expressionless, and she felt as if she were looking at someone she only guessed she used to know.

"I should be getting back. Ulma needs me," Eloise said softly, though she made no attempt to move. There was some part of her that felt she was making an irreversible choice, that after she climbed up and out of the Oak Rocket, she would look back and see only a fallen tree.

"I don't think I'll ever be able to look at Margaret again after today." Benjamin weakened. "I'll never be able to unsee it."

Eloise didn't want to think about what would have happened today if she had come upon Margaret when she was alone in the woods. "You saved her life, Benjamin." Eloise knew she spoke the truth.

When he didn't respond, Eloise braced her hands on the oak tree and pushed herself up and out of the wood. It was time to go home.

"I could tell him." Benjamin's words were like the venom that invaded Eloise's bloodstream when she was bitten by the snake in the river. "My father. I could tell him what you and Ulma do up there. He would stop you."

Eloise swallowed. She was chilled by Benjamin's threat, but she had learned to hide her fear well. It was the one thing Joan had given her, all those years ago. Eloise made her voice hard. "And how would he do that?"

Benjamin looked sad for a moment and then, quite deliberately, he made his finger into a gun and brought it to his head. Eloise stared at him, their eyes firmly locked, until Benjamin let loose a breath of air and laughed. He shook his head and let his chin fall to his chest. He looked defeated then, and Eloise breathed a sigh of relief. Benjamin wouldn't be talking about what he had seen inside Whitmore Halls. He would go home, strip out of his blood-covered clothes, and tell his father that he skipped out on church to go hunting. Killed a buck in the woods that was too heavy to bring back home. He would spend the evening taking apart a rifle that he would never learn to shoot quite right. But that would be later. For now, Eloise knew, he would stay inside the Oak Rocket, his fingers clenching and unclenching, and his head hung back to look up through the branches at something just out of reach.

The wind blew through the woods, and Eloise shook. When everything was silent again, she made her way back up the hill, pausing only when she heard the lonely call of the barred owl. And then, like a prayer, Benjamin's voice.

"Blast off."

Mae's Soap and Spool Shop looks different in the dark. It is evening when I return from the facility, and I carry with me a hollowness I didn't shoulder when I first went up to Dusty Hills earlier that afternoon. I am haunted by Eloise's story, by Benjamin's pale face that I'm certain was reflected in my own as I listened to Eloise tell me about how my grandfather held the woman pressed against him while she gave birth to a child that was already gone.

I sink into a chair in the shop and jump when a soft pressure pushes against my leg. Cougar looks up at me and mews. Stupid cat.

Mae is in the room in the back, and I am thankful for the silence. I pull the notepad out from my bag and read over my notes. The notations are written carelessly, the words misspelled and sneaking over lines. I have additions scratched in the margins, places where Eloise backtracked and added in details she had forgotten. *Ulma's hair was red, did I mention that? Darker than you're imagining, like the skin of a ruined peach. And Benjamin's nails, bitten to the quick.* Eloise's speech slowed when she talked about Benjamin, like it was harder for the words to form.

I feel like I know both everything and nothing about my grandfather. I see him with Eloise, the two sitting in the Oak Rocket. They are pressed shoulder to shoulder. They are children and adults at the same time, and the world is both small and large, and nothing makes sense. At this point in the story, Benjamin is no longer a boy, and his life is nearly half over. I wonder how surprised he would have been if someone had told him at that moment that the girl sitting next to him in the hollowed-out tree would one day kill him. Would he have believed it? Would he have stood, run back to town, and told his father everything he now knew about what the women did up at Whitmore Halls?

The long shadows of the streetlamps creep into the shop, and the old grandfather clock chimes. I turn at the sound. It stands at the opposite end of the room, its thick pendulum swinging back and forth. I can't say why I walk toward it, why I am drawn to this sound that pulls from somewhere deep inside myself. Yet as I reach out and grasp the smooth body of wood, all I can think about is how much Dad would love something like this.

I rest my forehead against the cool glass and let the deep baritone bury the image of Margaret Owens lying in the woods. When the clock quiets, I turn the gold key and open up the face to look inside. It's a

117

trick Dad taught me when I was small. In some clocks, you can see the gears twisting and turning. That's how you know the age of the piece.

The moonlight shines in from the window on the upper beam inside the clock, illuminating a small gold plaque nailed to the wood: Dunn Furnishings, 1948. This piece was made the same year that Benjamin died.

Dunn. Valerie Dunn.

My grandmother.

"Dunn Furnishings," I whisper aloud. "It can't be . . ."

Cougar saunters into the beam of moonlight shining down through the shop window, and his great orange body casts a long shadow into the room. Strange, I think, my gaze roaming from Cougar back to the plaque printed on the inside of the clock, how the moonlight can make such a small little cat grow into something large.

MISSING

MRS. GERTRUDE REY. MISSING SINCE AUGUST 12, 1946. WIFE OF REED REY. Last seen at Dee's Market in Bluestone, Kentucky.

MR. REY IS OFFERING A $150 REWARD FOR ANY PERTINENT INFORMATION ON THE WHEREABOUTS OF HIS WIFE.

DESCRIPTION OF GERTRUDE REY FOLLOWS:

Age: 40 (forty) years. Brown eyes. Red hair. Wearing long red-and-white dress, black patent leather shoes. Wears a large sunhat.

Eleven

Van's Furniture is in a barn behind a large farmhouse. A sign hangs over the door with letters painted the same shade of red as the old barn itself. To the right of the stable lies a long pasture with three grazing horses, and to the left are the same pines that stretch up into the mountains, cutting Darren off from the hills. Somewhere, not far from where I stand, sits Whitmore Halls.

I found Van's Furniture in a thin phone book inside Mae's shop. I flipped through, looking for the name Dunn. It wasn't listed. When I sifted to the back, paging through the yellow sheets lined with business numbers and locations, I found only one name under Furnishings: Van's Furniture. It was a mile from the town square. I could walk there within the hour.

The days in Darren are getting shorter and darker, and the edge of winter is already giving the town its cold shoulder. I wrap my scarf tighter around my neck as I walk up the gravel drive. The doors to the barn are open, and I look around to see if anyone is wandering the grounds. The property is large, the pasture stretching out for acres over the hills. There is a farmhouse closer to the road with a tall metal windmill creaking its arthritic arms in lazy circles. Farther back is the garage. It is set up as an old gas station with two pumps from the early 1940s standing on either side of the door. *Charming*, I think.

The barn is full of furniture. I wander through the doors and into a maze of wood, a man-made forest of pine and cherry and oak. The smell is overwhelming, all bark and soil. Toward the back, tables and chairs and benches and stools all sit in neat rows, as if a show is about to begin. On the far side, near a ladder that leads up to what was once a hayloft, stands a trio of rocking chairs and a baby crib made from dark oak that has been smoothed and polished. On the railing, carved with minute detail, is a circus parade of animals.

There are no aisles in the barn, so I weave my way into the space slowly, letting my fingers glide over the rounded edge of a kitchen hutch and the bony knuckles of a vanity mirror. All the pieces here—the bedposts, the dressers, the tall grandfather clocks that stand proudly against the barn walls, and the buffets with their delicate drawer pulls and decorative carvings—are crafted by a talented woodworker. They are exquisite.

"Looking for anything in particular?"

A woman stands near the door. She wears a dirty apron over jeans and a T-shirt. Her hair is cut close to the scalp and spiked into thick tufts that give it an untamed look.

"No." I circle closer, sidestepping the sharp corner of a large table. "I'm actually here to ask if you knew someone, or knew a company, rather."

The woman doesn't move as I stumble toward her.

"I'm looking for information on an old business called Dunn Furnishings. They made grandfather clocks in the 1940s." I hold my hand out toward the woman. "Sorry," I apologize. "My name's Tig."

She steps forward into the barn. Out of the sunlight, I realize she is older than I thought. Older than Dad, certainly, though not quite as old as Eloise.

"I'm Benjamin Costello's granddaughter." I guess that she, like everyone else in Darren, knows that I am here. "I'm here for the monument."

Her gaze is blank. It's unnerving, and I feel the hope of finding something here, of finding out more about my lineage, bleed away.

"He married a woman named Valerie Dunn." I'm not willing to give up just yet. "She was my grandmother, though she died recently." I pause, hoping that I might have gained some sympathy. I didn't. The woman is still and rigid with crossed arms and an unreadable expression.

"So they brought you in for the memorial, after all," she finally says, her shoulders relaxing.

I wait.

"Heard they wrote to someone up north." She looks up at the high beams of the barn, as if Ann Arbor were somewhere above, just out of reach. "Didn't know when you'd be getting in, though. I don't visit the center of town much. Like to keep to myself."

"I saw an old grandfather clock in a shop in town," I tell her. "Inside, there was a metal plaque with the name Dunn Furnishings printed on it. It led me here."

"It was a bit of a joke really." The woman shifts and drops her arms. "Dunn's Furnishings. Never sold a thing." She holds her hand to her forehead and squints as if she is looking for something up in the loft. "Used to make pieces for family and friends. Occasionally, someone in town wanted something—a chair, an end table, a clock."

My hand slides over the smooth corner of a china hutch. The dark, stained wood, the lacquered edges, the detailed carvings decorating the upper ledge.

"You're the clockmaker." I already know I'm right.

"I'm Rita." She selects a chair, sits down with a sigh, and gestures to the seat across from her. "Used to be Rita Dunn," she says as I sit. "Valerie was my sister."

❁

Rita Dunn tells me that she was seventeen years old when Valerie married Benjamin. "It was a beautiful wedding, all right. Had the church all dolled up in roses and lilies. The whole town was there. It was a big affair. The Costellos were *extravagant* people." Rita pulls a leg up over her knee and smooths the pad of her thumb over a bare ankle.

"Valerie was in a fit that day because someone hid her veil. It was probably those Johnson brats." Rita laughs. "They were always playing pranks. My father had them by the scruff of their neck more times than you could count. I don't remember much more. Everything went fine. The ceremony was beautiful, and Valerie looked stunning in her dress. She always looked good in anything."

I hadn't known my grandmother had a sister, though I had never thought to ask. Just as Dad never mentioned his father, Valerie never spoke of her childhood in Darren. In fact, I had never known if her parents were even still alive. I didn't see Valerie much and, when I did, I was consumed by the sound of the waves and the smell of the sand and of being a young girl standing in front of the ocean.

"My grandmother lives in Maine," I announced on Grandparents Day in elementary school. "She collects sea glass and wears orange shirts that fly open in the wind. She always loved the color orange. She prefers waffles to pancakes and drowns them in honey. She likes to draw trees on the backs of receipts, and her breath always smells sweet."

"She never talked about Darren," I admit to Rita. I don't say this to hurt her, though her eyes become heavy as if she is suddenly overcome with exhaustion.

Rita tells me she isn't surprised. "I spent so many years wondering what happened to her after she left." Rita uses the corner of her nail to pull at a wooden sliver cracking off the rim of the tabletop. "Where did she go? Was she coming back? Was she alive? I looked for her for a while and then gave up. I knew Valerie didn't want to be found."

Valerie didn't keep in touch with her family when she went to Chicago. She packed up her childhood and left it on the banks of Mud River, just as I had done when I left the city. It was easier that way, to try to start over.

I tell Rita that Valerie lived in Chicago for twenty years. That she worked in a diner and raised my father in a neighborhood on the northern edge of town. They lived in an apartment, on the third floor, right next to a Chinese restaurant that was never closed. They had blue curtains, I tell Rita. I try to remember everything Dad told me about growing up in the city.

"She moved to Maine after Dad went to college. Lived in a cottage on the coast and collected sea glass that she kept in blue bottles hanging from the ceiling." I think this detail will please Rita, but she only frowns, as if I've told her something that doesn't seem true.

"Valerie was always the town sweetheart, the angel of the house." Rita chuckles, and the sound is bitter. "She was the oldest daughter, and she had the softest voice—sometimes you had to lean in to hear her. Made the sweetest pies and preserves. Our mother used to say that she had sugar pouring from her fingertips. Nearly broke Daddy's heart when she left." Rita smiles half-heartedly, and I know it's been many years since she has told these stories.

I think of Dad's face in the days after Valerie's death. He said he was fine, that his mother's death was something he could endure, yet his features thinned after that. New crevices and lines appeared on his face; an old dimple became more pronounced.

"Why did she leave?" I ask. The question has been pestering me for weeks.

"Death changes things for people. It's hard to stay in a place that is consumed with grief." Rita blows out a breath, and I think of what it would have been like for Valerie after Benjamin died. I think of the way I ran from Chicago after the city became a place that no longer felt safe. Perhaps I have more in common with my grandmother than I knew.

"After she married Benjamin, Valerie didn't come around to the house much, though we lived only a few miles away. My mother would go to her place, especially after the baby was born." Rita shakes her head as if warding off an oncoming headache.

Mae must have been right. There was another child.

"Valerie never let Mom stay long," Rita continues. "She was in a bad way. And then the baby died, and Valerie became no more than a ghost. No one ever saw her around town. Benjamin said she was just adjusting, busy with housework. A bunch of rubbish if you ask me."

My head snaps up. "How did the baby die?"

Rita rubs the tops of her thighs. "No one knows for sure what happened. Everything was kept quiet around that time. Didn't even know she was pregnant again until after she left."

She laughs to herself, an inside joke that I can't understand. For the first time, I realize that Rita is not just some woman who knew my grandparents and makes beautiful woodwork, but she is the first real blood connection to my father that I have met here. Rita is Dad's aunt, my great-aunt. The hairs on the back of my neck rise, and I feel a sudden warmth toward Rita that feels new and exciting.

"Rita." The sound of her name has more meaning now. "What do you remember about Benjamin?"

A crow flies up to one of the loft beams and caws. Rita looks up as she talks. "Benjamin was a charmer. He was so . . . large. I don't mean that he was a big man. He wasn't. But when Benjamin was in the room, he was the center of gravity. He didn't even have to say anything; people just crept closer to him."

Rita runs a finger over the tabletop and draws a shape onto the wood. "She was always going to marry him. Valerie. Everyone knew it. He was going to be mayor someday, after his daddy died."

"Did Valerie want to marry him?" I ask.

"Oh yes." Rita doesn't hesitate. "She always wanted to marry Benjamin Costello." There is a certain inflection in her voice when she says Benjamin's last name, as if he were an heir to royalty or something of the sort. "I'm not sure Valerie ever thought of any alternative. Her life seemed to be set for her before she was born. I was glad she never resented me for it. Had I been eldest, I would have been the one with all the expectations. I was lucky in that way."

The crow spreads his wings and flies to the other side of the loft.

"Valerie always wanted to be a Costello. She felt she knew Benjamin better than most. I think it made her feel special. Until he married her, that is. Like I said before, things changed when they got married."

Outside, the sun breaks through a thin line of clouds, and a beam of light shines into the barn. It casts a long shadow over the side of Rita's face. The sunlight warps her features, and I feel as if I'm seeing her for the first time. *A person will rarely reveal who they truly are,* Dad once told me. *You must always be ready for that rare glimpse of a person when their true self is revealed. Where the light shifts, and for an instant, you see a person, vulnerable and exposed.*

"I only saw Valerie once while she was married to Benjamin." Rita's voice is quieter now, as if she is recalling a memory that can only be told in whispers. "One time. And it was more of an accident really. I was at the hardware store, in the back, where they keep all the wood. They let me back there sometimes in the evenings after they closed. I used the scraps for projects, practice, that kind of thing.

"I was coming out of the back, carrying an armload of wood, and there, in one of the last aisles, looking at nuts and bolts and things she would have no use for, was Valerie. Just standing there." Rita focuses on something off in the distance, and it's as though Valerie is here, in the barn, just behind my left shoulder. I nearly turn around myself.

"She looked so thin. Her clothes just hung off her. A yellow dress that looked filthy, a shawl over her dark hair. Everything about her looked worn. She turned when she heard me. And her eyes. I'll never forget them. They were so vacant looking, so hollow. She always had these brilliantly blue eyes," Rita says. "My father used to call her 'Bluebird' when she was small. But that day in the store, they were nearly gray. Everything about her was faded. It was like seeing a ghost."

"What do you think Valerie was doing there?" I ask.

Rita shrugs. "Not a clue. She wasn't carrying anything, didn't have a basket. She was just there, just standing in that aisle, and then she walked away. I was so startled that I didn't even think to follow her."

"Did she see you?"

"Yes." Rita takes a deep breath. "She saw me. We stared at each other for only a moment before she lifted a hand and put a single finger against her lips."

The ball of Rita's foot is bouncing up and down. "At first, I thought she was blowing me a kiss. But later, after I had gone home, I thought about it again and supposed it could have also been a sign to tell me to keep quiet. To tell me to hush."

Twelve

Everyone in town knew about the Dunn sisters. They were the daughters of Victor Dunn, great-grandson of the founder of Darren who was the captain of a sea ship that sailed from Europe to America in 1817. When Ulma first came to town, it was Victor, as mayor, who greeted her. He was a sour-looking man, unfriendly and abrasive, and the town never flourished under his care. The Dunns were all wrong for Darren, this family bleached in wealth. Victor had no ambition, no fuel to drive Darren into prosperity. It was no wonder that he and his wife left after Benjamin's death, after Valerie fled to the north.

Valerie and Rita Dunn were the town darlings, Victor's pets, and doll-like miniatures of their mother, a mouselike woman who had such a tremendous laugh. One only had to be walking down a neighboring street to hear the dry cackle.

Rita Dunn, the younger of the two, was an audacious child. She was always playing in the river, coming home with her dress torn and covered in mud. She was the deep crease in her father's forehead and the blemish on her mother's perfectly polished silver. Valerie, however, was the child every parent looked at wistfully, wishing she were their own. It was something about her hair, perfectly curled, and those soft, baby-blue eyes that made her look young and angelic, even when she waltzed into adulthood. And she was lovely. She glided through town each morning with her polished shoes and hair in neat plaits.

She always stopped to pet the heads of dogs, didn't matter if they had just rolled in mud or scratched their hinds. Valerie Dunn never met a dog she didn't take to. It was no wonder that the strays followed her home. She was a tender child. Soft in speech and quick to tears. So kind, so terribly innocent. That was why it was such a shock when she stood on the doorstep of Whitmore Halls, her sister's hand wrapped tightly in her own as she pounded on the old wooden door.

Eloise was down in the cellar and covered in blood. She was skinning a rabbit and draining the blood into 5-milliliter vials she placed in twin lines on the wooden shelves. It was a dirty job, but Eloise didn't mind. One teaspoon of rabbit blood taken twice a day did wonders for the kidneys. Suppressed the immune system and kept the white blood cells from attacking the organs. When Ulma had lower back pain, complaining her kidneys were inflamed, two weeks of rabbit blood did the trick. She was up and walking through the woods in no time at all.

Eloise was busy digging dried blood out from under her nails when she heard the knock at the door. Ulma was out back, gathering thyme and lavender, and Eloise listened to Charles's slow steps as he went to the foyer. It was a heavy gait, awkward and loud, carried on from his younger years of dragging his left limb. The sound of muffled voices mingled above as Eloise picked up the rabbit carcass. She flung it over her left forearm just as the cellar door opened.

"Better come up here," Charles called down.

Eloise sighed. She hoped Ulma would be back soon. She was in no mood to look at some old woman's rashes and bumps.

Eloise stiffened when she saw the Dunn sisters standing in the hall. Valerie, the pillar of piety, who spent most of her time up in the church, hanging banners and arranging altar flowers for Sunday service, was standing in the foyer. What was she doing, coming up to Whitmore Halls?

Valerie paled when she saw Eloise standing before them, a dead rabbit flung over her arm, drops of blood peppering the floor. Eloise bit her lip to keep from laughing. She hated the Dunn sisters and their white dresses tied with blue ribbon around the middle. She hated their curled hair and smooth white skin. They reeked of wealth and elitism and entitlement, and Eloise couldn't stand the smell.

Benjamin was sweet on the oldest. Just the other day, he'd left Eloise at the side of the river to go to a community church picnic.

"You're going to hook worms wearing those trousers?" Eloise laughed when Benjamin sauntered over to the riverbed wearing dress pants and black shoes so covered in polish that they shined brighter than a dead trout's body baking in the sun.

"Can't fish today," he said. "I'm going to the picnic." His chest puffed out, and he looked more like a man than a boy.

"Why'd you want to go and do something like that?" Eloise hooked a worm on the end of the line. The bass were jumping this time of year, and she couldn't wait to bring home a few for Ulma to fry up for dinner.

Benjamin stuffed his hands deep inside his pockets. "Just do, that's all."

Eloise snorted. Fine, let him go to the picnic. She would never want to do something like that, anyway. All those stuffy, prim church ladies with their chunky potato salads and rubbery green Jell-O. She cringed at the thought.

"Go on then," she groused, tossing the line into the water. "I bet Valerie Dunn would love to cut you a piece of pie."

Benjamin flushed, and Eloise knew she was right. All the boys were sweet on Valerie with her clean petticoats and smooth, fine-looking hands. What did Eloise care, anyway? Benjamin was a lousy fisher. He could hook worms, sure, but she'd catch more fish without him. Let him go sit with Valerie and her ridiculous pies. What kind of girl spent all her time baking pies, anyway?

The kind of girl who came to Whitmore Halls midmorning on a cool November day, it turned out.

Valerie's eyes flickered from the dead rabbit back to Eloise, her mouth tightening. For a moment, Eloise thought she might turn around, take her sister's hand, and run them both back down the hill. But Valerie simply took a breath and stepped forward.

"I'm here to speak to Ulma." Her voice was louder than it should have been, as though she was trying to mask the undercurrent of a nervous tremor.

Eloise glanced at Rita, trembling behind her sister. Her fingers winding and unwinding in front of her. *So delicate,* Eloise thought. *So afraid.* Eloise sighed. She had seen this look before. It was the look of a girl in trouble.

"Go get Ulma." Eloise handed Charles the dead rabbit. "She's out back," she said, "and take care of this."

Once he was on his way, Eloise turned to Valerie and asked, "Your daddy know you're here?"

Valerie shook her head.

Of course not, Eloise thought. Girls like the Dunn sisters shouldn't be up in the hills. "Come along then." Eloise led the sisters into the kitchen and sat them down at the old oak table. Valerie was still as a statue, her body erect and poised, teetering on the edge of the chair with her hands in her lap. Rita slouched next to her sister and wedged her shaking fingers under her thighs. Her eyes roamed the room, taking in the clotheslines of drying herbs and the pots of lemon and ginger boiling on the stove. Ulma must have started them before she went out.

Eloise turned down the burner and leaned against the counter. Normally, when a woman came up to the house, Eloise offered them water or warm tea, but she couldn't stand the thought of catering to these girls or, even worse, hearing them reject her offerings as if they wouldn't think of drinking from a glass given to them by a witch.

"So." Eloise crossed her arms in front of her chest. "What brought you up here? Surely you've been warned about these woods." A ruinous smile crawled across her face. She was being cruel.

Valerie straightened. "We'd really rather talk to Ulma."

Eloise blew her shaggy bangs off her forehead. "Fine," she huffed. "Suit yourself." She looked at Rita. She was fourteen, she guessed, though she looked younger. Her face was clean, not powdered and painted like her sister's, and her eyes were dark.

"Doesn't she talk?" Eloise nodded at Rita, though her question was directed to Valerie.

"She talks just fine, thanks," Valerie answered stiffly.

The back door opened, and Valerie pulled Rita to her feet with a sharp grip on her shoulder. Ulma bustled in with a wide gasp of cold air. The clotheslines swung and the dried herbs shimmied in the breeze.

"Mighty cold out there," she announced. "Get that kettle on." She nodded at Eloise, shooting her an annoyed glance.

"Sit, sit," Ulma urged the girls as she set down a basket of greenery. Ulma had walked through thornbushes, and her pant legs were covered in sharp prongs and burrs. The girls sat. Ulma pulled up a chair and held her hand out to Eloise. She wanted tea.

"So," Ulma began, once she was sipping from the steaming mug. "What can I do for you?"

Valerie hesitated when Eloise jumped up onto the counter, sitting on the hard wood and swinging her legs back and forth casually.

Eloise couldn't wait to hear what ailments these girls had. An itch of some kind, maybe a rash. Or a wart. A wart! Valerie Dunn with a big, red, pus-filled wart spreading between her legs. Eloise could already see the look on Benjamin's face when she told him. He wouldn't be spending any more time with Valerie Dunn after that. No, sir.

"I need some medicine," Valerie said, her voice quiet but firm. "For"—she glanced at her sister—"termination."

Eloise's legs stilled.

Ulma took another sip of tea. "You're pregnant." She set the mug on the table with a dull thud.

Valerie swallowed. "It's for my sister."

Rita Dunn paled. Until now, Eloise hadn't thought much of the girl. She was simply Valerie's shadow, sitting in the room like a doll Valerie carried on her hip up into the hills. She had a pasty look about her, like she was covered in flour, and she looked awfully timid and young. How had this girl gotten pregnant?

Ulma turned toward Rita. "You're pregnant?" she asked.

Rita nodded, wiping under her nose with the back of her hand.

"Are you sure?"

"Yes." Rita's voice was a low alto, the voice of a woman trapped in a child's trembling body.

"How long now?"

"About ten weeks," Valerie answered. "We think."

Rita looked at the floor. She had a cowlick on the back of her head where the hair swooped to the right. She brushed her hand over the spot as if she knew Eloise was staring.

Ulma glanced at Eloise. *Did you know?* her eyes asked. *Get the pennyroyal. The ginger. There is so little time.*

Eloise was still.

"Does anyone know you're here?" Ulma asked, though Eloise knew there was no need. Everyone in the room knew these girls were here surreptitiously. They had climbed the hill alone and afraid.

"No," Valerie said softly. "No one knows."

Ulma bent her head to catch Rita's eye. The young girl looked up.

"How old are you?" Ulma's voice was kinder than Eloise expected. Ulma was never rough with the women, but never tender either. She was straightforward, professional, and curt. Eloise was taken aback by her aunt's gentleness.

"Fourteen," Rita replied.

Ulma frowned. "You sure you don't want this baby?"

Of course she doesn't want this baby, Eloise thought. *She's not yet a woman.*

Rita shook her head. "No," she whispered. "No, I can't have this baby."

"She's barely fourteen," Valerie added. "This never should have happened."

Tears filled Rita's eyes, and she couldn't look at Valerie. The space between the two widened across the room.

Eloise jumped down from the counter and set a pot of water on the stove to boil. Rita Dunn was pregnant, she thought. Fourteen-year-old Rita Dunn.

"Get the pennyroyal, Eloise." Ulma stood. "And the coltsfoot."

Eloise didn't need to be told what to do. She had made the tea before, many times. It was always the same. Pennyroyal. Coltsfoot. Fleabane. A pinch of ginger. It tasted like pond scum, but it made the blood come. The cramping would last for a couple of days, the blood longer.

"Come with me. I need to take a look at you." Ulma led the Dunn sisters down the hall and into the far room while Eloise went to the cellar. *Lie down,* Ulma would tell Rita, leading the girl to the bed where she would take off her underwear. Ulma would work quickly, not wanting to keep the girl in a vulnerable position for long. She would feel the curves of her hips, press down on her soft abdomen, and slide her fingers inside the girl's vagina to feel for swelling. The vaginal walls were always thicker when pregnant.

When Ulma was sure, she would ask the girl again whether she was certain about termination. She would watch the girl's body language, the way her shoulders tensed and her fingers shook. She would ask whether anyone in her life was pressuring her to terminate, whether this decision was really her own. If Ulma sensed any wavering in the girl's words, in her decision, she would tell her to get dressed, to go back down the hill, to come back when she had fully decided.

The tea didn't take long to make, and by the time Eloise came back into the room, the exam was done and the Dunn sisters were sitting side by side on the bed with Ulma standing beside them.

Valerie looked up at Eloise when she entered. She seemed so small sitting on the bedspread, so defeated and helpless, that Eloise felt a sharp pain of sympathy for the girl. What had it taken for her to bring her sister up the hill? Surely there were risks, not only for Rita but also for herself, the daughter of Victor Dunn. What if she had been seen? What if her parents found out what their daughters had done?

"Two years ago, I was visiting a friend for the summer," Valerie began as Eloise handed Ulma the tea. Two sets of eyes followed the steaming mug of liquid. "We were staying at a summer house out on the bay. She had a beautiful older sister who was also staying there."

There was a bowl of moonflowers sitting on the nightstand beside Valerie. Eloise had collected them that morning, setting them in the room to dry. Ulma wanted them for their sap and leaves. Valerie reached over and plucked a flower from the bowl, cradling the white bulb in her palm. "One night, while her parents were out, she told us she was pregnant. She couldn't have the baby, so she needed to terminate. She found a knitting needle in the closet. Said she had a friend who did this same thing. It would be messy, but she would be fine in the morning."

Eloise had heard Valerie's story before. She had heard it from many women who came up to Whitmore Halls asking for terminations, telling stories of others who had no other options. Women using knitting needles, coat hangers, long metal kitchen utensils, shoving the sharp instruments into their bodies to bring the blood.

"She made us lock the bedroom door while she lay on the bed covered with towels. She cried out and there was so much blood." Valerie was glassy-eyed now as her finger moved methodically over the white flower petals.

"We tried to clean her up the best we could, but the blood kept coming. She lost consciousness after that. When her father came home, he burst in the room and found us still rubbing at the body. He told us to get out and to never speak of this ever again." Valerie's finger stilled. When she looked up, Eloise startled at the look of rawness in Valerie's blue eyes, like an open wound that wouldn't close.

"It wasn't until hours later that we realized she was dead," Valerie said. She looked directly at Ulma holding the cup of warm liquid in her hands. Valerie shook her head. "I couldn't let that happen to my sister."

"I'm sorry that happened to you." Ulma sighed. "That's a terrible thing to carry."

Rita placed her hand on Valerie's shoulder, her small fingers so white and tender. Eloise's eyes narrowed. It was strange seeing this young girl comfort her older sister when she was so clearly the one who needed her sister's touch.

Ulma stood in front of Rita and handed her the mug. "Drink this," she said. "And then you can go. You'll need to stay in bed for a day, maybe two. There will be some cramping. It'll be worst tonight. The blood will be heavy."

Rita nodded and took a sip. Her nose puckered at the taste, but she drank the tea greedily, like a child. She handed the empty cup back to Ulma.

"You should go now," Ulma said. "It'll be dark soon, and it's a long walk back to town."

Eloise stood on the front steps of Whitmore Halls and watched the sisters run quickly back down the hill. Their cloaks were wrapped tightly over their heads, and they looked like twin nuns hurrying away from a dark, looming convent. Eloise knew Rita would be fine. She would bleed the next morning, and in a week's time, she would begin to heal.

The girls would keep this a secret, their visit to the witch doctor. Years would pass and the secret would curdle. They would think about it at odd times, certainly, while Rita sanded the face of a cherrywood grandfather clock, while the sisters stood at the bus station waving to the train that brought home the boys who had turned into men while at war, while Valerie stirred the last bit of lemon into a frothy meringue so sweet it was nearly bitter on the tongue.

It was Eloise who was haunted by the Dunn sisters. Yet it wasn't the termination that struck her, or the girl's youth or even Valerie's harrowing story. It was Rita's small hand reaching out to lie on the soft curve of Valerie's shoulder, squeezing gently, as if whispering, *It will all be okay.*

✿

That afternoon, I receive a package.

I am sitting in front of a blank easel, straining to see my grandfather's face somewhere inside the white canvas, when there is a knock on the door. I hurry across the room to open it, and there, standing on the top step, is Mae. She is holding a large manila envelope in one hand and wearing a tight-lipped scowl across her face. The apologies rise in my throat.

"Package was dropped off for you," Mae says curtly. She thrusts the envelope toward me, and I am reminded of the night Dad and I sat at the dining room table with the letter from Mayor Grant stretched out between us.

My brow furrows. Who would be sending me a package? I look down at the wrapping and see only my name scrawled across the front of the envelope. There is no return address.

"Who is it from?" I ask.

"Didn't see," Mae answers. "Was sitting on the front step outside the shop when I came back from lunch." She turns to leave, and I catch a whiff of her perfume. The scent is raw and ripe, as green as the pines growing alongside Mud River. I think of the vial Valerie wore around her neck when Dad and I went to visit her in Maine. The bottle was small, barely larger than a thimble, and the liquid inside was jade green.

Why do you wear it? I asked her once.

She rolled the glass between the pads of her fingers, and for a moment, she looked lost, her face as blank as a freshly unwrapped palette. *It reminds me of home,* she said finally, pulling the cork from the bottle and inhaling the scent.

"I went to see Eloise Price," I say suddenly.

Mae pauses halfway down the stairs.

"At the penitentiary," I confess. The envelope feels heavy in my hands. "She's been telling me stories. About Benjamin. About her aunt and how she came to care for her up at Whitmore Halls." I'm not sure why I am telling Mae these things; I only know that I feel like I am searching for something, something both foreign and familiar, something that I can't seem to find.

"You were right," I tell Mae. "She does know Benjamin better than anyone."

Mae doesn't turn around. Instead, she wraps her fingers around the stair railing, and her shoulders square as if she's steeling herself for the inevitable fall. "I shouldn't have told you to go talk to her."

I take a step closer to the stairwell. "Why?" I ask.

Downstairs, the grandfather clock chimes just as the door to the shop opens and the voice of a young woman calls out.

It's not until Mae stands on the last stair, one foot already submerged in the shop's warm light, when she glances up at me and says, "Some stories are better left untold."

And then she is gone, swallowed up by the bars of soap and spools of yarn that Cougar spent the day unraveling. Mae greets the woman downstairs, and the sound of laughter, fake and abrasive, rushes up the stairs to chase me back inside the apartment.

I close the door with the side of my hip and rip open the envelope. Inside, there is a small book. It is barely larger than the size of my palms. For a moment I think it is a child's prayer book, but when I look closer, I see that the leather is old and worn and made soft by time and handling. This isn't a child's book at all, I realize. It is a journal, and when I open up the front flap, a pressed white moonflower falls to the floor.

Thirteen

The milk won't come. The baby cries and cries, and still the milk won't come. It hasn't stopped raining for days. The river is so high. It covers the rails, and the whole town smells like sewage. Davy cries when the rain hits the tin. His tiny feet and fists are red and swollen. The milk won't come. Benjamin says there's something wrong with the baby. Storms out of the house. He goes down to the bar that used to be that dirty apothecary shop. There isn't anything wrong with Davy. If I could just get him to latch, he would be quiet. But the milk stays sealed up inside me. It curdles inside my breasts. I feel it hardening.

The milk still won't come and Davy hates the bottle. Warm it up. Massage the nipple. Wrap in a swaddle. Nothing works. Davy is like ice one minute and on fire the next. My breasts are so full. I can't stand the weight. Benjamin slams the door, and the windows rattle like the teeth in the jar in my grandmother's bedroom. Not all are hers. I rock the baby at night. Shove the bottle in his mouth. He screams. The veins in his feet are so blue. If only the milk would come and the baby would latch. I rock Davy in the bathroom. Turn the faucet on. I don't look at myself in the mirror. Davy settles when he hears the water, but he doesn't sleep. He just looks at me with those pure blue eyes. He is always watching me with his daddy's eyes. He knows I'm going to do something wrong. I'm so tired. I rock Davy in the bathroom and the water drowns out my thoughts. And the tiredness makes everything else small.

Mama comes and tells me I look terrible. She tells me to give her the baby, but I won't let go. Davy is mine. The milk leaks slowly from my breasts but the baby still won't latch. He thinks I am poison. Benjamin has been gone for days. Two. Three. I don't count anymore. I know where he is. A bar in Morehead. The Lazy Daisy. Cheryl's Place. Liquor. Women. It's better when he's away. He doesn't like to see the milk stains on my dress. Mama tells me she will take the baby while I rest. I will never give her Davy. Davy is mine. I rock him in the bathroom in the darkness. All the faucets are turned on, and it's like we are underwater. I tell Davy we are swimming a thousand feet beneath the surface. His feet are so blue.

Davy is dead. The milk comes fast now. It pours from my breasts. I don't even bother to clean it up. Benjamin screams at me. What happened? I don't know. I was rocking Davy in the nursery, and his eyes closed. His lips suckled at his finger, and he stopped crying. He stopped crying. I told Benjamin again and again. The baby was asleep. The animals on the dresser were acting strange. An elephant and a zebra and a giraffe. They were moving. Dancing and spinning. And then Benjamin was there, grabbing the baby from me. Davy was blue everywhere, and the animals were still. "What did you do?" he screamed at me. *Whatdidyoudowhatdidyoudowhatdidyoudowhatdidyoudo?*

Benjamin tells me that I killed the baby. I fell asleep in the rocking chair and pulled the baby too close. He was pressed against my milk-stained breast. He couldn't breathe. Benjamin tells me this again and again. Davy is buried somewhere in the cemetery on the hill. Benjamin tells me this too. But I still find Davy in the crib. His body is wrapped in blankets. The milk is everywhere. At night, I fill the bathtub with cold water. I lie in the tub until my skin turns blue. I tell Mama not to come to the house anymore. Benjamin doesn't like it. He doesn't want people around. I don't go into town. Send Anna. She says a woman went missing a few days ago. Marjorie Thomas. She was having an affair with a fellow up north. It was one of those things that no one is supposed to know about, but everyone does. She disappeared. Missing posters up all over town. I tell Anna to bring me one. I keep it in the dresser right beside the baby crib.

Benjamin was going to make Davy a rocket ship. They were going to build it in the woods. All out of red oak. It would have a fuselage and a cargo hold and a real pressure gauge. Benjamin had the plans all drawn out. The Oak Rocket was what he called it. I used to make things. Pies. I could always make a damn good pie. The truth is, I never liked to eat the pie myself. Everyone always liked my lemon meringue best. Won the county fair contest a half dozen times. I don't make them anymore. I was going to make a pie for Davy. And Benjamin was going to build an oak rocket. The rain won't stop. The river is so high. The rails are ruined. Benjamin tells me he wishes I were dead.

We have a rat problem. That's what I told Anna when I left to go to the hardware store. She could hardly believe it. Me! Leaving the house! But why shouldn't I? Benjamin leaves all the time. I was standing in the middle of the shop when I saw Rita. At first I didn't recognize her. Her hair is so short. She looks like a boy. There was a time I would have teased her about it. I was so surprised to see her that I couldn't think to do much of anything. Until I remembered where we were and what I was doing. I think about Rita more than the others. We were always very close. She never came with Mama to see Davy when he was born. Benjamin never allowed it. He always thought something was wrong with the baby. I remember the day I took Rita up the hill to see Ulma Price. Rita was so young, and all I could think about was Tracy Randell's body lying on that bed covered in blood. Rita was too young for all that. I wonder if Rita will tell Mama that she saw me in the hardware store. I should have been more careful. Oh well. We have a rat problem.

There's a strange plant growing along the rails. I see it sometimes when Benjamin is gone and I take my walks. I like to walk on the railway alongside the river, mostly at night. The trains don't come by anymore. The rails are too rusted. It looks like a weed. But it has little white flowers on the head. At first I thought it was baby's breath, but then I smelled it. It smells awful. Still, I like the little white flowers, put in vases all around the house. Benjamin is getting suspicious of Eloise Price. Some woman in town has been running her mouth lately, saying that girls have been up at Whitmore Halls. Talk of dead babies buried in the woods. Benjamin doesn't like it. He's upset about the rails. He's upset about the talk. He's upset about Eloise Price. He says that something has to be done. Benjamin says he's going up there. He's going to give Eloise a talking-to. I almost laughed.

Benjamin says I'm coming with him up to Whitmore Halls. He's tired of everyone in town thinking he's not doing enough. It's time he has a talk with Eloise Price. I guess he thinks that my being there will make things better for him. He says he and Eloise are going to come to some agreement. I want to tell him that Eloise Price never agreed to anything she didn't want to do. Benjamin says I need to make a pie. Lemon meringue. He used to love it before I quit baking them. I have so many of the little white weeds now. They look nice. The green stains and makes my hands itch. But I still like to look at them, those little white weeds that I have placed all over the house.

Fourteen

Eloise and I walk the grounds of Dusty Hills, looking for leaves. It is two weeks before Christmas, and the sky is swollen with snow. It's the last day we will be able to find red oak leaves before the snowstorm, Eloise told me when I arrived, burying herself in the embrace of a brown wool coat.

Dusty Hills sits on a few dozen acres of land that is fenced in by tall iron rods. The residents of the facility are only allowed outdoors when accompanied by staff or during visiting hours. A long gravel walkway runs along the outer rim of the property, closing in the facility's residence halls, supply sheds, and the tall smokestack puffing out large plumes of pollution into the air. The residents stroll along the path, walking around the edifice in perfect squares. No one is allowed to leave the compound.

"The mountains smell like snow." Eloise bends to pick up an orange leaf. The edges frill, and she tosses it back on the ground. "Next time you come here, it will be too cold to walk outdoors."

I am quiet today as I stroll alongside Eloise. I came to Dusty Hills with my grandmother's words still ringing in my mind. It was her diary that had been in the large manila envelope left for me on the steps of the shop. It had been startling to see Valerie's words written on the pages in the leather binding. Even more so than reading about the baby, about his death, about the hardware store where Valerie saw Rita in the aisle and told her to hush. I read the diary three times, tracing my grandmother's words with my finger and bringing the open book to my nose to inhale. I was never as close to my grandmother as I was in those hours.

I tell this now to Eloise.

"A diary?" She almost laughs. "I wonder who kept that thing around for all these years." She chuckles again, but there is a charcoal hue to the sound that gives me pause.

"It was written after the baby was born. The boy who died." I watch Eloise, but her eyes are locked firmly on the roots of the fence as if she is looking for something buried there in the soil.

"She talked about Benjamin." I am speaking more to myself than to anyone else. "About his depression after everything that happened. About how the baby was sick, about how she collected flowers and put them in vases around the home." I don't tell Eloise that Valerie mentioned her, that the last page of the journal was covered in words about going up to Whitmore Halls. "Her voice was so different in her writing."

Eloise is distracted, bending over to pick some weeds growing by the fence line. I close my eyes and imagine my grandmother sitting down to write in the leather-bound book over fifty years ago. There was a bite to her voice that seemed so different from how I remembered her standing out by the sea. "She was always so happy looking out at the ocean," I explain to Eloise.

"Marriage changes people." Eloise straightens. "As does death." She holds a fistful of green stalks. They look like the ones that grow near the wooded trails back home. Eloise touches them gently. "I can't tell you much about Valerie," she states. "I never saw much of her before or after they married. Our worlds were very different, as you know."

I think of Valerie stretched out in the bathtub full of cold water. "Losing the baby seemed to ruin her." I suddenly wonder whether Dad knew about the baby who died before he was born. Whether he knew about the grief that consumed his mother before she again became pregnant and packed up her bags to run from memories that were too heavy to bear.

"Yes," Eloise says simply. "There was nothing Valerie wanted more than to be a mother."

"I can't believe those are still alive." I nod toward the plant in Eloise's hand. Few white wildflowers remain on the green stalks, but I can already see the careful way she will place the heads into her notebook and gently press down on the leather.

"Some plants live longer than others." Her gaze stays firmly set on the plant as she uses her thumb to press under the head. The white petals fall to the ground. She sticks the rest in her pocket. "I saw her once holding a dead fox cub."

"Valerie?"

Eloise hums. "She was about nine years old, give or take a year, and it was a cold spring morning. I don't know why she was out by the river, but a fox had made a den under the old railcar that was left to rot over by the trailer park. I can only imagine she found the cub by mistake." Eloise licks the pad of a finger, and her nose furrows.

"She was sitting there with the dead cub held in her arms like a baby, rocking it back and forth and singing some hymn they teach you in Sunday school. I wouldn't have bothered going over to her, except a mean-looking dog was staring her down and the buzzards were starting to fly overhead. I asked her what the hell she was doing, and she just looked up at me with those blue eyes that were better fit for a baby doll and said, 'No creature deserves to die alone.' I was sure she had gone mad."

"What did you do?" I asked.

"I ran right home." Eloise laughs, and the sound is so unexpected that I almost join in.

Eloise starts walking again. The gravel crunches under her slippers, and the clouds hang low above us. "How is the portrait going, Ms. Costello?"

The portrait. I sketched my grandfather on a large piece of canvas, using a dark pencil to etch the lines and angles of his body. I drew him in profile only: a long nose, thin lips, broad shoulders, thick neck. My finger smeared the charcoal from his jawline to his chin. The image looked wrong somehow. I threw it away the following morning.

"Painting is slow," I confess. "I feel like I don't know my grandfather yet, and I like to know a subject before I paint them." These are Dad's words, not mine, and they feel strange in my mouth.

"Can you ever really know a person?" Eloise asks.

I think of my father sitting inside his office, lost in the pages of a book born long before he was. I think of Valerie standing in a river that runs the length of Kentucky, of *The Woman in the Woods* locked away in my closet nine hundred miles away.

"There was a time when I thought I knew Benjamin better than I knew myself," Eloise says. "In a way I did, I suppose. We spent so many days together as children."

I imagine Benjamin and Eloise running through the forest, the world only as tall and wide as the branches of the red oak trees.

"After the day we found Margaret Owens in the woods, Benjamin stopped coming up through the trees." Eloise's voice staggers. "And by the time Valerie and Rita came up to the house, it had been years since I had sat inside the Oak Rocket with Benjamin. I saw him from time to time, sure, but he never looked quite right to me anymore."

The wind blows across the courtyard, and I pull my coat tighter around my neck as snow swirls at my feet. It makes me think of the snow globes Dad sets atop the living room mantel on the day after Thanksgiving. I loved to tip them upside down and watch the flakes surge and spin and swirl until they settled once again.

Eloise rubs snow over her hands as if she is washing them in a kitchen sink. Her skin is red with cold. "I saw him in the park once. Standing with a group of three boys. They would all go off to war together, later. They were smoking cigarettes, laughing at something that I'm sure wasn't in the least bit funny. Benjamin saw me and his face just turned. I can't quite explain it. He looked at me with such . . . *disgust*."

I remember the man smoking outside the general store the day I first arrived in Darren, how he had looked at me, with smoke streaming out of his nose, and smiled.

Eloise shakes off the memory. "I wanted to scream at him, to tell him that it wasn't long ago that he had spent every afternoon with me inside the woods, catching frogs in the pond. But it wasn't worth it. He wasn't worth it. I felt a certain loss then. It surprised me." Eloise's lips thin. "To look at him and feel sad."

I don't know what to say to Eloise, so I simply look up at the hills, so tall and wide and harrowing.

"You look so much like her," Eloise says, and it takes me a moment to realize she is speaking to me. Her hand reaches up to touch the side of my face, and her fingers are wet and cold and horribly tender. Eloise is looking at me with such intensity I am certain she is no longer seeing me but seeing another woman, from another time, standing on the steps of Whitmore Halls.

The facility bell rings, stark and shrill, alerting the residents that recreation is nearly over. Eloise pulls back sharply, a wounded expression on her face.

I rock on the backs of my heels and look out toward the parking lot as if I can already see Jason's old green truck parked just outside the gate.

"I'm going home for a couple weeks," I tell Eloise. "For the holidays." Christmas is coming, and I finger the train ticket folded in my coat pocket. "I'll be back after the new year."

I imagine Eloise alone on Christmas Eve, watching the snow fall just outside her bedroom window as she drinks tea made from dried dandelion wrapped in nylon.

"My father and I have a tradition," I disclose. "There is this funeral home a couple miles from our house, and every year they cover it in lights. All in the trees, on the building. They make an ice rink and have a lit-up Snoopy sliding into a five-foot-tall Grinch. That kind of thing." I'm not sure why I'm telling Eloise about the lights at Donovan's Funeral Home. It's ridiculous when I think about it. Going to a funeral home on Christmas Eve.

"It's absurd really." I shake my head in embarrassment. "It's something Dad likes. Going at midnight, being there when it changes into Christmas Day."

How silly, I think.

"Ruth would love that," Eloise says. "She always loved the holiday lights. Used to make us put them up in the trees around the house. Big colorful bulbs that had to be replaced every year."

"Ruth." I let the name sit on my tongue. This isn't the first time I've heard it. "Ruth lived in Whitmore Halls." I remember suddenly. Stan had mentioned her in the bar.

Eloise nods. "That's right." Her face is flushed with memory. "She lived at the house for a time. After the war."

"Will you tell me about her?"

"Let's go inside," Eloise says to my surprise. "I'll make a cup of tea."

For the first time, I am able to read Eloise's face perfectly. The relaxed muscles shaded pink, dry lips slightly parted, rounded eyes softened at the crease and painted in watercolor. It is the face of someone who has sidestepped into memory, and the unexpectedness of it is unmooring. There is pain there, undeniably, but also happiness and love. Ruth is important to her, I realize. Ruth is an important part of this story.

Fifteen

The war came slowly to Darren County, slower still to the women in the hills. For years, talk of the war overseas was boiling, America's lack of participation hotly debated over pints of beer in the taverns. The old apothecary shop was turned into a bar by then, and at night, the tables and benches were full of men who hated the Germans. And they wanted to fight.

Their time came shortly after the attack on Pearl Harbor. America was at war and, by Christmas Eve of '41, most of the men in town had already registered for the draft. They left before the start of the new year, and those who stayed, those hesitant to leave their wives and children and homes behind, would shortly follow. By fall, nine months after the first draft, all men between the ages of eighteen and sixty-four were required to enlist, leaving Darren, like so many towns around it, a township of women.

For months, not much changed for the residents of Whitmore Halls. Charles, because of his bad leg, was kept out of war and gave his services by driving to Louisville and back, bringing supplies to the hospitals and sending blankets and food rations to the post. Ulma and Eloise kept to themselves, foraging through the woods each morning and collecting herbs to store for the winter months.

Women stopped coming up the hill, their time spent working in the town and their minds flooded with concern for those overseas. And with the men gone, Ulma's and Eloise's services were rarely needed.

Occasionally, there would be a knock on the door. A woman asking for a balm to heal a burn. A young girl asking if the berries she found growing by the river were safe to eat.

Eloise was nearing twenty years old and was well versed in the world of herbal medicine and midwifery. She had diagnosed illness, alleviated symptoms of venereal disease, rid skin of rash and fungi, and delivered babies with ease. She was quick with her hands, swiftly offering prognosis and treatment plans. Where Ulma practiced with knowledge, Eloise relied almost purely on instinct, something that had earned her more than one harsh scolding when she was young.

Two years after the first draft, Ulma became ill. A lung infection that resisted mullein and Osha root and sent Charles on a weekly drive to Louisville in search of peppermint oil. It was there, in Louisville, that Charles first heard about the old medical facility in Darren being used to home patients.

"The general is full up," he told Eloise over dinner. "Can't house the overflow of soldiers. Too many wounded."

The Twenty-Fifth General Hospital was in the heart of Kentucky and where injured soldiers returning home to the Midwest were first sent. News of the staffing issues and equipment shortages littered the newspapers and radio channels. The hospital couldn't take any more patients, yet they kept being airlifted in.

"They're using that old hospital up in the hills as long-term care. The one they kept those tuberculous patients in. Going to start sending the overflow up there next week," informed Charles.

Dusty Hills. It had been closed for years. Eloise could see the building from the top balcony of Whitmore Halls, the old widow's walk that Richard Price once stood on to look over the town. When Eloise was young, Ulma would send her up to that balcony when a woman came to the house.

"Watch for rustling in the woods," Ulma directed. "Listen for branches breaking, for footsteps."

Eloise had known what her aunt was asking. *Watch for the men. Watch for the men coming up through the trees to get their wives.*

"Who's going to work up there?" Eloise asked Charles.

He shrugged and lifted the rim of his soup bowl to his lips. "Gonna need nurses, I suppose."

A week later, Eloise left Whitmore Halls and walked the long miles through the hills toward the hospital. Ulma's condition had stabilized, and Eloise was assured that she was needed more at Dusty Hills than she was here in the Halls. So, armed with a basket full of oils, ointments, and herbal balms, Eloise joined a group of sixteen other women who volunteered their services. Out of the sixteen, only two had any medical experience.

When Eloise stood at the front door of Dusty Hills, she looked up at the stone angel carved above the frame. *It won't be long,* she told herself. *The war will be over soon.* Eloise would stay at Dusty Hills for seven months. Fifty years later, when she stood on the same steps, looking up at the same carved angel, she would tell herself once again, *It won't be long, now.*

Eloise Price would never leave the facility again.

Ruth Ames was sent to Dusty Hills to supervise the nurses in training. Naturally, the wounded came in at such a startling speed that there wasn't much time for teaching. Ruth was from Chicago, where she'd worked as a trauma nurse in the inner city. She wasn't used to the hills, and the thick humidity left her breathless and flushed.

Ruth wasn't much older than Eloise and had a warm beauty about her. She was one of those women you just have to stop and look at, with her soft auburn hair and her small, inconsequential nose. It was always a bit pink at the end, raw, like she had been crying. She was brown-eyed and had long, dark eyelashes that exuded youth. There wasn't a single soldier who came through Dusty Hills who didn't fall in love with Ruth.

She had that quality about her, that special something that made you believe she really cared about you, that you could be someone whom she could deeply love.

Eloise took to Ruth instantly. She had seen pretty girls—Darren was full of them—but she had never seen one so knowledgeable, so intelligent, so capable as Ruth. Those first weeks spent at Dusty Hills, Eloise watched Ruth stitch up incisions angry with infection and dress seeping wounds with ointment and fresh gauze. When Ruth caught her staring, Eloise quickly turned away, busying herself with wiping down a soldier's sweaty face and rewrapping an abdomen wound that was soiled through.

See, Eloise thought, *I can mend the sick too.* But Eloise knew it was a farce. How silly it seemed now, coming to the hospital with herbal teas and oils. The ointments were useful, sure, and the cooling balms were used to treat burn victims, but Eloise knew these therapies couldn't mend the organ damage done by the grenades or the wounds still seeping from where pieces of shrapnel had been lodged deep within. It was Ruth and her modern medicines that would save the lives of a thousand soldiers.

The nurses slept in the halls. The rooms were full of soldiers—men and boys, some injured, some dying, a few stabilized. There was rarely a day when more soldiers weren't brought in for long-term care. Ruth rang the hospital in Louisville and pleaded with them to stop sending patients, but more still came.

At night, Ruth walked through the hospital like a ghost, floating from room to room. In all her time spent at Dusty Hills that year, Eloise saw Ruth rest only once. It had been a particularly trying day, with a dozen men brought to the hospital. The nurses had been told that the men were stabilized, but many were in critical condition—a distended stomach, broken limbs. By nightfall, the nurses were exhausted. They sat in the halls, faces pale and hands covered in dried blood. Ruth sat on a stool at the far end, her arm wrapped around her stomach as if she were holding something growing in her womb. She leaned her head against the wall and closed her eyes. Moonlight streamed down on her from the window, and Eloise saw her face was wet with tears. Quite suddenly, Ruth lifted her head, stood, wiped her hands on the front of her skirt, and turned down the hall to begin her evening rounds.

Eloise followed.

Just as Eloise had trailed behind Ulma when she was young, she shadowed Ruth down the halls of Dusty Hills. The other nurses were quick to notice.

"There she goes again, getting in the way," they whispered.

"Who does she think she is? Some country girl from up in the mountains."

"Follows Ruth around like a stray. Needs a good kick in the rear."

Ruth paid no mind to the other girls and simply handed Eloise a roll of gauze and bottle of iodine and told her to get on with it and dress the wounds.

Eloise moved from bed to bed efficiently, changing dressings, emptying bedpans, and monitoring patients' physical and mental stability. She learned to use her knowledge of plants and herbal therapies as supplemental forms of pain management, mixing lavender and coconut oil when the morphine and oxycodone ran dry. And slowly, under Ruth's guidance, Eloise Price became an effective medical practitioner.

"No," Ruth said when Eloise wanted to follow her on nightly rounds. "You must sleep."

Eloise bristled. For much of her life, she had resided in darkness, sleeping during the day and roaming the grounds of Whitmore Halls at night. She wanted to help, she told Ruth, but again, Ruth denied her request.

Now, the nurses in the hospital were not indestructible, though it may have seemed that way to the soldiers in their care. Ruth, in particular, appeared to be invincible as she moved from patient to patient. But Ruth, like many of the women in the hospital, was horribly sad and lonely. People do not become immune to death, they just become better at burying it.

So on the next night, when Ruth stepped out into the hall, there stood Eloise, holding a fresh roll of gauze and bottle of iodine in her pale hands. They stared at each other for a minute, and then a small smile tugged at Ruth's mouth. She tilted her head, only slightly, and beckoned Eloise forward. From then on, the two were always together, walking the halls of Dusty Hills like ghosts, roaming through the rooms, making their nightly rounds.

❁

Eloise took Ruth to the edge of Mud River where the willow trees grew. The morphine supply was nearly gone, and it would be days before Louisville would send another shipment. "The boys can chew on willow bark," Eloise told Ruth. "It's a natural pain reliever. There are willow trees near the river down the hill."

The hospital was quiet that day, and the two women carried woven baskets and wore heavy shawls. Eloise was bubbling with energy, ecstatic to be alone with Ruth and talking wildly about the mountains, the river, and the plants that grew among the trees. Ruth was quiet and content, happy to listen to Eloise drone on about these mysterious Kentucky hills so different from the flat plains of Illinois.

Halfway down the hill, there was a clearing in the woods. The ground was flat, and deer paths stretched out like fine cracks spreading along a frozen lake. A large boulder sat off to the side, and Ruth set her basket on its cold face as she leaned back against the rock, resting.

The woods here were ripe with coltsfoot, and Eloise gathered bunches in her fists. Deep under the red oak trees, just outside of the clearing, were thick bushes full of ripe purple berries. Eloise thought of the day she met Benjamin; how he had eaten the red yewberries outside of Whitmore Halls, and of how his eyes filled with horror as he realized the trick that had been played.

The smile faded from Eloise's face as she thought of him now, marching somewhere overseas. Was he dead? she wondered. There was a sudden pressure in her chest, a tightening. She didn't like to think about Benjamin. He was a part of her childhood she preferred to keep buried. Still, she couldn't deny the dull warmth that radiated inside her when she thought about the days they spent exploring the woods, the afternoons spent beside Benjamin in the Oak Rocket. It was startling, when she thought about it now, how sitting behind Benjamin in the wooden cockpit had made her feel a little less alone.

"What are you doing over there?" Ruth called out.

Eloise stood. What *was* she doing, thinking about Benjamin? She didn't want him anywhere near her, not now, not when she was with Ruth.

"Take a look at what I found." Eloise pranced over to Ruth, holding the black beads out in her hand. These berries, usually so dull and unimpressive, were ripe with sweetness and left red stains on Eloise's skin. How long had it been since she had tasted fresh fruit? The market in Darren had closed shortly after the war began, and Ulma's gardens were sparse. Even the soil seemed to experience the barrenness of turmoil.

Ruth peered down at the berries in Eloise's hands suspiciously. "What are they?" she asked. Eloise had taught Ruth well. Never eat anything in the woods that you can't identify.

A slow, devious grin pulled the corners of Eloise's mouth taut. "Pokeweed berries," she said soberly. "Very dangerous when they mature. And these . . . well"—Eloise tilted the berries in her hand, squinting her eyes—"these are the ripest I've ever seen. You'll stop breathing in less than a minute." Eloise tossed her head back and popped the fruit into her mouth in a manner not so different from Benjamin Costello, all those years ago.

"No!" Ruth cried out, grabbing Eloise by the hand and smashing the phantom berries from her palm.

Eloise howled with laughter, Ruth's white, horror-stricken face only spurring on her outrageous charade. How good it felt to laugh, to let loose the stream of pent-up energy and exhausted emotion. Eloise nearly doubled over by the ferocity of it, the sound of her own laughter swallowed up by the red oak trees.

"I'm kidding, I'm kidding!" She held her hands up in surrender, catching her breath. "They're blackberries, Ruth. Blackberries."

Ruth was not amused. Her eyes were round and lips slightly parted. Her shawl had fallen to the ground.

"I'm sorry, Ruth." Eloise sobered. "I was only playing a prank. An old prank. It was stupid, anyway." Eloise was shy now, Ruth's stricken face washing away the last strands of nerve.

She's seen so much death these last few months, Eloise thought. *How careless of me. How insensitive.*

"I'm fine," Eloise reassured her, reaching into the basket to pull out another handful of berries.

Ruth eyed them suspiciously.

"No berry will ever hurt me." Eloise worked to ease the tension. "Try one, they're delicious."

Ruth's fingers trembled as she placed the fruit on her tongue. Her eyes closed, and Eloise knew she was tasting the sweet juice everywhere in her mouth.

They sat down under the branches of the red oak trees and ate blackberries until their mouths were purple and their stomachs churned from sweetness. Eloise told Ruth stories about Whitmore Halls, about Ulma making teas and balms for the women who came up the hill, about Charles and his bad leg. She told her about Joan being brought to the house as a small child and about Richard, years later, disappearing into the night.

And Ruth told Eloise about Chicago, about streets lined with buildings so tall they would block out the sun, about yellow taxicabs and lights that stayed on all night long. She told Eloise about the clinic she worked in, about the group of women who had been gathering to talk about the changes needed in modern medicine. "It is a man's field," Ruth said, "but women are ready to play."

When the air cooled and the afternoon light waned, Eloise stood. "Let's get to the river. We'll get the willow bark and head back before dark."

Ruth looked down at her hands, palms stained, and then up at Eloise. Her eyes were wet, and Eloise was struck by all the colors she saw in Ruth's dark irises.

"It's not right to feel like this," Ruth said quietly.

Eloise didn't understand.

"To be here with you, right now, when there is so much suffering." A tear fell down Ruth's cheek, and she shook her head, looking downward. "Happiness doesn't belong in this time," she whispered.

Eloise felt a jolt of pleasure surge through her, much swifter than the shimmer of the red oak trees and sweeter than the juice of the blackberry. Ruth was happy sitting here with her, speaking of places that now seemed foreign. She was happy. Eloise, with her wild laughter and twisted pranks, had made Ruth happy. These years, this war, were awful, yes. But Eloise would be damned if she had ever felt more alive than on that afternoon, sitting in the woods with Ruth. The world was terrible, of that much Eloise was sure, but oh, how terribly wonderful it felt, in that moment, to be as timeless as the hills and as alive as the red oak trees swaying in the breeze.

Sixteen

"All right, Ms. Price. It's time for your vitals." A nurse walks into the room. She has a scowl scrubbed on her face, and I recognize her from the first day I came to Dusty Hills. She had been smoking outside. Her name tag read ALICE.

Eloise's lip shifts upward and her shoulders tense.

Alice looks around at the walls and ceiling as if she is disgusted. She carries a lunch tray in one hand and pulls a small cart behind her.

"Looks like it's your lucky day," she mutters, setting down the tray and flipping through a file of paperwork. It's thick and worn and the name "Eloise Price" has been written and crossed out numerous times on the front flap. "Blood draw."

Alice looks up and seemingly sees me for the first time. "You're back again. We've all been wondering about you. A girl crazy enough to come talk to Eloise Price."

Eloise scoffs. "Save it for the lounge, Alice."

The nurse's nose twitches.

Eloise wipes a hand through the air when I tell her I can wait outside. "She won't be but a minute. She can't stand to be around any of us *criminals* longer than that."

The tension in the room keeps me firmly seated. Alice's eyes darken.

"Let's get on with it then." Eloise pulls up her shirtsleeve, and I am horrified to see a constellation of purple and yellowing bruises freckle the inside of her arm. Most are caught in the bend of her elbow where a needle has been repeatedly jabbed at her brittle veins. Her wrist is also bruised, the skin rubbed into a sickly yellow that nearly looks green in the sunlight. I swallow a gasp when Alice takes out a pair of handcuffs and Eloise holds out her arms.

This is the first time I have thought about the care Eloise receives at Dusty Hills. It is easy to imagine her isolated in this bedroom, sitting at the desk, drinking tea, and staring out at the hills from her window. It is harder for me to imagine Eloise being handcuffed, leashed like a dog, and led down the hall. She may now be in a medical facility, but she is still incarcerated.

Alice pokes and prods at Eloise's veins, the needle biting at skin again and again. After the fourth try, I have to turn away.

"Veins are no good," Alice mutters, more to herself than to anyone else.

Eloise glances at the leaves we collected earlier, at the bowl of green and white wildflowers she picked up by the fence line. *Good for the sinuses,* she told me. She would let them dry out a bit and then make herself a strong cup of tea.

Eloise looks old to me now, lifeless, her hair frayed and eyes dull. Her fingers jerk as if she is about to reach outward, until she remembers that she is restrained by the metal cuffs locked around her wrists. It's a childlike movement, vulnerable, and I wonder about all the things that Eloise keeps concealed, all the parts of herself that she had to let go when she pled guilty and was taken into prison almost fifty years ago.

Alice whoops when she hooks the vein and the vial begins to fill with blood. "Nasty bugger."

And then she is gone, unlatching the handcuffs and pushing her medical cart out into the hall with a firm grunt.

"The care here certainly has deteriorated." Eloise pulls her shirt-sleeve down over her bruised arm and settles back into her chair. Her fingers reach out to caress the green weeds. She takes a breath, and when she begins speaking again, Dusty Hills transforms.

❀

Eloise was scrubbing bedpans when Benjamin Costello was brought into the facility. The ambulance drove seven men over from Louisville, all stable but with substantial injuries. One had lost a limb, two more had broken bones that weren't set right. Benjamin was among those who had internal injuries, organ damage, and internal bleeding that required long-term care. He had been shot in the abdomen during a raid and was lucky to be transferred back to the States at all.

The soldiers were put in a room at the far end of the hall. This was where the most critical cases were placed because of the proximity to the nurses' station. Eloise was working the front rooms that day, and it wasn't until she was making her evening rounds, carrying bags of fluid and bottles of liquid pain reliever that she saw him, lying on a stretcher in the middle of the room, talking with Ruth.

Eloise was so stunned to see Benjamin that she nearly dropped the basket of medical supplies. He looked nothing like the boy waving from the train car as he and 256 other men rode the rails south, all wiry arms and widespread smiles as the train wheels churned away from the station. How long had it been now? Two years, three. Eloise lost count a few seasons back.

She had been fishing the day Benjamin enlisted in the war, and when he came to the river, he wore a crooked and creased, dark-green garrison cap on his head.

"When are you leaving?" Eloise wasn't surprised that Benjamin had enlisted. He was a Costello. She figured his father had walked him to the post office with a heavy hand placed on his shoulder.

"Day after tomorrow." He reached into his pocket and lit a cigarette. "Going to Georgia for training in the morning. About a couple hundred of us."

The fish were slow to bite, and Eloise jerked the pole to make the worm squirm. "It's going to be quiet around here for a while."

"The men won't be gone too long," Benjamin said. "Now that the Americans are fighting, those Germans will be pissing their pants."

Eloise scoffed. She wasn't sure why Benjamin was bothering to come around and talk with her, anyway. He would be better off having tea with Valerie Dunn.

Benjamin ground the cigarette into the dirt with his heel. "I'll be seeing you," he said. He turned but stopped several paces back. "Eloise." He looked back at her over his left shoulder. "Don't be treating any women while the men are away. You and Ulma have caused enough trouble as it is."

Eloise balked. Who was Benjamin Costello to tell her not to cause trouble? Arrogant, self-righteous bastard. She didn't remember him complaining when Ulma stirred him up a strong pint of eucalyptus and chamomile leaves to calm a bad bout of diarrhea.

"Seems like the trouble will be across seas!" Eloise yelled. Her words fell like thrown rocks on his back. "With all you men gone, this town might actually become something!"

Eloise was disappointed when Benjamin just kept walking toward town, reaching up to straighten his cap.

Now, years after Eloise had last seen Benjamin, he lay before her with his face badly battered and skin sallow with malnutrition. His hand clutched the same garrison cap he'd worn that day by the river.

Ruth turned when she saw Eloise standing at the door. "Come over here and meet our new patients," she called out. "This man says he's from Darren. You might know him."

Benjamin tried to raise his head but flinched.

"I know him all right," Eloise said under her breath. "What have you gone and done to yourself?" She came to Benjamin's bedside and looked down. Benjamin's face contorted, and for a moment Eloise thought something inside him had come loose and Ruth would need to cut him open to stop the bleeding.

"Eloise?" His voice was hoarse. "What in God's name are you doing in a hospital?"

"I'm fixing you up, that's what." Eloise swelled with pleasure at the look of horror washing across Benjamin's dirty face.

"Don't worry, Benjamin." Eloise bit back a smile. "Yewberries aren't part of your treatment plan."

❋

Over the weeks, Benjamin became a demanding presence at Dusty Hills. He favored Ruth and was irritable and coarse when another one of the nurses came to change his dressings and administer his daily medication.

"Stop being such a pig," Eloise scolded him. "Ruth has better things to do than sit here listening to you drone on."

But Ruth took to Benjamin. She was charmed by his playful stories and sweet smile. She sat with him while he drank the watered-down chicken broth and laughed when he told her it was the best meal he'd had in years. She spent extra time wrapping and rewrapping his abdomen, checking the wounds for pus and infection. And in the evenings, Ruth perched on the edge of Benjamin's bed and hummed a song she used to play on the piano when she lived in Chicago, her fingers tapping on phantom keys in the air.

"He's getting married, you know," Eloise told Ruth one evening while they were folding linens.

She was feeling irked by Ruth's playful smile. Ruth was teasing her, Eloise was sure, but she was sick of watching Ruth laugh at some joke Benjamin made while he drank lukewarm tea. Only Eloise was allowed to make Ruth laugh like that.

"He's a sweet kid." Ruth pressed a towel into a tight crease.

Eloise recoiled. "He's a conceited pig. Really, Ruth, you should have seen the way he walked around Darren, watching over the town as if he owned the place."

Ruth hauled a stack of towels into her arms. "You are being dramatic." She sidestepped the table and stood close to Eloise, stilling Eloise's hand with her own. "And you have nothing to worry about."

❀

Eloise loved to stand over Benjamin. She liked seeing his weakened body and fragile mind work through her presence. Though he preferred Ruth with her soft voice and gentle fingers, Benjamin asked for Eloise. He was eager for stories about Darren, to know about the people back home. And though things had never been the same between them since the day in the woods when they heard Margaret Owens's screams, Eloise found herself sitting on the edge of Benjamin's bed and telling him about those still in Darren. It wasn't because she wanted to be close to Benjamin, she told herself, or because she forgave him for that day in the woods. It was because she knew for all the war took that it sometimes gave something back, and while sitting with Benjamin in the old crumbling hospital, Eloise felt that the thin mattress and stained linen sheets were no softer than the hollowed-out center of a dead tree.

"They had a nice funeral when he died."

Benjamin's face stayed blank while Eloise told him about his father's death.

They buried him in the cemetery on the hill beneath a stone statue. "It's an obelisk nearly as tall as me," Eloise said. "It looks like a stone bishop. Your father would have liked it, I think."

Ralph Costello had hated Eloise. He was always suspicious of the women living in Whitmore Halls, warning people to stay away from the hills. Only once did he come up to the house himself. It was a winter evening, and Ulma was pressuring Charles to keep up on his arithmetic. Eloise was tired after spending the day working on the Oak Rocket.

There was a hard knock at the door, and Ulma paused. It was a man's knock, bold and persistent. Eloise looked at her aunt with wild eyes. There were no women here. They had been so careful.

Ulma rose and went to the door with Eloise quick at her heels. Standing on the doorstep was Ralph Costello, his face white with anger and eyes black with malice.

"I don't want you anywhere near my boy, you hear?" He looked past Ulma and shook a large meaty finger at Eloise. "If I get word of you two together, I'll come up here and burn this place to the ground." He looked up at the blue-shuttered windows and long, protruding widow's walk. "Like your father should have done all those years ago. Murderous bastard."

Eloise boiled and her small hands churned into tight fists.

Ralph looked back at Ulma and sneered. "Don't think I don't know what you're doing up in these hills."

Ulma straightened, wiping her hands on the front of her apron. She had been busy canning peaches, and the white fabric was stained yellow. "You can go now, Mr. Costello. Eloise won't be playing with your boy anymore."

Ralph took a step back and wiped his nose with the back of his hand. "You're trash, Eloise Price," he spat. "And my boy doesn't go anywhere near trash."

The next day, Eloise was out in the woods gathering acorns when Benjamin came wandering over, carrying an old metal trash lid. "Look what I found!" he called out. "It's the perfect steering wheel for the rocket!"

"You shouldn't be here," Eloise said, bending over to pick up a stray nut. The squirrels were careless this year. "Your daddy wouldn't like it."

"What do I care?" Benjamin rolled a snowball in his hands. "I'm not scared of him, anyway." He threw the snowball against a tree, white snow smashing back into flakes.

Eloise grimaced. The right side of Benjamin's face was swollen and purpled, his eye red and angry.

"What are you staring at?" he demanded. His voice was strained, hinging on a man's deep tenor. How many days were left, Eloise wondered, before Benjamin sounded just like his father?

"Come on." Benjamin started climbing up the hill. "I want to try out the wheel."

✦

Eloise thought of this as she stood beside Benjamin's hospital bed, talking about his father's funeral. She hadn't gone. Ralph Costello would have rolled in his grave. But she had watched the procession from the branches of a red oak tree overlooking the town. It was strange to see a funeral in a time when death was everywhere and nowhere all at once. It was stranger still to see the line of unaccompanied women walking the streets like a row of black ants crawling toward the cemetery. Eloise heard their sobs and knew that most of these women weren't crying over the body of Ralph Costello. No, the body carried in the coffin had been one of many that day, buried in the soil of a small rural town.

"I'm going to be mayor when I get back home," Benjamin declared, coughing. "It's what my father would have wanted."

"That what you want?" Eloise asked.

Benjamin's face hollowed, and Eloise saw a glimpse of the boy who'd come running into the woods carrying a rusted lid, his eye black from his father's fist.

"I'm going to make Darren into something," Benjamin affirmed. "If I'm going to run the place, it's not going to stay the old dump that it is. I'm going to create a trade route. Build a railway line right along the canal."

Benjamin coughed, a syrupy sound that shook his whole body. "It will make the town rich," he exclaimed after catching his breath. "Darren won't just be another poor town where people can't find work and kids are going hungry. I'm going to make sure of that." His knuckles were as red as the ripe apples he'd tossed into the air the day he and Eloise first met.

Things won't ever change in Darren, Eloise thought. Build rails along the canal, create trade routes that stretch from the north to the south. It was a pipe dream at best. It would create jobs, she admitted, at least for a little while. But what happened when the work ran dry, when the river rose and the rails became impassable, when the metal railways sunk two feet below muddy water?

"Maybe Ruth would like to come." Benjamin looked around the room as if Ruth were suddenly standing there, leaning against the doorframe. "Come back to Darren, I mean."

Eloise stiffened. Of course she wanted Ruth to come back to Darren. She already envisioned the room she would have in Whitmore Halls. Eloise would make it beautiful for her. Candy-apple-colored curtains and a flower-print bedspread. There would be a vanity near the window and a stained-oak armoire opposite the bed. Eloise would put vases on the shelves and fill them with fresh lilies each morning, and there would be a music box Ruth could open with a twirling ballerina inside. Eloise would buy an old piano from the shop in Morehead, and Charles would deliver the instrument to the house. They would put it in the sitting room, and Ruth could play there every night before she went to sleep. Eloise saw it all perfectly. Ruth would be happy at Whitmore Halls. Eloise would make sure she was happy.

"She'll have a big house." Benjamin was getting excited now.

Ruth wouldn't live in the town. She would never. Just hearing Benjamin say these things made Eloise furious.

"What do you care, anyway?" she said loudly. "Aren't you marrying Valerie Dunn?"

Eloise had taken to mentioning Valerie whenever she could around Benjamin, liking how his face hardened when he heard her name. *That's right,* Eloise thought. *Remember her? The woman you're engaged to. Spend more time thinking about her.*

"Ruth doesn't give two hoots about you." Eloise turned on her heel. She didn't want to listen to any more of Benjamin's fantasies. Put Ruth in a house in the town. It was ridiculous.

"You're just jealous, Eloise Price!" Benjamin yelled as she left the room. "Just a jealous hag!"

✦

The war ended almost as abruptly as it began. Germany surrendered and the soldiers were sent home. The patients at Dusty Hills were discharged or transferred to hospitals throughout the States, and the nurses at the facility eagerly packed their bags. Dusty Hills, though functional, was not a working hospital. It would be years before the facility was renovated and new patients were brought in.

Eloise was eager to go home, to see Ulma and even boring old Charles. She could already taste Ulma's rabbit stew boiling on the kitchen stove. Three days after the war ended, Eloise and Ruth sat outside Dusty Hills, waiting for an ambulance to come and take a half dozen men back over to the Twenty-Fifth General in Louisville.

"I was thinking," Eloise began as she sat on the base of the stone steps beside Ruth. The air felt cooler now, but Eloise was hot with nerves. "Maybe you'd like to come back to Darren with me. We could use another doctor in the house, one with the right medical training. We could start a real practice." Eloise couldn't stand the thought of Ruth going back to Chicago, of being states away in a city with buildings as tall as the sun.

"Oh, Eloise." Ruth drew in a sharp breath.

"You know the war isn't really over," Eloise pressed. "For women, I mean." *Especially in places like Darren,* she wanted to add.

"I can't just leave Chicago. You know Dr. Ross needs me."

Eloise knew all about Dr. Ross, the physician who worked with Ruth in the city. He had a small practice and worked primarily with women. He was a gentle man with kind eyes and a soothing voice. Women traveled for hundreds of miles to see him, his medicine passed on by word of mouth. Whispers travel swiftly in a city. He was quick to fix venereal disease and to fit women for diaphragms. He was also one of the only doctors who performed abortions. Of course, he never called them that.

"Ruth." Eloise turned so she could look at her directly. "The women in Kentucky need you too. Probably even more than they need me or Ulma. We can make teas and balms, but you've said yourself that those aren't good enough. That women need access to safe medicine, safe terminations." Eloise was pleading now. "We could help them."

Ruth looked up at the heavy sky, pregnant clouds crawling overhead. The crisp spring air blew strands of dark hair across her face, and Eloise was once again struck by her beauty. A strange, not altogether pleasurable feeling churned inside her stomach.

When Ruth spoke again, her voice wavered. "Dr. Ross had a partner once. A woman. Elizabeth. She wasn't a licensed physician because she was female, but she could perform any procedure that Dr. Ross could do. I worked with them both for two years before a group of people found out about the practice."

Down the hill, an ambulance siren wailed. *They'll be here soon,* Eloise thought.

"The protesters didn't know where we were located, but it wasn't long before they found out that Elizabeth was one of the doctors."

"What happened?" Eloise asked when Ruth paused.

"They followed her. Threatened her. Found her at the train station and wouldn't let her board. They yelled obscenities. They terrorized her, Eloise." Ruth turned and her dark eyes were raw. "And then they killed her."

Eloise shook.

"It was never proven. She was found in the river. But Dr. Ross and I knew what had happened. I almost quit that day." Ruth tucked her hair behind her ear. She leaned back against the step and crossed her legs in front of her. The back of her shoe popped off her heel.

"It's a dangerous life. It's nearly impossible to have a family, to have children," Ruth said. "Important work, certainly, but so dangerous."

"What happened to Dr. Ross?" Eloise asked. "Did the protesters go after him too?"

"Of course not," Ruth said nonchalantly, rolling her eyes as if the question was absurd. "He was a man."

Of course not, Eloise thought. Elizabeth's crime was not only that she was performing terminations, albeit illegally, but also that she was a woman.

"I'd never let anyone hurt you, Ruth," Eloise said solemnly. She felt helpless, like she was a small child sitting beside someone so much older, so much wiser. How different they seemed now, Eloise and Ruth.

Eloise shuddered.

✿

Eloise returned to Whitmore Halls. For weeks, she was intolerable, sulking around the rooms and halls, petulant and dismissive of Ulma's questions and wonderings. Ulma's health had improved over the months Eloise was gone, though she couldn't rid herself of the persistent cough that plagued her in early mornings. Charles seemed to be thriving. He enjoyed his drives to and from Louisville and kept up the trade long after the war had ended.

Benjamin Costello did indeed become mayor. He stood on the front steps of the courthouse one Sunday morning in the piercing light of early summer and spoke about the prosperity of the town. Valerie Dunn was at his side, holding a bouquet of sunflowers and waving out at the crowd. They would be married in the spring.

Benjamin made good on his word to bring the railways to Darren. In May, three weeks after his marriage to Valerie, long lines were drawn along the canal and, by the time winter came, men were eager for work.

For a long while, Whitmore Halls was quiet. The rooms seemed larger now, Eloise thought, after her stay in the crowded halls of Dusty Hills. With Ruth back in Chicago and Benjamin standing with his arm wrapped around Valerie on the front steps of the courthouse, loneliness consumed Eloise. Ulma tried to ask her about medicine, about the procedures and equipment she used up at the hospital, but Eloise was a half-hearted teacher, and Ulma was tired, leaving them both exhausted and disheartened.

Life at Whitmore Halls was draining, and the days stretched long and wide. Yet it was on one of those mundane, unassuming days that Eloise Price opened the front door and there, on the doorstep, was Ruth.

Seventeen

The Christmas lights at Donovan's are bright and brilliant this year. It's a large funeral home that sits on a square plot of plowed land in the suburbs of Ann Arbor. The building is situated a quarter mile off the road, and the paved drive is flanked with two stone pedestals, each holding a lit angel playing a trumpet. The red ribbons wrapped around their waists flutter in the breeze. The rest of the driveway is lined with ropes of white light. Dad turns the dial on the radio station, and the car is full of Mariah Carey.

"Donovan's really outdid themselves this year," Dad says as we drive toward the building. The roof, windows, and pillars are all covered in strands of colorful glowing orbs.

When I arrived back in Ann Arbor yesterday afternoon, the house was dark and empty. I went up to my room, the stairway seeming too large and sturdy after my stay at Mae's. I was surprised to find that I missed the deep crease in the third step and the musty smell rising from the floorboards and walls. I found so much of home in Darren County. I wondered where I would find Darren here.

Locked in my room, I pulled out *The Woman in the Woods*. I cringed at the girl's shredded body, remembering what it had felt like to take the edge of my key and scratch the surface of the canvas. The rest of the painting was the same: the dark forest trees with thick trunks and widespread branches, all the deep saturated colors I had used to paint them, the olive greens, the burgundies, the fire-roasted reds and charcoal gray.

I ran my finger over the canvas's terrain, the pad of my thumb gliding over a trunk. The paint was heavy there, and its hardened crust felt like the bark of the red oak trees. There was something wrong with the painting now, something that left me feeling hollow. I sat back on my knees and tilted my head. The girl was gone, shredded into a ragged hole that couldn't be painted over. But the trees, the forest, the soil that was painted with blacks and browns and watered-down greens felt off somehow, like they belonged in a different portrait completed by a woman who saw trees only painted in green.

I thought of the portrait of Benjamin Costello. I had started it after my talk with Eloise, and it was now sitting in the far corner of Mae's living room, pushed away from the windows and any light that could turn its colors. It was a terrible painting, one I'd never show Dad. *I suppose it would be fine,* he would say, placing one hand on the base of his spine and leaning back, *if one wanted to look at a corpse.*

I've been home for nearly two days and still haven't had a chance to talk with Dad about Darren. *Later, Tig,* he would say when I brought up the smell of Mae's apartment, the sound of Mud River running beside the rusted rails, the feel of the bronze statue of his father.

"Mae likes to say that the only good bird is one that is cooked in an oven," I told Dad over dinner the previous night. We were eating pesto chicken. It was a staple in the Costello house because it only required three ingredients.

Dad grunted in reply, standing to clear his plate. "Need to get these finals graded before tomorrow." He wiped his mouth with his napkin. "Just leave your dishes in the sink. I'll get to them later."

I sat alone at the dining table, wishing for a glass of Mae's sweet tea. Would it taste as sweet here in Ann Arbor? I looked at my plate of half-eaten chicken breast and overcooked asparagus. "The only good bird is a cooked one," I said aloud. My voice echoed in the empty room.

✦

"They have a new scene." I point to the ice-skating rink that is built to the right of Donovan's Funeral Home. It is next to the makeshift snowball fight between Charlie Brown and the rest of the *Peanuts* gang. Charlie Brown has his arm wound back, ready to launch a wet snowball at Lucy from across the lawn.

"Always did love the Grinch best." Dad nods to the lit figure gliding across the pond. His body is made from red and green lights. To his left, Winnie-the-Pooh and Piglet circle past, their skates locked on a track that keeps them on a continuous loop.

Dad eases the car into a turn. Donovan's sits in the middle of a roundabout, and it's easy for cars to circle around the building and view all angles of the attraction. Dad likes to joke that the holidays are always its busiest time of year.

"Dad," I begin. "Did you know Valerie had a sister?"

Dad stiffens. His fingers wrap around the top of the steering wheel, hands moving back and forth over the smooth leather.

"She never mentioned having a sister." Dad is resigned to the conversation now that he is stuck in the car without his office to scurry off to. "There was a lot she never mentioned."

"Sounds familiar," I mumble. I sink lower in my seat, and I'm suddenly ten years old, peering out at Donovan's Christmas lights for the first time. There is the family of deer grazing to my right, the fawn with its ears perked forward, ready to flee. And there, behind Snoopy's lit-up doghouse, is a blow-up Santa Claus, his burgeoning red belly full of air.

"But I knew." Dad twists the radio dial to the left, and the music stops. "I found a photograph once," he says, "tucked inside her dresser drawer."

Dad slows the car, and his gaze locks on the Nativity scene: the wood-carved manger, the plastic Mary and Joseph kneeling on a bed of hay. I hold my breath. Dad is telling me something. Dad is telling me something important.

"I was looking for cigarettes." Dad snorts, and the sound belongs to someone else. "I was maybe fifteen years old. I didn't like being in her bedroom. She was always very strict about personal space. Which was part of the reason why it was so hard to clean out her house after she died. I knew she hated the thought of anyone digging through her things."

The manger is lit from behind, and the wood glows. It is a softer light than the colorful bulbs that shine brilliantly from the rest of the diorama.

"I found three photographs, actually. Two were of my father. One was a photo of him standing by the train station, ready to go off to war, and the other was from when he was a boy, sitting on a rock in the middle of a large field." He runs a hand over his chin. The hair has grown into a rough stubble, and I wonder how long it has been since he's shaved. Dad has always been such a clean-shaven man.

"The last photo I found was of two girls," Dad continues. "They were standing in the river with arms around each other, laughing. One was my mother, and the other was so familiar she could only have been her sister. They looked identical. They couldn't have been more than ten years old."

"It was Rita." I am certain that it had been the two of them standing in Mud River. "Why didn't you ask Grandma about it?"

Dad presses on the gas, and we roll along the backside of Donovan's. "I asked her about my father once or twice, and she got this pained look on her face. It was like I slapped her. I don't know how else to explain it. I didn't even know he was dead until I was well into my twenties, and then it just didn't seem to matter anymore. Look at the polar bears." Dad points to twin polar bears standing by a tree. Both have red scarves wrapped around their necks.

"It didn't seem to matter?" I can't understand my father's lack of interest in his own father's death. "If I found out Mom was murdered some years back, I would be starving for answers. Don't you want to know why?"

Dad puts the car in park and looks at me. His face is strung with Christmas lights. "Tig," Dad says, his voice all watery yellows and greens. *A dusty sky,* Mae would call it. "I think my mother was running from something the night she came to Chicago," he says. "I think she was running from Benjamin."

It's discomforting to hear him talk like this, and I don't understand what he is trying to tell me. "B-but Benjamin was dead," I stammer.

Dad furrows his brow in the same way he does when studying a portrait that hasn't come out right. "He was dead," Dad finally concedes. "But I think she still felt she had to get away. That she was in danger in some way."

A strange wave of unease swells in my stomach. "Why did you let me go there?" I ask. My voice is timid, as if sending the words out into the air suddenly made them true. Dad sent me to the town his mother ran away from. "Why would you let me go to a dangerous place?"

Dad's lips are a tight line. He looks troubled, and instantly I know I have it all wrong.

My hands unfold and the knuckles are bone white.

"Your grandmother loved Darren County."

I watch Dad's reflection in the glass of the window.

"She talked about the hills and the trees. There were so many trees. She said she always wanted to take me there." He turns to look at me directly. "But we both knew she never would. There are some places you just can't go back to, no matter how much they try to pull you in."

I think of Chicago, of the purple elephant painted on the cement wall inside Graffiti Alley. Would I ever run my hand over her long trunk again?

"As I grew, there were times my mother looked at me and her whole body went still." Dad breathes through his mouth, and I smell tobacco on his breath. "I knew that she wasn't seeing me in those moments—she was seeing someone else. Someone who hurt her."

A car rolls past us, and the lights are bright in the rearview mirror. The twin beams make our eyes drop to the floor. "She grew distant as I got older," Dad says. "It was harder to talk to her, and she stopped looking at me. I spent so many nights thinking about her eyes. They were this piercing blue, like the hottest part of a fire. You only see eyes like that in paintings, in Lorrain and Salvator Rosa. Those who were in love with color."

Dad wears a face so unfamiliar that I struggle to memorize the lines and angles, the shadows under his eyes and the clean sweep of gray that runs from jaw to earlobe.

"I wanted you to go to Darren to see the trees," he confesses, finally. "To see the place your grandmother always wanted to see again but couldn't."

I think of the photograph of Valerie standing in the river, her dress bunched in her hands, a wild smile on her face. Even when standing with her feet in the ocean, she never looked that free. *Sometimes one must find their own way to escape.* Eloise told me this during our last meeting, after the nurse had left and Eloise sat stirring a packet of sugar into a cup of tea.

"Dad." The word slips off my tongue. "I've been talking with people about Benjamin, about Valerie."

My father's face is blank. It's as if these names, these people, are merely characters in a book, references he's not able to place.

"I went to Darren to find out more about Benjamin, and I certainly have, but I'm also learning more about Valerie. And her sister, Rita." A warmth sifts through me. Rita. My great-aunt. A woman who makes clocks that chime together every hour. Suddenly, I want to go home and find my old sixth-grade genealogy tree, rolled up under the basement stairs. *It has another branch,* I want to say aloud.

"I'm visiting with a woman who has been telling me stories about the people in Darren." I am cautious, unsure how Dad will react to me talking with his father's murderer. "Her name is Eloise Price."

"Eloise Price?" Dad chews on the name, and I know he is searching through the files inside his brain. The name is familiar to him. I wait until he finds it. "The woman who killed him?"

I take a deep breath. "Yes."

Dad flinches.

"She was friends with Benjamin. She's been telling me about what it was like to live in Darren County all those years ago."

Dad is contemplative for a moment, his thumbs tapping on the steering wheel. "The reindeer were always my favorite."

I look out the window at the twelve wooden reindeer lined up in the snow. They are painted white and harnessed together with red ropes covered in golden bells. Behind them is the sleigh. It is empty now, but soon, on Christmas morning, it will be full of presents ready to be sent to the children's hospital.

"Eloise helped women," I begin again. "She and her aunt were midwives around the time of the war. Women from town came up to see them when they had menstrual cramps or rashes or when they needed an abortion."

I see Valerie standing on the steps of Whitmore Halls with Rita's hand clutched in her own. *We're here to see Ulma Price.* I see her sitting on the edge of the bed, hands wrung tightly together, voice barely louder than a whisper. *We tried to clean her up the best we could, but the blood kept coming.* And then I see Valerie standing in the hardware store, thin and gaunt and holding a finger to her lips to keep her sister quiet. *Hush.*

"Courageous work," Dad says. "It was dangerous to be an abortion doctor at that time. Still is."

"They helped so many women." My voice tapers off as I think of how I sat on the ground in the alley, leaning against the dumpster, a cow jumping over a moon painted above me. The man had run off, down the tunnel like a feral cat. There was a bag of trash on the cement. The plastic blue ring from a milk carton. A brown banana peel. This was what I would remember most in the days after.

"Is that why she killed him?" Dad asks. I know that he is asking about Benjamin. "Did he find out about it?"

I asked myself the same question many times. "I don't know," I admit.

Dad nods, just once, and I feel the distance between us stretch wide. He presses on the gas, and the car rolls forward. A cardboard cutout of a small boy in a pink Easter Bunny suit waves goodbye. My body suddenly feels bloated. The lights of the funeral home are as bright as the Chicago skyline, and my mouth is wet with saliva and a cow is jumping over the moon and I want to tell Dad what happened to me in the alley.

"Dad." I grip the hemline of my skirt. The bunched green fabric holds me steady. "Something happened in Chicago."

The car turns, and we are once again at the front of Donovan's. The lights on the large pine outside the door dance white drops over my hands, freckling them with specks of color.

"I went to a bar," I tell Dad. "And there was this guy." Wide-legged stance. Cheap cologne. Damp hair. Those straight white teeth that peered out from a wry grin.

"He took me into an alley." I say the words fast, like ripping off a Band-Aid. "I didn't have a chance to say no."

Dad presses on the brake, and the car grumbles. He looks at me with eyes that are round and vulnerable, and I think of the panther we once saw at the zoo when I was small and the world still felt kind. The cat was caged in a large enclosure surrounded by a tall chain-link fence. Inside were stone slabs and a tree that stretched out over a small pool of water. The panther lay on the slab farthest from the fence, looking down at the cat toys strewn across the ground: a purple tube, a stuffed mouse, a plastic bucket that was empty and turned on its side. I told Dad that I was bored and wanted to go, but he held up his hand, telling me to wait.

We stood together, outside the metal fence, for nearly an hour before the cat yawned and stretched its front legs forward, rearing its hind end into the air. Dad curled his lips together and made a noise that sounded both mechanical and childish at the same time. The panther cocked his head and jumped down from the stone, his sleek black body coming near. I held my breath as Dad knelt, his eyes level with the cat's. The two stared at each other so intently that my body burned hot with jealousy. I was relieved when Dad stood, turning his back to the animal. "Let's go," he said. When I glanced back, the cat looked wounded. His gold eyes were milky with loss.

"I just couldn't stay in the city, after what happened," I say now. "I just couldn't."

Dad rubs the back of his hand under his nose and sniffs, reminding me of Jason. "I didn't know," he says quietly.

Suddenly, I feel like I am the adult and Dad is the child coming to me after he was caught drinking in the schoolyard parking lot, his eyes so full of shame. I look out through the window at the ground covered in snow. *It's almost too perfect,* I think. *All that white.*

The first week I was back in Ann Arbor, I went to a support group for women who had been raped. I went into the room expecting it to be a collection of teenage girls and young, college-age women with thin faces, flat stomachs, and rounded breasts. And some of them were, but others were large women, older women, women with stretch lines on their stomachs and deep laugh lines creasing their skin. One had been raped by her uncle. One by her coach. A handful by brothers, friends. One woman had been raped repeatedly by her husband, who then drove her to the emergency room when she wouldn't stop bleeding. I made it to the stairs just outside the door before I vomited.

Dad reaches across the car console, and his fingers curl around my hand. I'm so startled by this tenderness that I nearly pull away.

"I'm glad you came home, Tig." Dad's face looks less refined in this light. If I were to sketch us now, side by side, I'm certain we would look the same.

I squeeze his hand lightly, and it is enough. For now, it is enough.

Snow has begun to fall outside, and everything is covered in white. *Ruth would love this,* Eloise had said. *She always loved the snow.*

"Should we go around again?" Dad asks.

"Yes," I answer. "Again."

MISSING

MRS. DANA FIELDS. MISSING SINCE DECEMBER 13, 1946. WIFE OF CARL FIELDS. Last seen at her residence in Reynolds, Kentucky.

MR. FIELDS IS OFFERING A $75 REWARD FOR ANY PERTINENT INFORMATION ON THE WHEREABOUTS OF HIS WIFE.

DESCRIPTION OF DANA FIELDS FOLLOWS:

Age: 22 (twenty-two) years. Blue eyes. Blonde hair. Wearing flower-print dress. Sandals.

Eighteen

The train pulls into Morehead, and I wipe the last flakes of Ann Arbor off my cap. I look out the window and marvel at the way the white makes the rounded mountain peaks look larger, more majestic with the pines covered in ice. The sky is a mix of whitewashed gray, and the smoky-colored palette rests heavily on the mountain's shoulders. I'm eager to be back in Darren, to breathe in the fresh air. The train car is stuffy and hot and smells of Burger King wrappers and week-old fries.

Jason stands outside the green pickup. The bed of the truck is heavy with snow. There is a plow head attached to the front, and I know Jason has been busy.

A young girl stands beside him, sucking the end of a candy cane into a sharp point. She has Jason's round face and straw-like hair tucked under a red wool hat with a pink puff ball on the top.

"No rollers this time?" Jason teases, gesturing to my duffel bag.

I laugh. "Wasn't going to make that mistake again."

Jason introduces me to Lilly, his eldest daughter. "She wanted to come along for the ride."

Lilly tugs on the end of the open zipper of her coat. Beneath her jacket, she wears a Power Rangers T-shirt with the pink ranger kicking outward. I want to tell her to zip up, that it must be below freezing out here and she will catch a cold, but I stay quiet.

Jason takes my duffel and throws it behind the driver's seat. I hesitate when Lilly goes to open the passenger-side door. Jason's truck has only two seats. Why didn't Jason think of this before?

Lilly is unfazed by my hesitation and simply swings her body over the center console, straddling the plastic arm with her legs. She places her hands on the shifter as Jason starts the engine. I slide into the truck, careful not to press my body against Lilly's. I'm not good around children, and I crowd close to the door.

"All right, Lil." Jason is oblivious to my discomfort. "Shift us into first."

I clutch the handle of the car door as Jason presses on the gas and his nine-year-old daughter, gripping the round knob of the shifter, pushes it into first gear. Lilly's candy cane hangs limply from her hand, the gummy edge sticking to my jeans.

Lilly talks incessantly. She got a dollhouse for Christmas. It wasn't a surprise; her daddy built dollhouses for many of the girls in town, but hers is the biggest. It has eleven rooms, and the roof is made from real shingles. Daddy cut them with a razor wire. She has one more week until school is back in session, and she's planning to make an igloo with an ice table inside. She'll sell bowls of snow for fifty cents. You can eat them with a spoon made from an icicle. Wasn't that a great idea?

"You should come by." Her mouth is sticky with red sugar. "Daddy said we can even use food coloring, and it will be like eating a snow cone. You know, the kind you can get at them carnivals in the summertime."

Lilly is loose with her words, nothing like her father. The sentences roll off her tongue with ease, and I see the woman she will become. She will live in Darren all her life, just like her parents. She will marry young, raise two or three children, host biweekly cribbage clubs with the other women in the neighborhood, and on Sunday afternoons, she will invite her parents and sister over for dinner. Chicken, mashed potatoes, and biscuits soaked in a bowl of gravy will be her specialty. It will be a simple life but a happy one. I feel a pang of jealousy jab the right side of my ribs.

"Look!" Lilly points out the windshield. "There's Whitmore Halls!"

"Yep, there she is." Jason winks at me from across the seat. "Lilly always loves when we pass the old house."

"Mom says it's haunted." Lilly shoves the last hard end of the candy cane in her mouth.

"But you know better than that, don't you?" Jason squeezes her knee, and she erupts into a fierce fit of giggles.

From here, Whitmore Halls does look haunted. The house looks dark and bleak in the hills, the eaves lined with long, sharp icicles larger than my body is tall. The roof is sagging with snow, and the widow's walk is nearly crumbling under the added weight. It won't be long before the boards crack and the home is swallowed by the hills.

"Does anyone go up there anymore?" I ask.

"Can't." Jason shakes his head. "The road's closed off. Been that way for years now. Too dangerous."

"I don't think it's haunted one bit." Lilly's voice is clear and loud. "I think it's beautiful."

I look up at the tiered peaks, the stone turret that must have once seemed so grand and majestic when Richard Price first looked up at Whitmore Halls on that early-November day. *Ruth always loved holiday lights,* Eloise had said. Had they hung strands along the windowpanes? Had they set candles on the front porch at nighttime? What did it look like that afternoon when Ruth first came up the hill, knocking her knuckles against the hard oak door, waiting for Eloise to open it?

"I think you're right," I say to Lilly, letting her chubby leg rest against mine. She is wearing tights that look like two long strips of bubble gum. "I think it's beautiful too."

❀

Room 402 is covered in leaves.

When I arrive on the fourth floor of Dusty Hills, Eloise is missing. She isn't sitting at her desk, isn't lying on her bed, isn't rooting through her closet, looking for a sweater she misplaced months before. Instead, there are dried leaves covering the surfaces and floors, as if I have just stepped outside after a windy fall morning.

"I've been waiting for you."

I turn, and Eloise stands in the doorway in much the same way that I once stood at the entrance to room 402 only weeks earlier. It's strange to see her standing there, caging me in.

The corner of Eloise's mouth pulls up. She is happy to see me.

"What is all this?" I gesture to the red and yellow and orange leaves. I notice the small bouquet of white wildflowers Eloise picked when I saw her last; they're sitting in a mug on the corner of the desk. They are pretty, sitting there in the sun, and I like to think of Eloise waking up each morning to see the small white flowers staring back at her.

"It's been snowing." She walks awkwardly toward the window, side-stepping the leaves with catlike precision.

When she turns, her body is etched with a dull pencil, and the white of her hair blends into the gentle curve of her collarbone. "Today we hang the leaves."

It never occurred to me that Eloise had further plans for the dried red oak leaves other than placing them in stacks inside the shoeboxes she keeps lined up around the room. But as she tells me about how we will plaster them to the white walls, the popcorn ceiling, the glass of the dirty window that looks out over the courtyard, I begin to realize that Eloise doesn't just press leaves for the hobby of it. No, she has been collecting the red oak leaves for the past decade and now, in room 402, she is ready to display them. Eloise is ready to build a forest.

"You will do the ceiling," she instructs, looking up at the fading paint. A large brown stain blooms over the door.

She tells me to stand on a chair, handing me a child's glue stick and a shoebox filled with the driest leaves that has "1991" written on the side.

"Does the nurse know you're doing this?" I pull the cap off the glue and smirk at the purple stick.

"This place is falling apart." Eloise gathers a handful of leaves in her hands and sets them on the desk. She will start with the wall closest to the window. "No one cares what is stuck to the walls. Not like in prison. You couldn't hang much of anything in there."

It's harrowing to think of Eloise locked in a cell. She must have been forced to wear a jumpsuit. I bet she hated that. Eloise wipes a stripe of glue on the back veins of an orange leaf, careful not to rip the delicate skin. A streak of gold sunlight creates a perfect square of white on the back of her wrist. It must have stung when they snapped the metal handcuffs around her thin bones that first night. Did she cry out? No. Eloise Price would never cry in front of a man.

"We are at a turning point, Ms. Costello." Eloise presses the leaf onto the wall. The room suddenly expands. "Last time we spoke, I believe I ended with Ruth."

"Yes," I confirm. "With her coming to Whitmore Halls."

Eloise smiles, and her face is that of a twenty-year-old woman opening the door to see someone she loves standing on the other side. "Yes, Ruth decided to come and stay. Ulma hated Ruth those first few months." Eloise chuckles. "The first thing Ruth did when she came to the house was go right down into Ulma's cellar and toss anything that she thought was no good. This, as you can imagine, set Ulma off in a rage.

"When Ruth pulled out her bag of medical instruments, stethoscopes, hooks, and scalpels, well, Ulma about sent her right back down the hill." Eloise holds a yellow leaf up to the light before setting it aside. "But I saw Ulma looking at those metal tools one night, digging through Ruth's bag like it was a bucket of Halloween candy. She was curious. And it wasn't long before she was asking Ruth questions."

"Just like you did." I remember the way Eloise followed Ruth around Dusty Hills, around the same rooms we stood in now. I press a leaf onto the ceiling, surprised when it doesn't come fluttering back down.

"Things changed after the war," Eloise continues. "Work, medicine, family. Benjamin did what he said he was going to and built a railroad going right through Darren. I'm sure you've seen the rails running alongside the river. That started with Benjamin."

I nod.

"The railroad gave the men work. Jobs that weren't as dangerous as working in the mines and the tobacco fields. Things were good for a while, or at least they seemed to be. But things are rarely what they seem."

I think of how the rains were heavy the year the rails were built, how the river came up and rusted the steel and warped the wood. The tracks didn't get to working right until after Benjamin's death, the mayor had told me while we stood and looked up at my grandfather's upturned face. It isn't until just now that I realize that Benjamin's bronze back is to the rails. He won't ever have to look at them again.

Eloise drops a leaf and curses.

"Ruth changed things when she came up to Whitmore Halls," she reveals. "No one knew she was an abortion doctor. They couldn't. Ruth would have been killed. We had to be very careful. With Ulma and her teas, it would have been hard to prove that the plants did much of anything." Eloise shoots me a glance that tells me I should know better, that the plants did quite a lot. "But with Ruth . . . Well, Ruth brought medical equipment, tools and medicines that made terminations safer but also undeniable. If anyone came around the house searching, they would find what they were looking for."

I drop a leaf onto the floor, and Eloise scowls. I must be more careful.

"No one understood why Ruth lived up in the hills, but they loved her all the same. She was kind to them, enjoyed their company. I was never sure why." Eloise shrugs her shoulders in bafflement.

"Ruth must have been terrified." I think of her walking through town, smiling at the woman selling rusted gas cans for twenty-five cents and waving at Benjamin Costello from across the street.

"Ruth knew the work we were doing was important," says Eloise.

I think of young Valerie cleaning the body of a girl who was already dead.

"All of us living up at Whitmore Halls knew that there was never a day when we weren't in danger. Perhaps never more so than on the night that Marjorie Thomas came up the hill."

"Marjorie Thomas?" The name sounds familiar. I've heard it before. "Marjorie Thomas," I repeat, my body chilling at the realization. "Isn't she one of the women who went missing?"

Eloise nods. "Well, that's one side of the story."

✪

It was a cold, damp night, and Ruth was busy teaching Eloise how to play the piano. Nearly four months had gone by since the end of the war, and Whitmore Halls was waking. Ulma was back in the woods, picking and gathering herbs. Charles had bought a pair of Rocky Mountain horses and was teaching them to trot in circles and ride through the fields. He never got over the limp in his leg, but he rode beautifully. Ruth and Eloise spent many of their days in the far end of the house, where Ruth set up a medical practice in the same rooms Richard Price once used to house his patients.

"You're in the wrong key," Ruth scolded Eloise, pushing her hands away from the instrument.

Eloise hated playing the piano, much preferring to listen to Ruth, but she loved the game of practicing. She bit the inside of her cheek to keep from laughing when Ruth huffed her displeasure. Eloise knew very well that she was in the wrong key.

"You're just testing my patience, Eloise Price." Ruth pushed back from the foot pedal, her face flushed with annoyance. "You don't want to learn, fine."

"Come on, Ruth," Eloise whined. "You can't give up on me now!"

Ulma raised her eyebrows from the armchair across the room.

When there was a knock at the door, Eloise jumped up to answer. The house was cold, and she pulled her sweater tight around her shoulders as she made her way down the hall. A sharp cut of laughter rang out from the den, and Eloise was sure Ulma and Ruth were mocking her musical skills.

Marjorie Thomas stood on the doorstep. She was a middle-aged woman, just over forty years old, and married to Christopher Thomas, a quiet but violent man who spent much of his life working in the mines three towns over. Marjorie was slight in stature, but had large, fossilized hands that were dry and chapped. As she stood on the doorstep of Whitmore Halls, they were white with cold.

"Hello, Marjorie," Eloise greeted her, holding the door half-ajar. Her voice was casual, conversational, for this was not the first time Marjorie had come to the house. In fact, over the years, Marjorie had been up to Whitmore Halls at least a half dozen times.

"Eloise." Marjorie nodded curtly. She reached up to pull the collar of her coat tight around her neck. Her dark hair, drawn back behind her head, was wet with rain. "I need to come in," Marjorie said.

"Of course." Eloise pulled back the door, and Marjorie hurried through.

There was something different about Marjorie that evening. Before, she had come to the house in the same way that many of the women came, standing on the doorstep with bent shoulders and furtive, fear-filled eyes that were never still. She spoke in whispers, stumbling over symptoms with her face flushed. But tonight, she didn't wait for Eloise to lead her down the halls. Instead, she marched straight for the den, her brown Mary Janes leaving wet footprints on the wooden floor.

When Marjorie stepped into the room, Ulma and Ruth quieted.

"Good evening, Marjorie." Ulma folded the newspaper that sat on her lap into four squares, placing it on the side table. "How are you tonight?"

The room seemed smaller with Marjorie standing in the doorway, and Eloise had to press against the wall to sneak back into the den. Marjorie tightened her hold on the wool collar of her coat.

"I'm in a bad way," Marjorie said. "I'm pregnant . . ."

Marjorie stumbled over the words, and Eloise noticed the fingers on her left hand were trembling. *She needs a termination,* Eloise thought. *It will be easy enough. She can't be more than three months. There is laminaria in the storeroom, and the forceps and curette have been cleaned and sterilized.*

Marjorie's voice caught and she shook her head as if waving away a gnat. "My husband is going to kill me."

Ulma rose from her chair, and Marjorie took a step back, her eyes hard.

"Now, Marjorie . . . ," Ulma started.

"It's all right." Ruth sat perfectly poised on the edge of the piano bench. "You're safe here." Her voice was soft and soothing. Eloise knew the tones well.

"Many women come up here just like you, and we help them," Ruth continued. "We can do the same for you, and you'll be home in a couple hours. Now, does your husband know you're pregnant?"

Marjorie's eyes flitted from woman to woman. "I don't think you understand," she finally said. "I can't go back home ever. My husband is going to kill me." She let go of the coat collar, and a red rose bloomed on her neck. The angry skin was raised and brittle, like dried flowers pressed between the pages of an old book.

"Jesus," Eloise swore. "Christopher did that to you?" The burn was fresh, not more than a few hours old, and like roots hidden under soil, only partially visible under Marjorie's smock.

"Get the aloe, Eloise." Ruth stood.

"She needs the calendula lather," Ulma said. "Take her to the back room."

"My husband is going to kill me," Marjorie repeated as she followed Eloise to the far end of the hall. "I can't go back there."

Eloise didn't know much about Christopher Thomas, only that he had lived in Darren all his life and worked in the mines. He'd been in the army for the duration of the war and was stationed with Benjamin in Belgium. He lost two fingers from frostbite during the Battle of the Bulge, Marjorie had said.

"What happened?" Eloise asked Marjorie as she sat her down on the edge of the bed while Ruth filled a glass basin with cool water.

"Christopher has always had such a temper." Marjorie's fingers quivered as she worked the buttons of her dress. She grimaced as she pulled back the two folds of fabric, revealing a withered vine of red, blistering skin that stretched across her chest and stomach.

Ruth gasped. "Oh, Marjorie."

"Lie back," Eloise instructed, gently pressing on the woman's shoulder. The skin was hot to the touch, and Eloise knew Marjorie was feverish. The wounds were dirty, as if Marjorie had been pushed to the ground. They would need to be cleaned and sterilized before Ulma could apply the lather.

Marjorie hissed when Eloise touched her abdomen. "He came home in a rage," she cried. "Slamming the door, throwing things around the room. I didn't know what set him off."

Ruth soaked a washcloth in the basin of water and sat beside Marjorie, wiping the dirt off her shoulders, avoiding the burns.

"He found me in the kitchen. I was making tea to bring over to Leona's house. Her mother just died two days back, and I wanted to check in on her. Suddenly, Christopher comes storming in, screaming at me. Calling me a whore."

Ulma entered the room holding a tray of aloe and a thick paste the color of margarine. "Good Lord," she breathed, shaking her head at the ugly wounds. "Need to get those cleaned up before the calendula."

"He grabbed my hair, slapped me, beat me. He ripped off my clothes." Marjorie was upset now, tears running down her pale cheeks. "I didn't even see the kettle until he was pouring the water on me. It felt like ice."

"This is going to sting a bit," Ruth apologized, working the cool water over Marjorie's raw skin.

"He threw me outside on the ground." Marjorie's voice shook. "He told me he doesn't allow whores in his house. I lay there in the snow and dirt until he got in his truck and left. That's when I knew I had to get out of there."

"You walked all the way up here?" Eloise marveled at the will of a woman who was afraid.

"Didn't have no choice," Marjorie said. "I didn't know where else to go."

"Put the lather on thick after those wounds are clean," Ulma told Eloise. "I'm going to the widow's walk. Someone needs to keep watch. Christopher could be anywhere."

It was wintertime and the woods were bare. It would be easy to see someone coming up the path, creeping up through the trees.

"Is the baby all right?" Marjorie asked. Her hand reached up to caress the underside of her stomach.

Marjorie was pregnant. Eloise had almost forgotten. "Hand me the Pinard."

Ruth placed the stethoscope into Eloise's outstretched hand. Eloise bent over Marjorie's stomach, holding the wooden bulb against her abdomen and tilting her head to the right. The heartbeat was strong.

Eloise nodded. "Baby's fine."

Marjorie sighed in relief.

"Does Christopher know about it?" Eloise asked.

Marjorie shook her head, biting her bottom lip while Ruth rubbed a strip of black dirt from her chest. "It's not his," she said.

Eloise froze.

"I can't go back there," Marjorie pleaded. "He'll kill me."

✦

By the time Ruth and Eloise were finished, Marjorie had calmed and her eyelids were heavy. The wounds were glossy with a thick lather of aloe and calendula cream, and the fever had subsided. Ulma was still up on the widow's walk. Her rhythmic steps paced overhead when Eloise pulled Ruth out into the hall and shut the door behind her.

"We can't send her back," Eloise stated. "I think she's right. He will kill her, especially when he finds out about the baby."

Ruth leaned her back against the wall. She looked tired, like a woman who had just told a man his wife had died on the operating table. *There was nothing more we could do.*

"She doesn't want to terminate," Ruth affirmed.

"I'm not talking about termination, Ruth," Eloise said. She was flustered and frustrated. Let the town think the women in the hills were performing witchcraft, stewing potions, and chanting rhymes. The women needed them. "She's a woman who needs help," Eloise asserted. "That's all there is to it."

"Then what, Eloise?"

Ulma's footsteps grew quiet above them, and Eloise glanced upward, holding her breath. Did Ulma see something? Had she heard a tree branch snap in the woods?

"What is it?" Ruth whispered.

Eloise held out her hand to silence her. The tick of the grandfather clock. The purr of the refrigerator. The sound of mice scratching inside the walls. And then, from above, Ulma's footsteps. Eloise let out a breath of heavy air.

"We need to get her out of Darren," Eloise said firmly. "She can't go back to that angry bastard."

Ruth frowned. "Out of Darren?"

"She can't stay here much longer. Christopher will be up here soon, I know it. Men like him, they won't be gone from home for long, and when he comes back and she isn't there, it will be hell. She can't stay here. We need to get her to the station. Get her on a train to . . ." Eloise was rambling now, a slur of words that circled around her feet as she paced back and forth, mimicking Ulma's solid paces above.

"To Chicago," Ruth finished, pushing back from the wall to stand erect. "She can go to Chicago."

"Chicago?" Eloise repeated.

"Yes." The edge of a smile pulled at Ruth's lips. "I know a woman there. Amy. That's right. Amy Jones."

Ruth snapped her fingers. "She owns a safe house. A shelter for battered women. It's very hush-hush. She worked with Ross, back before Elizabeth's death. Practiced women's medicine until it was no longer safe, and then she formed a boardinghouse for women who are victims of domestic violence."

"Chicago." Eloise tasted the word. She thought of Marjorie, a woman who had never left Darren, living in a boardinghouse in one of the largest cities in the States. "Yes." The idea was taking root in her mind. "I'll bring her over to Morehead tonight. Get her on a train. She can be in the city by morning. We can send her with a letter and some money."

Ruth placed a palm against her own cheek as if feeling for a fever. "You know this is dangerous, Eloise Price. You know what you're risking."

"Everything we do is dangerous," Eloise replied, indignant. "But a woman needs help."

"And what if he finds her?"

Eloise shook her head. "He won't," she said. "It's Chicago. It's easy to get lost in Chicago."

✦

"I took Marjorie up to Morehead that night after the dark had settled in." Eloise pastes another leaf to the window. There are nearly a hundred now, covering the wall and ceiling. It is late afternoon and nearly time for me to leave. We will work on the leaves another day.

"Wasn't Marjorie in pain?" I cringe at the thought of the hot burns scarring her skin. Once, when I was barely old enough to stay home alone, I pulled a frozen pizza out from the oven. The baking sheet slid from my hand and pressed the back of my forearm against the lip of the grate. I reared back in a fury, the red burn the size of my thumb pad. The wound never healed quite right, and even now, the back of my forearm has a white scar of waxy, raised skin. My thumbprint, Dad always teased.

"Certainly!" Eloise exclaims. "A tremendous amount. But you'll be surprised what a woman can do while in pain. After all, women live through childbirth every day. I drove her up to Morehead. She was shaking the whole way." Eloise sets the glue stick on the desk and brushes her palms together. She is done for the day. "We waited at the station for over four hours until the train arrived. We were both anxious. Certain that Christopher was going to appear at any moment, come through the door with his hands in fists. But he never did.

"The train came. Marjorie got on with her bag of ointments and pills and one of Ruth's old dresses. I gave her fifty dollars, which seemed like too much and not enough at the same time, and the letter for Amy, Ruth's friend who owned the boardinghouse. We told her to call if she ran into trouble, and we would send Charles to fetch her. She never did call, though. In fact, we never heard from Marjorie Thomas again." Eloise lets her eyebrows fall; her hands rest limply in her lap.

"You don't know what happened to her?"

She shrugs in a casual way, and her bottom lip pushes forward. "She was safe. Made a life in the city."

I think of the posters that must have hung around town in the days after Marjorie went missing, how her husband must have gathered men together and sent them trampling through the woods. I think of Stan sitting in the bar down the hill. He must have been about twenty-two years old then, just back from war, used to the weight of a gun slung over his shoulder. Eloise killed those women—he sounded so sure.

I imagine Marjorie sitting on the train in a back row, where she could easily nestle down into the pulled-up collar of a worn jacket that was too large. Amy's address, written on a piece of folded paper clutched in her fist, must have gone soft after being rubbed so many times between her palms.

A gust of wind blows against the window, frosting it in white. "Snow's picking up again," Eloise says, though she is looking up at the leaves. "You should be getting back to town. We can finish this next time."

As a child, I hated the snow. It was cold and wet and never looked as beautiful on the muddy streets of Ann Arbor as it did now in the hills. I think of Lilly and her café, making bowls of red- and blue-colored snow to eat with an icicle spoon. It would be so dirty, the snow rolled into balls, but the kids would still take large bites of the colored water. I think of Jason's lopsided smile as Lilly hands him a bowl. He would eat it without hesitation. And Lilly would erupt into sugary giggles when he asked for seconds.

"Whitmore Halls is covered in icicles," I say, thinking of the house on the hill. "I saw it when I was driving in from Morehead. It looks beautiful."

Eloise perks up at the mention of the house. "Have you been up there?"

I shake my head. "The road is closed off. No vehicles can get through."

"Well." Eloise places a handful of leaves into a shoebox. "That doesn't mean you can't go."

I think for a moment. Of course, I realize, I don't need a car to get up to Whitmore Halls. How many times has Eloise told me about the women walking up the hill? It would be a long hike, sure, but no longer than it was fifty years ago when Valerie and Rita and Ruth and Marjorie hiked up the long gravel road to stand on the doorstep.

"See if there are still holly trees up close to the house," Eloise instructs as if she already knows I'm going. "They were always ripe around this time of year."

A slow smile creeps along my upper lip. I will go to Whitmore Halls, I decide. I will go to the house where my grandfather was killed.

Nineteen

The path to Whitmore Halls is covered in snow. I shouldn't be surprised; the road is barred off with old metal poles that have long since rusted. A No Trespassing sign hangs from a single brown screw, and the square flap of metal creaks as it shuffles back and forth in the wind. When was the last time someone was up this way? Surely it's been years since the road has been passable.

I sidestep the gate and walk along the edge of the path, my arms outstretched to hold my balance as my body sinks in the snow. It is heavy and seeps over the tops of my boots until my socks are wet and chilled.

It's an arduous climb, and the path twists and turns as the jays call down to me from the snow-covered tree branches. It would be beautiful if I were entirely certain I would make it to the top before my lungs constricted and I was forced to fall into the snowbank, a sad excuse for a snow angel, as the white flakes slowly drifted over my frozen body.

The red oaks quiver around me. It is midmorning, and the hills are exhausted from last night's storm, the fresh blanket of white leaving everything clean and bright. It occurs to me that even if there had been footprints going up the hill, they would be covered now. I look behind me, keenly aware of how alone I am.

"I shouldn't have done this," I say aloud. Anything could happen up here. A wild animal. Are there bears in the hills? Wolves, coyotes, wildcats. And what if I'm not alone? Someone could be watching me, following me, hiding in the forest. My heartbeat quickens.

Somewhere, up above, sitting in a tree branch I can't see, a bird calls out, and I think of the night when I met the man at the bar. It was nearing midnight. The art show had ended, and I left *The Woman in the Woods* hanging alone in the dark as I met a group of students at Cello's, a small pub that sported cheap beer and half-price shots after ten o'clock. It had been raining all day, a lazy drizzle that left the city soggy. I was exhausted just thinking about the long walk home through the April puddles.

The room was loud and bloated as I wove my way around arms and legs, wedging myself onto a stool beside the bar. It was a hot night, the rain exacerbating the heat instead of alleviating it. A woman wearing a short skirt made of colorful geometric shapes pressed against me. "Hey, honey!" she called to the bartender. "I'm thirsty!" The man behind the counter waved her off with a flick of the wrist. Cubism, I decided. I would paint her in blocks of color.

"Hard to get a drink, isn't it?"

The man's voice was everywhere and nowhere, and when I glanced back over my shoulder, he was standing close to me, his wide-legged stance and sly grin less than a foot away. His hair was damp. It made him look innocent somehow, standing there with those rain droplets that refused to be shaken off.

"Just leaving, actually," I said.

"Monet." He pointed to the tattoo of a water lily on the inside of my wrist. It was an old memory, one that didn't amount to much. A group of friends, reckless and naive and terribly young.

"A boring story." I waved my credit card in the air. "I don't think it would interest you."

"Try me," he said.

I turned to look at him fully. He was attractive, sure, but in a bland way. Nothing about him was striking, just perfectly symmetrical. He would be easy to sketch in a beginner class. Why not let this man buy me a drink? I was just awarded a fellowship. I deserved to celebrate.

I nodded and the man smiled. He reached past me, pressing his body close as he raised his hand, a wad of cash clenched in his fist. He smelled of fresh rain. I resisted the urge to run my hand up the front of his green polo, just to feel the fabric.

He talked of small things, inconsequential stories that left me nodding and laughing when nothing was amusing. The drinks came quickly, pink and sugary and achingly sweet. I dreaded the hangover that would plague me in the morning.

"I'm an artist," I told him, three drinks in, four. "A painter."

Half-off shots. What could I say?

"I go to an alley sometimes." I thought of Graffiti Alley, the paint-covered tunnel only one block over from the "El." I hadn't been able to visit in over two weeks, and my hands felt dry. "There is a purple elephant painted on the wall."

He set his glass down. The brown liquid whirlpooled toward the rim. Was it rum? I couldn't remember. "Sounds dangerous," he said. His voice was like sinking into a freshly made bed.

"No." I shook my head. "No, it's the only place I feel . . . I don't know. Free."

He reached across the table and used his finger to trace shapes on the back of my hand. How soft his skin felt, how warm and new.

"You feel like Monet when he sat in front of those water lilies," he said.

I looked down at the flower inked on the inside of my wrist. *Yes,* I thought. *Yes, that's just how I feel.* The man's eyes bored into my own, and a flush of desire coursed through me. For a moment I worried that I was going to be sick.

He raised his glass of liquor into the air. "To water lilies!"

I lifted my half-empty drink, and the glasses kissed.

I look back down from where I've climbed. The path is a white sheet stained by the irregular beat of my footprints. I take a deep breath. I am alone, I tell myself. And I want to see the Halls. I turn back up the hill and then, up ahead, there is a tree with red berries. The holly tree. I am close.

My lungs are burning by the time I reach the rounded summit and the hill levels off. I am red with exertion, and my breath tastes frosty and metallic. I bend down and place my palms against my knees before looking up at the face of Whitmore Halls. The house is so much larger than it appears from the road: the stone-faced tower rising up from the West Wing where Richard Price first homed patients nearly eighty years prior; the crumbling gables with a dozen blackbirds perched on their frozen peaks; the broken windowpanes missing plates of glass, giving the house a wide-eyed, stricken appearance. Above, protruding from the bow of the home like a wild cowlick, is the widow's walk where Ulma and Eloise stood, pacing back and forth, waiting to see if trouble would come spiraling outward from the pines.

It feels surreal standing in front of the house, like I am suddenly placed in a picture book, staring up at a place that sits somewhere between reality and imagination. *Dad would love this,* I think. The architecture, the history, his history. This was the place where his father was killed, after all.

I walk over to the stairs, four stone steps that lead to what was once a front door. Now there is only a broken screen that hangs limply from rusted hinges. I am surprised that there are no signs hanging on the house, no posts warding off intruders or warning people of danger. Who owns this place now? If it is the city, surely they wouldn't want people coming up here and getting hurt? The whole house looks one gust of wind away from toppling down the hillside.

I step onto the front porch and peer inside. "Hello," I call out softly. When no one answers, I follow my voice into the house.

Inside, everything is trashed. The wallpaper is rippling from the walls, hanging in loose tendrils that bleed faded color. There are shards of broken glass and bits of crumbling drywall on the floor. Crushed beer cans and sandwich wrappers are tossed into corners, and a broken mattress is laid out on the floor of what was once a formal sitting room. I'm not the first person who has come up to this place. People must come up here to party, to tell stories, to see if they can conjure up the ghost of Benjamin Costello.

I want to see this magnificent purple elephant. A chill sweeps through me as I remember how the man at the bar asked me to take him to Graffiti Alley.

I did.

I took him down to the subway, stumbling and incoherent, Chicago swirling around me in odd shapes and colors I couldn't hold. I was on a carousel. I was walking through the city with the ringmaster. How marvelous it was to be alive.

The alley buzzed with sound. A man sat on a milk crate, picking at a guitar. A couple leaned against the stone wall smoking, both with headphones over their ears. A homeless man lay curled under a blanket, the word RAD painted above him and a bottle of half-gone Coca-Cola in his hand.

He took me deeper, the man whose face was just a set of perfectly straight white teeth. There was a dumpster at the far end of the tunnel. It was hard and sharp and cold when he pushed me against the steel.

"I know you want this," he said.

His body was heavy against mine, and the zipper on his jacket raked across my neck. Chicago had cooled, and the cold was biting at my skin, sharp and chilling. Surely I had a coat when I went into Cello's. Where was it now?

My arms wrapped around the man's waist, pulling him closer. His body was so heavy and warm, and my head lolled back against the rim of the dumpster. Wet lips pressed against my neck. Where were we? A painted cow jumped over a half-full moon above me. Yellow five-pointed stars blinked. Teeth bit and licked and tore my skin.

I know you want this.

A rough hand pulled at the strap of my dress and fingers dug into my thigh. Something was wrong. How did I get here? The man grunted, his breathing labored, the fog of his hot breath like smoke. I coughed, and the man pressed harder against me.

"A cow." I looked up at the painted sky. "A cow jumping over the moon." My voice was all wrong.

The man glanced up. The whites of his eyes were streaked with red. He laughed, a hoarse and mocking bark. "Hey, diddle, diddle." His mouth was back on my ear. "The cat and the fiddle."

The cow jumped over the moon.

❀

I swallow the memory of Chicago and the alley and the cow that jumped over the moon as I walk farther into the bowels of Whitmore Halls. This was once the home of Eloise Price, I remind myself. There is nothing to be afraid of.

I'm not brave enough to try the stairs, not sure if I'm more afraid of the house crumbling or of what I will find in the upstairs bedrooms. I decide to find the dining room where Eloise sat Benjamin down to chat.

I pass broken picture frames hanging lopsided on the wall like the eyes of the cockeyed blackbird standing on the porch rail. The walls here have been torched in graffiti, and they are covered in lewd drawings and vulgarity. Nothing like the work inside Graffiti Alley.

On the floor is a long hall runner that stretches from the east to the west. It is faded brown and squishes under my footsteps. It was once red, I guess, sprinkled with white flowers. I will have to ask Eloise. They must have once been cherry blossoms.

I find the dining room easily. The space, like the rest of the house, is a palette of trash and broken glass. There is a china cabinet pushed against the wall—all the drawers are missing—and an old chair with a cracked leg. In the center of the room is the table, the wood scratched and gouged with the same words and drawings that bleed across the walls. The room smells like urine, and I imagine the boys who come in here with their bottles of spray paint and booze, laughing as they urinate on the walls. From the looks of it, it's a popular area. I'm not surprised. Benjamin's body may have been found out in the woods, but this is where he was killed.

I run my finger over the lip of the table and try to imagine what the wood looked like fifty years ago when the house still smelled of cinnamon. If I were to paint this room how it is now, the canvas would be covered in gray.

Next to the dining room is the den with the stone fireplace, the charcoal heart of the home that is no longer beating. On the floor is Ruth's piano. The legs have all been sawed off, and the black and white keys are covered in dust. The left side of the instrument looks burned, as if someone tried to light the old wood on fire but it didn't take.

I kneel and place my hands gently on the keys, my thumb resting gingerly on middle C. When I press down, the piano exhales a hoarse whine.

Hey, diddle, diddle.

There is a sharp sound behind me, the loud creak of the front screen opening, and I gasp. I'm not alone in this house.

I scramble to my feet and stumble over an empty beer can that goes sliding across the wooden floor. When I turn, an old man stands in the doorway of the room.

"You in trouble?" His voice rattles as if it's gone unused for some time.

He is dressed in a heavy wool coat and stocking cap that is pulled low over his head. In the hall's darkness, he looks like a cutout figure of a man, a dark silhouette barring the door.

"Sorry." I find my voice. My body radiates with fear. There is a broken window to the right. I could climb out if I had to. The ground would only be a few feet away. How fast could I run in this snow?

The man grumbles. "Best get out of here," he says. "This place isn't safe." He turns, and I know he expects me to follow. He favors his left leg as he shuffles back toward the front door, a distinct limp in his gait. My eyebrows lift. *No,* I think, *it can't be.*

I follow him out of the house.

Outside, the old man turns, and in the daylight, I notice his face is carved with age spots and deep-set wrinkles. It's the face of a man who has lived a lifetime out in the sun. "You in trouble?" he asks again.

"Charles?" The tremors in my voice dissipate in the wind. "Charles Price?"

He seems startled by the sound of the name, and I know that I'm right. I'm standing at Whitmore Halls with Charles Price. Why didn't Eloise mention that he still lives here?

"My name is Tig," I tell him. "Tig Costello."

Charles's face remains expressionless.

"I'm Benjamin's granddaughter," I try again, searching for a spark of recognition. Surely, he remembers Benjamin. "I've been talking with Eloise up at Dusty Hills. She has been telling me stories about Whitmore Halls."

Charles shifts his feet. "Eloise," he says softly. "She always did have some good stories."

He can't possibly live in this place, I think.

"I was just finishing up in the back," he says. "Going to make a hot toddy if you want one."

Charles doesn't wait for me to respond, just turns and starts walking away from the house, back toward the barn. I quickly follow.

The forest lines all sides of the property, but it is thickest around the back. The rear of Whitmore Halls faces the pond. The water is frozen over and covered with a fine dusting of snow. We walk toward the barn, the only part of the property that looks maintained, and I know instantly that this is where Charles lives. There are three grazing horses out in the pasture, and I remember what Eloise told me about Charles raising Rocky Mountains. *He was always such a beautiful rider.*

"Have you lived here all along?" I pant, struggling to keep up with Charles's quick gait. He may have a limp, but he is well versed in traversing the snow-covered ground.

"All along," he repeats. I'm not certain if he is answering or simply clarifying.

We pass the stone wall that borders the southern end of the pond, and I imagine Eloise sitting on the rocks, swinging her legs back and forth, wrapped in a sticky web of boredom when suddenly a young boy appears from the woods. He is carrying a red apple in his hand.

"Careful of the ice there." Charles points to a frozen puddle near the barn door as he pushes open the iron gate and leads me into the field. The horses raise their heads.

The barn is bright with light and hay, and I revel in the instant warmth, suddenly acutely aware of the way my fingers have long since frozen together. I realize that I left my mittens beside Ruth's piano. How long will it take for the Halls to consume them with dust?

"I didn't realize someone still lived up here," I call out to Charles, who stands in a small kitchen built into the side of the barn. The door is propped open, and I hear the clink of the spoon hitting the side of a glass mug.

When Charles comes back, he hands me a steaming cup of tawny-colored liquid. I can nearly smell the fiery Kentucky bourbon. "Not many people do." He sits on the edge of a hay bale, gesturing for me to do the same. The barn doors are open, and a chestnut-colored horse walks in.

I turn to look over my shoulder. "She's beautiful."

Charles grumbles.

I wrap my gloveless hands around the hot mug. "Eloise has been telling me about this place," I begin. "About Ulma and Ruth and the women who used to come up here."

Charles sets his glass on the floor beside his feet and pulls an army knife and bright-green apple from his coat pocket. The horse comes closer.

He cuts the fruit in half once and then again. "Surprised she's talking to you," he says.

"I'm helping her with something." I don't tell him about the leaves. "I think she's lonely."

Charles hands a slice of apple to the horse standing at his shoulder. "Eloise don't get lonely."

We sit in silence together, and I think about Eloise staring out the window in room 402, sipping tea.

"You look like her," Charles says without looking up.

"Valerie?" I think of the way Eloise touched my face, her warm palm pressed against my cheek. "I've heard."

"Women came up here all the time." Charles takes a bite of the apple, and the horse snorts in displeasure. "Men too. Some angry, some scared. Some leaving things."

"Leaving things? Like gifts?"

He nearly laughs. "If you could call them that." His fingers work the knife around the apple with ease. "Broken dolls left on the doorstep, baby bottles filled with blood, rope tied into a noose hanging from the porch rails. Anything to give us a scare."

My throat burns. "I didn't think people from town gave you much trouble."

"They gave enough, for a while. Old man Costello came up once or twice when I was a boy, and then Benjamin when he was running things. Always told Eloise to leave well enough alone, to stop treating the women." Charles pauses. "The women who came up here didn't talk much."

"There were rumors about the abortions." I think of Stan sitting in Mitt's, spitting out accusations that were dirty with decades-old filth.

"Sure," Charles agrees.

"Were things better after Eloise went to prison?" I ask.

The mare noses Charles's head, and his stocking cap falls to the side. "When Eloise confessed, the people in town left us alone for the most part. Eloise was put behind bars. My mother and I stayed in the house with Ruth. Things were quiet for a while."

Charles looks over at the stalls as if he were trying to remember where he placed something long ago. "But Ruth was lonely here. She missed Eloise. Never did meet a couple more devoted to each other."

Charles sips at the bourbon in his glass and licks his lips. They are raw and chapped from the cold. "Any woman needing help was too afraid to come back up the hill at that time," he says. "So Ruth left. She took a train to Chicago, and she never appeared in Darren County again."

I'm stunned. Ruth went back to Chicago. Did she go to work with Dr. Ross? Did she continue to practice women's medicine? When I ask Charles this, he stands and walks over to the tack bench. There are leads and harnesses hooked over wooden knobs. He pulls what looks to be a horse brush out of a basket. I know nothing about horses, but the teeth of the comb look like they could rip the mats out of an unruly mane.

"Do you know much about red oak trees?" Charles places the brush in my hand. The handle is thick and textured and various shades of brown bark.

"Made that from the root of a red oak." Charles sits back beside me. "Oldest trees in these hills. Some have been here for over five hundred years. Descended from the roots that have grown on these lands long before people settled here. The thing about red oaks is that they have a shallow root system. You can dig only about a foot or two before you can't dig no more. But the roots stretch outward for miles. In fact, some say that the roots that grow in this area are all part of a system that stretches north, up through the Midwest. You may have a tree growing right here in Darren that feeds off the same water that first fed those up in Illinois."

I run the pad of my thumb over the smooth curve of the brush handle and imagine the smooth wood buried underground.

"Just because Ruth left Darren doesn't mean a part of her wasn't still rooted here," Charles says.

I lift my head. "You were still in contact with her?"

Charles rests his hands on his knees. "After Ruth left, the people in town got bored with Whitmore Halls. They figured they had won. Eloise was in jail. Ruth was gone. Mom was sick by that time. Her cough worsened over the winter, and she died that spring. I buried her out by the gardens." He nods toward the eastern side of the house, toward the same plot of land that Joan once rolled in as a small child.

"I didn't have nowhere to go and couldn't imagine leaving this place, so I stayed. Bought another horse, made a small loft in the barn. Lived here ever since." Charles pulls a flask of bourbon out from his breast pocket and uses his teeth to unscrew the cap. "You want a topper?"

I shake my head when he holds the bottle out toward me. "Why don't you stay in the house?"

Charles's face wrinkles. "Too big for one person. Never did like it much anyhow. I've always preferred the barn."

"But people just come in and vandalize it. Doesn't it bother you that the place is trashed?" I want to place a fence around the home, to hire a contractor to stabilize the foundation, to right the widow's walk, to put glass back in the old windowpanes.

"The house is a crumbling mess of stone and plaster." Charles takes a long sip of bourbon straight from the mouth of the bottle, shaking his head as the alcohol goes down his throat. "It wasn't built right. It will fall off this hill one of these days."

"What about Ruth?" I ask again. We have gotten off topic. "What happened to Ruth when she went back to Chicago?"

"Ruth." Charles says her name slowly, and for one fear-filled moment, I think his memory has failed him, that Ruth is only a phantom in his aging mind. Then he cocks his head and his eyes refocus, become alert.

"Well, after a bit of time, women started coming back." Charles smacks his lips like a horse. "It wasn't just women from Darren that came here. It was women from all over the state. Women couldn't find anyone to do the things that Ruth and Eloise did, so when one found out about the house, well, word travels."

Charles takes another sip from the bottle. "Eloise went to prison. Ruth went to Chicago. Ulma was sick with the cough. But the women still came, needing help."

"But no one was here." A sinking feeling settles in my stomach.

Charles looks baffled. "I was here," he states. "I'm still here."

Are you in trouble? Charles had asked when he first saw me standing in Whitmore Halls. He thought I had come up the hill for help.

"You brought the women to Chicago," I slowly realize. "You brought the women to Ruth."

Charles sucks in his left cheek. "More or less," he confirms. "I brought them to the train station, sent them upstate with an address and a few bucks. Rang up Ruth and told her about it. She never once told me not to send them. She must have been terrified each time a woman was sent up to her, but she never once said no."

"She was an abortion doctor up in Illinois." I tap the top of my mug with the palm of my hand.

"She and a few other women were part of a network. Created a facility for women who had been beaten," Charles says. "One of the first in the Midwest. Most of the girls who came around before the '70s came because they were pregnant and didn't want to be. If you've been talking to Eloise, then I'm sure you've heard the stories."

I think of Valerie wiping the blood off a dead girl's body. Knitting needles, garden tools, tumbling down a flight of steps. There was always so much blood.

"No safe way for a woman to get that kind of care," says Charles. "Ruth wanted to change that."

I think of Charles living all these years up here in the hills. I think of the women who must have come up through the woods. How they must have stood on the front porch of the decaying house and thought, *No, this can't be the right place.* Charles would come out then, ask them if they were in trouble, and they would be comforted by his presence.

They would have been told to look for an old man, an old man who would drive them to Morehead, set them up with a train ticket and send them four hundred miles north to meet a woman who would help save their lives. Then I think of the snow-covered road, of the No Trespassing sign hanging on the rusted gates.

"The road is closed," I say, as if he doesn't know. "How did you get the women to the station."

"You think that road is the only way out of this place?" Charles nearly laughs. "Got a truck at the bottom of the hill, right through the trees. The horses help some."

I imagine Charles bringing a woman down the hill, through the woods. How terrifying and beautiful the red oaks must look.

"Called them moonflowers," Charles says. "The women who came up here."

"Moonflowers?"

He nods. "A kind of code word. Something Ruth and Eloise came up with long ago. A woman would come to the house needing help, and I'd send her to the city with a moonflower tucked in her pocket."

I think of the moonflower that fell out of Valerie's diary and how I had picked it up and held the gossamer petals in my palm.

"When the train stopped in Chicago, the woman would go to the address I gave her and show Ruth the moonflower. Ruth would then show her one of her own." Charles looks at me fully, and I feel a certain tenderness toward him, as if I were his granddaughter coming up to the barn to hear a story about a woman he used to know.

"That's how they would find each other," he clarifies. "That's how they would know they were safe."

"Why moonflowers?" I can't help but ask.

"They only bloom at night," Charles says simply.

He rubs a knee with his hand and then stands. "Feeding time."

Charles moves over to the wheelbarrow filled with hay. The horses neigh and stomp and thrash their heads in approval.

I swallow the last burning sip of whiskey and think about all that Charles has told me. The moonflowers. They were Eloise's favorite, she told me that first day when I had gone to Dusty Hills knowing nothing about Benjamin and Eloise and Ulma and Ruth. Now I understood. The women came at night. They were wrapped in shawls and cloaks and had furtive eyes as they spoke in whispers. It was only under the moonlight that they could stand on the steps of Whitmore Halls, fingers shaking as they lifted a hand to rap on the old oak door. These women alive in the darkness, these flowers that only bloomed in the night.

I am halfway down the hill when I see Jason's truck. It's parked in front of the old metal poles I climbed over when I steadied myself on the No Trespassing sign and began my ascent up toward Whitmore Halls and all I would find there.

"Damn it," I curse. I may have found more to the story I was searching for up in the hills, but now, inevitably, Jason's found me.

I practice excuses in my head as if I'm reciting the lines to *Hamlet*, a play Dad and I acted out on the nights when I was young and sleep felt futile. *I just wanted to see the place where my grandfather died,* I rehearse as I slow my descent. *Come on, Jason, you know you would want to see it too.*

The sky is a lazy, tired gray when I reach the bottom of the hill, and the truck door opens. I am just about to call out and tease Jason about the way he's always waiting around for me. *Don't you have better things to do than follow me like a lost Labrador?* And then suddenly I stop because the man who steps out of the truck, arms folded across his chest and eyes twin slits spread across his face, is not Jason at all.

It's Mayor Grant.

Twenty

Mayor Grant drives me back to his office in silence. When he pulls up alongside the curb in front of the courthouse, he turns and rubs his hands over the steering wheel in a way that reminds me of Jason, though the thought gives me no comfort.

"I think it's time you and me have a little chat," the mayor says, and I feel like I am sinking into the mucky waters in the lake just outside Ann Arbor.

We walk through the courthouse and into the back office that I once stood in, asking the mayor for a car to use during my stay in Darren County. It looks just as it did months ago, and when the mayor asks if I would like a glass of water, I stare at the same old baseball and crooked photo of a woman and two boys as I shake my head no. I don't need a glass of water. I need to get the hell out of here.

"So, Ms. Costello." Mayor Grant sits across from me and folds his hands together atop the large wooden desk. "Did you know that trespassing is a state violation? I could put you in the county jail for six months, at least. Fine you a thousand dollars."

I think of Eloise sitting beside her window at Dusty Hills. She would probably get a good laugh about this one. A young woman comes to a small town to talk to the old lady who murdered her grandfather and ends up in jail herself. I cross my legs and wedge a hand under my thigh. I don't know why I am so nervous, but sitting in Mayor Grant's office, I feel Darren closing in on me, as if a hundred people have circled the courthouse, knowing I am inside.

Mayor Grant leans toward me. "What were you doing up there?"

I let the story fall from my lips slowly, like a child admitting she stole her mother's blush just because she wanted to feel what her mother felt when she rubbed the color on her cheeks. "I wanted to see the place where my grandfather died. I thought it would make me feel closer to him."

For an artist to paint a portrait, he must truly understand his subject. This was something Dad once said while studying Picasso's *Portrait of Dora Maar*, Picasso's lover for nearly a decade. The two met one evening in Paris, and Maar was wearing a pair of black satin gloves. As they talked, she placed one gloved hand on the table and held a penknife in the other, digging the pointed tip into the wood between her outspread fingers. She missed several times, and when she did, drops of blood appeared on the black glove. At the end of the night, Picasso asked Maar for the bloodstained article, and he kept it in a glass showcase inside his home. *This is why Maar's fingers are painted bright red in the portrait,* Dad told me. Most would look at her and think her nails are simply stained red, but that's not it at all. They didn't know her like Picasso did. Her hands are covered in spots of blood.

I tell this now to Mayor Grant, and he chuckles in the forced way that tells me he doesn't know why I told him this story. He sits back in his chair, and the air is thick and stale around us. When the sun streams in through the window, dust mites swirl through the air. "I hear you've been to see Eloise Price."

The mayor shoots the words across the room, and they land hard against my stomach. Who told the mayor I had been to Dusty Hills? A sick pull of nausea fills my mouth with saliva. Was it Jason? I wonder. I don't have to wait long for an answer.

"I have to say, I'm quite disappointed, Ms. Costello." Mayor Grant shifts and the chair groans. "When Alice told me that you had been coming around during visiting hours, I could hardly believe it. Now why would Benjamin Costello's granddaughter be talking to the woman who murdered him in cold blood? Is that any way to honor his memory?"

Alice. The nurse who stuck Eloise's veins with the needle that left bruises on her fragile skin.

I stay silent.

"I should have known you were going to be trouble." Mayor Grant rubs the side of his face, and the sunlight reveals the fine line of stubble growing on the soft curve of his jaw. "And don't think you can get away with anything around here, sweetheart. When Alice told me about you going on up to talk to that wicked woman, I started asking around. Sure enough, nearly a dozen others saw you and Jason driving on up that way. Don't know what that boy was thinking."

I take a deep breath. I've gotten Jason into trouble. "It wasn't Jason's fault . . ."

"Damn right about that," the mayor interjects. "Boy's always been a coward. Mae wasn't too pleased, either, when she found out. Yes, I talked to her, too, so you can go right ahead and wipe that tortured look off your face. Mae said she knew nothing about it, but she would be giving you a firm talking-to later."

I cringe. The mayor is right about one thing: Mae is not pleased with me. The sharp teeth of guilt bite against my chest when I imagine how the mayor must have barged into Mae's Soap and Spool Shop, his heavy steps loud and angry as he pushed up against the counter and asked if she knew what I had been doing up at Dusty Hills.

In the hall, a door slams, and the light fixture above my head rattles. Something shakes loose within me. I unstick my hands from underneath my thigh.

"Eloise has been telling me about Benjamin." I am surprised by the dark-purple nuances in my voice. "Seems to me like she knows him a hell of a lot better than you do."

I am pleased by the look of shock that pales the mayor's face, and I wonder where this sudden surge of courage stemmed from. Did Eloise plant it while we hung leaves on the white walls of an old hospital room, or was it buried inside me long ago in another place, another town, and only here, in Darren, Kentucky, had it finally begun to grow?

Mayor Grant's nose twitches. "And what's she been saying? Eloise *Price*."

There is nothing the mayor could give me that would make me tell him all that I had learned from Eloise. Hers is a story that wasn't meant for him. "She says that Benjamin was a corporal in the war. That he was injured and sent back to Darren as a hero. He became mayor and built the first railroad through town." I sound like I am listing a set of tired facts pulled from an eighth-grade textbook.

"Is that so?"

I don't know why the mayor looks surprised; all this could be read in the articles he gave me that first day we stood together in the park.

"You want a story about Eloise Price?" There is a tremor in the mayor's voice, a bitter rise in his cadence. "I have one for you."

The mayor closes the door, shutting us in the office. The buds of courage that had so recently begun to sprout inside me now wilt in the thick humidity of the room as Mayor Grant stands by the window. He stuffs his hands in his pockets and looks through the dirty glass. "I was there the day they brought her into this courthouse," he says. "I was just a boy then, but I remember it like it was just last Sunday."

The mayor's voice pins me to the chair, and I rearrange myself on the sticky plastic.

"The county judge was Jeffrey Perkins back then. Such a small town, most of what he did was settle cases about stolen chickens and car parts. Maybe a case of trespassing every now and again. Something you should know a bit about, Ms. Costello." Mayor Grant talks to the window glass more than me, and I wonder if he would notice if I just stood up and left. *Sorry, I have an appointment to get to. Maybe we can catch up later at Mitt's. Best Reubens in town, I hear.*

"I was about ten years old, sitting in the back of the courthouse with my pop. They brought her in wearing handcuffs. She was dressed in some housedress that probably wasn't even hers. Had a sort of wild look about her. And she just walked right up to that table and sat herself down." The mayor shakes his head at the memory. "The courtroom was dead silent. All I could hear was the fan they had hanging on the ceiling. It kept going around and around, and it was downright freezing in that room."

I imagine Eloise at the prosecution table, sitting much the same way she sat at the desk up at Dusty Hills, her eyes locked on nothing but seeing everything.

"It was over so fast," says Mayor Grant. "Judge read off the charges and asked Eloise her plea. She looked straight at him and said, 'Yep, I killed him.' It was like she was admitting to stealing a candy bar from the station or something. The way she said it. I'll never forget it."

Eloise's voice is everywhere in my head, and I try to imagine the confession sitting on her lips. Had she practiced it? Had she thought about the words she would use when the judge asked her if she killed Benjamin?

Mayor Grant turns from the window, and his shoulders sag. He sits back in his chair heavily. "I think folks expected more to happen that day. Expected Eloise to curse the town or to shout and holler. Expected to see some guilt or even some promise of revenge come out of her. But nope, Eloise Price just looked over at the judge and said, 'Are we done now?' and then she was taken out to the jail."

"Was Ulma there?" The question slips from my lips faster than I can catch it. "Charles?"

"Nope." The mayor shakes his head. "They were hiding out up at that house. Too scared and ashamed after everything Eloise had done."

I think of Ulma sitting alone in the kitchen, holding a hot mug of tea and looking up at the herbs drying on the lines above her. I think of Charles out in the barn, leading a horse into a stall. Both would have been thinking about Eloise, about what was happening inside the courtroom. Whitmore Halls must have trembled.

"Ruth came down, though," Mayor Grant says. "She stood in the back by the door, shaking with fear when Eloise confessed. Ruth was

Abigail Rose-Marie

downright terrified of her. I figure that was the first time she really saw
Eloise for what she was—a murderer. Left town soon after that."

The mayor is quiet as the story settles like dust on the desk between
us. There is a hollowness in my stomach as I think of Ruth standing
there in that courthouse, watching Eloise Price give herself so readily to
cuffs. I am about to ask the mayor if I can leave when he says, "I spoke
to Eloise Price that morning. Before the guards took her away."

I settle back in the seat as Mayor Grant speaks evenly. "The moment
Eloise pled guilty and the verdict was read, the courtroom was busy with
sound. Eloise Price was going to jail. Justice was done in Darren that
morning. That sort of thing. My pop hollered that they should bring
her out back and shoot her, an eye for an eye. She deserved it.

"In all the commotion, it was easy to grab her hand. I was ten years
old, remember. I think I was more surprised than she was, that I had
really reached out to touch her. But I had to know."

My eyebrows bend inward. "Know what?"

"What she did with my mother."

I hold my breath as the mayor tells me about his mother. She lived
in Darren all her life. Worked at the public library on weekday mornings. A quiet woman but had a laugh you could hear from three houses
down the street. She was a natural beauty, one that turned the heads of
men. His father hated that and was quick to set her right when he had
a bad night with the bottle. A mean drunk.

One night, when the mayor was eight years old, he came home after
dark and knew there had been trouble. There was water and blood and
glass on the kitchen floor. His father was gone, which wasn't unusual,
but his mother was also nowhere to be found. He put up posters around
town. Tacked them to trees and telephone poles, but his mother never
came home. There were rumors about what happened to her. No one
believed she was dead. But she was never seen again in Darren, leaving
the eight-year-old boy alone with a father who liked to drink a bit too
much. And when that boy got older and his old man died, the boy

222

went and gave himself a new surname. Began to go by Grant, after his favorite war general. And a bit after that, he became mayor of this town.

Mayor Grant reaches forward to pick up the framed photograph on his desk. The picture is of a woman, older than the one who hangs on the wall. This photo was taken a long time ago. The mayor looks down at the woman who is smiling up at him as if they are sharing a secret through the glass. "I knew Eloise Price had something to do with my mother's disappearance," Mayor Grant continues. "So when I saw her in that courtroom about to be taken away, it was my last chance to know for sure. I grabbed her hand and asked her, 'Where is she?' She looked down at me, and it took her a moment to realize who I was. But when she did, her eyes turned dark as night. I'd never seen anything like it."

Mayor Grant talks more to the woman in the photo than he does to me. "'Where is she?' I asked Eloise again, and then, and I'll never forget it, the way she smiled. This kind of sneer that almost made me stumble over right there in the courtroom. 'You'll never find her,' she said to me. 'You'll never find her.'"

The mayor sets the photograph down on his desk and folds his hands in the same way he did when we first sat down in the office. "And that was when I knew that Eloise Price had the devil inside her. She is a dangerous woman, Ms. Costello. And if I hear that you've been talking to her again, that you've been snooping around in places you have no business being in, I'll have you on the next train back to Ann Arbor."

I am shaken. Not by the mayor's story, or by his threat that now hangs heavy around us inside the office walls, but by the harrowing knowledge that Mayor Grant is not only the mayor of this small town sitting in the Kentucky hills but also Marjorie Thomas's son.

Twenty-One

Costello House is everything that Whitmore Halls is not. After Mayor Grant effectively banned me from seeing Eloise, I decided it was time to see the home my grandparents once lived in when they were not much younger than I am now. They give tours of the property, Jason told me on my first day in Darren, as we drove down the street lined with flags. Now, three days after I spoke with Charles Price while drinking hot toddies on a hay bale, I am more than ready for that tour.

The property surrounding the house is barren, lacking in trees and greenery, but well kept. The home itself is freshly painted, and a set of stairs greets the wood door standing between a pair of bay windows. Above, four perfectly square glass panes stare out toward Darren, their clear eyes peering through the pillars. I'm surprised to see no fence, no signposts, nothing that marks this property as owned.

"Benjamin inherited this home from his father when he came back from the war," the tour guide tells me. She is old, and her white hair is pulled back in a loose bun on top of her head, reminding me of the lunch ladies who serve watery soup and packets of oyster crackers at the elementary schools. When I arrived, she looked up at me and moved her glasses to the top of her head, pressing her hair against her scalp. Her name tag stated ANNA.

"Sergeant Ralph Costello, Benjamin's father, died while he was at war." Anna leads me into the high-ceilinged foyer. I nod as if I'm learning this for the first time. I haven't told Anna who I am, saving that ace of spades in the back pocket of my jeans.

"When Benjamin came back from service, he inherited the house. This was in 1945, when the war ended," she says, making sure there are no holes in my history lesson. "His mother lived here as well, and in 1946, he married Valerie Dunn, the great-great-granddaughter of the founder of Darren."

Anna's speech is well rehearsed, and the lines are delivered with enthusiasm and reverence as I follow her through the wide hallway and into the sitting room. The home is bright and clean, the crown molding scrubbed and freshly painted. Much has been restored to its original condition. The furniture, though many pieces have been replaced, is modeled to look just as it did when Benjamin once lived here.

"Who owns this place now?" I stop in front of a painting hanging in the hall. It's of a man and woman, both staring straight ahead. The man is standing behind the woman, who sits on a formal dining chair, his hand placed firmly on her left shoulder. He wears a military coat with a service medal covering his heart. His shoulders are squared, and his dark irises are locked on the eye of an invisible camera. The woman looks less severe, though her face is lifeless. Her skin is pale, and her hands are wound tightly together atop pressed pleats. They are painted with a dark palette of oils, heavy paints held in an ornate gold frame. Beside the portrait, a metal plaque is screwed into the wall: SERGEANT RALPH COSTELLO AND HIS WIFE. 1934. My great-grandparents, I realize. They look as if they were made of wax.

"After Benjamin died, the county retained ownership of the house," Anna explains. "It was empty for many years. Just the caretaker lived in the room in the back. Then Mayor Grant started his term and decided the space could be used as a museum. Since then, it has been restored to its original condition. Well, the bottom half, that is." She glances at the ceiling. "The upstairs is still a mess."

I think of Whitmore Halls, sitting up in the hills, a refuse for trash and empty beer cans. "Can I see what's up there?" I ask. A large red velvet rope blocks the staircase to the upper floor.

"Visitors aren't allowed in restricted parts of the house." Anna opens a door on the right and leads me into a study where a large desk sits proudly under the window on the far side. "This is where Benjamin wrote all his speeches."

The room smells like lemon furniture polish, and I know the wooden bookshelves lining the walls have been replaced. They would smell earthier if they were the originals. Still, the study is grand and beautiful. The floors are hardwood, and the tiered chandelier spits cylinders of white light onto the ground. It must be crystal, I think. Strange, in a place like Darren, to have this pellet of wealth. There is a fireplace built between two bookcases, a bed of logs displayed in the open mouth like rows of dirty teeth.

"May I?" I ask Anna, gesturing to the desk chair.

Anna hesitates. She has a child's mouth, small and thin, like she is still growing into it. "I really shouldn't . . ."

"I've always loved history," I try, thinking of the way Dad's whole face lifted whenever I showed interest in his studies. When I was young, if I wanted something, I had only to feign interest in a seventeenth-century armoire, crafted by a French artisan in Venice and selling at an antique shop two towns away, and Dad would agree to anything I asked. Look at the intricate carvings along the outer rims. Wouldn't it look gorgeous sitting in the foyer? It was flawless.

"Okay," she relents. "You can sit there for a minute. But be careful. That chair is the original. Made in the eighteenth century, long before Benjamin was even born."

I sit on the smooth oak and run my hands up and down the armrests. It's a sturdy chair, finely made, but nothing like Rita's pieces. Her work is more refined, rich with character. I look at the desk and wonder what's inside the drawers, wonder if somewhere inside is a piece of my history that isn't curated for me by the people of Darren.

A phone rings inside the house, and it's no longer 1945, the shrill tone interrupting the facade.

Anna frowns, looking back over her shoulder. "I should get that," she says. "Do you mind?"

"Not at all," I answer, relieved to be left alone, if only for a couple of minutes. Anna leaves the room, and I look around at the green-and-white-striped walls. A clock chimes, and I am pulled back out into the hall, searching for the sound. Would the clock be one of Rita's? Anna is still on the phone, her voice bouncing off the paneled walls. To my left is the staircase, roped off like the aisles in the old theater Dad used to take me to in the city.

Anna laughs from some room far away.

I step over the red rope and climb the stairs, careful to keep my balance on the narrow staircase that is without a handrail.

Upstairs, all the doors are shut, and the floor is covered in saw-dust. My feet leave white footprints as I walk along the hall, trying knobs that are frustratingly locked. On the walls, old photographs hang in glass frames that are fogged with age. Most are of Benjamin, adorned in medals and shaking hands with men in suitcoats standing in front of the Darren County Courthouse. Sitting beneath a faded red-and-white-checkered quilt is a small table with a glass case on it. Inside is a silver pistol.

At the end of the hall, a single door is left ajar. There is a hammer on the floor and a pile of long screws. The tip of my shoe slides over a sharp nail, and I jump back, imagining the metal stem piercing through the bottom of the sole and up into my skin. I need to be careful, I remind myself.

Inside the room, a large four-poster bed is placed in the center of the space, across from a stained wardrobe and oak vanity. Three small glass bottles sit on the tabletop. At the end of the bed is an old hope chest. Its lid is cracked across the top as if something large was set on it in a rush. A painting of orange lilies hangs over the mirror. The creamy-colored petals bloom on a white backdrop as if they are growing up from a bed of freshly fallen snow. This was my grandmother's room, I realize. She always loved the color orange.

I glance behind me, listening for Anna's voice, or her slow, haphazard footsteps below. Everything is silent. I step into the room.

The radiator shudders on, and a blast of heavy heat puffs from the teeth. I look at myself through the mirror on Valerie's vanity. *You look so much like her,* Eloise said. I pick up an old perfume bottle. It's a dark maroon with the word "Sumatra" written across the center in swirled calligraphy. When I press the round nozzle up to my nose, it smells like rotten flowers, like fruit lying in the bottom of a dumpster.

The vanity has two drawers that open easily and one that sticks, closed with a layer of paint that has hardened over time. It's missing a handle, and I wonder if it was painted over before or after the house was sold.

I glance back over my shoulder before pulling a pocketknife from my bag. I slip the sharp edge of the blade into the crease of the drawer and split the paint. It is like cutting open the crate full of art back in Ann Arbor, my heart beating wildly as I reached in to pull out *The Woman in the Woods.* The paint gives, and I wiggle the tip of the knife back and forth until the drawer unsticks with a soft gasp. I set the knife on the tabletop and use both hands to guide the drawer outward.

"Hello?" I hear Anna call out from below. "Where did you go?"

I pull harder, and the drawer comes free. It leaves a square hole in the vanity, as if a bullet has ruptured the left ventricle of the heart. Paint chips cover my hands as I peer inside the drawer.

It's empty.

"What in God's name are you doing, Ms. Costello?"

I turn quickly, surprised more by the sharp sound of my name than by Anna, who stands in the doorway. Her body is as white and rigid as if she were seeing the ghost of Benjamin Costello himself sitting at his wife's vanity, holding a split-open drawer in his hands.

I am covered in a dusty film of guilt and confusion. "How did you know my name?"

"I've been waiting for you to come visit me." Anna's face loosens, and I am left perplexed. The tension in the air settles at my feet.

"I'm sorry," I stumble. "I don't understand . . ."

Anna steps into the room, and she seems instantly more relaxed, as if this room, Valerie's room, is a place that stirs up good memories. "I have to say, I thought you would have been here ages ago."

My lips part in confusion.

"Costello House would have been the place I first began." Anna ignores my bewilderment. "It is a historical site, after all. And full of your grandparents' things. If you know where to look." Anna nudges my ribs with her elbow, and I lean away from the intimate gesture. If she thinks we are sharing an inside joke, I have been embarrassingly left out.

Anna strokes one of the wooden bedposts. "I've lived in this house since I was fifteen years old. More than fifty years now."

Fifty years?

"But that can't be—"

Anna waves her hand to shush me in the same manner Eloise has become so accustomed to. Thinking of her now spurs a sudden ache in the center of my chest.

"I worked for the Costellos," Anna explains. "For your great-grandparents first, and then after Benjamin and Valerie married, for them as well. Took care of this place after they were all gone."

I think of Valerie's diary. She mentioned a woman named Anna. She brought rumors home with her every day when she went to town. My head is swimming with the past and present, and I hold on to the back of the stool to steady myself.

"I see it now." Anna reaches out as if she is going to touch me but lets her hand drop back to her side. Her fingers are like the bones of a hummingbird, all veins.

"You look like him." Anna's gaze scurries over me. "Same dark eyebrows. He was always so good looking."

It's disarming to hear her say that I look like Benjamin. He still doesn't feel real to me, only like a figure waving from far away.

"The mayor gave me some of Benjamin's things." The dusty shoebox sits beside the bed at Mae's. "Newspaper clippings, a marriage announcement. It wasn't a lot," I admit.

Anna looks excited now. "The mayor doesn't have much," she confesses. "That's why I sent you that diary."

My eyes widen to twin spheres. "It was you."

Anna nods. "Someone had to point you on the right track."

I am dizzy with revelation.

"Come on, now." Anna turns and waves for me to follow. "We have a lot to discuss."

Twenty-Two

Anna tells me to wait in the hall while she pulls down a ladder that leads up into what I assume to be an attic. The ladder is old and filthy, and I cough into my shirtsleeve as Anna's head and torso are swallowed by the attic's open mouth.

"It's right here," she announces. I am surprised when she shimmies back down the ladder carrying a cardboard box.

She motions for me to follow her back into Valerie's bedroom and sets the box on the vanity. "This is full of old documents. Most are from Benjamin's study. Some from here in the bedroom."

Anna hovers over my shoulder as I pull apart the flaps of cardboard. Inside are stacks of papers and files. It will take hours to go through all this. Anna rattles on behind me, talking about the typed pages of Benjamin's speeches. Home deeds, land deeds, all the paperwork pertaining to rail sales. Ralph Costello was a businessman and meticulous when keeping records. I think of Richard Price writing notes in the upper wing of the manor, charting patient moods and activities.

There is a large manila envelope near the bottom of the box. It's the same kind that was sent to me with Valerie's diary buried inside. When I pull it out from under the pile of business transactions and receipts, I see the edges are brittle with age. The seal is broken, but the flimsy metal clasp is held tight.

"Birth certificates, titles and deeds, all in those folders." Anna gestures to the envelope in my hand while sifting through the box.

I open the winged clasp and pull out a stack of papers. They aren't titles and deeds, like Anna said, but instead are a stack of missing person flyers, each one printed with a sketch of a woman's face. MISSING is written across the top in bold, capitalized ink. Dana Fields. Joyce Hammond. Gertrude Rey. Marjorie Thomas.

"Valerie kept those," Anna says, glancing over. "Poor souls. Not one of them was ever found."

The women staring back at me from the flyers are both young and old, beautiful and lifeless. I don't recognize the names of most, and only Marjorie and Joyce are from Darren County, but I can guess what happened to them. They went to Whitmore Halls, battered and bruised and desperate to escape. They met the women who lived up in the hills and cried with relief when Eloise told them that they were going to be okay. They climbed into the back of Charles's old Chevy Coupe pickup, and Eloise drove them to the train station, where they got on a train that took them to a city so much larger than the one deep in the valley of the Appalachians.

"Valerie was deeply bothered by the disappearances," Anna says reverently. "Especially when another woman from Darren went missing. Mae's aunt, in fact. Joyce was her name."

I quickly look up. "You know Mae?"

"Of course I do. Her sister is married to my cousin. They moved out of here about two years back. Henry was sick of the mines, and they went west. Haven't heard from them since." Anna plays with the gold ring on her finger, swirls it around her knuckle. "Everyone is connected to someone around here. By blood or marriage. It's all the same now."

"When did her aunt disappear?" I brush my finger over the face of a woman I have never met.

Anna knots her fist under her chin. "Shortly after the war, thereabouts." She riffles through another stack of papers.

I think of my first evening in Darren, sitting with Mae as she made soap. That was the night she first told me about one of the women who went missing, the night before I first met Eloise Price. I think about how the words slipped from Mae's mouth involuntarily, how the admission made her push back from the table and stand abruptly.

Anna sits on the corner of Valerie's bed, and her hand strokes the quilt beside her. "Do you know why I stay here, Tig?"

It's a relief to hear Anna use my first name, and I find myself comfortable being with her here in my grandmother's old bedroom, a place that feels oddly familiar.

When I tell Anna no, that I don't know why she has stayed here in this house for all these years, she looks sad for a moment. "Most people think it is because of Benjamin. Out of loyalty. Out of wanting to preserve the home and his memory."

I press my hip against the edge of the vanity.

"But it was never about Benjamin." The quilt is covered in stitched birds, and Anna traces a threaded wing. I think of how Valerie once sat on a bedspread in Whitmore Halls, her fingers smoothing the petals of a moonflower as Ulma made Rita a cup of tea.

"I never cared for Benjamin." Anna closes her eyes for a beat. "But I was dedicated to Valerie."

Anna tells me that she worked for the Costello family for twenty-five years. Her mother, Nettie, had been the Costello housekeeper when they lived in Texas. Anna was five years old when she and her mother moved to Darren County. By the time Anna was ten, she was cooking and cleaning right alongside her mother, and when Benjamin and Valerie married, Anna was sent to live with them.

"I still remember the day we all moved in here," Anna says. "Valerie was so happy. A house to make into a home. She was already talking about all the pies she would bake in the kitchen, all the flowers she would put in vases on the windowsills. They went on their honeymoon, somewhere in the west, I don't remember now, and while they were gone, I spent every day scrubbing this house. I wanted it to be beautiful when they came back. Not for him, but for her."

"Why?" I ask.

Anna thinks for a moment. "Valerie was special. Fragile. She felt things more than other people."

I think of Valerie holding the body of the dead fox cub in her arms, tears streaming down her round cheeks.

"There was a certain warmth about her that made you want to make her happy, to make sure that when she looked at you, she smiled. Benjamin and Valerie were the same in that way. When one of them was in a room, you wanted to be the person standing next to them."

"I feel closer to her now," I realize aloud, "closer than I ever felt to her while she was alive." I think of Valerie laughing in the river, her dress bunched up in her hands. She always loved being near water. I came here for Benjamin, in the hopes that his story would reveal more about my own and my father's. But standing in my grandmother's old bedroom, I feel that it is Valerie who is trying to tell me something, who is standing somewhere near but just out of reach.

"She's dead now, is she?" Anna sucks in a breath.

"Yes," I tell her. "Pneumonia."

Anna closes her eyes, and the room swells with emotion.

"I didn't want to come here," I confess. "The letter was sent to my father, and he asked me to go. He said he couldn't do it himself."

Anna hums and nods like she understands.

"It was a photograph of Valerie that made me get on the train," I say. "She was standing in a river, laughing. All around her were trees, and I wanted to see them. I wanted to see the place she had been when she was a young girl. After you sent me that diary, I read through it a dozen times. There was so much about her I didn't know. I had no idea about the baby."

Anna smiles sadly. "Valerie couldn't wait to be a mother. She knew she was pregnant about two months before the wedding. A real scandal. The day she told Benjamin about the baby was the first time he hit her."

Benjamin's bronze hand turns to a fist in my mind.

"You see, Benjamin was in love with Ruth. I suspect you may already know something about that." Anna doesn't pause when I nod. "He was engaged to Valerie when he went off to the war. Wrote her letters, sent her pieces of tarp to make into dresses. But then he got wounded and ended up at Dusty Hills. That's where everything changed."

"He met Ruth." I tell this to Anna as if she doesn't already know.

"He came back to Darren County, and things were expected of him. Barely given any time at all to work through what he had seen overseas before he was thrown up in the mayor's seat, looking over a town that was stricken by death." The energy has slowly seeped out of Anna's pores.

"He wasn't the only one changed by the war." Her shoulders sag. "They were just boys when they left, and when they came back, well, some days they were not much more than ghosts. Many took to the bottle. Benjamin too. It was hard to blame them. But Benjamin had more riding on his shoulders. People were looking to him to fix things, to make right what the war had taken. And then Ruth showed up."

I scratch the inside of my palm as I think of Ruth, of my fingers resting on the same piano keys she had once played inside Whitmore Halls.

Anna continues. "Benjamin was still engaged to Valerie, of course. The wedding was being planned, but then he saw that Ruth had moved to town. Well, everyone could see what that boy was thinking. And that was about when Valerie got pregnant. There was just no getting out of it then. So they got married, moved to this house, the baby came, and then . . ."

"The baby died," I finish. This is a story I've heard before.

"Yes," Anna confirms. "The baby died, and most days it felt like Valerie went right along with him. See, nothing was going right for Benjamin around that time. Those tracks he worked so hard to build kept getting washed out by the river, and the people around here were getting restless. Everyone was worried about money and food and jobs, and it felt like life was flourishing everywhere but in Darren County. Benjamin was in a bad place. And he took it all out on Valerie."

"He blamed her for the baby's death," I say quietly, remembering the words I read in the leather-bound journal.

Anna nods in confirmation. "He used to lock her up in the nursery. Say she was forgetting about what she did to the baby. He cut the electricity to the room so she had to sit in darkness. He liked to put her in there when I was gone for a couple days visiting my mama. She lived up in Lexington back then, and I would come home and find Valerie shut up in the baby's room. No sign of Benjamin. I never knew how long he kept her in there, but I had a good feeling he shoved her in that room right when I left, and then he took off to Morehead." Anna cringes from the memory.

"I found her once, lying in the baby crib. When I looked down at her, I thought she was dead. Her eyes were just staring up at the ceiling, her face was ghostly white, and she had dried blood on her mouth and her hair. She smelled like urine and bile, of things you can't scrub out no matter how hard you try."

I close my eyes and turn my head away from Anna's story. I think of the suitcase Dad keeps under his bed. It is small and brown and full of Valerie's things. I found it when I was young, and when I opened the case, it was filled with a menagerie of strange curiosities: a half-used tube of lipstick, a mold of teeth painted lime green, a Zippo lighter with a wolf howling at a full moon printed on the side. There was a drawing of a horse scratched on a napkin, an unlabeled cassette tape that was wrapped with masking tape, and a palm-size rock painted with red roses and twisting vines. Throwaways, Dad would say, yet he kept them all in a child's suitcase shoved under his bed.

"Why are you telling me all this?" I ask weakly.

Anna comes close to me, taking my hand in hers. "Because you should know, Tig." Her eyes bore into mine. "You should know that Benjamin may have survived the war, but he isn't the only survivor who lived in this town."

Back at the shop, Mae hands me a rag and says we need to talk. "Wipe down that table over there." She points to the large circular table in the middle of the room. It is Sunday and the shop is closed. The best day for cleaning up the place, Mae once told me.

"The mayor came around, looking for you." She is wiping down the cash register, and the room smells like lemon and bleach.

I scrub at a piece of dried soap that is stuck to the tabletop. "He found me. I was up at Whitmore Halls." There is no point in lying to Mae. "He told me he doesn't want me talking to Eloise Price anymore."

Mae snorts, and I think of what Anna told me while we looked through papers and deeds inside my grandmother's bedroom. Mae's aunt was one of those girls who went missing.

"Not surprised he doesn't want you talking to her." Mae opens the cash register, and the sound makes Cougar jump from the bench he's napping on and scowl. "The mayor's never quite gotten over what happened to his mama all those years ago."

Mae knows about Marjorie Thomas.

"He's afraid of her. Eloise Price," Mae claims. "Afraid of what went on up there in the hills. Why people went to see her."

There's a liquid quality to Mae's voice, and she speaks in that languid way people do when they have something they want to talk about but just aren't sure how to slip into it. It's the syrupy stream of Mae's words that makes me stand straight and ask, "People like your aunt?"

The silence feels sticky between us as Mae grabs the spray bottle full of cleaning solution. "She was in a bad place," she says.

I scrub at the gummy film of melted soap that is pasted onto the tabletop as Mae tells me about how Joyce was married to a man who was no good. It was Mae's mama who told Joyce she had to get out of Darren if she wanted a chance at any sort of life. She needed to go talk to Eloise Price. After Marjorie Thomas went missing, there were rumors about Eloise, about how she could make women disappear. So Joyce left one night, walked up the hill, and knocked on the door of Whitmore

Halls. Her sister stood at the bottom of the hill, hidden in the shadows of the trees, but Joyce never came back down.

I reach into my bag and pull out the missing women posters that I found in the old cardboard box at Costello House. When I asked Anna if I could take them, she simply nodded and said, "Take whatever it is you need." I find the poster of Joyce Hammond and show it to Mae.

"My mama had this printed," Mae says softly, holding on to the edge of the paper in the same way Dad holds photographs. "Just to prove that someone out there was looking for her. Someone cared that she had disappeared."

I think of Eloise driving Joyce to the train station. *There's a woman in Chicago who can help you,* Eloise would have said, handing Joyce an address, an envelope with fifty dollars inside, and a white moonflower.

"It was best that way." Mae walks back around the counter and hands me the spray bottle. "No one wanted to be associated with Eloise. It was dangerous to talk about her. Turns out, it still is."

The corners of my mouth pull up in a tight smile, and I think of all the afternoons I have spent with Eloise, listening to her voice, hanging red oak leaves on her walls. After all these weeks, Eloise still hasn't told me about the night Benjamin died. I feel us creeping up to it, sneaking up on March 27 in the timeline, but it seems inconsequential somehow, like Eloise's story was never really about that night at all.

"Benjamin was horrible to Valerie," I tell Mae. I push the image of my grandmother lying in the crib from my mind. "Was that why Eloise killed him?"

On my way back from Costello House, I stopped to see the statue. I hadn't been to the monument since my first day in Darren, and Benjamin looked smaller now. It had snowed the night before, and his bronze cap had a palmful of white flakes sitting on the flat lip. The sun left a shadow along the left side of his face, hollowing out his cheek and leaving him with a playful grin. I hated him in that moment.

I used the underside of my glove to brush the snow off the words carved into the stone base. "Courage, Bravery, Honor." It seemed like a cruel joke. The sun peered out from behind a cloud, and the bronze overcoat reflected beads of light, the snow making everything brighter. A gust of wind swept in from the hills, and the flags lining the street shook.

"Seems like there is only one person who knows why Benjamin died that night," Mae says. It takes me a minute to realize she is talking about Eloise.

"It doesn't matter now, anyway." I spray a shower of bleach on the table. "The mayor won't let me go back to Dusty Hills. I doubt I'll see Eloise again."

I am surprised when Mae starts chuckling. "You're going to let old Mayor Grant scare you?" When I tell Mae that he threatened to send me back home, she simply shakes her head. "Why are you here, Tig?" she asks.

Before I can respond, she takes a step closer to me and looks me in the eye. "Is it really to paint a picture?"

It sounds like an accusation, and I gulp. I'm suddenly unsure myself of why I am standing here in this room with Mae in Darren. "That's why I came," I say numbly.

"But why are you *here*?" Mae asks in a way that tells me I'm not here to paint a portrait, that maybe I was never here to paint at all.

I set the spray bottle on the table and let my gaze settle on the grandfather clock in the corner of the shop. Its thick pendulum sways back and forth, as lazy as a heartbeat. I think of Rita sitting inside the barn, the smell of sawdust everywhere. I think of the photograph of Valerie standing in the river. "I'm here to learn more about my family," I say slowly. The words don't taste quite right on my tongue.

"I came here searching for something. Searching for something for Dad, for Valerie, for all the parts of me that still feel unknown. My world had been so small," I conclude. I think of all the quiet holidays, the empty bleachers, the barren branches of my genealogy tree. "And I wanted Darren to make it bigger somehow."

Mae pulls out the chair across from me and sits down. "I've spent my whole life trying to be small," she says, "to make the world a little more manageable, to stay out of trouble. Trouble finds you anyway."

Mae is quiet for a moment. "Go on back to Dusty Hills," she instructs, surprising me. "Let Eloise finish her story. Seems to me that there still might be something left for you to find here in this town."

"But I thought you said—"

I don't get to finish before Mae holds out her hand to stop my words. "When I knew you had gone up to see Eloise, I felt a terrible trembling in my chest. Like I had helped put something big into motion, something that this place wasn't quite ready for yet.

"I was afraid," Mae admits. "I was afraid of old ghosts." She holds the poster of Joyce Hammond in her hands, and I see the raw emotion stretched across her face. "But then I thought of Joyce. Of her strength and her courage all those years ago, and I thought to myself that this place's history, this town's story, is so much more than that bronze statue. And it's about time for that story to be told."

Something inside me ignites at Mae's words. "What about Mayor Grant?" I ask.

Mae simply shrugs. "Next week is the memorial retreat up in Morehead. He'll be gone for a few days. Too busy to be bothered by much of anything else."

I consider all that Anna has told me and all the things that are starting to come together, that I am starting to understand, and my body feels heavy with memories that belong to someone else. And then I think of all that remains unknown, and the backs of my knees begin to itch because I know what I need to do. A slow grin spreads across my face, and I settle into the warm knowledge that soon I will be back at Dusty Hills and that, if I am sure of nothing else, I am certain of two things: I need to hear more of Eloise's story, and Mae is full of surprises.

MISSING

MRS. JOYCE HAMMOND. MISSING SINCE JUNE 22, 1947. DAUGHTER OF LESTER WILLIAMS. Last seen on the corner of Marshall and Baker Avenue in Darren County, Kentucky.

MR. WILLIAMS IS OFFERING A $150 REWARD FOR ANY PERTINENT INFORMATION ON THE WHEREABOUTS OF HIS DAUGHTER.

DESCRIPTION OF JOYCE HAMMOND FOLLOWS:

Age: 31 (thirty-one) years. Brown eyes. Black hair. Wearing yellow dress. Brown shoes. May be carrying a large canvas bag.

Twenty-Three

Dusty Hills is chilled. It's been nearly a week since I was last up to the facility, and in that time, the building has fossilized. Long icicles clutch the eaves and hang over the front entrance like sharpened teeth. Even the stone facade is coated in a thin sheet of ice, and I recall what Eloise once told me about the bad ventilation. I shiver at the thought.

Jason drops me off at the front door. I found him earlier in the day, shoveling snow in front of the courthouse. When I told him that I needed a ride, he simply looked at me for a moment and then let his head fall in a way that told me he already knew.

"Be careful, Tig," Jason says as I step out of the truck. I glance back at him and know that he isn't talking about the icy walkway leading up to the front door. I nod.

Inside, I wipe my feet on the mat and pull off my hat, shaking away the snow. I can see my breath in the air. When I go to sign in, I still. Alice is sitting behind the counter.

Her top lip pulls upward when she sees me, and I think of the Doberman that liked to chase me down the street when I went running back in Ann Arbor, teeth bared and a line of saliva foaming at its gumline. *He's harmless!* the owner would always call out. The dog seemed as harmless as the sea twenty minutes before a tsunami crept to shore.

"You're not supposed to be here, Ms. Costello," Alice says. Her voice is a deep ebony stirred too long with the tip of a paintbrush. It smears all across the room.

I gather my courage and remind myself not to be afraid of Alice or the mayor or the people in Darren who watch me through shuttered windows. They have all heard by now. I am the girl who talks to Eloise Price.

I take off my mittens. "I see you got put on desk duty."

Alice's jaw shifts to the right, and I know I've hit a nerve. I bite back my smile.

"Wait until the mayor hears about this," she mumbles just loud enough for me to hear.

I raise my eyebrows. "Thanks for telling him, by the way. He has been so supportive." I sign my name across the top of the sign-in sheet. There is only one other name written above mine, and I realize how quiet Dusty Hills must be in the winter. Not many people are willing to drive up this way. How lonely it must become for the people trapped inside.

"Stanley was right about you," Alice says then. "He always could spot the rotten ones."

Alice must notice the confusion etched on my face because she smiles unkindly. "Said he met you over at Mitt's a couple months back."

Of course Alice knows Stan. I can see it now, the two of them sitting at the bar, drinking lukewarm beer and trading nasty stories about the girl who goes to talk with Eloise Price.

"Said you're no better than those women up in the hills." Alice spits. "Maybe we should lock you up here as well." She laughs, a low growl of a sound that makes me reel.

I set down the pen and take a step backward. I am chilled by Alice, by the bitter malice in her threats. I turn to go, eager to put some distance between myself and the front desk, even though I know it is fruitless. Inside Dusty Hills, Alice is everywhere. I think of the No Trespassing sign hung limply on the gate leading up to Whitmore Halls. How quickly I disregarded it. Would I do the same if it were hung outside the door of Dusty Hills?

"Three days, Ms. Costello," Alice calls after me as I trek quickly down the hall. My shoes leave sticky wet prints on the floor. "Three days, and the mayor will be back. Don't you think he won't find out about this. Then you'll be gone! You'll be run out of this town, you'll see!"

Alice's voice chases me to the staircase. *Three days,* I repeat. Three days to gather the rest of this story, to find the truth that I have been searching for. Things must move quickly now. This story must soon come to an end.

❀

Eloise is not pleased.

"You didn't come see me last week," she says coldly when she notices me standing at the entrance to room 402. "Have you forgotten our deal, Ms. Costello?"

Of course I haven't forgotten. She tells me a story. I help her hang leaves.

I tell Eloise that the mayor found out about my visits to Dusty Hills, that he threatened to send me back to Ann Arbor for good if I came back here.

Eloise purses her lips, and I can almost hear the word "coward" slide across the floor and stop at my feet.

The room is now nearly covered in color, though many of the leaves have fallen in my absence. I imagine Eloise in bed, looking up at the canopy of red and orange above her, watching as a dried leaf unsticks from the paint and flutters down to lie on her chest.

I tell Eloise that I went to Whitmore Halls, that I met Charles, and that we sat together in the barn. I don't tell her about my conversation with the mayor, about how I learned that he is Marjorie Thomas's son. When I thought about it, kneeling by the open bedroom window in the upstairs apartment above the Soap and Spool Shop, I felt a peculiar pity for the mayor, for the boy who came home to find his mother had disappeared. Did Eloise know then that Marjorie had a child? Did she know that by driving Marjorie to the train station, she was taking her away from not only a cruel man but also a small boy?

"Charles," Eloise says softly. "How is he?"

I tell her Charles is doing well.

Eloise looks as if she wants to say more, but she simply shakes her head, and I wonder if she feels the same urgency that I do. "Well, let's get on with it then," she says. "We have already wasted too much time."

★

Benjamin watched Ruth.

Ruth, unlike the Price women, enjoyed going into town. She made easy small talk with the women in the market and was always quick to compliment a new haircut, a freshly painted front door, a polished shoe. The people of Darren didn't know what to make of this soft-eyed woman from the city who now lived up in the hills. If it weren't for her choice to reside in Whitmore Halls, Ruth would have assimilated right into the heart of Darren County.

People liked Ruth. They didn't bristle at her sudden appearance in shops or whisper as she walked down the street. They bought her cups of coffee and helped her with her coat as she rose to leave, watching through perplexed eyes as she walked back up the hill, the tail of her red coat trailing behind her. Why was she living up there with crazy Eloise and Ulma Price? Ruth was such a kind and tenderhearted girl. She really belonged in the town. No one to keep an eye on her up in those woods.

Benjamin never quite gave up on getting Ruth to move into Darren. "Come on down out of those hills," he said. "Live with the better half."

He accompanied Ruth to the market while she perused the crates of red tomatoes and fuzzy peaches brought in on big trucks from the city. He tossed apples into the air and caught them in his mouth, a trick that made Ruth laugh. He bought her coffee at the diner and told her about his plans for the town that would one day be a railway hub even larger than Morehead. And when she was ready to leave, he walked with her along Mud River until she came to the base of the hill. "Are you sure you don't want to stay down here?" he asked. "Dana Fields's house is empty now. You could move in by morning. I'm sure of it."

Ruth simply smiled and shook her head, patting Benjamin on the shoulder before she climbed back up toward the Halls.

Eloise didn't go to Benjamin's wedding, but Ruth did. Ruth had been back in Darren County only two months by then, and she sat in the back of St. Mary's, the only church in town, which meant that everyone was either Catholic or damned. It was a grand affair. The church was covered in white ribbons and bouquets of roses. Candles lined the windowsill, and the old crucifix of Jesus, warped and in need of a good scrub, was draped with a curtain of lace hanging around his neck like one of Isadora Duncan's scarves.

"She looked terrified," Ruth told Eloise that night. "Valerie's blue eyes were positively wild with fear."

"Why'd you go then?" Eloise couldn't understand Ruth's tenderness toward Benjamin. Why would she want to spend a perfectly good summer afternoon sitting in some stuffy church watching Benjamin Costello get married? "He and Valerie will get married, live in that square house close enough for him to be town mayor, but far enough away that he doesn't have to smell the stench from Mud River." Eloise snorted. "He should spend more money cleaning out that water instead of putting more oil and waste into it."

Ruth thought for a moment. "He's a good man, Eloise," she said. "A good man who's had a hard life."

"Sure." Eloise shrugged, dumping out her half-full cup of tea that had gone cold. "It must have been just terrible having a four-course meal every night and a nanny making your bed and cleaning your filth."

"Be careful, Eloise Price," Ruth warned. "The house in the field is no larger than the one in the hills."

Eloise dropped the glass in the sink with a loud crash, whipping around to look Ruth in the eye. "I'm nothing like Benjamin Costello," she shouted as she stormed out of the room.

Ruth sighed. "You know what I mean."

But Eloise didn't know what she meant at all. The way she saw it, Benjamin was the epitome of privilege, and she didn't give one hoot or holler about the boy's black eyes or the way his father squeezed his shoulder tightly as he led him to the station to enlist in war. Benjamin was mayor now, and all Eloise cared about was keeping him far from Whitmore Halls and even farther from Ruth.

"He gave me the strangest smile," Ruth had told Eloise as she hung up her coat after the wedding. "During the ceremony. It was as if he were trying to tell me something he couldn't say aloud." She shook her head, musing over the puzzle Benjamin had set before her.

Eloise had stilled, knowing then that while Benjamin had been repeating his vows to Valerie Dunn, he had been looking at Ruth.

The woods were wild the year after Benjamin became town mayor. It had rained for weeks on end, and the river was high, pouring muddy water over the fresh rails and flooding the valleys. Tobacco crops were lost, and money was tight for most of the people in Darren County. The rails were finished and there wasn't much work. The men were forced to either travel upstate for jobs or to stay home and wait out the flooding. Neither option was any good.

After the rains relented, it took another week for the river to retreat, leaving trash and diapers hanging from the low branches of the trees that had been submerged in water. The hills were green and fragrant, moss and brush growing lush from all the rainwater. Eloise stood on the widow's walk one morning and frowned. The paths through the woods were much too overgrown. She would never be able to see if anyone was coming up, not with all the branches and leaves obstructing her view.

She grabbed the hedge clippers from the shed and made her way into the woods, chopping down branches and trimming bushes, clearing the deer paths that wove through the forest. *If it were only the deer using these tracks, I wouldn't have to bother,* she thought.

"Have Charles do it," Ulma had said when she saw Eloise hefting on the old flannel coat, but Eloise had bristled. Charles was no good at keeping the paths clear. He missed low-hanging branches, those that were perfect for men to stand behind, just out of sight. No, it was better to do it herself. Eloise didn't mind being in the woods. She felt they were hers, after all.

"I know what you do up here, Eloise Price."

Eloise whipped around, the metal shears clutched tightly in hand. She relaxed when she saw Benjamin leaning casually against a tall oak, a bottle of Kentucky whiskey held in one hand. He looked tired, his eyes red and face long, but she could still see the boy he had been, meeting her in the forest, holding an old garbage can lid. *We can use this for the steering wheel and get the hell out of here.*

Eloise bent down and chopped a limb off an overgrown bush. A fistful of red berries fell to the ground.

"You're going straight to hell, you know that?" Benjamin took a swig of whiskey. He was a careless drinker, sloppy and loose. "Up in these woods, mixing teas and plants that are probably nasty with disease. I won't even say the worst of it."

Eloise nearly rolled her eyes. People had been talking more about what went on inside Whitmore Halls. Whispering speculation and making preposterous accusations. *They cut babies straight out of a mother's stomach. Bury butchered infants in the fresh-turned soil.* It was enough to make Eloise's own stomach churn.

"I'd kill my wife if I ever heard of her coming up here." Benjamin shook his head at the thought. It was strange to hear Benjamin use the word "wife." He had favored Valerie as a young boy, but Eloise saw the way Benjamin looked at Ruth now, the way his eyes followed the curve of her palm as she lifted a hand to brush dark hair away from her face.

"Heard the ceremony went well." Eloise picked a berry from the bush and rolled it between two fingers. *No,* she thought. *Too easy.*

Benjamin staggered forward before leaning against another tree. The sapling fought against his weight. "Things will be different around here now," he said. "Those rails are going to bring in all kinds of money. Just have to wait until the water goes back down."

"I was talking about your wedding," Eloise quipped. She had no interest in Benjamin's business endeavors. *Let the river boil up and flood this town,* she thought.

"The railroads," Benjamin slurred. "That's where the money is. Soon, people aren't going to be running out of food. I'm sick of seeing the kids around here picking through garbage bins and fighting off dogs for a piece of bologna. Things are going to change."

Eloise snapped upright. "What do you know about it? You and your big dreams. This place is a piece of shit."

Eloise waited for Benjamin to strike back, to spit out some half-witted retort that she could smear back in his face. Instead, he nearly bent over laughing, his lean body convulsing. For a moment, Eloise was sure he was about to be sick.

"You're right, Eloise Price!" He laughed. A dot of saliva glistened on the corner of his mouth. "This place is shit. And I'm running it, goddamn it."

Eloise normally would have been quick to agree but was so struck by the absurdity of the moment, of Benjamin Costello laughing hysterically in the woods, that she felt a pang of sympathy for the boy she once knew. Benjamin was always going to be town mayor, to inherit this town from his father's violent hands. Maybe Ruth was right about him. Maybe life for Benjamin Costello hadn't always been grand.

"She's pregnant," Benjamin said, the muscles in his face loosening. "Valerie."

Eloise nearly laughed. "Good thing you married her then."

Something shifted in Benjamin's demeanor, and he took a step closer to Eloise. "What happened to Gertrude Rey, Eloise?"

Eloise stilled. Gertrude Rey was a middle-aged woman who'd come up to Whitmore Halls one night about a month ago. She was from Bluestone, a town five miles south of Morehead, and had heard about the women who lived on the hill from a friend of a friend. Someone's aunt or cousin, Eloise didn't know which. Gertrude stood on the steps with a broken cheekbone, a black eye, and three fresh cigarette burns tattooed on her stomach. When she lifted her dress, a whole constellation appeared on her back.

"I can't go back to that house." Gertrude pleaded with Eloise to help her. She lived with her husband and father-in-law. It was hard to say who had treated her worse.

After Marjorie, Eloise and Ruth had been careful. People in Darren were already suspicious, and Christopher Thomas was fuming that his wife had yet to be found, though most assumed she had drowned in the river by that time. But Gertrude Rey wasn't from Darren. It would be so easy to make her disappear. No one in Darren County would bat an eye.

"What are you going on about, Benjamin?" Eloise laughed, reaching up to chop a low-hanging branch from the red oak tree.

"Ah now, Ellie," Benjamin taunted. His voice was as sweet as the rotting peaches they'd picked from Morrison's orchard as children. "Don't play with me. I've seen the posters hung up all over Morehead Station. I know you've done something with the girl."

Benjamin talked to Eloise like a child, and it made her want to take the clippers and snap at his hand like a rabid dog starved in the woods. "You spending a lot of time up in Morehead now? I hear you've been seen over at Cheryl's Place more than once." Eloise nearly purred when Benjamin's lips thinned. *See?* Eloise wanted to say. *It's not just me they're talking about.*

"I could put you in prison," Benjamin said smugly. "You and Ulma. I haven't forgotten what I saw that day when I brought Margaret Owens up to the house."

What Benjamin saw that day was nothing more than bottles of herbs and lotions made from oils and crushed powders that Ruth had long ago thrown out. Nothing like the equipment they had in the house now, the forceps and the speculums and the cervical dilators and the syringes and the curettes. Eloise didn't want to think about what would happen if Benjamin came into the house now and saw these things. The look that would cover his face as he whispered, *What have you done, Eloise Price? What have you done?*

"And Ruth," Eloise fumed. "You gonna send Ruth to prison too?"

A cockeyed smile bent Benjamin's mouth, and he lifted the bottle to his lips before placing a palm on the nearest tree and looking up into her womb of branches. "You remember the Oak Rocket?"

"'Course I do," Eloise answered.

"Would have made a fine spaceship." Benjamin looked sad then, the evening sun darkening the lines on his face. He would look just like his father in a couple of years.

"Never would have gotten off the ground." Eloise began chopping limbs off the nearest bush. The branches were tough and covered in thorns. Devil's snare.

"The wooden wonder," Benjamin said reverently. "Called them the mosquitos. Fastest aircraft in the world and made almost entirely out of wood."

Benjamin never talked of the war. Not like the other men who spent long afternoons mulling over what they had seen, trying to make sense of it all. Benjamin never showed interest. It was like he had no recollection of the fields, the dust, the bombed buildings, and the burn of ash stamped inside his lungs. Eloise wondered if he had been in the war at all or simply hid in a ditch, playing solitaire over and over again, until he was shot in the abdomen and sent back to the Kentucky hills.

"You fly in one?" Eloise asked nonchalantly. She didn't care one way or another what happened to Benjamin overseas.

Benjamin's face contorted, lips pressed together and eyes squinting in pain. Eloise wondered if she had accidentally clipped him with the cutting shears.

"I'm going to build my kid one of those ships." Benjamin's face relaxed. "Made of pure red oak. It will fly right out of these goddamn trees and up into the clouds. He won't ever have to be stuck here on the ground."

Benjamin took a long drink from the bottle and coughed. The harsh sound rattled the leaves. When he looked back at Eloise, his face was stained with tears. *A sorry drunk,* Ulma would call him. *A wounded soldier,* Ruth would say. They were everywhere these days, crawling into the bar. Mitt's business was booming.

Eloise set the trimming shears on the path. Benjamin was harmless. He could never prove she knew anything about Gertrude Rey or what happened to Marjorie Thomas all those months ago when Eloise had driven her to Morehead and watched her board a train that would take her far away from the hills. Eloise and Ruth had been careful. There was nothing to worry about.

"Come on," Eloise said. "I think it's time you got back home." She looped Benjamin's lifeless arm over her shoulders and started to lead him back down the hill, back toward his river-ravished town.

Twenty-Four

"Six months after the wedding, Valerie gave birth to a baby boy," Eloise says. "His name was David."

A sadness pulsates within my abdomen when I think of that baby. He lived only three months. Anna told me this up at Costello House as I held the boy's death certificate. It was strange seeing his name, the same as my father's, written on the piece of paper. I thought of what Dad would say, if he saw his name marked as deceased.

Eloise continues. "Benjamin said the baby was premature, though everyone knew this was a lie. The whole town whispered about when the baby was conceived. It was Ruth who delivered the infant, when it came."

I imagine the town's surprise. "I can't believe Benjamin allowed that."

Eloise raises her eyebrows, and her mouth twists. "Any excuse to be near her, we used to joke at the Halls. Though it was never very funny."

Eloise reminds me that Ruth was a medical practitioner who had performed hundreds of deliveries. And though not many people trusted Eloise or Ulma, sometimes Ruth would be called to do a home birth when the drive to Morehead was just too far.

I think of how many people in Darren County don't have transportation.

"The baby came fast," she says. "And when people asked Benjamin why he chose Ruth to deliver the infant, he was quick to answer, 'Ruth took care of me up at Dusty Hills. She will take good care of my boy.'"

❀

David was a sickly-looking child. There was a yellowish hue to his skin, and when he cried, the sound was hardly louder than a whisper, though that didn't stop him from wailing. His little gray face turned red with anger.

"It's like he was screaming for days inside the womb," Ruth told Eloise. "By the time he came out, his voice was all used up."

Valerie didn't leave Costello House after David was born, and people started to wonder about the child. They had been so excited when Valerie announced she was pregnant, even more so when Benjamin said the baby was about to arrive. But in the weeks since his birth, Valerie and David had yet to be seen. And this started all kinds of rumors.

"Now, Ruth, you've seen the child. Tell me the truth, what's wrong with the little bugger?" the waitress at the Morning Diner asked as she poured Ruth another cup of coffee. Ruth often stopped at the restaurant when she was running errands in town. *Best coffee in all the Midwest,* she liked to say.

"Leslie, it's not uncommon for new parents to want to keep their child indoors in the winter." Ruth took a sip from her mug. "We've just had about a foot of snow."

"Come off it, Ruth." Leslie set the coffeepot on the burner. "We all know something's wrong with that baby. I reckon it's deformed, and old Benjamin don't want no one looking at it."

Ruth simply waved a hand in front of her face and set the empty cup back on the tabletop, shrugging on her coat and waving to Leslie as she left the diner and started her walk back up the hill. Ruth didn't have time for town gossip, though she did wonder about the Costello boy. A week after he was born, she'd seen Benjamin standing by the edge of the river. The snow had melted, and the icy water was dangerously close to the newly built rails.

"How's that baby of yours doing?" she asked, coming up to stand beside him.

Benjamin startled when he saw her and looked dazed, as if he had never met her before. There was a wide swatch of dried mud streaked across the bottom half of his jeans, and his hair was in need of a good washing. Ruth smelled alcohol on his breath.

"You're out early this morning," she said.

A sly smile of embarrassment crept across his face.

"Baby must be keeping you up. You look like you need a good night's sleep," Ruth teased, though Benjamin tensed at her words.

When she'd told Eloise about this later, Eloise frowned. She was never as sure as Ruth about what was happening at the Costello residence. Ruth was certain the baby was only fussy, crying and hungry and mad at the world for being born in Darren County. But Eloise knew that something had been uprooted, and when Benjamin showed up at Whitmore Halls three months after David was born, carrying a half-empty bottle of rum and stumbling through the front door, she knew that something was about to shift.

"I'll get Benjamin fixed up in the kitchen," Eloise said, eyeing Ruth. *Clean up the back room. I'll keep him away.* There had been a termination that morning. A young girl who had come from three towns over. Her uncle came into her room at night. She didn't even know what was happening until she felt the pain. No one believed her. Her uncle was a math teacher and such a kind man.

Eloise sat Benjamin down in the same chair Valerie once sat in when she brought Rita up to see Ulma. He looked large sitting there, head bent and body curving in on itself. The bottle of amber liquor hung loosely from his fingers, Old Rip Van Winkle swaying back and forth over the floorboards.

"Baby's dead," Benjamin said to the bottle. Rip Van Winkle's white beard hung to the left, and his magician's cap nearly slid off his head. Benjamin took a drink.

Eloise placed a hand on her stomach as if she could feel the baby's dead body settling inside her like a rotted peach pit that she'd forgotten she swallowed. She pulled a bottle of whiskey from the top shelf and set a pair of shot glasses on the table. Old Rip Van Winkle wouldn't last another hour.

"What happened?" Eloise flipped a chair around and straddled the back half, her arms hanging over the chairback. She filled the glasses to the brim. Benjamin glanced at the alcohol before bringing the cup to his lips and finishing it off in a single gulp. Even dead fish are thirsty for water.

"Valerie was rocking him to sleep. He was always crying, and then he wasn't anymore. He just stopped crying." The hollows of Benjamin's cheeks were nearly purple in the dimming kitchen light.

The baby was dead. It happened sometimes. Babies are sleeping and then they're not. "There was nothing you could have done," Eloise told Benjamin. "It's just the way of nature."

"She was rocking him to sleep," he repeated. "And she . . ."

Eloise thought of the snowballs Benjamin used to make in the forest in wintertime. He always packed the snow so tight, crunching the balls between his hands and then hurling them at the trees. The snow splattered against the trunks.

Eloise poured another shot of whiskey into Benjamin's glass and glanced out into the hall to look for Ruth. Did she get everything put away? Was Ulma still outdoors?

"I was going to finish the plans for the rocket with David. When he got a bit older." Benjamin's voice slid down an octave. "It would have been a fine ship."

A sharp kick of pity struck Eloise in the center of her stomach. The Oak Rocket. *The rocket will save us,* Benjamin had once claimed. *We can blast into the sky and never have to come back to this place again!*

Darren County would never be prosperous. It was barely holding its head above water. Benjamin would be a fool to not realize that the railroad tracks set beside the canal would never work. The river had already sunk them twice in the last three months. Soon the rails would be rusted, impassable.

And now Benjamin's baby was dead. And the Oak Rocket was abandoned somewhere in the woods, buried under two feet of snow.

Eloise poured herself another round.

"She was rocking the baby," Benjamin repeated, his own shoulders rolling back and forth. "She just fell asleep."

Valerie.

"Then the baby fell asleep?" The pads of Eloise's fingers felt cold.

"He was so light when I picked him up. I barely felt him in my arms at all." Old Rip Van Winkle was empty now, and Benjamin's face soured. He set the glass down hard on the table. "I came into the room, and they were both asleep in the rocking chair. David was cradled against Valerie's chest. I couldn't see his face. It was turned toward her. His whole body was pressed against her, and she was just sleeping."

Eloise heard Ruth's footsteps somewhere down the hall and then the sharp snap of a door shutting. Everything was hidden. They were safe.

"She woke up when I took the baby. His skin was blue. Goddamn blue." Benjamin shook his head. "I didn't think that could happen to a baby."

"Benjamin." Eloise swallowed. "Where is Valerie?" She thought of Rita's small hand pressing against her sister's shoulder that day when they came up the hill. *It's okay*, Rita had whispered. *It will be okay.*

There was no white left in Benjamin's red eyes when he looked up. "Who the fuck cares?"

He shoved back his chair and stood, swaying on weak knees. He stumbled to the kitchen sink, gripped the metal basin, and leaned far forward until his forehead pressed against the windowpane. His red eyes locked on some invisible speck hanging in the sky. It was as if he were looking for something. It was as if he were searching the black sky for the bright streak of fiery gold, the hot sparks of the Oak Rocket blasting off into the night.

✦

"I left Benjamin at Whitmore Halls and went down the hill to find Valerie." Eloise tells me this part of the story sitting down. She toys with the same orange leaf she was holding when she began, twirling the stem between her fingers.

"After all these years, I'm not sure why. I certainly never cared much for the girl. But there was something that seemed to tether us together." Eloise pauses, reflective. "I felt protective of her in some way. Even then. Even on the night when the baby died."

"I don't think my dad knows he had a sibling." It's curious they named Dad after the baby who died.

Loss and grief make people do things they wouldn't normally do, Tig, Dad told me on the car ride back from Maine when I asked him why he wanted to stop at White Castle to pick up a dozen mini hamburgers. Dad never ate fast food, and he hated chains. My grandmother's ashes sat heavy on my lap. I couldn't stand the thought of putting them on the floor.

We used to get White Castle burgers every Thursday night in Chicago, Dad said. *There was a place right down the street from our apartment, and after eight o'clock, they were always half off.* It was hard to imagine Dad eating a greasy White Castle hamburger, but on the car ride home, I watched him swallow nearly a half dozen. The following week, in a graduate drawing course, I was asked to draw a picture of grief, and I sketched Dad, sitting in the front seat of a 1987 Honda Accord on Interstate 90, his face and hands covered with hamburger grease.

"I found Valerie by the river," Eloise says. "She was cradling something in her arms. Just like she once held that dead baby fox. At first, I worried it was the baby. But it was only an armful of brush. She was going to make a fire and needed to collect kindling. Grief is an odd bear, Ms. Costello."

I nod. The car smelled like hamburger grease for days.

Eloise tells me that she didn't mention the baby when she saw Valerie. Instead, she just walked along the river, helping her collect branches and twigs to bring back to the house in the field.

"There were a hundred things I could have said to her that night," Eloise says. "But none of them would have made any difference. The baby was dead and she was alive, and Benjamin was up at Whitmore Halls letting Old Rip Van Winkle take the sting out of his grief.

"Valerie didn't pay me much mind, just nodded when I told her I would help carry the wood back to the house. Make sure she got home okay. Mostly I wanted to make sure she didn't get too close to the river. The water looks awfully inviting when you're looking at it through grief-stricken eyes."

Valerie moved to Maine because she loved the sound of the ocean. *It drowns everything out,* she told me when I was small and the world was only made with different shades of blue. *The water makes everything else hush.* She loved to tease me, splashing a handful of water at my feet, smiling when I shrieked.

"Autumn has always been my favorite time of year." Eloise draws me back from the ocean. She is looking up at the ceiling, nearly all covered with red oak leaves. I stand on a chair in the far corner under the last white halo of paint. It's disorienting to look at the leaves pasted above me, and I sway lightly.

"I shouldn't have left Whitmore Halls that night." For the first time, Eloise's voice is heavy with regret. The leaf I'm holding slips from my fingers and floats to the ground.

❀

When Eloise came back to the house, Benjamin was gone. The halls were eerily quiet, like they had been left to rot for the past decade.

Charles was out in the barn. Eloise had seen his shadow pushing a wheelbarrow toward the trough and heard the high-pitched whinnies of the Rockies as they trotted after him toward the stables.

Eloise stepped into the kitchen. The room was a mess. The chair she had left Benjamin sitting on was lying on the ground, turned on its side as if he had stood abruptly when someone came into the room. There was glass on the floor, and the empty Rip Van Winkle bottle had rolled under the table. Had Benjamin thrown his cup against the hardwood to watch it shatter?

The window above the sink was fogged, and the space felt smaller than it was, as if Eloise were standing in the room not as a twenty-five-year-old woman, but as a child scanning the cupboards for an afternoon snack. A rug was pushed up against the wall, its green-and-blue weave gathered like a closed fan. There was a cast-iron skillet on the floor. It looked odd sitting there, so far from the stove.

Eloise found Ruth and Ulma in the back room. Ulma was making the bed, pulling a clean sheet tight over the corner of the mattress. Ruth was sterilizing the medical instruments, wiping the cold metal with a cloth soaked in rubbing alcohol. Both were silent.

"Where's Benjamin?" Eloise asked. Every nerve inside her body was rubbed raw, and she felt as she had the night she brought Marjorie Thomas to the train station in Morehead and the two had sat in the hard pews for over three hours, waiting for the rails to quiver.

Ruth wouldn't look at Eloise, but Eloise saw the angry red bruise darkening along Ruth's neck. When Ruth set the scalpel back on the silver tray, a set of five purple bruises circled her wrist as if someone had forcefully grabbed her arm and didn't let go.

"Ruth . . . ," Eloise breathed, but Ruth turned away.

Ruth told Eloise that she had work to do. Three girls were coming up tomorrow morning. They were in a bit of trouble. Everything needed to be sterilized and set out to dry. Ruth grabbed the tray of tools and walked out of the room. The buttonholes on her dress were inside out.

Eloise looked at Ulma through the same eyes she'd worn when Ulma first came to Whitmore Halls and Eloise had hid under beds and behind curtains as she watched this strange woman walk into her home and make it bright. *Fix this,* she pleaded. *Fix this.* But Ulma only shook her head, her eyes heavy with the weight of the last ten years.

I'm not good with the hard stuff, Benjamin had said on the day he came to the river to say goodbye before going to war. *I don't like the feel of it in my body.*

Benjamin Costello. The dead baby. The bottle of Rip Van Winkle lying on its side under the kitchen table. The buttons on Ruth's dress.

Eloise stormed up to the widow's walk, climbing onto the balcony and glaring out into the woods. Benjamin was out there, hiding in the trees. She was sure of it. And she would wait, she decided. She would wait for Benjamin Costello to come stumbling out through the trees.

✦

"Benjamin raped Ruth."

The canopy of leaves trembles, and I bend down to grip the back of the chair. I'm not prepared for this disclosure, and I carefully step down from the seat. My hands are shaking.

"She never spoke about it," Eloise says. "I asked her, once or twice. She got this look on her face that was so . . ." Eloise searches for the right word. "Haunted. It was the same look my mother wore when she walked to the pond the night the moonflowers bloomed."

Hey, diddle, diddle.

I'm going to be sick.

"Ruth wasn't the first woman to walk through Whitmore Halls looking that way. I saw it all the time back then. I see it still." Eloise tilts her head, studying me.

She knows, I think. *She knows that I brought the man into the alley.*

Eloise relents, her eyes shifting to the quilt of leaves above. "Ruth was never quite the same after that. Yet, she kept up her practice; the work was more important than ever to her. Women needed her. This was worth the risk."

There was glass shattered on the sidewalk in the alley. A blue bottle some kid threw out a car window. Cerulean, aqua, indigo, teal, cyan, periwinkle. So much color bleeding into the gutters.

"Are you all right, Ms. Costello?" Eloise asks. "Am I upsetting you?"

I shake my head as I grip the notebook in my hands. "No," I whisper. Something inside me pulls tight, and I think of Dad's face when he saw me that first evening when I came back to Ann Arbor. *I can't go back to that place,* I said. *I can't go back.*

"Should I go on?" Eloise asks.

I tell her yes. I'm fine.

Eloise continues. "Ruth quit going to town, stopped caring what people thought of her. She spent a great deal of time up on the widow's walk. Ruth felt truly unsafe, and nothing I did was going to change that."

Eloise cocks her head to the side as if waiting to hear the final chords of a song that started long ago. "She stopped playing the piano," she says. "After a while, Charles just shut the lid."

I think of Ruth's piano, still up at Whitmore Halls, broken and covered in dust.

"For the first time since Joan roamed the rooms of Whitmore Halls, the house once again had a ghost," Eloise states. "And eight weeks after Benjamin Costello came up the hill, cradling a bottle of Old Rip Van Winkle in his arms, Ruth came down the stairs and said she was pregnant."

Twenty-Five

The light pierces through the windshield in bright, hot slashes. Ten minutes have passed since I stumbled out the doors of Dusty Hills, my hands gripping my knees as I gulped icy cups of air so cold they burned the back of my tongue. I felt numb as I climbed into Jason's truck, as if I had spent the afternoon sitting outside without a coat or gloves in the bitterest part of a Northern Michigan winter.

"Tough session?" Jason asks.

I tell him to just drive.

My stomach feels painfully full, distended with Eloise's words. Ruth was raped. I hear Eloise say it over and over in my mind. It is no wonder that she killed Benjamin. Benjamin raped Ruth. The boy who wanted to build his son a spaceship made of oak, a rocket that would blast into the air and fly them far from the hills, was a rapist. And here I was, his granddaughter, brought to this town to memorialize him in paint.

"Pull the car over," I tell Jason.

"What?"

"Pull the car over now!" My hand is already releasing the clutch, and the door spreads open as the truck rolls to a stop alongside the road.

"Tig!" Jason yells as I stumble out. "What the hell?"

I stagger into a field of dead cornstalks. Rows and rows of brown sticks bent and trampled on the ground. There is a wooden fence post shooting up from the snow-crusted earth, and I grip its square head. My stomach clenches and I heave.

"Jesus," Jason swears. When I stand, he is beside me, handing me a worn handkerchief printed with red and white stripes.

I cough into the fabric.

I think of Benjamin catching apples in his mouth to make a girl laugh. It was a good trick, one that made my grandmother giggle. This is what I would have told my sixth-grade class as I was presenting my family tree. He was going to make a spaceship for his son so he could fly to the moon. The Oak Rocket.

Eloise is wrong, I think. *She is wrong. She is wrong.* I say the words over and over again in my mind. But then I think of my grandmother. Of Valerie locked in the dark nursery, of her ice-blue eyes looking up at the white ceiling as she lay curled up in the crib. I think of Dad, of the tortured way Valerie looked at him as he turned into a man.

I don't think my father was a very good man, Dad said to me in the car as we drove around Donovan's Funeral Home.

Dad knew about Benjamin. Dad knew what I would find here in Darren. And still he asked me to go. A fresh wave of nausea crests inside me. The snow on the ground is blinding.

"Hey, diddle, diddle."

I whip up at the sound, horrified when I realize the words are seeping from my own mouth. I plug my ears.

The cow jumps over the moon. It was a full moon. Wasn't it supposed to be a half-moon? The blue paint was chipping, and the smell of rotten banana peels and urine and half-off drugstore cologne was everywhere.

"Tig!" Jason grabs my shoulders, squeezing too tight. I wrestle away, catching myself before I stumble to the ground. Jason stares at me incredulously, his eyes as large as two sweet gum seeds, but he doesn't try to touch me again. His face is wrecked with confusion. *The girl from the city has gone mad,* he must be thinking. How terribly cliché.

"I . . ." The rich mountain air is too pure, too raw, and my teeth pulse from the sweetness of it.

"I shouldn't have come here," I realize aloud. I'm not ready for this. I'm not ready to hear this story set so close to my own. Dad was right. There are some things about a person's history that must be told to them through a funnel. I want to hold out my palm, to stop the flow with the underside of my outspread hand.

"It's okay, Tig," Jason soothes, though he keeps his distance.

"It's not okay!" My eyes focus, and I see the world as if I have only recently emerged into it. The dust-colored hills, the naked branches of the trees shaking under the white snow. They can't weather the weight of it. Thousands of oaks fall every year. Somewhere deep in the woods, a gunshot rings out.

"None of this is okay!" I cry. "Benjamin wasn't a hero! He wasn't even a good man. Thank God Eloise killed him." The words fall like grenades into the barren field.

Jason looks insulted. "What the hell are you talking about?"

"He raped a woman." My chest heaves. "He abused my grandmother, and he raped Ruth." Now that I've said it aloud, I know it's true. My grandfather raped a woman, and Eloise killed him. It was justice.

Another gunshot goes off, and geese fly overhead. "It's hunting season," Jason says. "Let's get out of here."

But I'm not finished with this field yet.

"This place is shit!" My arms spread wide, as if I mean to gather the hills and the trees and the field of dead stalks all in my embrace. "Eloise is right." My voice drops in defeat. "Benjamin couldn't save this town. He isn't some hero who came back from the war and built a railroad that made this town rich. He gutted this place, used up any money and cheap labor he could find and built rails that the river washed out in one bad rainstorm." I reach down and pull a piece of dried feed corn from a stalk, throwing the rotted ear across the field. It feels good, to break off the dead seed and fling it across the barren plot of land, like throwing a snowball against the bark of a tree.

"Now I know why Valerie left this place." A corn husk hurls through the air. "There's nothing here but predators and rapists. And men"—I launch another corn missile at the sun—"who build statues of other men who attack women." I'm panting now, my arm sore from the overextension. "And do you know what the worst part is?"

Jason looks at me as if I were Lilly throwing a tantrum in the middle aisle of the supermarket, all tight-jawed and raised eyebrows. It makes me want to hurl a piece of corn at his chest.

"Mayor Grant was right about one thing." I huff. "This town belongs to Benjamin." I repeat the mayor's words from when we stood together looking up at the statue. "Benjamin is Darren. Benjamin belonged here. He belonged here, but I don't." I say this with a finality that makes me stumble, like I've shot a bullet into the air and the kickback has taken me by surprise.

"Damn it, Tig!" Jason snaps, and I see orange flecks of anger blur the whites of his eyes. "Not all men are murderers and rapists and wife beaters!"

Jason shifts his feet, and I think he, too, is about to reach down and grab an ear of corn, see how far he can throw it across the field.

"Christ." Jason looks at me as if I've hurt him somehow. "You know, maybe Benjamin Costello wasn't such a stand-up guy. Maybe there shouldn't be a statue of him in the middle of the park. And maybe Eloise Price did all of us a favor the day she killed him. But Jesus, Tig, Eloise Price ain't no saint."

Jason has no idea.

"You know that Marjorie Thomas had a kid?" he says.

What does Jason know about Marjorie Thomas?

Jason tells me the same story that the mayor told me in his office only days ago. Something tightens inside me as he speaks, and I know before Jason can tell me that Jason does not just work for the mayor, but that he is Mayor Grant's son.

"Marjorie left my pop when he was just a kid, but everyone knew that Eloise Price had something to do with it. So don't go putting her on a pedestal," Jason says angrily. "She took my pop's ma from him, and that's a missing piece that he's still trying to fill."

I could tell him, I think. Tell him about the night when Marjorie came up to Whitmore Halls. She was pregnant. She was terrified. She was burned. Eloise must have known she had another child in Darren. Did she ask Marjorie about him when she took her to Chicago? Did Marjorie cry and say she wanted to go back for her boy, or did she simply place a hand on her stomach and watch the lines of the road become small?

"All I'm saying is that not all of us are bad." Jason kicks a corncob with the tip of his shoe.

"You don't know what it's like, Jason." I am calmer now, but the anger still burns the back of my neck. "You don't know what it's like to walk down the street always glancing over your shoulder, to hold a bottle of pepper spray in your hand on the subway just in case someone tries to grab your ass while you're waiting for the next stop. And you don't know what it's like to go to a bar and to wonder if the man sitting across from you plans to take you into the back alley, to hold his hand around your throat while he unbuckles his belt."

I'm suddenly exhausted.

"I do." I choke out the same mixture of a laugh and a cry that has plagued me for weeks. "I took the man back there, to the one place where I felt most alive, and he . . . he . . ." I'm crying now, wet tears that taste bitter with salt. I can't say what he did to me. I can't say it, but Jason understands just the same.

"Shit, Tig," he says softly. "Shit."

And I was lucky, I want to say. I was lucky.

★

Mae makes me a glass of sweet tea.

When Jason dropped me off at the Soap and Spool Shop, Mae took one look at my ashen face and told me to go on upstairs as she swung the sign on the door from Open to Closed.

She stands in the kitchen now, in the worn place where the tile fades from yellow to brown. It's odd to see her there, dumping a great heap of sugar into the cup of tea, until I remember that I am the stranger here. I am the one who doesn't belong.

I sit on the green-and-pink-striped couch and stare at the wall, feeling both numb and unnerved at the same time. It felt different this time, telling Jason about what happened to me in Chicago. When I told Dad, there hadn't been space for my anger, the car barely able to hold the two of us and the weight of my words. But today, with Jason, the field had been large enough to absorb my emotions, and it had been a relief to yell, to hurl the words across the crops like dead corncobs.

"Never can have too much sugar." Mae hands me the cool glass and sits down beside me. The green and pink stripes pull taut under her weight.

The tea is devastatingly sweet, and I devour it.

I set the glass on the end table and tell Mae everything. I tell her how Eloise and Ruth and Ulma had to stand on the widow's walk to keep watch for the men. I tell her about Marjorie, how Eloise brought her to the train station and sent her to Chicago where she would be safe. I tell her about Ruth, how she loved Christmas lights and played the piano every evening after dinner. I tell her about Charles and his wooden horses, about the Rocky Mountains he still has up in the hills. I tell her about Benjamin, how he could catch apples in his mouth and of how he dreamed of building a rocket ship that could fly him away from this place. And I tell her about the night the baby died, the night he stumbled into Whitmore Halls and attacked Ruth.

I tell her all these things, and it's still not enough, so I tell Mae about the painting of *The Woman in the Woods*, how I took a key and shredded her body. I tell her about Dad and how his face looked as he stared out the window at a thousand strands of light, about Valerie's diary that is lying on the nightstand in the other room, and about Valerie locked in the nursery, her blue eyes staring up at nothing at all. And then I tell her about the night in Graffiti Alley, how I met a man at the bar and let him buy me too many drinks. The man took me into the tunnel. There was a purple elephant painted on the wall and a cow jumping over a moon.

I tell Mae all these things, and when I'm done, when the words have finally stopped flowing from my mouth, I feel vacant somehow, like there is still so much of me left to be filled.

Mae listens to all this in silence, and then, after the burn in my chest has begun to release, she tells me about a woman who once came to stay in the same apartment we are in now. "This was about twenty years ago," Mae says, "and I had just started renting this room. She only came for two days. I can't even remember how she found out about me."

Mae's eyes search the space as if the woman is here with us now, just over in the kitchen pouring herself a glass of tea. "She was older than me by a few years but had a youthful face, and when she spoke, you listened. She was dressed all wrong. Not all that different from you when you first came around."

Mae and I share a smile.

"She worked in some corporate office somewhere. Made a lot of money, had a family. Two daughters, I think she said."

"Why did she come to Darren?" I wonder.

Mae looks at the MISSING posters spread out like a deck of cards on the coffee table. I had set them out the night before, had spoken their names aloud, just to fill the space. Marjorie Thomas. Joyce Hammond. Gertrude Rey. Dana Fields.

"She came to see Eloise Price," Mae reveals.

I am surprised, and my cheeks flush as I realize that I'm not the first person to come a long way to talk with Eloise.

"Eloise was still in the prison then, but this woman had traveled over eight hundred miles to visit with her. To thank her."

Mae lets the words settle. "She told me that she had gone up to Whitmore Halls when she was much younger. She had lived over in Reynolds, that's over five hours from here, but she had heard that there was a woman who lived in the hills and could help those who were in trouble. So she hitchhiked the three hundred miles across the state."

I stare at the half-finished portrait of Benjamin as Mae speaks. The woman came to Darren to tell Eloise that she saved her life all those years ago. That she was able to stand in the same apartment where I now sat because of the night when Eloise took her to the train station and sent her to a woman in Chicago. When I ask Mae what the woman's name is, Mae simply smiles and nods down at the MISSING posters fanned out on the table.

"Her name was Dana Fields."

I brush my finger over the face of Dana Fields printed on the yellowing paper. She looked so young, the lines of her profile harsh and deliberate. I want to ask Mae if she looked this angular when she came to Darren or if time had softened her. When I glance up, I see the eyes of the half-finished portrait of Benjamin Costello watching me.

"I won't finish the painting," I tell Mae. "I can't."

There is no definition to Benjamin's face, no contours, no refined lines and angles to his incomplete frame. He will stay that way, dazed and unfocused, until I throw the canvas into the dumpster and it's brought to the Darren County landfill, where it will be buried.

"I came here and completely failed." The realization slides into the hollow places inside me, and I wrap my face in my hands. I am consumed by exhaustion.

"Tig." Mae places a hand on my shoulder. "You were brought here to contribute to the memorial. To help create a monument that reflects who Darren County is. To tell people that those who live in this town are brave, courageous, and honorable."

I lift my head. "I just can't do it. I don't believe Benjamin is any of those things. I'm ashamed to call him my grandfather." My voice raises an octave, and I feel as if I'm on the verge of losing any resolve that still clings to my skin.

"You're not hearing me, Tig." Mae tries again. "I didn't say anything about Benjamin."

I stare at Mae with a face that I'm certain is a washed-out palette of color, but Mae is no longer looking at me. Her gaze is locked firmly on the faces of the women printed on the posters. I glance down at the papers and then up at the half-finished portrait of Benjamin, watching me from across the room. *What are you going to do, Tig?* I hear him ask from across the room, but it's not Benjamin's voice at all. The words pierce through me and above me and all around me, and it's not the voice of my grandfather, but the voice of Marjorie Thomas standing in the living room of Whitmore Halls asking for help, and the voice of Dana Fields telling a man in a pickup truck to take her to Darren County, where she will walk to the old house up on the hill. I hear Gertrude Rey trembling with gratitude as Eloise helped her board a train with a moonflower tucked in her pocket, and I hear Joyce Hammond whispering to her sister, the same words Rita once told Valerie right before she drank a cup of tea.

What are you going to do, Tig?

I hear Ulma laughing out in the garden and Charles asking a young woman if she is in trouble. And I hear Eloise. Eloise whispering the names of plants inside an old apothecary shop. Eloise walking up the front stairs of Dusty Hills, arms full of medical herbs, meeting a nurse from Chicago for the first time. I hear Eloise and Ruth laughing together under the red oaks, and later, sitting side by side on a piano bench inside a house that overlooks a small town in Kentucky. I hear all these things as Darren County sighs and expands and, when I look back at Mae, I smile because I now know exactly what I am going to do.

★

I go to the General to buy flour. I haven't been to the store since the day I arrived in Darren County and Jason stopped to pick up a few things for his wife. There had been men standing outside, and I remember the way my hands trembled when one looked at me and smiled.

Inside, the store smells like tobacco and something that I can't quite place but feels familiar, and I know that when I smell the earthy scent again, away from the hills, I will think of Darren County. The store is larger than it looks from the outside, and I wander through shelves that hold half-off bath towels and plastic soap dispensers. To the left is a display of toy cars and five-dollar kites and stuffed animals that look out at me with glass eyes. They make me think of Valerie lying in a baby crib, and I have to turn away.

The dry goods are toward the back, and I find the flour easily. *Two bags ought to do it,* I think. A fine dusting of powder covers the paper, and when I set them down on the counter to pay, my hands are chalked with white.

"Just this?" the woman behind the register asks. She is young, about my age, and has her thick hair tied back in a braid.

I am about to tell her yes, when I notice the jars of candy lined up along the wall. Bubble Gum Cigars. Candy Buttons. Chocolate Coins. Cinnamon Bears. "I'll take a bag of Cherry Sours as well," I tell her. They had always been Dad's favorite. And Valerie's. On our trips to Maine, Valerie would take Dad and me to the candy store near the bay, where the walls were covered in plastic dispensers. As a child, I liked to take my time filling a bag with an assortment of sugar while my grandmother and Dad went straight to the Cherry Sours, teasing each other about how they should try something new. I wonder now if Valerie's affinity for the sweet began right here, inside the General, when she was just a girl looking up at the rows of candy and already tasting the tang on her lips.

"You're the one who came for the memorial," the woman behind the counter says, and I know she has just recognized me.

"That's right," I admit reluctantly. So few have been happy by my presence lately. I set a five-dollar bill beside the flour. I am eager to leave.

The woman glances quickly around the store and then back at me. "You've been talking to Eloise Price?"

Her voice lowers as she says this, and I pause. I know she is nervous. I open my mouth to reply, but before I can say anything, the woman interrupts me.

"My grandmother grew up here," she says. "She knew Eloise a long time ago, and—"

"Janey." A man comes up behind the counter. "Having any trouble?" The man is about Dad's age, and he wears a red apron tied around his waist.

The woman shakes her head, and I know our conversation is done. She hands me the bag filled with flour and Cherry Sours and smiles tightly at me as I turn to go. Her grandmother knew Eloise, I think. Was she one of the women who went up the hill so many years ago? I want to ask her to tell me more, to tell me about this woman who knew Eloise Price and who, perhaps, also knew my own grandmother, but I know this is a story that is meant for someone else. My time in Darren is nearly over.

I open the General's screen door and bump into someone standing on the other side.

"Hey, now! Watch where you're going there, honey."

"Oh, I'm sorry . . ." I start to apologize when I realize that the two men from my first day in Darren have returned. And they are not alone. Sitting on the old wooden bench beside them is Stan. A cold fist of January air lodges in my throat, and I swallow. A chill runs through me.

"Well, Tig Costello, I didn't think I'd be seeing you again." Stan sneers as I try to forget the sound of my name on his lips. Seeing him outside of the bar feels wrong somehow, like seeing Dad at a hot dog–eating contest at a county fair.

Stan licks the front of his teeth. "I thought you'd be long gone by now. Mayor will make sure of it when he gets back."

"Maybe she's just sticking around for a little farewell present." The man leaning against the building winks. "Come on around to my place, and we'll send you off real nice."

The men laugh. I wait to feel the icy knot of fear gather inside me, but it never does. Instead, something red and yellow and orange unfurls within me, and my feet root themselves into the ground. *I will not run from these men,* I tell myself. *I will not be afraid.* The hot breath of anger ignites inside my stomach and surges outward until I no longer feel the winter chill and my skin is flushed with heat.

"What you got in the bag, hun?" the man sitting next to Stan asks. He sits with his knees spread and his shoulders wide. His teeth are tobacco stained when he smiles. "Something for Eloise Price?"

Stan knocks a hand against his knee as if he has just heard a joke. "Maybe you can give her a little present for me. I think I saw a bit of rat poison inside the shop that I'd like to send on up to her. Put it in her tea."

I let the bag of flour and candy slide down to the crook of my elbow as I look down at my hands, still covered in flour. I am pleased to see that they do not tremble. I step toward Stan, one foot in front of the other, until I am directly in front of him. My body towers over his slight frame, and I like how he has to look up to keep my gaze. He is no longer smiling.

"You are a coward, Stanley." I am delighted when Stan sours at the sound of his full name. "You and all your talk about Eloise Price. You aren't half the person she is." I am done hearing men joke and jeer and sneer at women walking down the street.

"I'll be gone soon enough," I say, "and when I leave, why don't you go take a look at that statue in the park and think about what it really means to be brave and honorable." I take one last look at Stan, so old and worn and tired, and rub my hands against one another. Together, we watch as the flour dusts his shoes.

Twenty-Six

Thursday, on my way to visit Eloise Price for the last time, I stop to see Rita. With the mayor's return only a day away, my time in Darren is waning, and I have something for Rita, a gift that should have been hers many years ago. I find her in the barn, sanding down the round hooves of a long buffet. "I have something to show you," I tell her. There is sawdust streaked across her face. She lifts a hand to her forehead as if to shield her eyes from something bright and faraway.

We sit together at the table where we first talked about the two sisters growing up in a small rural town beside a slow-moving river, and I place the diary between us. "It's Valerie's," I tell her, though she looks like she already knows.

We read through the book together, and when we're finished, Rita leans back and says, "I always wondered if Valerie was there that night."

My body sinks. I don't have to ask Rita what she means. I already know she is talking about the night that Benjamin died. The diary has no dates scrawled out on the upper half of the page, but it isn't hard to piece together the timeline, not now, after everything I've learned. The night that Benjamin brought Valerie up to Whitmore Halls to have a talk with Eloise Price was the night he was killed.

I'm not sure what to say to Rita. I feel like we have walked through the same forest, glanced up at the same trees, yet our paths have never crossed. For the first time, I feel a saturated sadness stretch through me. It bruises my insides an oily maroon. There was so much more to my grandmother than I ever guessed, and the thought both terrifies and astounds me at how much of a person can remain unknown. I'm about to tell Rita these things when she clears her throat and pushes farther away from the table.

"Valerie came to the house the night after the funeral." Rita looks different now, like someone familiar I would see on the street but not feel sure enough to wave. "I was the only one home. The doorbell rang, and I thought it was someone stopping by to drop off flowers. We received so many in the days after Benjamin's death. But when I opened the door, Valerie was standing there. Still thin and gaunt, but her eyes were brighter than ever before. There was some part of Valerie that I recognized.

"'I'm leaving,' she said. 'Don't come looking for me.' And then she was gone into the night. I stood there staring after her for a long while, and then I closed the door. I suppose part of me was angry with her. What did it matter to me if she left Darren for good? She left our family the day she married that man. I had seen her at the funeral. She didn't even stand by us, her family. It was like she was already gone."

I imagine Rita at eighteen years old, closing herself inside her bedroom with an old radio to drown out her sister's voice. "Did you tell your parents that she came by?" I ask.

"No, I thought it would only hurt them, and I was scared. Maybe a part of me thought it was all a dream. Seeing Valerie on the doorstep like that, telling me not to look for her. And there were questions about Benjamin's death. It was ruled accidental suicide at the time of the funeral. Did you know that?"

Rita doesn't let me answer before she says, "Hypothermia and death by the bottle. Benjamin wasn't the first."

I can't hide the confusion on my face. "I thought Eloise confessed right away."

Rita shakes her head. "A couple days after, if I'm remembering right. Right around the time Valerie went missing. I thought Valerie was dead for a long time. That she was so cut up by Benjamin's death that she took herself to the river one night."

Rita takes a deep breath. and I think about how this conversation has aged her. The clouds shift, and the old barn creaks in the wind. "I never planned to see a play in Chicago," she says, "the night of the art show."

I look at her quizzically. The night of the art show?

Rita stands, and I wonder if she is going to turn and walk right out of the barn, but she simply reaches in her back pocket and pulls out a square of sandpaper. She folds the strip in half and then rubs the rough teeth over the edge of the tabletop. "Needs quite a touch-up," she says.

Rita's hands are sure and steady as she works the edge of the wood. "I never liked the city." Valerie's diary rocks back and forth atop the table. "Never had any need to visit it until I got the letter."

Rita tells me that a letter came a couple of months before I got to Darren. It was mailed in a large manila envelope, much like the one I received at the end of summer. It was postmarked one week before Valerie died, and the return address was from somewhere in Maine. Rita didn't know anyone in Maine until she opened the envelope and out slipped a double-sided letter and a newspaper clipping. Valerie was sick with pneumonia. She was writing to Rita to tell her that she had lived a good life out by the sea. She wrote that, though she had made many mistakes, leaving Darren that night all those years ago was not one of them. She told Rita that she had a son; he was a professor over in Michigan. He, too, had a child. A girl. Rita would like her. She was an artist, Valerie had written. It was the first time Rita had heard from Valerie in over fifty years, and by the time the letter arrived in her mailbox, her sister was already dead.

Rita is down on her haunches now, gripping the wooden leg of the table and sanding the hard, bulbous foot. "I always knew that if I waited long enough, I would hear from Valerie."

I think of my grandmother lying in the hospital, sealing up an envelope stuffed full with a letter that had taken her fifty years to write.

Fifty years is a lifetime, I think, maybe several. How to fit it all on a two-sided piece of paper? I wonder then how many times Valerie had thought about what she would say to Rita. *Infinite,* Dad would say. He's always loved that word.

"It wasn't enough." There are drops of anger in Rita's voice. "I read Valerie's letter a dozen times, and I still knew almost nothing about who she had become. And then I looked at the newspaper clipping."

Rita leans back and looks at me now, fully. Her face is blotchy from exertion, and the tops of her cheeks shine. "It was an article about a young girl. An art student in Chicago who had just won a fellowship for a painting. It would be displayed at a show at the Art Institute."

It was printed in the *Chicago Times,* two days after I'd gotten the award. It wasn't a long article, but Dad had bought ten copies of that week's press, cutting out the newspaper clipping. He must have sent one to Valerie.

And then, suddenly, I know. I know why Rita looked so familiar the first time I met her inside the barn. I know why her voice made me pause, why her stance made me furrow my brow. I had met Rita before. It was the night of the art show in Chicago. A woman in a yellow coat came and stood in front of *The Woman in the Woods* and said, *I know these trees.*

"You were there." I am astonished by how far the roots of these branches stretch. "You were there the night of the art show."

She wipes her hands on the front of her overalls. "I wanted to meet you," she says. "If Valerie was dead, I thought, why not meet someone who can tell me more about her? Fill in the gaps a bit. That's why I asked the mayor to write to you."

Rita shrugs as if this were an obvious realization.

"You told Mayor Grant about me?"

"More or less." Rita sits on the edge of her chair and places her elbows on her knees. "I heard he'd been talking about the memorial, wondering if someone could paint a portrait of Benjamin. No one around here knew he had a granddaughter. Then Valerie's letter showed up in my mailbox, and I thought, here is this girl, a relative of Benjamin's and an artist; why doesn't she do it?"

"But the letter was addressed to Dad?" I uncross my legs and cross them again.

Rita's pupils roll upward. "Once Mayor Grant found out that Benjamin had a son, a professor at a fancy school no less, he thought he would be better at the job."

I smirk, imagining Dad here, in Mae's upstairs apartment, painting a portrait of his dead father.

"You brought me to Darren." A wash of affection colors my cheeks pink.

Rita says, "I suppose I did."

"Why didn't you say anything earlier?" I am both bewildered and incredulous that I have met Rita before, that she could be both here in Darren County and in Chicago, the bridge holding together the pillars of a life I am still unearthing.

"Didn't seem to make any difference how you got here. Besides, Darren County and I have a sort of agreement." She stands and walks over to the small refrigerator, pulling two bottles of Coca-Cola off the bottom shelf.

"An agreement?"

She sets the sodas on the table and uses a lighter to push off the bottle caps. "I don't bother no one in Darren, and they don't bother me. No more questions about Valerie, about my parents, about Benjamin." She tips the soda foam onto the barn floor. "And I let them think whatever they want about good ole Ben. Let them build that damn statue without a fuss."

"I take it you don't think much of the mayor then?" I tease.

Rita snorts.

"And what about Eloise Price?" The question slips from my lips before I have time to catch it.

Something shifts inside Rita, and she sets the bottle of soda on the table, folding her hands in her lap as if she were a small child getting ready to pray. She looks out over the wooden jungle that she has created in the barn, at the half-finished headboard leaning against the far wall, at the trio of grandfather clocks all sanded and in need of polish, at the log bench that is just ready to be cut and carved.

"Eloise saved my life," she says finally. "Valerie's too."

This is the first time Rita has brought up her visit to Whitmore Halls, and my heart quivers at her words.

"I'll never forget it," Rita says. "I was fourteen, and our father's friend had been staying with us that summer. He was a . . . *business associate*."

There's no need for Rita to tell me the rest of the story. I already understand.

"When I told Valerie what had happened, and that I hadn't bled, she didn't think twice about it. 'We need to go to Whitmore Halls,' she said." Rita swallows thickly. "I didn't even know she was scared until we got back home. She sent me right up to bed, told Mama I was sick, got right to helping with dinner. But when she came up to check on me later, her hands were shaking so bad she couldn't even pour a cup of tea."

I think of Eloise sitting in Dusty Hills, mixing lavender and dandelion petals into her mug. *The taste of spring,* she said.

"She was always stronger than me," Rita admits. "I don't know if I could have done it."

Confusion settles on my face.

"Leave," she clarifies. "Leave Darren. She must have been terrified. There is still so much I don't know about her."

I reach across the table and take Rita's hand. Her skin is hard and sun-stretched. She is so different from Valerie, made of hard edges and sturdy angles, yet holding her hand in mine feels like slipping my fingers into my grandmother's warm palm. "I can tell you," I say. "I want to tell you."

As the icicles drip off the old barn door, Rita and I sit at the half-sanded table and drink the sugary sodas while I tell her everything I remember about Valerie. I tell her about the small white house with the pink door. Valerie painted it herself the day after she moved in. I tell her about the collection of glass turtles she kept on her dresser, the way she took all the bulbs out of the ceiling lights because she preferred the soft yellow glow of lamps. I tell her about the chip in her left eyetooth; she once baked a cherry pie and left a pit in the filling.

I paint the portrait of Valerie from a palette of memory, dipping the brush into faraway details to narrow the bridge of her nose, to deepen the shades of laugh lines that held together the corners of her mouth. And when I'm finished, when the verbal portrait of my grandmother is as detailed as I can make it, I feel closer to her somehow. It's as if Valerie is sitting here beside us, at the table her sister built, drinking a can of cold Coca-Cola while listening to the story of her life.

When I have told Rita all that there is to tell, she walks me to the end of the drive, and I wave goodbye. I look back once, as I start down the dusty road, and Rita is still standing there, holding Valerie's words in her arms, the barn a striking red sun behind her. I think Valerie would be glad to know that Rita still lives in Darren, that she's made a life here in this small Kentucky town. I shrug my bag higher onto my shoulder and quicken my pace. It's Thursday afternoon, and Jason will be waiting in front of the courthouse to take me to Dusty Hills. This will be the last time I go to visit Eloise. Only a few handfuls of leaves remain to be hung. *It's time,* I will tell her. *I'm ready to hear the end of the story. I'm ready to hear about the night Benjamin died.*

Twenty-Seven

Ruth wouldn't touch the baby.

She gave birth inside Whitmore Halls on a silent, cloudless night. It was an easy birth, the baby boy sitting low in the womb. He was ready to be in the world, and when Eloise cut the umbilical cord, his brown eyes were like twin searchlights, trying to see everything all at once. Ulma had never seen anything like it. A baby born with his eyes open wide.

Ruth didn't want to hold the infant. In fact, she got this peculiar look on her face every time he was brought in to nurse. It was like she was seeing the babe for the first time and thinking, *Whose child is this? How did he come to be inside this house?*

Eloise never much cared for babies, but she took to the boy. She liked to play with his tiny toes and watch him squeal with delight when she blew bubbles on his stomach. He was an easy child, rarely fussy and quick to suck on the top knuckle of her smallest finger. Ruth refused to name him, so Eloise took to changing his name once a week just to try it out. None of them ever seemed right.

Three weeks after the boy was born, Eloise found Ruth sitting on the widow's walk, perched on the same wooden stool she used when women came up the hill. It was night, and Ruth faced away from the window, looking out toward the trees. The moon was nearly full, and the white light fell on her skin in drunken pools. It was cold, much too cold for Ruth to be sitting outside in a thin paisley-print dress meant for a picnic.

"Ruth," Eloise said softly, not wanting to startle her. She startled so easily these days. "Ruth."

But Ruth paid Eloise no mind. Not even the curve of her shoulder lifted in response to her voice.

Eloise worried. She thought of Joan, the woman who first came to Whitmore Halls so long ago, brought by a man who promised her dolls and a garden full of flowers. Joan, who gave birth to a child she did not want, who wouldn't look at the girl, who wouldn't feed her, who wouldn't even turn when the child cried in the middle of the night. *She had such troubled eyes,* Richard had liked to say. *Such alluring, troubled eyes.* Eloise could see them now. Her mother's haunted gaze, those eyes that saw nothing at all. Joan had walked the halls at night. Eloise remembered the sound of her footsteps. Eloise always kept her door propped open. Just in case. And the night when the moonflowers bloomed, Joan had walked so slowly toward the pond. Eloise could have stopped her.

"Ruth," Eloise whispered.

Ruth kept her eyes trained on the trees.

When Benjamin and Valerie Costello showed up at Whitmore Halls, Eloise knew there was going to be trouble. She had been seeing Valerie from time to time, not in town, but at night when she went to the river to collect the plants that were growing up and around the rails. Hemlock. A plant that could kill.

Eloise was startled when she first saw Valerie, wandering like an orphaned shadow in the darkness, bending down to pick handfuls of weeds that grew between the wooden slabs of the tracks.

"You don't want to be messing with that," Eloise said. She herself was collecting the weeds for Ulma. Hemlock favored the rails, liked to grow along tracks and fence posts. Ruth said it was too dangerous to keep around the house, but Ulma liked to have a jar or two dried out in the cellar. Good for the joints when used right. Add a pinch too much and a body would be convulsing on the floor within minutes.

Valerie stilled on the tracks, and Eloise was shocked by the woman's fragility. She had heard rumors about Valerie. She didn't leave the home after the baby died. She looked no more than a ghost sitting inside Costello House, like a doll locked in a glass case.

It was springtime, and the air tasted of wet soil as Eloise told Valerie that the plant was most dangerous about now, after the rains. It will leave a nasty rash on your skin. A tea bag filled with only three leaves could leave you gasping for breath as your lungs swelled. Wouldn't take much until you were down on the ground in respiratory failure.

"Don't say I didn't warn you." Eloise shook her head in dismay as Valerie bent to pick up another fistful of the herb. "One bite of that could kill a cow."

Valerie looked amused, and Eloise had the unsettling feeling that Valerie was pleased, that she was delighted to know that the white flowers she held in her hands could kill her in an hour's time.

Eloise hadn't seen much of Benjamin since the night the baby died. Good riddance. He had stayed away from Whitmore Halls. Eloise liked to think it was because he knew if he were ever to come back up the hill, he wouldn't be making it down again with all his limbs. That was partly why she was so surprised to see him standing on the other side of the door on the night of March 27, a rather smug, unsightly smirk on his face.

"Eloise Price!" he exclaimed as if he were greeting an old friend. "Why, we thought we'd come up here and bring you a pie."

"You've gone mad if you think I'm letting you back in this house." Eloise held her hand on the edge of the door to block him from pushing it open. It was strange to see Benjamin and Valerie together, stranger yet to see that Benjamin, though his eyes were red and sunken, hadn't been drinking. Still, Eloise didn't like the way he stood on the doorstep.

He was too sure of himself, standing there in an overcoat that made his shoulders look wide and waist thin with that wily, cockeyed grin that was bent just a bit too much to the right. No, Eloise didn't like it one bit. She gripped the edge of the door a little tighter.

Benjamin chuckled. "Your time is up, Eloise Price," he said. "You haven't been as careful as you should have been. I had a chat with Jenny Cox the other day, and she had some real interesting stories for me about what you've been doing up here in these hills."

Jenny Cox.

A twine of terror wound around Eloise's wrist. Jenny had been up at Whitmore Halls three days ago for a termination. She had four kids who already didn't have enough to eat. Her husband hadn't found work in months. They couldn't have another child. Jenny had been so sure. She told Ruth that this child just wasn't possible. They would never make it with one more empty belly to fill. She'd cringed when she heard the baby crying in the next room. *Jenny would never tell Benjamin,* Eloise tried to assure herself. *She would never.*

"A person will tell someone almost anything when they're needing work," Benjamin said as if he were reading her thoughts. "A couple of details for a job in Morehead." He shrugged innocently.

Valerie shivered, and Eloise's gaze flicked to the right. She had almost forgotten that Valerie was there, standing next to Benjamin, holding a lemon meringue pie.

"Eloise." Valerie's voice was barely above a whisper. "Please."

Why are you even here? Eloise wanted to ask her. It was dark outside and late. Valerie should be sleuthing along the rails, collecting handfuls of hemlock. Yet Eloise knew she had no choice. Send Benjamin away down the hill, and he would be back in an hour with a group of men.

"Well." Eloise put on a smile. "Never want to let a perfectly good pie go to waste." Eloise led them to the dining room, gesturing for the couple to sit while she went to the window and tied the waists of the heavy set of curtains. Charles was in the barn. The light from the loft shone brightly across the field. *Look this way, Charles,* she willed. *We have visitors.*

"Where's Ruth this evening?" Benjamin asked.

Eloise gripped the edge of the windowsill. "Oh, she's retired early," she answered. "Has a bit of a head cold."

Ruth was upstairs. Ulma and the baby were in the nursery. They were safe, Eloise told herself. She pulled a bottle of wine from the shelf and began pouring glasses. It was jarring to see Benjamin and Valerie sitting at the table. Ulma had set the room for dinner, and three place settings were arranged on the white linen tablecloth, as if the dinner had been prearranged. Valerie had taken off her coat and was clutching it against her stomach. She had gotten so thin in the last few months, and the candlelight caught strands of gray in her dark hair. She looked frightened as she sat across from her husband in a house that didn't belong to them. Eloise wondered whether she was thinking about Rita.

Benjamin, however, looked perfectly comfortable sitting at the head of the polished oak, leaning back in the chair and looking around the room at the china cabinet full of Joan's dolls, the long cherry-blossom floor runner, the painting of a black horse running in a field. It had always been Ulma's favorite.

Benjamin nodded when Eloise handed him a glass of red wine, and he sipped the alcohol loudly. Benjamin Costello was not used to drinking port. *Cheryl's don't offer that on special, now do they?* Eloise wanted to snipe, but she held her tongue.

"So." Eloise rounded the table, pulled out a chair, and slid into the seat beside Benjamin. "What did old Jenny Cox have to say? Trading lies for work?" Eloise clucked, shaking her head. "Sounds a bit risky, I would say."

Be careful, Eloise. She heard Ulma's voice as if she were standing right there beside her.

Eloise reached for a glass of port and took a sip. It was terribly bitter on her tongue. In the kitchen, the back door creaked open. *It must be Charles,* Eloise thought. *He's done with his evening farm chores.*

"The thing is"—Benjamin smacked his lips—"I've known for quite some time what you all are doing up here."

Eloise glanced quickly at Valerie. No, she thought, Valerie would never talk about it.

"We both know what I saw all those years ago. Don't care much about that." Benjamin's face soured as if the port had turned.

"Cut me a slice of that pie." He pointed a calloused finger at Valerie, who quickly stood, picked up the knife Eloise had set on the table, and cut the soft meringue into neat lines.

"But I know what else you all do up here." Benjamin turned fully toward Eloise. "I know about the pregnant women, have always known. They come up here, from Darren, from Morehead, hell, probably even from Lexington! They come here pregnant, and when they leave, they aren't pregnant anymore." Benjamin ran his fingers up and down the stem of the wineglass.

Valerie sliced another clean line through the pie.

Eloise forced herself to look directly at Benjamin, to dig into his blue irises, to grip on to those same eyes he wore as a young boy stumbling out from the woods with an apple in hand. *You want to see a magic trick?*

There was a kettle boiling in the kitchen. Eloise could hear the water begin to roil.

"Benjamin . . . ," Valerie started. Eloise wondered if it was a warning.

"Shut up!" Benjamin snapped.

"Your pie." Valerie slid the plate toward him.

Benjamin took a forkful of the dessert in his mouth, uncrossed his legs, and leaned forward. "I could put you in jail, Eloise Price." Benjamin's voice was eerily quiet, and Eloise knew he was bluffing. He wouldn't put her in jail. He was after something else.

Eloise lifted the fork that sat on the table beside her, letting the silver prongs swing like a pendulum between her fingers. A door slammed and the baby cried out. Three sets of eyes snapped toward the hall.

"A baby," Valerie said quietly.

Another door creaked open, and the crying stopped. Eloise closed her eyes briefly. *Count to five,* she told herself. A trick that calmed her down when her body was riddled with fear.

"Why now?" she asked Benjamin. The pie sat perfectly in the center of the table.

"Is that . . ." Benjamin jammed a thumb over his shoulder.

Eloise told him it was nothing.

"Why?" she asked again. "If you've known all this time, why bother throwing me in jail now?" Eloise knew there was always a chance one of the women would talk. That was why they were so careful with the medicines and herbs. *Let them talk,* Ulma used to say. *They won't ever get any proof.* But now, with Ruth, with all the equipment in the back room, it would be so easy for someone to come in and search. It would be so easy to open cupboards, to look under beds, to open dressers and closets. The practice could be dismantled in minutes. And Ruth. Eloise had nightmares about the stories Ruth had told her about Elizabeth, the abortion doctor Ruth worked with in Chicago. *She was found in the river,* Ruth had whispered. Eloise couldn't stomach the thought.

Benjamin rubbed the backs of his knuckles together. "The thing is," he said, "Jenny Cox told me something kind of funny. She said, well, she said there is a baby staying up here."

Eloise stilled.

"And I got to thinking that was rather odd because I don't remember seeing you pregnant, Eloise, and that aunt of yours is too old to be pushing out any babies." Benjamin looked over his shoulder once again.

Dread trickled down the back of Eloise's throat. Ruth hadn't been to town in quite some time. Ruth had been avoiding him. It must have been so easy to piece together. And now.

I was going to build my boy an oak rocket. Wasn't that always Benjamin's plan? Suddenly, it was like the baby was back from the dead. And hadn't Benjamin been in love with Ruth for years? He had locked eyes on her as he recited his wedding vows, had begged her to move into town, had brought her into his home to deliver his child and now, now that he knew about the baby, what was stopping him from claiming them both as his own? Certainly not Valerie, Eloise thought. No, Benjamin never cared for Valerie the way he cared for Ruth, and Valerie would be easily disposed of. Brought to the state asylum. *She's hysterical. Can't get over the loss of the child.* They would put her in a room with white walls and fluorescent lighting. How easy it would be for Benjamin.

Expose Eloise.

Institutionalize Valerie.

Take Ruth and the baby.

Eloise was going to be sick.

"A baby," Valerie said. Her voice was firm and weighted, and Eloise was sure that she was just now realizing what Benjamin had pieced together not too long before. When Eloise looked up, she saw that Valerie's gaze was not on Benjamin, but was settled on the kitchen doorway where Ulma stood, holding the baby boy in her arms.

Benjamin pushed back from the table, standing. "Is that him?" His face was that of a father seeing his child for the first time. Eloise couldn't stand it.

Ulma pulled the child closer to her breast. "I was just getting some milk," she said to Eloise, but her eyes were wide. She knew she had made a mistake.

"He's mine, isn't he?" Benjamin looked from the baby back to Eloise, a tilted smile fitting awkwardly on his mouth.

Eloise told Ulma to take the baby upstairs.

"He's mine, I know it."

Eloise cringed when Benjamin took a step toward her as if he meant to grab her by the shoulders and squeeze.

"Take the baby upstairs, Ulma."

"Wait," Valerie exclaimed. Her arm reached out toward the child. "Wait." She made her way to Ulma in the same steady way Eloise saw her balance on the rails late at night. Valerie reached out and placed a hand on the baby's head. The baby cooed.

"Don't," Benjamin snarled, but his voice was no louder than a far-off echo.

"What's his name?" Valerie asked.

Lionel. Samuel. James. Artemis. Eloise listed them all in her head. *How about Joseph?* Eloise had asked Ruth the night the boy was born. Ulma was in the forest, planting the placenta under the red oak trees. Ruth was lying in bed, staring at the painting of the Virgin Mary that hung on the wall. She had brought it with her from Chicago. The painting had faded over the years, but the young girl's eyes still looked as sad and lonely as the day she was first hung in the bedroom. Eloise never understood why Ruth loved the painting so much. Mary looked so young. She was just a kid herself.

Joseph is a good name. Eloise pulled the blanket tighter around the baby's small frame. When she'd looked up, she'd seen a tear fall down Ruth's cheek.

"Don't you dare touch him!" Benjamin was across the room and wrapping his long fingers tightly around Valerie's wrist. "She killed my first boy."

Valerie wrenched away from Benjamin. Her chest was heaving, and for one silent moment, Eloise thought Valerie was about to spit in his face.

She killed my first boy.

This wasn't the only time Valerie had heard this accusation hurled at her from across the room. It couldn't be, Eloise realized. She was far too calm. It was as if the words sounded dull to her, an old knife that had never been sharpened.

"Sit down, Benjamin." Eloise was surprised by the steadiness in her voice. She told Ulma to take the baby upstairs. This time she went.

"That's my son," Benjamin repeated. The words turned Eloise's stomach.

There were footsteps above, and Eloise knew that Ruth had come in from the widow's walk. Benjamin needed to leave.

The kettle in the kitchen whistled. The water was boiling. "I'll get it," Valerie said. She was wearing her coat now, and Eloise wondered if she was going to walk through the kitchen and out the back door.

"I'll make a cup of tea. It calms Benjamin down." Valerie spoke as if she were going to warm up a bottle for a fussy baby. She nodded when Eloise told her there were lemons on the counter.

"I'll burn this place to the ground, Eloise Price," Benjamin warned. He sat on the edge of the chair, the wooden legs scraping against the wood.

Benjamin took another bite of pie as if the sight of the golden meringue reminded him that he was here to celebrate the birth of his son. He was going to build his boy a rocket ship. How fine life must have looked to him then.

"That boy has nothing to do with you."

Be careful, Eloise.

Benjamin sniffed. "I guess Ruth never told you about that night a year ago."

The night the baby had died. Eloise twitched with anger. Benjamin stumbling into Whitmore Halls, the bottle of Old Rip Van Winkle lying under the kitchen table. The overturned chair. Valerie picking up sticks beside the river.

"It was always supposed to be me and Ruth." Benjamin looked down at the pie as he spoke, his voice cracking. "I've always loved her."

He had always loved Ruth, and Eloise hated him for it. She wanted to scream at Benjamin, to overthrow the dining room table that was too heavy to lift, to pick up the cake knife and jab it in the center of his chest, to expose the warped, diseased heart that beat with a love that looked like bruises on a woman's neck and broken glass on the kitchen floor.

"Go to hell, Benjamin Costello," she swore softly.

Benjamin sat up slowly, a look of amusement on his face.

There was a clatter in the kitchen, and Benjamin turned. Valerie. She was making tea.

"I think I'll go see what's taking her so long." Eloise stood. Benjamin took another bite of pie.

In the kitchen, Valerie stirred a cup of tea. There was a slice of lemon beside the sink, and the room smelled mustier than usual. Charles needed to clean out the pipes.

Valerie turned and nodded when Eloise asked her if she was all right.

"Just coming back out," she said, holding the cup of steaming liquid in her hands. "I made it just how he likes it. Lots of lemon."

There was something different about Valerie now. She stood there, in the middle of the kitchen, in the same place where Ruth had stood the night Benjamin came to Whitmore Halls holding the neck of the Old Rip Van Winkle bottle in his hand, but her face was flushed, and her eyes were bright and alert. It was unbearably hot in the room, as if someone had turned on the furnace, but Valerie still wore her long dark jacket. Eloise saw that the stove burner was lit. Beside the sink lay the paring knife, a half-squeezed lemon, and a green leaf. The spoon held a pool of tea in its silver belly.

Eloise took a step closer to Valerie and peered inside the cup. A teaspoon of green leaves sank to the bottom. Hemlock. Eloise would know their shape and scent anywhere.

Eloise didn't need to look up at Valerie to know what she was doing. Valerie Dunn, the young girl who once brought her sister up the hill to have a termination that would save her from having to wash the blood from Rita's body. Valerie, the young woman who married a man who spoke his wedding vows to another woman. Valerie, who so badly wanted to be a mother, who gave birth to a fragile baby that wouldn't sleep, was now standing in the kitchen holding a glass of poisoned tea. It would kill Benjamin within minutes.

Eloise thought of Valerie on the night the baby died, how she walked beside the river collecting sticks for a fire she would never build. How she would continue to walk along the tracks, night after night, gathering tufts of hemlock. Why hadn't Eloise asked before? *Why the plant, Valerie? What are you planning to do with all those weeds?*

Because she had known, Eloise realized. She had known from the moment she told Valerie about the plant. *It would take a cow down in one bite.* Valerie hadn't looked horrified at all, and Eloise had known. Valerie was only waiting for the right time. When Benjamin told her that they were going up to Whitmore Halls to have a chat with Eloise Price, Valerie must have looked over at the bouquets of weedy white flowers around the house and thought about the manor, about the home that had always been a place for women needing help.

Valerie looked at Eloise for only a moment before gliding past her, the steaming cup of tea as hot as a beating heart. Eloise stayed rooted in the kitchen as she heard Valerie place the tea in front of Benjamin. "Goes perfect with pie," she said. Her voice was as soft as a lullaby. "Brings out the lemon."

By the time Eloise came back into the dining room, Benjamin was already drinking greedily from the glass. He was never a man who could say no to a drink.

Valerie leaned against the doorframe of the room as Eloise slid onto the chair opposite him.

"Bitter." Benjamin wrinkled his nose before folding his hands on the tabletop. "Here's what I've been thinking," he said. "I'll give you two weeks to close down and clean up whatever you have going on here. I don't want any more talk of women coming up here to this house."

There was a large manila envelope in the top drawer of the bureau. Inside was a hundred dollars and an address written on a thin sheet of paper.

"I'm tired of people thinking I do nothing around this town. Letting a place like this operate under my nose." He coughed and swallowed. A wet sound.

Valerie couldn't stay in Darren now. No, there would be too many questions. She wouldn't be safe. But she would need to stay for the funeral. People needed to see her mourn. Then Eloise would take her to the station.

"Now, I'll admit the rails were a mess." Benjamin shook his head, smacked his tongue on the roof of his mouth as if to rid a bitter taste. "Built too close to the river. That damn river."

Eloise looked out the window. Charles was back in the barn, leading a chocolate-colored horse into the stable to feed. He would have to come in soon. Eloise needed him.

Benjamin's face was red, his hands starting to tremble. "Damn hot in here." He pulled at the collar of his shirt. A drop of red wine stained the fabric. He coughed, stumbled off the chair, fell onto the floor in the dining room. His whole body quaked.

"He'll convulse soon," Eloise said to Valerie, who hadn't moved from the doorway. "You need to be getting on home."

Benjamin pounded his fist on the wooden floor.

Eloise told Valerie to go into the other room, to find Ulma. She would stay with Benjamin. It wouldn't be long now.

Eloise sat in the chair closest to where Benjamin laid. His body was rigid and eyes wild with fear. *Yes, Benjamin, you are going to die.* There was no antidote for hemlock. Eloise couldn't stop the poison if she tried. "You remember that day we found the Oak Rocket?" she asked. Her voice sounded peculiar in this room, like she was just a stranger visiting a house for an evening dinner. She hated the wallpaper in here. Green and white. She would tell Ulma to change that, after she was gone.

"The red oaks were all changing colors, and the woods felt large, even to us." Eloise and Benjamin had been roaming through the forest, looking for rabbit holes. Ulma wanted to make stew that night, and Eloise had gotten pretty good with the slingshot. The winds had been bad the month before, so when they found the red oak, fallen on the hillside, they knew there was a good chance for rabbits. Rabbits loved dead trees. It was Benjamin who saw the hollowed-out trunk.

Look at this! he called, climbing into the open hole. *It's a cockpit!*

Eloise didn't care much for planes and motorized vehicles, but she climbed into the tree just the same. The trunk was large and infested with mold and black ants. Still, Benjamin was right. With the tree landing on the incline, it did feel like they were in the cockpit of a plane, the old trunk itching to speed along the forest floor until it burst up from the hills and into the sky.

Benjamin clutched the edge of the bark in his hands, his body bouncing up and down. Loud, motorized sounds peeled from his mouth. *Three, two, one! Blast off!* His body rattled against Eloise, making her laugh and clutch the side of the tree.

Here we go! Here we go! Benjamin yelled. The trees rushed past them in a blur of red and orange and yellow. The roots of the red oak, a web of gnarly limbs rising up behind them, were fueled with red-hot fire. Any moment now, and they would blast through the hills. The sky would be everywhere. Eloise held her breath, peering over Benjamin's shoulder and waiting for the moment when everything would become small.

"It felt like we were flying," Eloise said, "when we were in that tree."

Benjamin's body was still now, his eyes blank. She would need to check his pulse soon. Just to be sure. Ulma and Valerie were in the hall. Charles was in the barn. Where was Ruth? Eloise knew things would have to move fast. Valerie had to get back home. The body would need to be moved. The kitchen had to be cleaned. The poison thrown away. Valerie would need to call the police in the morning to tell them that Benjamin was missing. They would search for hours until they found him alone in the woods. They would say Benjamin died of hypothermia at first. There would be no need for an investigation. Until the autopsy results came back. An autopsy was sure to be done on a town mayor. But Eloise knew that by then there would be no need for people coming up and poking around Whitmore Halls, because six days after Benjamin would be found in the woods, two days after the body was buried, Eloise would walk down to the courthouse and say, *I did it. I killed Benjamin Costello.*

Twenty-Eight

"I sent Valerie back down the hill, and Charles and I brought Benjamin out to the woods." Eloise tells me this part of the story as we sit together under the forest of red oak leaves. It took us just over two months, but today Eloise and I have turned the last square of white into a branch of fiery foliage. It seems fitting that we finish today, just as Eloise's story is meeting up with my own.

Eloise tells me how they laid Benjamin beside the fallen red oak tree, the back of his hand pressed against the old, worn bark of the Oak Rocket.

I think of how in the week after Valerie died, Dad and I drove to Maine to retrieve her ashes. We hadn't visited in over two years, and the house looked smaller than it had when I was a child. Dad fumbled with the keys, and I sat in one of Valerie's old wicker chairs on the front porch and thought about how strange it was that her absence felt so much heavier than her presence had.

Inside, we were greeted by dozens of glass bottles. They hung from the ceiling on various lengths of thread and were full of sea glass. Some were from beer and wine; others were glass jars and jugs that hung from handles. There were bottles larger than ceramic vases and ones that could fit in the palm of my hand. Some were chipped and cracked; others were perfectly pristine.

Jesus Christ, Dad swore. *Someone is going to have to clean this mess up.* He walked along the edge of the room toward the window, careful not to touch any of the glass. When he opened the blinds, the light rushed in, and I reached out to stroke the blue bottle closest to me. It spun on the thread as I walked into the forest of glass.

"They found Benjamin's body within two hours." Eloise inhales shakily, and I realize that this one trembling breath is the first time she has felt frail to me. I imagine Eloise standing over Benjamin, how she must have looked down at his face and thought of the boy she once knew, of how quickly love can turn to hate.

"What did you do then?" I ask.

Eloise smiles sadly. "Then I went to talk to Ruth."

Eloise knew there could be no investigation. Not in Whitmore Halls. Not with Ruth.

She stood inside the dining room, in the place where Benjamin had sat only hours before, and looked around the room. The crystal bowl sitting on the buffet. It was full of rotting apples. The old wooden clock hanging on the wall. Eloise had never noticed that it didn't chime. The glass chandelier. The white trim over the doorways.

Eloise picked up the pie and brought it into the kitchen. She didn't like the way her hands shook when she set it down in the sink. The scent of rotting milk was everywhere.

Ulma and Ruth could continue the practice. They would be okay here, up in the hills. Benjamin was dead. Eloise would be locked up. Ruth's life wouldn't be in danger.

"Eloise."

Eloise turned. Ruth was sitting at the kitchen table, and Eloise wondered how she had missed it, how she had walked right by Ruth's wide-open face on the way to the sink.

"Eloise," Ruth whispered. "What did you do?"

The sound of Ruth's voice split something inside her, and Eloise thought of the first time she had seen Ruth cry. A single tear sliding down her cheek as she sat in the bold strip of moonlight slicing the halls of Dusty Hills.

"Ruth." Eloise knelt and placed a hand in Ruth's lap, grasping at the soft cotton. "I need you to go upstairs," she said. "Help Ulma hide the equipment. We will need to be quiet for a while until things calm down. I need you to call Amy and tell her a woman is coming to the city. A woman who needs help."

Eloise knew that Ruth understood. Valerie would need a train ticket to Chicago. Talking to Ruth now, Eloise felt herself harden for what was to come, and she gripped on to this bitter resolve. She would need it in the coming days.

"Valerie needs to stay for the funeral, and then I'll bring her to Morehead." It was a good plan. No one would suspect Valerie of killing Benjamin. After all, she was only a grieving widow. So much loss. The baby and now this.

"After Valerie is safe"—Eloise took a breath—"I will call the police."

Ruth's eyes shot upward, and Eloise knew she hadn't been expecting this. "And tell them what?" she demanded.

When Eloise didn't respond, Ruth asked the question again, her voice wavering. "And tell them what, Eloise?"

Eloise couldn't bear to look at Ruth's face, so withered and destroyed. Everything inside Eloise was coming undone. "We can't have an investigation up here, Ruth. You know what they will do to this place. To Ulma. To you." She didn't need to remind Ruth about Elizabeth's body found in the river. "If I confess . . ."

"No."

"It will be over."

"Why?" Ruth asked quietly, and Eloise thought of all the afternoons she and Ruth had walked along the halls of Dusty Hills, of the day they had sat on the stone steps, waiting for the ambulance to take the men away. The war was over, and Eloise insisted that Ruth come back to Darren County with her. Eloise thought of the story Ruth had told her, of Dr. Ross and Elizabeth and of a life where one was never safe. *I will never let anything happen to you,* Eloise had promised. Now, kneeling in the kitchen, knowing that Benjamin's body was out in the woods, Eloise cringed. She had pleaded with Ruth that day on the steps, begged her to come to Whitmore Halls. Had Eloise been breaking her promise, even then?

Eloise reached up and cupped Ruth's face in her hands. "I need you to be okay," she said softly. "You are too important."

Ruth looked away, and Eloise felt herself scraped raw when she realized that it was always going to end like this. It was always going to end with Eloise having to make a choice that wasn't a choice at all and with Ruth looking away as if she had always known that one day she would be left sitting in the hills without her.

❀

Eloise tells me how on the day after the funeral, she drove Valerie to the train station.

"It was the next morning when I confessed," she says. "Went to the police station and told them that I did it."

I try to imagine the moment when Eloise walked into the sheriff's office. They would have been surprised to see her. Eloise would have gone right up to the sheriff and held out her arms. *I did it,* she would say, her voice bloated with authority to hide the way she shook. *I killed Benjamin Costello.* It wouldn't have taken much for the men to believe her. I want to ask Eloise these things. I want to ask her to tell me about the moment she stepped inside the courtroom, about the fan that spun and spun from the ceiling, about the smell of rot and decay that the river had left behind as it receded into the banks. I want to ask Eloise to tell me this chapter, but instead she simply turns her head and says that she brought the baby with her to the train station.

"He rode in the back seat next to Valerie," she says. "She was as white as a ghost."

"Why did you bring him?"

I am surprised when Eloise hesitates, when she bites the corner of her lip and fidgets with the loose skin above her knuckle. "The night before I brought Valerie to Morehead, I found Ruth sitting beside the crib. The baby was screaming, and Ruth was just *vacant*. She sat not two feet away from the boy, and I wasn't sure she even heard his cries."

Eloise was surprised to find Ruth in the nursery. She rarely went in there, into the room that Eloise once called her own when she was a small girl and Ulma first came to Whitmore Halls all those years ago. The baby was wailing when Eloise stepped inside, his skin wet and hot from exertion.

Ruth sat two feet from the crib, in the rocking chair Charles brought home from three towns over. It was strange to see Ruth sitting there, her foot rhythmically rocking the wood back and forth. Eloise was sure this was the first time Ruth had been in the nursery.

"I can't even look at him," Ruth said as Eloise went to the crib, picked up the baby, and gently cooed. He settled against her chest.

The days had been long since Benjamin's death, and still, they weren't long enough. The funeral was set, and Eloise felt herself growing small within the Halls. She and Ulma had placed all the medical supplies in the old cellar they once used to store the jars of herbs from Erika's shop. They took down the dried leaves and flowers that hung on lines strung across the kitchen, scrubbed the dining room floor that would never quite look the same after Benjamin Costello had writhed on the warped wood. Eloise helped Charles with the horses, brushed their manes and ran her fingers down the slope of the mare's back.

And she walked through the woods. For hours, Eloise roamed the hills. Her bare feet sank into the soil, and dried branches and leaves cut into her skin, making her bleed. She didn't notice until she was back inside Whitmore Halls and a soft ache punctured each of her steps. In the woods, she thought of everything and nothing at all. She ran through deer trails like she had when she was young and wild and ferocious, climbed the low-hanging branches of the red oak trees and sat nestled in their arms as she looked over the town. She sat on the ground and grabbed fistfuls of soil just to feel the earth in her palms and thought of Joan licking dirt from her fingertips. Eloise longed for the ripe juice of berries horribly rich on her tongue. And in the evenings, while Ulma rocked the baby beside the fireplace and Ruth sat, hollowed-out, on the widow's walk, Eloise lay in the forest and looked up through the brittle branches, wishing for autumn.

"Ruth," Eloise whispered helplessly. She had no idea how to ease Ruth's suffering, to ease so much of the pain that Eloise felt she had stoked herself.

The rocking chair creaked, and Ruth gripped the wooden arms tightly. "I hate myself for it," she said softly, unmistakably.

Eloise juggled the baby on her hip and let him suck the soft tip of her finger. The air in the room felt stale, and she longed to open a window, to let out the seedy stench of despair that moved from room to room within the home.

Ruth looked at Eloise, her brown eyes so dark and round that Eloise felt the horrible pit of grief settle deep inside her.

"What kind of mother can't even hold her own son," Ruth cried.

Eloise stiffened as she thought of all that had been done to Ruth, all that had been taken from her. Even this. Even motherhood had left her bare. Eloise looked down at the boy and thought of the life that stretched out before him. He would grow up in the same house she had traversed as a small child. He would wander the halls and play in the forest. Ulma would teach him about plants. Charles would teach him about horses.

And Ruth. Ruth would sit on the widow's walk and stare out at the trees. The boy would grow, and Ruth would fade. She would slowly stop coming to the door when a woman stood on the other side and knocked. She would forget to change her clothes each morning, forget to wash the dirt out from her hair. Over the years her skin would become a dull sort of gray and her eyes a muddy shade of brown. She would become quiet, until one day she would just stop speaking altogether. Eloise had seen it happen before. And then, one night when the boy was about six years old, he would see Ruth walking beside the pond in the dark. And when she walked into the water, sinking below the surface, he would be so full of hate. He wouldn't think to stop her.

Unless.

Eloise studied the baby sucking at her thumb. His brown eyes looked up at her as if he knew what she was thinking.

"He has your eyes," Eloise said quietly.

Ruth stopped rocking and, when Eloise looked up, her eyelids had already slipped shut.

✿

At the train station, Eloise handed Valerie a small envelope. Inside was money and the address for the safe house in Chicago. "A woman will answer the door," Eloise explained. "You must show her this."

Valerie took the moonflower from Eloise's outstretched hand. She fingered the white petals just as she had on the day she and Rita first came up the hill for a glass of tea. How long ago that now seemed. "She will show you one back," Eloise instructed as she walked to the back door of the truck, pulling it open. "That is how you will know that you are safe."

Eloise pulled the baby out from the basket in the back seat. He was wrapped in a blanket, one Eloise found inside Joan's old hope chest that still sat against the end of the bed in the upstairs room. He fussed as Eloise tucked the gray weave tighter around his body.

Valerie's lips parted as Eloise placed the baby in her arms.

"Take him." Eloise had never been so sure and so unsure of anything in her whole life.

"I don't understand." Valerie trailed her finger over the boy's small white fist, the short length of his nose.

Eloise felt very far from the train station as she told Valerie to take the baby with her to Chicago. "He is yours now. He never belonged inside Whitmore Halls, anyway."

Somewhere, out in the darkness, a train whistle blew, and a bright dot of white light pierced through the black belly of night. The train would be here soon. Valerie pulled the baby closer to her chest, and his lips pursed as if he were ready to suckle at her breast. Eloise thought of all the times she had held the boy, of all the times he had sucked on her finger. She swelled with emotion. And then Eloise thought of Ruth. She had brought the baby to Ruth earlier in the afternoon. He cooed as she sat beside Ruth and told her of what she had planned.

He will be safe with Valerie, Eloise whispered. *He will go with Valerie to Chicago, and he will live a good life.*

Ruth reached her hand out to stroke the baby's soft head, and Eloise felt herself split in two. *I always wanted to be a mother,* Ruth had said quietly. *But he was never mine.*

"He will be okay," Eloise said aloud. She took a step backward, away from Valerie and the child in her arms. "We will all be okay." The wind swept through the trees and, in the darkness, Eloise saw the green buds just starting to bloom. She looked down once more at the baby and nodded. "Give him a name," she said.

Gordan. Christopher. Lawrence. Adam.

Eloise said them all in her head.

"He already has one." Valerie swaddled the baby closer to her heart. "It's David. I'll call the baby David."

Twenty-Nine

"Dad."

Eloise nods. "He was such an inquisitive baby. Always looking around, always studying."

"Dad was born in Whitmore Halls." I feel like this is both a startling shock and something that I've always known. "Valerie wasn't pregnant when she went to Chicago."

"No," Eloise confirms.

I try to imagine what it was like for Eloise that night, placing the baby in Valerie's arms, knowing that soon she would call the police, but all I can see is the way my grandmother's face must have lit up, how she must have felt her heart crack in two as she held the small boy who looked so much like the child that was buried in a grave.

"I knew that Ruth wouldn't survive motherhood." Eloise is sitting at her desk in much the same way as she was the first time I came into room 402. *I'm here to learn about Benjamin Costello*, I had said.

I will tell you the story you need to hear.

"He's lived a good life," I tell her. "Dad. He grew up in Chicago with Valerie. Went to good schools, graduated at the top of his class. He's a professor now, did I mention that?"

"You did," she tells me. All the autumn leaves reflect in Eloise's irises.

"Valerie kept the name Costello." I ponder. "I would have thought she would change it when she went away. Less likely to be found that way."

Eloise chuckles. "Ruth used to say it was easy to get lost in the city. It was like the forest in that way."

"Eloise," I begin. There is something about the story that I don't understand. "Why didn't Ruth terminate?" *She must have considered it,* I think.

Eloise sighs, and the room fill with loss. "Ruth didn't talk about it much. She always wanted children." She reaches across the desk and picks up a notebook. This one is smaller than the others, barely larger than the diary I left at Rita's earlier in the day. Eloise holds it in her lap.

"Termination wasn't the right choice for her," she says finally. "That's all we were ever really trying to do up in the hills. Give women a choice."

"That's why you took the blame," I say. "For Benjamin's death. You couldn't let anything happen to Ruth and the clinic."

"It was the hardest decision I ever had to make"—Eloise smiles sadly—"and the easiest. There was nothing I wouldn't do for Ruth. Even if she hated me for it." Eloise's voice is raw, and I know that something she has kept buried inside her has now been unearthed.

"Everything Benjamin knew and had seen died right along with him. And the people stopped caring about Whitmore Halls after a while," Eloise clarifies. She is finishing a story I first heard up at the house in the hills.

"Ruth left soon after the trial." I remember what Charles told me. How Ruth boarded a train for Chicago, riding the same rails that Marjorie Thomas and so many others rode only months before.

Eloise hums. "After I went to prison, Ruth stayed with Ulma and Charles for a while. They kept a low profile, and things were quiet. And then Ruth decided to go back to Chicago. Things were starting to happen there, underground. Word was spreading about the need for women's medicine. There was a woman who was starting a practice in the city. She had been performing illegal abortions for years, just as we had been doing up at Whitmore Halls, and she was overwhelmed. Ruth found out about it through Amy."

"The woman who ran the safe house?" I ask.

"That's right."

Eloise tells me that Ruth left for Chicago in the late forties, and by the time my father would have been ten years old, she was part of an underground abortion network that provided safe and effective medical care for nearly twenty-five women a day. The women running the program were always in danger. They wore disguises when they went in and out of the office. They dressed as men when they walked down the street. They carried knives in their pockets and never walked alone.

"They must have been so scared." I think of what Charles told me about the broken dolls left on the doorstep of Whitmore Halls. The baby bottles filled with blood.

"Yes," Eloise confirms. "But they knew their work was too important. And in that time, there was nowhere else for women to go if they had an unwanted pregnancy. They needed women like Ruth and Amy and the others. Without them, well, we would have too many stories of young girls and women hemorrhaging in bathtubs and on cotton sheets."

"And Charles." I think of how women still came up to Whitmore Halls, even now, fifty years later. *Are you in trouble?* he asked. *I'll take you where you need to go.*

"Yes." Eloise's face weakens. "And Charles."

I look up at the sky of leaves above me. It would always be autumn here, in room 402.

"Seven months before you came here, I received a letter in the mail." Eloise pulls a white envelope out from the book she is holding. As she fans through the pages, I see hundreds of pressed flowers threaten to slip onto the floor. Somewhere there is a moonflower, I think. It's bloomed for over seventy years.

Eloise hands me the envelope. The writing is small and fine, tight letters addressed to Eloise Price. Inside, there is no note, no letter. Only a single newspaper clipping. An obituary. At the top is a name: Ruth Ames.

She died in her sleep on February 22, 1997, in Chicago, Illinois. She worked as a physician in a small clinic on Maple Street for over thirty years. Ruth was a pianist, a woman's advocate, and a member of the Chicago Women's Liberation Union. She devoted her life to medicine.

"I knew you were Ruth's the moment you walked through that door," Eloise says. "Same dark, unruly hair, set shoulders, inquisitive eyes. It was like seeing her back in these halls the same as she was nearly sixty years ago."

Eloise touches the faded skin of her jaw.

"Why didn't you tell me then?" I ask.

She leans back in her chair. "Well, you asked for a story, Ms. Costello. Surely you aren't one of those people who reads the last page before the rest?"

I laugh. "No," I say. "I'm not." I flip the envelope in my hand. The obituary was sent from a woman in Chicago. Ms. Gloria Galley.

"Don't know her," Eloise answers when I ask who sent her the letter. "I figure she must have worked with Ruth. She knew enough to send me the clipping."

"This is close to the school," I say aloud. North Richmond. That was just on the east side of the city, a short train ride from the Art Institute. It's strange to think of Ruth there, living so close to me. If only I'd known.

"Can I keep this?" I hold up the envelope, and Eloise nods.

"Ruth would have loved this." She looks up at the leaves. "She has always been my autumn."

I imagine Ruth and Eloise sitting in the forest of red oaks, eating blackberries. It must have been fall then, the war nearing its end. The leaves must have looked just as red and yellow and orange as they did now, covering the walls of a room where Eloise and Ruth first met.

Eloise reaches over to the mug filled with wildflowers. The white buds have wilted, but the stems are still green and ripe. "It's such an inconspicuous plant," Eloise says quietly. "Hemlock."

Hemlock.

My lips part, and the insides of my palms burn hot at the sudden realization. The weeds Eloise picked along the fence line of Dusty Hills aren't Queen Anne's lace or baby's breath. They are hemlock. The same plant that my grandmother collected and bound in bouquets around her home, the same plant that she used to kill my grandfather fifty years ago.

"Do you remember the day you first came here?" Eloise takes advantage of my stunned silence. "When I asked you about your favorite flower?"

Yes, I think. Sunflowers.

I can only nod.

"I told you that the Appalachian forests are home to some of the rarest flowers in the country." She begins picking the dead flower heads off the plant, careful to set them back in the mug. I remember how Eloise had snapped at me when I had gone to touch the buds just the other day. *Don't touch those!* Her voice had been so sharp that I felt the cut of it still lingering on my skin when I woke the next morning.

"The forests are also home to the most common. Did you know that hemlock can be found in almost all the states? Some call it a garden plant." Eloise chuckles. "But it loves the hills. I first noticed it growing out by the fence line last spring when they moved us here from the penitentiary. I thought it was terribly fitting. The facility surrounded by enough poison to kill everyone inside."

"Why didn't you tell anyone?" I ask.

Eloise pulls leaves from the stems and sets them on a cut square of nylon used for making tea bags. "I knew it would come in handy one day."

I tremble.

"Last year, around this time, I learned something was wrong with my blood. Probably from some virus I picked up in the prison. It was a nasty, filthy place. Sometime after that, the obituary came. It was winter then, and I knew I had to wait for the buds. And then you showed up at my door," Eloise says, "and I knew it would soon be time."

"No." I shake my head slowly.

Eloise cuts a cord of string and ties the mesh around the hemlock leaves. She has made a bag of tea.

"My story is done, Tig," Eloise says. "And it's time for me to be rid of this place."

I don't need to look around to be reminded of the water-stained walls, the sterile lighting, the dishes of foul-smelling beans, and the flakes of potatoes poured from a box. I don't need Alice to come in with her needles and vials and watch Eloise hold out her bruised wrists to be handcuffed while the needle pierces her gnarled veins. The thin gray robe hanging on the doorknob, the slippers with a hole straight through the toe. The smell of urine. The cry of a woman down the hall. I have spent only hours here, in these halls, and each time I leave, I am surprised by the fierce rush of air that drains from my lungs when I step outside.

"This is why you told me," I realize. "This is why you told me about Whitmore Halls. About Benjamin and Ulma and Ruth. About Valerie."

This is the moment we were always coming to. Ruth was dead, and Eloise wasn't just telling me about Whitmore Halls because I was the granddaughter of Benjamin Costello. No, she was telling me because she knew, because she had known from the moment I first stepped into room 402, that at the end of her story, she would make a cup of tea seeped with the same poisonous plant that had killed my grandfather and that she would drink it.

"You had this planned," I say. "You always had this planned."

"I have spent fifty years locked in rooms, Ms. Costello," says Eloise. "I think it's finally time to be free."

My mouth is dry and chalky, and I want to tell Eloise that she can't. She can't just give up. She can't end her life in this way.

"My life has been full of strange and beautiful people," Eloise says. "And I think it's now time to sit under the red oaks and enjoy a cup of tea."

I look up at the leaves hanging above and around us, the burning color seeping onto the walls of an old hospital room in Darren County, Kentucky. When I look back at Eloise, her eyes are closed. The sun shines down through the window and onto her skin, and I see Eloise standing on the stone wall, meeting Benjamin Costello for the first time, the same girl who would grow into the woman who would place my father into my grandmother's arms and send them both to Chicago where they would be free.

There is so much I want to say, so much I am still trying to sort through, but the sun is bright and warm, and there is a steady pulsing inside me that tells me that my time with Eloise is now complete. And so we sit together, in the silence, among the leaves.

That night, I sit on the corner of the green-and-pink-striped couch, staring at a clean sheet of canvas. This used to fill me with a sense of dread, all this white space with no lines, waiting to be filled. It was like looking at a washed dinner plate, at a clear sky painted only in gray.

The portrait of Benjamin is in the dumpster. I brought it there when I came back from Dusty Hills earlier this evening. I'll give the mayor his money back. He'll have to hire someone else if he wants a portrait of Benjamin hung in Costello House. Still, I want to leave something behind in this town. Some piece of memoriam.

There are so many ways to start a painting, I thought on the night I first started painting *The Woman in the Woods*. It was late August, and the apartment on Dahlia Street was expelling great gasps of heat. The canvas was large, and it shifted from the right to the left as I worked, sweat trickling down the back of my neck. Thick tree trunks rose from the base of the canvas. There was something familiar about them, even then. The widespread branches, the dark green leaves. The girl in the red dress came last, almost like an afterthought. Her thin, outstretched arms. The moonlight reflected off the sphere of her upturned face. The hem of her dress cast a long shadow on the forest floor.

I glance at the blank canvas before me as I cover the wooden palette with dabs of color. Reds and yellows and oranges. I start slowly. I dip the fine bristles of the paintbrush into the watercolor. There are so many ways to start a painting. And this painting, like many before it, begins with the eyes of a girl.

MISSING

MRS. VALERIE COSTELLO. MISSING SINCE APRIL 1, 1948. WIFE OF THE LATE BENJAMIN COSTELLO. Last seen at her residence in Darren, Kentucky.

THE DUNN FAMILY IS OFFERING A $200 REWARD FOR ANY PERTINENT INFORMATION ON THE WHEREABOUTS OF MRS. BENJAMIN COSTELLO.

DESCRIPTION OF VALERIE COSTELLO FOLLOWS:

Age: 26 (twenty-six) years. Blue eyes. Brown hair. Tall and thin in build. She may be wearing a long wool coat and red scarf.

Thirty

The next morning, I call Dad. He answers on the first ring as if he has been waiting for my call. "Tig," he says. I see him pulling at the neck of his tie and wrapping the tips of his fingers around the rim of a sweaty glass. Suddenly, I miss him fiercely. In Chicago, I didn't have time to miss Dad. I was consumed with classes and art and the sound of Graffiti Alley in mid-July. But now, in the place where Dad was born, his absence is everywhere. It is like seeing his shoes sitting beside the front door and knowing that he isn't inside.

I tell Dad that I'm taking a train north the next day. I've done all I can here in Darren, and it's time for me to come home. Dad doesn't ask much about the project, and I'm grateful. Throwing the painting of Benjamin into the dumpster is hardly the conclusion he would expect. Still, there is so much to tell him. Not now, not over the phone, but in the days to come. I will tell him slowly, in the same way that Eloise told me. That way, if it all becomes too much, Dad can simply hold out his hand to stop the flow.

Dad is quiet this morning, and our conversation is full of stumbles. We speak at the same time with awkward pauses that stretch five beats too long. There is so much that each of us is holding under our tongues that the line between us sags under the weight.

"We should make the diorama," I say, "like we always talked about doing." Ever since I was young, Dad spoke of making a diorama of ancient Greece. The place where art began. We would make the model city in the dining room. The length of Athens would span the width of the old wooden table Dad refinished the year after Mom died. We would use real wood to make the Acropolis and clay to create the sanctuary of Dion. Dad would tell me stories about the ancient Greeks while we worked, stories I'd heard since I was a child: Pandora's box. The three sisters of fate. Theseus and the minotaur. And, of course, the great tale of Antigone, the young heroine who wished only for the proper burial of her brother. I, too, would tell Dad a story. One about three brave women who lived in the hills that looked out over a small rural town sitting alongside a muddy river.

Dad clears his throat, and I know he is ready to get off the phone. "Well." I take a deep breath. I'll let him off the hook, I decide. I'll be home soon anyway. "I guess I'll see . . ."

"Do you know why she left?" Dad asks dryly.

I don't need to ask to know what Dad is referring to. He wants to know why his mother left Darren County all those years ago.

I tell Dad I do.

He sighs, a thick mix of sadness and relief.

I press the phone closer against my ear. For a moment, I nearly tell Dad everything I know. I nearly tell him about the railways that Benjamin built alongside the river and how trains only ran on the steel bars for a few months before they sank beneath the water. I nearly tell him that I know there was a baby born before him, that Valerie was pregnant the day she got married, and that when the baby was born, he was blue in the face. I nearly tell Dad that his father dreamed of building a rocket ship from a red oak tree and that his mother had an odd habit of collecting hemlock in her coat pockets in the middle of the night.

"Dad?" All the things I know and think I know and want to know tumble inside me.

"In seventh grade, Mrs. Sorenson passed out a worksheet covered in Punnett squares," Dad says. The cord between us is stretched far and thin. "We were learning about genetics. Height. Weight. Hair color. Things like that." Dad pauses, and I think of my sixth-grade genealogy tree. Strange that Dad has a grade school project he remembers just as well.

"She told us to write blue, green, and brown along the left side of the chart. We were going to look at the probability of a child's eye color." A siren wails in the background. It drowns out Dad's voice. It's the first siren I've heard in Darren County, and it screams from hundreds of miles away.

Dad talks about the probability charts, about the monohybrid crosses between the paternal and maternal traits. The dominant and recessive genes. It all sounds both vaguely familiar and utterly nonsensical.

"I knew Benjamin's eyes were blue, just like Valerie's, but when I put them side by side in the chart, I couldn't make sense of it."

Dad is a twelve-year-old boy, sitting at a desk in the middle of a room covered in maps and the periodic table of elements. *An indecipherable language,* Dad liked to say. He never loved the sciences as he did the arts.

"I wrote the words over and over again. Paternal eyes, blue. Maternal eyes, blue. The probability of blue eyes was nearly one hundred percent. Green eyes, maybe five percent. Brown eyes, nearly impossible." Dad chuckles, but the sound is all wrong.

"Your eyes are brown." My voice cuts through Dad's memory.

"Yes," he agrees. "My eyes have always been brown."

Dad doesn't need to tell me for me to understand what this meant to the twelve-year-old boy filling in Punnett squares, over and over again. Blue. Green. Brown. Blue. Green. Brown. The percentages must have blurred his vision, the lines bending to the right and then back again. He must have looked at his eyes in the mirror, wondered if they could pass as blue. A dark hazel. A grayish navy. No. Dad's eyes have always been indisputably brown.

I lean against the wall in the shop. The phone cord is wrapped around my wrist. "Did you ask Valerie?"

"She took one look at those Punnett squares and told me that a better use of my time was to make that chart into a good game of tic-tac-toe. In fact, she was prepared to beat me in the game right then." Dad laughs, and I'm glad there is some angle where this memory appears sweet.

"But I knew," he continues. "I could see it. The fear in her eyes. It was like by me showing her that chart, she was seeing the color of my eyes for the first time. And I knew then that she wasn't my biological mother."

I'm not surprised that Dad already knows the ending to this story. He was always one of those people who liked to read the last page first. Just to see if it was going to be worth it. I tell Dad that there is so much more to say, that I will tell him about the woman who gave birth to him right here in Darren, and that her story and Valerie's story and even Benjamin's story are like the roots of the red oak trees that grow from the Kentucky hills in the south all the way up to the city in the north.

"Well, look at that," Dad says. "These Appalachians have made a storyteller out of you."

Any story worth telling has more than one storyteller, Eloise told me once. The pressed leaves were everywhere, and there was purple glue stuck to my thumb. I had come to learn more about Benjamin, yet hadn't Eloise been telling me all along that a story can't be told by one person? *Go to Whitmore Halls,* she had urged. *Let me tell you about the Dunn girls; one of them still lives around here.* Eloise, Valerie, Charles, Rita, Mae, Jason. All these voices, like branches of a tree, growing together to tell the story of a small town nestled beneath the Kentucky hills.

The door to the shop opens, and Mae calls out from across the room. Her amber-colored voice coats everything in honey. Cougar mews.

"It will be really nice to have you home, Antigone," Dad says. His voice is lathered in tenderness. "And to hear these stories about the women in the hills."

The night before I leave Darren, I visit my grandfather. It is just after midnight, and the darkness is heavy and thick around me. There is no moon, just a single streetlamp that beams a pale-yellow circle of light onto the road. The eyes of the boys of war follow me as I sneak down the street. Tonight, I am glad for the darkness. Tonight, it will just be my grandfather and me.

Earlier in the day, I went to the library. I told the librarian, a young man wearing wire-rimmed eyeglasses and red suspenders, that I had been to Costello House and met Anna, who had graciously let me look through some of Benjamin's documents. "I was wondering if I could make a few photocopies," I asked him. "Just for my own records before I leave."

The boy agreed, leading me to the photocopy machine before walking back to the front desk to write due dates on the backs of old note cards that would be tucked inside the front covers of books.

Alone, I took the posters of the missing women from my bag and placed one face down on the copy machine. *One hundred should do,* I thought. The machine shook as the face of Marjorie Thomas appeared before me again and again. When the copies were complete, I replaced the first poster with another. One hundred more. I pressed copy. I would return the originals to Anna. They belonged in Costello House, in the box with the land deeds and baby David's certificate of death.

I placed the copies in my bag and waited until I was back at Mae's to begin ripping the pages into long strips. It was quite a mess when I finished, but I was pleased.

Now, in the park, the strips of paper are carried in a plastic bag I set down before the statue. Beside it, I place the large bucket full of mixed flour and water that I stirred together before leaving the shop. It is thick and messy and the perfect consistency for papier-mâché.

"Hello, Benjamin." I look up at my grandfather's upturned chin. It was warmer during the day, and Benjamin no longer has snow on the lip of his cap. Excellent. The bronze won't be damp.

I work quickly, not wanting to be outside longer than I must and not wanting the papier-mâché to congeal in the bucket. I start with a thin strip of paper, dunking it into the paste and using two fingers to wipe off the excess before wrapping the poster shred around Benjamin's shoe. The right side of Marjorie Thomas's face looks up at me from the tip of the bronze boot. I reach for another strip.

While I work, I think of the sixty-two-pound papier-mâché uterus I made in Chicago. I kept it in the far corner of the apartment, under the window where the moonlight poured through each night. It was big enough to sit inside, to lie on my side with my knees curled into my chest. I did this sometimes, when I was lonely or when I felt too much of the world pressing in around me.

I stand on the stone pedestal and wrap a strip of paper around Benjamin's waist. The word MISSING is printed in black letters that cover the dress coat's gilt buttons.

When I left Chicago, the uterus was too heavy to carry to the dumpster, so I left it in the center of the living room. It was the last thing I saw before I stepped out of the apartment and closed the door.

I stand on my tiptoes to reach Benjamin's head, using my fingers to press the soggy paper onto his cheeks, the bridge of his nose, the curve of his bronze, lifeless eyes. A wet pearl of papier-mâché drips off the tip of his nose, and I wipe it off with the back of my hand.

When I've finished, my fingers are numb, and the bucket of paste has hardened. I take a step back and look up at the monument. It still looks like a soldier. The figure is tall and commanding and powerful. Yet the eye is no longer drawn to the stiff garrison cap or the pointed mouth of the musket, but to the printed words and the faces of the women. My gaze returns to them, over and over again, the eyes of Dana Fields pasted on Benjamin's bent elbow, the hollowed-out cheekbones of Gertrude Rey covering the gold medallion on Benjamin's chest, the thin, pursed lips of Joyce Hammond, almost bent into a smile on Benjamin's round kneecap. I have covered every part of the monument except for the stone pedestal where I have left the carved-out words: COURAGE, BRAVERY, HONOR.

The wind picks up, and I hear the restless river to my right. *She's never frozen over,* Jason told me while we were driving back from Dusty Hills.

My teeth chatter, and I know it's time to go. I place the unused strips of paper into the bucket. I will throw them out on my way back to the shop. I glance once more at the statue and nod in approval. This is what I will remember most about Darren. This is what I will take with me.

❀

The sun is a brilliant gold sphere shining over Mud River on the morning I leave Darren County. I pack up slowly, letting the warm sunlight rub the backs of my heels as I clean out the yellow-colored fridge, fold the worn checkered quilt, run my fingers through the wild pink fur of the toilet seat cover one last time. I will miss this place with its green-and-pink-striped couch and plastic flowers sitting in a vase on the kitchen table.

Jason is picking me up at the shop in fifteen minutes. He will take me to the train station in Morehead and drop me off at the same platform Eloise Price brought so many women to, many years before. It's sad to be leaving Mae's after all these weeks. I gather my bag in my right hand and the large canvas painting in the other. It is wrapped in brown paper and bounces awkwardly against my outer thigh as I struggle down the stairs. I am eager to drop it off at the courthouse on my way out of town. In my back pocket is the envelope with Ruth's obituary folded inside. I'm not quite done with it yet.

Outside, Jason loads my bag into the truck bed. "No wheels," he teases, though the joke feels worn. I am sad to be leaving Darren, though I know this won't be the last time I come to this town. I will bring my children here, someday. I will show them the river my grandmother stood in when she was a young girl and walk them up the hill to see what remains of Whitmore Halls. This is the home of three extraordinary women, I will tell them.

"Well now, I think I'm actually going to miss you." Mae stands in the doorway of the Soap and Spool Shop, holding Cougar, his great orange body draped over her forearm. "I got rather used to you walking around up there."

I laugh half-heartedly. It's strange how you can miss a person before you even say goodbye. "I'll be back," I promise, looking up at the gray January sky, all smoke and charcoal. It's cold this morning, and my breath hangs heavy in the air.

Mae scratches Cougar between the ears, and his leg stretches outward. Maybe I'll get a cat when I go back home, I think. I tell this to Mae, and she laughs. "I'd give you this one, but I can't stand the mice that come around."

Jason snaps the tailgate into place and tells me we're ready to go.

Mae sets Cougar down and waves me over, wrapping an arm around the backs of my shoulders and pulling me close enough to smell the sharp cologne of the castor oil she rubbed into her hair earlier this morning.

"I'll practice making soap." I plan to take the hobby back with me to Ann Arbor.

"Oh, Lord." Mae shakes her head and then says, "Send me some. After you have some practice."

Mae places her hand on my cheek just as she did my first day in Darren. *You have lonely eyes,* she said. I think of everything I told Mae that night we sat on the couch and drank sweet tea. It felt so easy to let the story fall from my mouth, to set it on the green-and-pink-striped fabric between us.

"You'll be okay, Tig," Mae says. Her hand is so warm against my skin. "You'll be okay."

✦

At the courthouse, I leave the wrapped painting on the steps outside Mayor Grant's office. He returned to Darren late last night, and I smile when I think about how this is the first thing he will find when he comes into work.

It is early, and much of Darren is still asleep. I tape a white envelope to the top right corner. Inside is the $500 stipend the mayor gave me when I came to Darren County and a folded note written on a blank piece of paper torn from the back pages of *To Kill a Mockingbird*:

You were right. This town is full of brave and courageous heroes.

"I'm sorry you won't get to give it to him in person," Jason says. He stands beside me on the doorstep. I know he is curious to see the painting, but he will have to wait. I have no interest in seeing the mayor's reaction.

When we drive past the statue, Jason slows. "What the hell . . . ," he says. I bite the inside of my cheek to keep from smiling. The papier-mâché has held up well overnight. A few strips have come undone and are waving in the breeze, but for the most part, the statue remains covered. Even from the road, I see MISSING pressed again and again over Benjamin's body.

"Did you do this?" Jason peers out the windshield in the same way that I once did to better see Whitmore Halls.

"I thought it needed a little sprucing up." My voice is playful.

Jason laughs and shakes his head. "Wait until my pop sees this." He turns to look at me. "You know they will just take it down."

"It won't matter," I reply. I know it won't be long before a hose is taken to the statue and the hardened papier-mâché is ripped and broken off. By afternoon, Benjamin will once again have his bronze physique reflected in the sun. "They won't be able to take it down before people see it," I tell Jason. "And once one person sees it, they all will." I think of how fast news travels in Darren.

"They can take it down," I reiterate. "But I'd bet one of Mitt's Reubens that people will remember it."

Jason bends the front of his baseball cap in his palm. "That's a sure bet you got there." He starts up the truck and pulls away from the park. I watch out the window as Mud River runs alongside us until we take a turn to the right and Darren becomes small.

"We never really got to talk about it," Jason says as we near Morehead. His gaze is set on the road, but I see the way his thumb taps against the side of the wheel. Jason is nervous, and I know he is thinking about the day in the field.

"It was a bad day." I feel the weight of the rotted corn husks in my hand.

Jason's mouth twitches. "I think of my girls sometimes. How they're getting older."

"They're barely ten." I laugh, but I quiet when the lines of Jason's mouth stay firm. Something is bothering him.

He continues. "Soon there'll be no more ice cafés. No more doll-houses. No more riding in the truck and teaching them to shift the gears."

"You'll be teaching them to slam on the brakes before you know it."

This time the corners of Jason's mouth pull upward. "Don't I know it," he says. "They'll be talking about boys and going out at night. Spending too much time by the river and hanging around Mitt's."

Jason taps a finger on the window glass. "There are so many scum-bags in the world, you know. And I don't . . ." Jason seems to rearrange his thoughts. "I just don't want them growing up thinking we're all bad."

I look out the window and watch the yellow lines blur on the road.

"I've been thinking about what you said. About the statue. How we have some big memorial to a man who did such bad things to women." Jason is talking faster now. "It's not right, and I'm going to make sure

The Moonflowers

my girls know that. I've been thinking about taking them on a walk up into the hills. Maybe go take a look at Whitmore Halls. Lilly is always saying how pretty it is with all the snow on it."

I imagine Jason traversing up the snow-covered road, his two daughters working to place their boots in his sunken steps. They would laugh as they followed him. Their arms would be outstretched and faces red with cold. Jason would make a game of it. Find a squirrel sitting on a tree branch. Spot a deer in the forest. Gather a handful of red berries. Don't eat them! And when they got to the house, the three of them would stand and stare at the broken window frames and rotting wood, and Jason would get down on one knee and tell them that this house used to belong to a group of doctors. All of them were women.

There are so many things for a woman to be afraid of, I think. Crowded bars. Empty rooms. Parking garages. Dark alleys covered in graffiti. It's so easy to think that much of the world is bad. Yet sitting here with Jason, listening to him talk about bringing his girls up to Whitmore Halls, I feel a certain calmness radiate inside my body.

"Jason," I say. "You're one of the good ones."

He flushes, and I know he understands.

"You're going to be a bit early." He checks his watch. It's digital and the green clockface looks childish wrapped around his wrist. "Train don't leave for another couple hours."

"In an hour," I reply as Jason pulls into the station.

He looks at me, confused.

"I'm taking the 8:20." I lift my hips and pull the folded envelope from my back pocket.

Jason frowns and tells me that train isn't going toward Michigan.

"I know," I say. "I have one last stop to make before I go home."

Thirty-One

I ride the train to Chicago in a railcar full of ghosts.

In the seat in front of me, to the right, is Marjorie Thomas. She sits erect beside the window, a bag placed on the chair beside her. She is wearing a dress that is two sizes too large, and the neckline bothers her. Every couple of minutes, she reaches up to pull the collar away from her skin. She clutches a children's book in her hands and, when she flips through the pages, tears run down her cheeks.

Gertrude Rey sits near the front. She is a nervous woman and continually runs a hand over a mane of red curls. She must be worried they will give her away if anyone comes looking for her. She will be fine once she reaches the city.

Dana Fields sits one seat behind me, the toe of her shoe knocking against the leather chairback in a steady rhythm. It sounds like a heartbeat.

I turn my head and see Joyce Hammond on a seat in the back half of the car. Dark bruises cover the left side of her face. She stares listlessly out the train car window.

And there, in the last bench in the back, is Valerie Costello. She's holding a small baby boy in her arms, and her body rocks back and forth with the rails. Her gaze is locked on the sleeping child, and I'm not able to see her face well, but when the sun streams through the window and streaks against her skin, her eyes are bright with motherhood.

✿

The clinic is located on the corner of an intersection, a mile from the Art Institute. It is nestled between a law office and a print shop, and the front walk is covered in protesters. They hold signs and Bibles and sit on fold-out chairs meant for camping. When I walk toward them, they rise and wave the signs above their heads.

"You don't have to do this!" a woman yells. Her jacket is unzipped, and she wears a black T-shirt that has a jagged line printed over her chest. A fetal heartbeat. "You don't have to become a murderer."

A man stops close to me, and I worry he is about to grab my arm. "Follow Jesus," he says. "He doesn't want you here, but forgiveness can be found in Jesus Christ." He clutches a sign in his hand: Rape and Abortion are Wrong.

I open the door of the clinic and slip inside. Everything becomes quiet. The waiting room is painted in pale blue. It's the same hue Valerie used on her walls inside the house by the sea. There is a welcome desk to the left and a coffee table covered with magazines and a box of tissues. On a shelf, above a fish tank, are three wooden giraffes, all lined up in a row. On a side table, a candle burns cinnamon and nutmeg into the air.

"Do you have an appointment?" A woman calls me over to the desk. She is small and soft-spoken and looks no older than I am.

I tell her no and apologize for coming unannounced. She waves away my apologies, and I see that her nails are painted to look like ten different flags. Mexico. Japan. Italy. Poland. Germany. I can't name the rest.

"I'm looking for someone." I tug the envelope from my back pocket.

The woman tells me she loves my coat. "It reminds me of Christmas," she says. "I love the red."

I show the woman the name on the envelope, and her face lifts. "Oh, of course," she says. "Dr. Galley. She's right in the other room. I'll get her."

While the woman is gone, I look at the shadow boxes that hang on the wall. They are large frames and filled with writing. They are letters, I realize, stepping closer. Hundreds and hundreds of letters sent to the doctors at the clinic, thanking them for their care.

The front door opens, and a young girl comes in. Her face is pale. The shouts of the protesters nip at her heels.

The woman with the flag-painted nails pops her head into the waiting room and asks me to follow her. "Dr. Galley will just be a couple minutes." She directs me to a patient room before closing the door and going back to the front desk.

I sit on a chair beside the doctor's stool and rub the cool envelope between my fingers. There is an examination bed in the center of the room, pink leather covered by a long white sheet of paper. A medical cart is placed close to the head, an ultrasound machine standing on the top shelf. Another cart full of supplies sits beside the sink. A tray with packaged needles, plastic prescription bottles, a speculum, cotton swabs, boxes of gloves. In the far corner, a floor lamp is turned on, and soft yellow light shines a halo on the white ceiling. There is a picture of a potted plant hanging on the wall. It's painted in watercolors.

The door opens and a woman walks in. She is tall and lean and built from the same mold as Dad. She can't be much older than him and wears a pair of lime-green scrubs under her white coat.

"Well, hello there." She straddles the small stool and rolls toward me with practiced ease. "Dawn says you were wanting to see me?"

I tell the doctor yes and hold out the envelope. "I saw you sent this to a woman in Kentucky. Eloise Price."

Her face relaxes and the lines around her mouth soften as if she has just heard that someone important to her is safe. She takes the envelope and peers in, pulling out Ruth's obituary and then tucking it back inside. "I didn't know if it would make it there," she admits. "I always wondered if it did."

Dr. Galley looks up at me. "You know Eloise?"

I tell her I do.

I think of Eloise sitting at her desk in room 402. She is gazing out the window, surrounded by leaves. The gray clouds saunter across the sky, large and lethargic, as she stirs a cup of tea.

"I spent most of the last four months in Kentucky," I say. "I was there to complete a project for a memorial, and I met Eloise. She told me a story." I tell Dr. Galley about Whitmore Halls, about Ulma and Eloise and Ruth, and how they helped women in trouble. I tell her about the clinic they set up in the back bedroom, about the widow's walk where they watched for men coming up through the trees. I tell her about how they sent women to Chicago and how, after Eloise went to prison, Charles continued the practice by sending women to Ruth from states away.

Dr. Galley nods, and I know this part of the story is familiar. "That's right," she says. "Women did come here from Kentucky. Still do from time to time."

Dr. Galley explains that her mother started this clinic in the seventies, after abortion became legal. She started it with another woman, a doctor who had been working in women's medicine for over thirty years. That woman was Ruth. The two were part of an underground organization that provided safe abortions and counseling for women throughout the late sixties. It was based in Chicago, but women from all across the Midwest came for medical care.

"My mother and Ruth knew the importance of the work they were doing," Dr. Galley says. "Do you know how many women died from botched abortions before 1973?"

I nod. The numbers are horrific.

"Hundreds a year," Dr. Galley states.

It's strange to be talking with Dr. Galley about Ruth, about the woman I never met yet whose blood runs through my veins. She was my grandmother, I want to say, but the word doesn't seem to fit in my mouth.

"I can't believe you knew Ruth," I say quietly.

"Oh yes," Dr. Galley confirms. "I knew her very well. When my mother died ten years back, it was Ruth who graciously let me take over the clinic. She sat with me for hours as we went through boxes of files. She told me about the dangers of the job, most of which I had already experienced. The stalking, the insults, the protesters following you home. She prepared me for it all."

Dr. Galley pulls out Ruth's obituary once again, and Ruth's face fills the room. She is younger in the photograph than she must have been when she died. A middle-aged woman with dark-colored eyes.

"It's funny"—Dr. Galley pushes her blonde bangs away from her forehead—"all these stories you heard from Eloise. Ruth told me the same ones. Right here in this clinic."

"She talked about Kentucky?" I'm surprised. "About Eloise?"

"All the time." Dr. Galley nods. "She always said that it was Eloise who made this place possible. That she was the reason why Ruth could come back to Chicago after her years spent in the South."

Dr. Galley hands the envelope back to me. "Eloise never came to this city, but her presence is everywhere. Take a look at those letters on your way out." She glances over her shoulder, and I think of all the notes pasted into the shadow boxes. "Some of them are over fifty years old. Ruth kept them in a shoebox and carried them with her on the train. I bet you'll recognize some of the names."

Eloise would hate the city, I decide, but I think she would like to know that places like this exist. One day, when I go back to Kentucky, I will tell the people of Darren County about Dr. Galley and the clinic that Ruth started in the city. I will tell them about the letters framed on the wall and the woman who works behind the desk with flag-painted nails. I will tell them about the blue walls and the pictures of flowers that hang in the rooms. I will tell them that the facility is clean and bright and smells like vanilla. I will tell them that it is a safe place. It is a place where you can get help. I will tell them all these things because it is important for them to know that there are so many strong and courageous women who are here to help them when they're afraid.

Before I leave Chicago, I go to Graffiti Alley.

I take the long way, winding through the campus green and walking beneath the university clock tower. To the north, a block away, is Dahlia Street. I think of the uterus and wonder if it still sits in the middle of the living room, waiting to be filled.

Later, I will take a train back to Ann Arbor and I will meet up with Dad for dinner. I will tell him more about the people I met in Darren and about the painting of Benjamin that I threw in the trash. He will laugh when I say this, and the sound will be so warm and familiar that when he asks if I'm going back to Chicago in the fall, I will nod a yes.

It's midday, and the streets are bloated with people. There is a crowd around the mouth of Graffiti Alley, and when I get close, I see a group of dancers performing beside a large boom box. One, a stocky man with a winter parka and shorts that look five sizes too big, is beatboxing while the other three spin and tap. The tallest of them, a woman with a bouquet of dreadlocks tied back in a red, black, and green bandanna, moves her feet so fast I have trouble telling which one is her right from her left. She does a backflip, and I feel like I'm home.

I walk into the alley expecting things to look different now, but the same menagerie of art welcomes me inside. The man twirling the world on his finger like a basketball. The pink unicorn hiding behind a jungle of vines. The boy playing a violin to a goat who sits on his hind legs like a dog begging for a treat. There are the painted eyes of the cheetah and the long tentacles of an octopus splashing in the water. And then, farther down, the purple elephant spraying flowers from her trunk. I stand in front of her great colorful body and am buried with relief when I still find her extraordinary.

I don't go any farther than the elephant. I have no need to see the cat playing the fiddle or the cow jumping over a half-moon. They are a part of the alley that doesn't feel like mine.

I pull my red coat tighter around my waist. The cold is biting here in the city. Yet my fingers itch to create. I stopped at the art store on my way to the clinic and bought a few cans of spray paint that I dropped into my bag. Just in case. Now, as I find a space in the alley that feels sparse, I'm glad I did.

It's been months since I've worked with spray paint, and my arm moves clumsily, my fingers instantly stained with a color that will take me days to wash off. I start with the trunk, thick lines of brown that spread into branches as high as I can reach. The leaves will make a difference, I tell myself. It just needs a little color. I open the red can of paint and then the orange. I save the yellow for last.

As I paint, I think of all the women who snuck away from homes and husbands and the strange comfort of consistency to climb up the hill and knock on the old oak door of Whitmore Halls. How terrified they must have been. I think of Valerie, standing on that front step with Rita's hand clutched inside her own and, later, leaning on the arm of Benjamin Costello, her pockets heavy with hemlock. I think of Ulma planting herbs in her garden and of Charles leading a black-bodied Rocky Mountain to a bale of hay. I think of Eloise and Ruth. I see them sitting together in the forest, eating berries under the red oak trees and speaking of happiness in a world that was mostly bad.

When I'm finished, I take a step back and stare up at the spray-painted tree.

The Red Oaks.

Their roots stretch from the hills in the south to the cities in the north. A whole network of roots lying just beneath the surface of the soil.

I raise my arms high above my head. A rush of cold air flows down the alley and blows the hem of my coat open in the same way my grandmother's shirt used to billow outward in the saltwater air. The tips of my fingers reach out toward the leaves.

To see Tig's painting, please visit:
abigailrosemarie.com

Acknowledgments

There was once a woman who lived in the hills who helped victims of domestic violence by opening her home to them when they had nowhere else to go. This is the story my mother told me when I was young. My mother was just a girl when she went to Kentucky and spent an afternoon clearing wooded pathways leading to an old house in the hills where a woman lived. I know nothing about this woman's mission, other than that her home provided a refuge for women who were abused. Eloise Price is a fictional character, but her courage and her bravery grow from the ghost of a woman I know nothing about. It is to this woman, and to all the fearless women who have lived in the hills, that I owe my deepest gratitude.

My profound thanks to the following people:

Lori Colvin, my agent. Thank you for believing in this book when it was still in its early stages. Thank you to Cindy Bullard and the Birch Literary team—this book is stronger because of you.

Erin Adair-Hodges and Chantelle Aimée Osman, my amazing editors. I am so incredibly lucky to have worked with you both. Your insights and support brought this book to life. My profound gratitude to Manu Shadow Velasco, who read this book many times over and whose advice and generous feedback shaped this story. Thank you to the Lake Union team and to Amazon Publishing. I am forever indebted to your guidance and kindness throughout the publishing process.

The Ohio University faculty members who have been not only my professors but also my mentors and friends: Eric LeMay, Edmond Chang, and Erin Schlumpf. Thank you for reading this novel in its embryonic state. Your comments and unique perspectives allowed these characters to grow and change in ways that I never expected. An enormous thank-you to Patrick O'Keeffe, who read this novel over and over again and never failed to offer invaluable insights that shaped this story into what it is today. Your support, knowledge, and friendship have meant so much to me.

My early readers: Anne Valente, you are such a wonderful person, and I feel so honored to have worked with you. Kelly Davis, in so many ways I feel like we started our writing journey together. Thank you for being the most loving, hilarious, and genuine person I know. Deb Van Duinen, you've probably read more of my stories, chapters, and ramblings than anyone else. Thank you for spending the last twenty-five years brainstorming, creating, and reading with me.

Monica McFawn: My life forever changed the moment I sat in your creative writing class all those years ago. Thank you for seeing something in me and for knowing that one day I would write a book. I hope you like this one!

My family and friends who have had to listen to me spout stories for years: If I listed you all here, the book would need another chapter. Know that your love and encouragement and generous ears have meant everything to me.

Bill Dykstra and Lisa Harju: Thank you for being the best parents a kid could ask for. Your love is endless, and I can't thank you enough for always supporting my creative endeavors and for instilling in me a love for lakes, trees, and literature. You are the roots that ground me in every way.

Morgan, my partner in all things. My best person, my best reader, and my best friend. Thank you for all the laughter, all the wisdom, and all the love. Thank you for being you.

And Sivvy: My favorite writing buddy. Thank you for all the times you sat beside me and purred.

Book Club Discussion Questions

1. What were your initial thoughts as you finished reading this book? What emotions did you feel?
2. Did the characters seem believable to you? Did they remind you of anyone you know?
3. What surprised you the most in the book? Were you surprised by any character's actions? By any plot twists?
4. What were the main themes in the book? How were those themes brought to life?
5. How important was the time period or the setting to the story? What would have changed if the book was set in a different time period or setting?
6. What scene would you point out as the pivotal moment in the narrative? How did it make you feel as you were reading it?
7. What do you believe motivates the actions of each character?
8. Were there times when you disagreed with a character's actions? If so, what would you have done differently in the situation?
9. How have the characters changed or grown by the end of the book?
10. How does the book's title work in relation to the book's contents? Does it feel like the right title for the book?
11. How did the book impact you? Are there any lingering questions you still have after reading the book?

About the Author

Abigail Rose-Marie is a writer from Grand Rapids, Michigan. She holds a PhD in creative writing from Ohio University and an MFA from Bowling Green State University. She currently lives with her wife and their very spoiled pets in Utah. *The Moonflowers* is her first novel.